RECESSIONAL
FOR GRACE

RECESSIONAL
FOR GRACE

∽

Marguerite Poland

VIKING

an imprint of

PENGUIN BOOKS

VIKING

Published by the Penguin Group
80 Strand, London WC2R 0RL, England
Penguin Putnam Inc, 375 Hudson Street, New York, New York 10014, USA
Penguin Books Australia Ltd, 250 Camberwell Road, Camberwell,
Victoria 3124, Australia
Penguin Books Canada Ltd, 10 Alcorn Avenue, Toronto, Ontario,
Canada M4V 3B2
Penguin Books (NZ) Ltd, Cnr Rosedale and Airborne Roads, Albany,
Auckland, New Zealand
Penguin Books India (Pvt) Ltd, 11 Community Centre, Panchsheel Park,
New Delhi – 110 017 India
Penguin Books (South Africa) (Pty) Ltd, 24 Sturdee Avenue, Rosebank,
Johannesburg 2196, South Africa

Penguin Books (South Africa) (Pty) Ltd, Registered Offices:
Second Floor, 90 Rivonia Road, Sandton 2196, South Africa

First published by Penguin Books (South Africa) (Pty) Ltd 2003

ISBN 0 670 04786 4

Typeset by CJH Design in 10.5/12.5 point Plantin
Cover design: Mouse Design
Printed and bound by Interpak Books, Pietermaritzburg

KoNkabiyamalanga
For my companions, 'the oxen of my days'

Chapter one

⌒◦

There is a saying in Zulu, *'If you were in my flesh, I could tear you out, but you are in my blood, which cannot be divided.'*

Which cannot be divided.

For her, it was the tragedy. For me, the consolation.

This is the story of the man I love. I have loved him all my life.

At every age, in any time, I know his walk, his voice. I know his hands, the back of his neck and the way he turns his head. I have always known the scent of him, from baby-nape to boy, soldier, man. Even at the moment before death: yes, perhaps I will know that too.

I have never met him.

I never will.

He has been dead for nearly forty years. He ceased when I began.

Or did he?

There is no need to explain the anomaly. It is quite straightforward.

I am his biographer: he is in my blood, which cannot be divided.

He lived here in the last days of his fieldwork. He returned only once: ten years later. It was November 1957. The visit was brief and to the point. He brought no luggage. He stayed one night.

Then he left. He may have looked behind him – a quick glance of appraisal, not lingering.

Had he gone one morning – one still morning with a fish-scale sky like today? Were the stars still out? He would have known them all, the planets and the constellations: here is the Dawn's-Heart star; here, the *gauun* flower in

1

the sky; here, the hunting lynx. This, the *aardvark* planet and this, the star of the hoeing season.

This is the star of Hunger. This of Famine. This of Death.

Then he'd have dismissed them – or himself. Wryly. He had had his Education.

Except, they moved him. They moved him enough to spend almost twenty years recording them.

And here, for the last three years, I have been recording him, with the same care, cross-reference to cross-reference, as he annotated the endless variations in his dictionary, dogged old lexicographer. He plays with me sometimes, testing me. *Did you take that lead, my dear? Did you catch that nuance?*

I follow the entries in the card index (pointed writing, grammatical markers penned in red), then track the clues, from card to card. There – tucked in square brackets:

[- *qolo (u(lu)qolo* n.)
i) Ridge. *Uqolo lwezimpungutye:* the ridge of the jackals i.e. in a lonely place; a place of weeping, lamentation.]

Weeping, lamentation.

Whose weeping? Whose lamentation?

Yes, I know the register, the faint mind-map he left for me. I have the faith to trace it.

My own cards are new, lined in cheap turquoise. His are old. They are brittle now and the blue writing ink has taken on a haze of brown round about the edges of the letters, as if they had bled, decaying down to the bones of the words. Corpse words: his voice has gone but I know it might have been quite slow – middle-register and warm – without hollows, with a question in its intonation: he was a generous man.

Just sometimes it seems that he is here – in the next room, out at the pump, sudden on the path. At first, he remained elusive. And then, he seemed to wait. But today, we will end it. Here. In this place. No one else remembers any more.

When I first came, the silence was oppressive. It drifts at different levels now. I am alert to it at last, knowing when to listen, when to let it carry me. Today, the air is breathless, the flat whiteness of late summer, quince-skin gold beyond the white. The ridge is featureless. There is a presence – old as the ironstone hills, the *krantzes*, the ancient river-bed. It is in this house as well.

I wonder if he felt it.

If he did, he would have examined it, quite unafraid.

He would have cranked the pump with strong hands and brought up water. He would have stoked the Aga and poured the anthracite in and whistled quietly as he worked, too sure to look behind him.

I look behind me all the time.

Last night, when I asked him to come – invoking him – someone knocked. There seemed to be a shadow outside. Yes, someone knocked. Small and urgent. But quiet: the tap of our own cipher. And I was too afraid to move. What would I have said? *There you are?*

'There you are. What have you to say?'

Instead it was probably Delekile, back from inspecting fences, come to ask for his money. But so late, so small, so insistent?

Lexicographer. Scholar. Philosopher. Sportsman. Farmer.

Idler. Lover.

He remained uncelebrated for almost fifty years.

The monk and the secular. The ascetic and the voluptuary. I think he was both. It is the monk and the ascetic I choose to scrutinise. The other? Half awake, half asleep, in the grey morning, I can invent him in many ways, but when the night turns in on itself, scenting a new day, the underbelly shows: there is a sense of desolation, an undertow of loss and dislocation. It has its signs. I know it well.

I felt it from the start, from the day when, coming back from the town with supplies, I saw a leguaan in the middle of the road – quite out of place, in the high light of noon – walking with the awkward gait of an amphibian far from water, all the grace of swimming gone. I stopped and, sensing me, it drooped across a bush, melting to it, without tension, only the black eye watching with a deep intensity. And the colours – they were burnished in the rusts and golds and greys of burned-out landscapes: so ancient, so tensely coiled to spring, under the slack reptilian ruse.

It was an emissary. Littoral. Ambiguous. Living at the interzone between the light and dark, the water and the land, reality and unreality. Deceit and Truth.

We watched each other in that barren place, the leguaan and I, where the road curves round the steel of the hillside and, below, the little house crouches – a small protuberance among the ironstone outcrops. When I had turned my eyes away to slip the brake and glanced again through the lowered window, it had gone. Though I searched, I could not see it, it was so cryptic.

Perhaps it had not been there at all – an intimation only, a trick of light and shade on earth and rock. Like his face in a photograph: a composition in light and shade as well. Those eyes cannot see me. They will not respond to my scrutiny. How can they? They are marks on a paper, tones juxtaposed. Where is the breath, the blood, the scent, the faint heat of skin? Here, a boy in cricket togs, ankles crossed, hands in the lap, hair well brushed, eyes direct, the suggestion of a smile. I had propped the picture against the pile of reference books – mostly his – and watched. If I absorb him long enough, may I claim him? Would he move? Would he – one day – walk in through the back door and speak to me?

And when the work is finished? What then?

Dr C J Godfrey MC (1898-1963)

I found him in a document.

It comprised a hundred and twenty pages of annotated diagrams and lists. The writing, the drawings – part of both design and composition – were meticulous.There was artistry in the simplest figure.

I came across it in the depths of the university library. There it was, relegated to redundancy, in the old teak bookshelves housing volumes taken from the new steel stack-racks to make way for more contemporary works. I was shown down a dark side corridor by a librarian too busy with the registration of first year students to worry with my foraging. In that corner, the light bulb had given out. I peered along the rows of titles, breathing spores of mould and dust.

And then I heard a shrike calling in the autumn morning far outside the louvred window where the hill rises from the Botanical Gardens and the aloes are dry and the old gum squanders leaves all across the shoulders of exotic shrubs. It must have been another of the voices I'd so often failed to recognise. I stood and listened, my hand resting on a set of folders in a row. I picked at one, pulling idly at the spine.

I prised the folder out.

It was old, cloth-bound in a faint maroon, a thin ribbon, like the binding for a lawyer's brief, holding the contents in. The lettering on the spine was flaking off: MS 125.003 (God).

The script was handwritten. Scrawled across the top margin of the first page, *'Field Notes: Aug. 1946':*

Colour-Patterns of Indigenous Cattle:
isomi – Redwinged Starling (Onychognathus morio): reddish beast with deep purple points.
intenjane – Crowned Plover (Vanellus coronatus) or kiewietjie; dun to grey beast with white patches. Black markings on head.

A photograph affixed. A *kiewietjie*-cow with a black coronet! A *kiewietjie* cow with white underbelly and cloud-grey flanks, black-harnessed at the chest.

Further on, another photo, the pattern clear despite the faded sepia of the print:

Inkomazi ezikhala zemithi – the cow which is the gaps between the branches of the trees, silhouetted against the sky.

4

I have seen a cow browsing among sweet-thorns, her points black as shadow-shards, the patterning of her side like the shade of branches on the ground. She backs from the brush, walks out into the open, carries the pattern with her, leaves its mirror-echo on the earth behind. 'I *am* the shadow of the trees . . .' – not – 'I am *like* the shadow of the trees'.

Simply, I am.

For pages, he notes the colour-pattern terms in his precise writing – suddenly thoughtful and deliberate, then swift, then measured, then impatient and abrupt.

'*The ox which is the stones of the forest.*'

How can an ox – so bland, so bovine – be a stone of the forest, or a cloud made of whey, or the eggs of a lark? How can an ox be vivid and poetic: the drowsing onomatopoeia, the lift and fall and grace of tone – so exact? A love affair in metaphor.

Here, in this worn cloth folder, dormant for fifty years, I had found the subject – not only for my doctoral dissertation but, despite myself, for something else as well. Looking back, I should have been content with the terms for colour-patterns, or star-lore or *veld*-lore – or any lore at all. I should have been content to make my dictionary of terms for *lobola* cattle, even dared the whimsy of poetry at the head of the chapter on marriage:

'*I could have wept and howled to see the bridal cattle pass,*
Not for me, but for Thathalasi,
Lovely, with a high-bridged nose.'

But I did not content myself. I meddled – and I allowed his secret subtext, his little markers and pointers and diversions to distract me. Here – he pencils in a riddle:

'*What is the great white bull of the sky and what the herds of white cattle?*'
The answer?
'*The full moon and stars!!*'

He likes that. He has punctuated it with two exclamation marks, making of the dots a set of circles.

'*Black cattle returning to the byre: dark thunderclouds drifting round the moon.*'

In time, I learn that all of his skies are filled with celestial herds, all the constellations red as a group of *utshezi* oxen, the colour of 'blanket clay'.

But no – instead of sticking to the task, I went beyond the gathering of words, images, finely balanced metaphor, rich allusion. Behind the carefully annotated entries, I saw him. C J Godfrey, the man.

The recognition was absolute. It could not be rescinded.

I held the folder to me. I did not have the librarian's cool detachment – thinking of tea-time and a bit-chat in the common room. I could feel its substance in my hands – the grain of it, the weight. I went to the old catalogue drawers and looked up the title. It is a small item in the vast corpus of his work: books, conference papers, articles, contributions to journals, an unpublished manuscript. Inscribed in the bottom right-hand corner of each relevant card, the date of acquisition – *June 1963* – and the name of the donor. Mrs Stella Godfrey.

His Wife?

There are many photographs of cattle – some haltered by a herdsman, an ox with its driver, a cow and calf, a bull.

But there is one – *one* – which I extract and put aside.

It is a small contact print of a heifer. She stands in front of the suggestion of an aloe-hedged byre and twisted stake of sneezewood at its gate, head slightly turned, faintly speckled on the rump, eyes dark-rimmed. Standing next to her, arm noosed to her neck, is a man. I know it is Godfrey. The shadow on the upper arm, the khaki shirt, indicates an afternoon of low, clear light. Like the beast among the thorns, he is sculpted – and created – by both sun and shade.

If the light changes, will they disappear – she with her skimming spots, her dancing hooves? Will he?

I examine the print under a magnifying glass, tilting it to the reading lamp.

The heifer is enchanting, there is something mythic in the light and shade that forms her – but it is the face of the man that arrests: the ascetic and the wry, the detached, aloof. And yet, there is an odd self-effacement in the tilt of his head, the deftness – and the humour – of his embrace. His eyes are set deep. It is a face from an old fresco, bearded, a little too lean, so fine-boned it might slip the perfect tension of its anchor-points and disembody. At first glance, it does not look as though it knows the silly tenderness of fingers. It is too patrician. And yet, again, perhaps it might: there is something in the upper lip of teasing.

It is also passionate.

I hold the picture in my hand, absorbed.

The cajoling pose, the fleeting glance – I sense that they are moments in a long-gone conversation. That look, so strangely intimate, has been received and pinned. And in the foreground, faintly stained across uneven ground, blurring at the edge of the print, the cryptic shadow of the photographer – it requires the magnifying glass to decipher – the shadow-curve of arms and crown which reaches almost to the toe of his boot.

It is a female form.

I take the folder away. I do not hand it over the librarian's desktop for the blue stamp – always running out of ink – but lodge it among my papers. I have never done that before but there is no pang of conscience. What does the librarian know of cattle with names like *'the fruit of the Wild Medlar'*, *'the fledglings of the owl'*, *'millet and amasi'*? What does she know of *June, 1963*? She will only miss the number in the sequence of the files and fret at the carelessness of students.

Besides, it is simple.

It has been left there for me.

I take the proposal for the dissertation to my supervisor.

'I've found it!' I am bouncing, slipping in my sandals from sweaty excitement.

He looks at me over his half-moon reading glasses, coffee cup poised, his mouth forming a kiss for the steam, a moist little 'o'. He dilates his nostrils gently, puts the cup down, leans back, fingers poised against each other. It is his 'all-ears' attitude. He is already forming objections.

'Listen to this.' I wave the folder at him, untie the string, fan the papers on the edge of his desk. ' "*Inkomo engamuntu elel' ephakathi*"!'

'I beg your pardon?' Not the usual 'What?' He is being formal now.

' "The cow which is the person lying inside".'

He picks up his coffee cup again and takes a sip. 'Which is . . .?'

'A cow,' I say triumphantly, 'which has a colour-pattern which looks like a person lying inside it.'

'Could be very uncomfortable.' He takes up the teaspoon and taps it reflectively in his palm. The pile of essay scripts in front of him is large. He is distracted by them, anxious I should go. I pass over a photograph. It is rather small and blurred. 'Looks an odd cow to me,' he says, 'especially as it is clearly a bull.'

'And this,' I say, ignoring the blunder, 'is *ezikhala zemithi*, which is the dappling, or whatever, of the trees. The silhouettes of them. You know, against the sky. It's just like branches. Don't you think it's amazing?'

He takes the print and looks. There is a flicker. 'Go on,' he says.

'I found this in the old stacks. It's lists and lists of the colour-pattern terminology in Zulu for indigenous cattle. Full of natural reference. It's all the most beautiful metaphor and association with birds and animals and plants. There's a comparative section with Xhosa terms. It's wonderful!'

He puts out his hand and draws the manuscript across. He turns the pages. I wait. His coffee stands. I can almost see the surface wrinkle now, a little bitter walnut-skin of cold.

'Nice stuff,' he says, conceding. 'But it's just a list. What do you propose to do with it?'

'A study of colour-pattern terminology. Indigenous cattle. There's a world of history and meaning.'

'Sounds good enough for an honours dissertation.'

Deflated, I draw the papers back. 'In everything that's ever been written about cattle in Africa, they're viewed as peripheral to people. I'm sure they

7

haven't been looked at with *them* as subject and focus. Cattle for their own sake
...' I am being vague, inarticulate: I know exactly what I mean.

He doesn't. 'This is supposed to be a language study.'

'Exactly. Metaphor, imagery and symbolism in naming. Onomastics. Your favourite subject!'

He is not as triumphant as me.

'I found some cattle poems,' I say. ' *"He comes in Beauty, Father-of-the-Morning. He stretches himself across the sky, this wonderful Bovine".* '

He pays no attention. I am being fulsome. He is not even a little indulgent. I want to laugh at him.

He wants to laugh at me. I can hear him – *stupid bloody girl and her cows.* Instead he says, 'I might have thought you'd take on something more contemporary, a little more challenging. Have you looked at Derrida's "Of Grammatology" yet? I bet you haven't. We have to examine the structures that generate meaning ...'

'These *are* structures that generate meaning.'

I have interrupted him – but he continues without missing a beat '– how the texts themselves subvert those very structures. Have you looked at deconstruction? This is all very well – but it's somewhat anachronistic.'

'What happened to beauty?' I say.

My ears burn. Imagine saying that to a professor: *What Happened to Beauty!*

There is a small silence. It lasts just a moment longer than it should. 'Pardon?' he says.

I start to gather up the papers. There is a place on my neck that glows like a welt when I am embarrassed. Perhaps he has noticed it. He takes off his reading glasses. Avuncular, he says more kindly, 'Who wrote this stuff?' putting out his hand and drawing over the title page.

'C J Godfrey.'

Despite himself, he is impressed. He makes an approving sort of snort, pulling the edge of his moustache in under his upper lip.

'Why? Do you know him?' I still do not meet his eyes.

'No, but I know his work on tonology.' He is scanning the pages again. 'Good on comparative stuff. Fine linguist. He was here, teaching. Fifty years ago, at least.'

The phone rings. He swivels on his chair to answer it. I tap the papers together and tie them into the folder.

He is making little signs at me to make more coffee. I want to go but he is insistent. I take his cup and walk to the door. I know he is watching me, that vague sort of gaze at retreating legs which is more a habit than appreciation.

'Tell me about Godfrey,' I say, when I return.

'I've just found this rather interesting coffee blend,' he muses, drifting his nose across the steam. 'I discovered it last week. Oh, by the way, you must give me those first year marks from the essay you set. Did you take the register? I can't find it anywhere.' He is lifting papers and books and putting them down.

'What blend?' I say.

'A sort of special that this fellow makes. A bit of this and that. I don't know the proportions. Quite a bit of mocha, I should think.'

As easily as he is diverted, he can be brought into line again. 'Godfrey,' I say, quite firmly.

'There's a picture of him in the Senate Chamber with all the dear-departed. Monkish-looking chap,' says the prof. 'What do you think of it?'

'I haven't seen it.'

'The blend.'

'The blend?'

It is all the same to him.

I put in my proposal. It is accepted, without murmur, by the Higher Degrees Committee. I am given access to all C J Godfrey's work. There are three letters from the Higher Degrees Committee to prove it. C J Godfrey's personal papers are mine to scrutinise whenever I like. On the way back from the Dean's suite, passing the pictures in the passage of the alumni who had died in two world wars, each suspended from the picture rail by a wooden rod, regimented against the cream stucco walls, I stop at the door of the Senate Chamber. The dark teak gleams. The brass handle is burnished weekly by a man in overalls, whistling quietly in his head, the tin of Brasso at his feet, the little scraps of newspaper that he has used balled into the wire bin he nudges before him with his foot from door to door. Gingerly, I pull the handle down, listening for voices within. It takes a moment to engage. I press my shoulder against the panelling.

No one is inside. The great-backed Edwardian chairs, leather-spined, hold consultation across the table. Above each – an echo of their present incumbents, different only by the style of their spectacles, the middle partings in their hair – are the portraits of long-gone professors who occupied them once. I go from face to face. No one smiles. They are distinguished by their age, their ubiquitous jowls, the thinning at the temples, the receding crowns. It is not hard to find him. Despite the pose – it seems the whole lot were exhumed and taken in a batch, framed in black – his face is distinctive. It is shadowed, a little smoky, as if he held his pipe just beyond the crisply bevelled mount. Black eyes, black hair, that cool intensity, appraising me. He should be sculpted, not drawn. The fine ridge of his lip, the delicately moulded counterpoint of nostril, the line angled down his cheek dividing the lean plane beneath the cheekbone, should be tactile. His hair is greying at the temples. He no longer has a beard. The jaw is not softened by age. His eyes are faintly humorous. The photographer's earnestness at so much eminence has earned a small unspoken riposte: it is Godfrey, laughing at himself.

Underneath, in brass:
Professor C J Godfrey
Department of African Languages
(1933–1947)

I wonder what the '*CJ*' stands for?
He has only one name for me.
Godfrey. Simply that.

I pin my proposal to my notice board to remind myself that this is to be a
language study, a doctoral thesis on colour-pattern terminology and naming-
practice in relation to indigenous cattle: linguistically sound, literary, with
full acknowledgement to the unfinished work and archival record of the
original researcher – *him* – but my dissertation, nonetheless. Biography has
nothing to do with it beyond an introductory paragraph – the polite reverence
for departed scholarship – a trite dedication, perhaps a picture.

'Not necessary,' says the prof briskly, 'this is not a literary work – and, while
we are about it, please take out that ox poem at the head of the abstract. It
interferes with the tone of the thing.'

I do not take it out. I have found lost fragments of ox poems, aphorisms,
proverbs – whatever – scattered all through Godfrey's extended text. They are
full of the enchantment that led him here in the first place.

That led me.

I secure my place in the postgrad reading room. I have laid out my territory.

'Thirteen boxes of manuscript, my dear,' says the librarian. 'All uncatalogued
and in a bit of a muddle' – checking the inventory – 'and so many of those old
index cards!' They squat on the desk with extraordinary detachment, lumpish,
divested of personality. Here, a scratched 'table of contents', there, a sheaf of
papers skewered with a brass hinge, the flanges splayed at the back to secure
them, the rust stain of years grainy against the paper. These pages are a carbon
copy, cheap purple ink, the 'v's' and the 'y's' vagrant, wherever they occur. The
stops and commas are punctuated firmly enough to pierce the paper. And, as if
– from all those years ago – he had anticipated my unknown supervisor, he has
noted:

'*The researcher may believe that he has fully grasped the actual nature of some
situation, but if he mingles his description of it with personal judgement and with
passion he will never properly convey that actuality to his readers, and, in truth,
he will not himself have fully grasped it. For the moment of dispassionate
understanding is not complete until it has been clearly communicated to other
men.*'

10

The moment of dispassionate understanding?

I do not believe him. Even by the vigour and the speed with which he thumped those 'v's' and 'y's' across the page, I know he was not dispassionate. He might have believed it once, defending himself – but he changed his mind in time. Oh yes, he changed his mind. In time he overturned his chilly dictum on dismissing passion and personal judgement. Perhaps it was the bravest thing he did.

The last time he lived here was just over fifty years ago. I know. Besides his *'Field Notes'*, I have a small suitcase of papers and photos. Among them I found a slip from the store, enumerating expenses:

25th November, 1946.
1lb tea
1 bottle paraffin
½ lb brown sugar
sm tin condensed milk
4oz tobacco
2 bxs matches

This is a desolate place, but without the glamour of real desolation: it is not set at the edge of a desert vista, there are no dark histories, no raging sunsets. The dusk is usually quiet and grey. *'Vaal'* is the only way to describe it. Dusty and *vaal* with a small cold wind. It is anonymous on the map as well – except for the symbol which denotes a post office and a police station. As far as I can tell, this house must have belonged to the original trader. The store is usually closed now, but the change is recent. Not long ago, thieves broke up the bars and took the till. Since I first came here, chicken netting has been erected, reaching to the ceiling. Between the shopkeeper and the customers is a roughly made port through which money and goods can be exchanged. The shelves are almost empty. There is a brand of motor oil and a brand of cooking oil. There is a substantial number of packets of tea. There are Lennon's remedies, there is some flour. The charm of a full trading store has gone. When he was here it would have been stocked with bolts of material, stacked to the ceiling. Now the upper shelves are empty. There is only a dusty statue of St Joseph holding the Christ-child and a lily. It watches over the chicken wire, a recluse in a niche of shadow. There is a glass display case: some mouth organs; two penknives in boxes, long ago rusted into their hasps; a wedding and engagement ring set. They have been there for years, waiting for a hasty marriage. Once, I nearly bought them, to put them out of their expectation in the velvet-lined box with its plastic dome, the diamond like an ice-cream cone, the gilt of the gold flaking off the band. There is duck-boarding on the floor, old pallets for heaving sacks. Outside, scraps of engine, long past repair, used to lie about a small square of pasture, incurious as old cattle. Now they are gathered in a rusty iron shed. They recall another entry which I found and filed:

– jendevu (umjendevu / imijendevu)
i) Old beast past further service.

These machines, forlorn and abandoned: *imijendevu.*

On either side of the shop, cream-washed, the colour of stale whey, red-roofed, corrugated, are the two sections of the dwelling. It makes one long building. The windows are small, mostly sash. A new steel frame has been put into the living room. It sits flush with the wall and there is no deep sill. The brown enamel paint flakes in shards, there is a crack like a star where a rock pigeon collided with the glass. I found it when I came, feathered in rust and roan, its eye like lizard-skin.

Now the shop is only opened sometimes.

Why would Godfrey choose this place, so detached from his usual haunts – the university, the museum storeroom, the old house of his childhood with its warren of rooms interleading, walls bolstered with fine, woven Indian cloth, stretched tight as a tympan, some fancy of his father's. School. Cambridge. Flanders. London. Paris. Cairo. The north-eastern bush country of the old Northern Rhodesia. The Masai Mara.

It ended here – and it is here that I will fix him. So small, so prosaic in comparison with where he'd been before – a man who'd looked out on the Cam every morning from his window in Clare, who'd ridden his bicycle along the old roads and lanes and byways, who'd drowsed at lunch-time recitals at St John's. All that antiquity, that scholarship, that poetry – for this.

And yet – it is this ridge, spined across the high white sky, bleached to bone, that held him. *Uqolo lwezimpungutye.* The ridge of jackals.

Is this the place of his epiphany? Or mine?

Choosing to live here was an eccentricity: candlewick bedcover in old worn cream, an eiderdown, a picture on the wall with a black frame, hanging on a chain, some dusty ledgers with shop entries. Did anyone else come here?

There is no evidence. This was a workplace, a place to write.

But I know that a writer's room is never empty. There is always someone. Perhaps not present. But there.

He may have kept some photographs of his wife, Stella, and their sons. Not on his desk though – he was not that kind of man. He was more likely to have framed a picture of his dog. And her? The faint presence in the photograph, the supple shadow at his feet?

No, he would not have kept a picture of her. There would be no evidence of

12

her in any of his possessions or in his speech. Not even in his breath, no undertone of talk in her absence to betray him. Perhaps, then, I am simply inventing her, some alter-ego for myself, now heroine, now rival. She may not have existed at all.

And yet, each small flourish, with his ubiquitous pencil in the margins of his dictionary cards, is addressed to another. The tone, the register, has the echo of a word exchanged. There is a sense of dialogue. And once or twice – just faintly – he has written '*G, check this . . .*' And once or twice, on entries about stars, '*The "aardvark of the sky" is a red planet which calls the flying ants out after rain! G, don't you like that?*'

When I found them first – a recognition so instant, so obvious – I needed somebody to know, to share the excitement of discovery. I telephoned my supervisor on the crank-handled phone in the shop. 'There is something fascinating in the dictionary index cards . . .' Was he listening, two hundred and seventy-three kilometres away in his cream-painted room overlooking the university quad and the fountain? 'It's a sort of dialogue. It's as if he's talking to someone.'

'Who's talking?'

'Godfrey.'

There was a small silence. Then he said, 'Concentrate on the cattle-terms and the dictionary. I told you, who wrote it, doesn't matter.'

'But you can't separate them.'

He did not choose to hear. He said instead, 'How far have you got?'

I say – perversely – 'To *"G"*.'

'*G*?'

'*Gxamanxa.*'

Another silence. This time, it is because he does not recognise the word. He does not say so.

' "That which is divided".' I was being pedantic.

'I thought you might be further.' He was irritable.

' "Irrevocably parted".'

Now he was pretending that the line was bad. 'What was that?'

'I've been in the field, where Godfrey had his herd,' I said quite briskly. 'Talking to a chap called Delekile who works at a run-down old store that's been here since long before Godfrey's time. He can't remember any patterns. Whenever I show him the photos he just says, "*bantom*", like a bantam, or "*i-bles le*", something with a blaze on its face. He's given me some contemporary praise-names, though. They suit the kind of boring cattle you get here now . . .' I rattle them off. 'There's a lovely one for aeroplane. *Flayimashini*. And *Kom-kom* – police van, you know. "*Kom, kom, kom, kom, klim in, julle vuilgoed*". Come, come, come, climb in, you rubbish.'

He tried to laugh.

13

'*Demfulu. Blatifulu.*' I said it rather too pointedly. 'Good names for oxen, don't you think?' Damn fool. Bloody fool.

We have missed each other. He is rather offended, impatient to be gone.

There is no one to tell after all.

Only Godfrey knows – and he has been dead for nearly forty years.

For hours I might be restless, shuffling cards, looking for signs. Once I came across an entry with a comment pencilled in the margin. I moved it to my own box, beaten from tin, decorated with the advertising logo for a brand of snuff. I bought it from Delekile. He was pleased, said he would make more for me. Godfrey's catalogue boxes are wooden with an elegant little brass port for an alphabet card. They are *objets* in their own right. But so are mine, made from the newer, bright detritus of the world he led me to explore. The lexicon stays in the wooden boxes, but when I find an entry that is 'Godfrey' more than word – I mark it 'G' as well – I copy it and keep it in the tin box:

BUTE SNUFF
Healing . Soothing . Quick Relief

I think he would have liked that. He liked simple things, honestly made. Things that worked. I found his old propelling pencil and his nib pen and compass box. Such a sturdy little box. Such precision in the way each thing lay in its moulding. The old plush inside has a well-loved nap, rubbed here and there to thread: he had used it often. He had scratched his initials on the lid. Small boy writing, fashioned – tongue slid to the corner of the mouth, hot concentration – not to spoil the dark gloss of the lid. I like to think he held these things in his hands. Boy hands, knuckled and undexterous; man hands, deft as a musician's . . .

'*Uchibidolo: abundance. An abundance of herds, a concourse of cattle.*'
He has written in the margin, in pencil:
First memory (2-3yrs? Maybe a little older) – being in middle of stampeding oxen. Great excitement!!

Again, implicit in the entry is exchange. This is not the work of a solitary man.

His first memory is of cattle.

He is running free, escaped from the custody of child-minders, through the fence and into a camp where outspanned oxen dip muzzles in a long stone trough. Whatever startles them, they turn as one. Small, very small, in the midst of the herd lumbering round him, ponderous and clumsy with horn and hoof, so close to trampling him, his child-minder shouting

14

– the high fearful voice of a woman – he stands at the still centre of their frenzy, breath-suspended, the underbelly-smell of cattle. Does he laugh in triumph when they have passed, exulting in his own storm of thunder-hooves, the lightning-scythe of horns, the flash of eyes, the spark of hoof on stone?

They became a passion. For him. For me.

This is something that my good professor does not understand. Magic eludes him. Passion. He remains stubborn. He repeats it often: *who* collected the material on cattle is peripheral to *how* it was done. I am fortunate to have discovered such a homogenous and thorough corpus of research, lucky that I do not have to do all the fieldwork myself. Despite his reservations about my motivation (the word 'beauty' hangs inadmissibly between us) and my lack of enthusiasm for Deconstruction, he has conceded the point, that – fortuitously – an archive, well-documented and scholarly, collected at a certain time, has turned up, ready for analysis and comparison with contemporary usage in more than one indigenous language.

'Turned up'. That's what he said.

I do not explain that it did not 'turn up'. It was there, in trust.

I do not say how incomplete it is. That it stopped. Suddenly. That the usual rigour, the unassailable scholarship of everything Godfrey ever wrote before, simply ends at '*v*', '*–valamlomo* (*what closes the mouth*)', the catalogue cards, stacked and equally divided between the letters following to '*z*', empty and slightly foxed.

It is my task to complete it.

Why Godfrey stopped will be between us. I will not mention it to Prof again. As he says – with a hint of condescension at my choosing an 'easy option' – it is a privilege to inherit the work. I was not registered, I do not pay my fees, just to act as voyeur.

So.

Through all the months of my research, I collate diligently. I check each synonym for colour-patterns in cattle again and again and marvel that mottled and speckled, that blotched and gashed and stippled can be classified at all, with so much precision. Like him, I am now acquainted with each carefully annotated photograph, each diagram, each and every beast in his forgotten herd. I know the grey-roan bull, the dun. I know the little *inala* cow – so particular – with the white face and painted eyes, black-lined and the red-speckled pattern of her hide: *I am the Kei apple, I am Abundance; I am the bridal party beast with the moon-white face.* He played with patterns as he played with words. He also had the soul of a missionary: such rigour is testimony to subjugation of mind and (in this paraffin glow) of his eyes as well. I am astonished at his industry. There are moments, though, when the writing

15

becomes vague. One senses a break, the turning of his pencil, his thoughts straying elsewhere – and a word falls, unthreaded.

It is these I must restore.

Not for the sake of the work. For him.

And so I am here, returning as he had once returned, so many years ago. Like him, I will set out on the road, travelling west.

Soon it will be sunrise: *kusempondozankomo,* the time of the horns of the cattle, dark against the dawning sky. The white light will rise behind the ridge, a lyre-horn of aloe transform from ironstone to dust.

Chapter two

I should start at the beginning. I should start with his birth. But that is not the way it works. Most biographies are elegies: it is only in reflection of the whole that meaning emerges. The story is elliptical – the writer knows the end before it is begun, has already wept and triumphed and despaired. Without it, who would be moved to commit to paper the words, '*In the Beginning . . .*' with all their grandeur and their promise? For the biographer, to explore a life before its final resolution, is to compromise the plot and invite a rival in.

There will be no addenda for C J Godfrey – mostly because I will not share him. In admitting that, do I forfeit the right to his story? Above all, a biographer must be objective. There may be no insinuating of oneself into the life of the subject.

And yet, from the day of finding the file in the library stacks, we begin to exist in the utmost dependence, he and I. We have the Afterlife between us. We overlay each other with our histories, layer by layer. First his, then mine. His. Mine. He beckons me. I follow. I beckon him – and he is there. It is only perfect faith that makes it possible, perfect trust that can permit this fragile, reckless shadow-dance of ours.

But he must wait. First, I must churn my way through the abstract for my thesis, the plan, the field of research. Methodology. I make graphs and schedules, meet my professor each week. Brew the coffee, listen to his discourse on direct and indirect metaphor.

'What is metaphor?' he says, intoning like a cleric.

'Everyone knows what metaphor is,' I reply.

He produces a volume – he has been waiting for this moment – 'Well, here is a book which proves that no one can give a satisfactory definition!' He tosses it to me triumphantly.

You will have to wait, Godfrey. You will have to wait for me to nail that definition down.

I am dogged as you would have been, working through the texts. I have hundreds of pages of notes. You have hundreds of catalogue cards. We make maps together: the movement of the herds down Africa. I follow yours, adjusting to the latest findings. Do you approve? Do you mind if I correct you sometimes?

And then the term ends and I am gone. I take a train to the town where he was born. It is the way he would have travelled from home to school and back again. I must go alone. My arrangements for my family are elaborate, bordering on indulgence. I tuck little notes of love about the house for children, husband (under the pillow, in a gym bag, propped against a CD player). I put flowers in every room for caretaker grandparents: my mother with her stock of counter-indulgences, my father with his toolbox for fixing up a year's worth of household neglect. He has the zeal of a Jesuit.

I promise to bring back presents. I promise to go shopping with our elder daughter on the day that I return. I promise the younger that she can have a ginger kitten. Or a puppy. Or a mouse. I know that I am rash – but I am guilty.

I go, uneasily, bargaining with God. But I know, as the stations pass, one by one, I will begin, half consciously to suspend myself within Godfrey's time. And I will slowly change from lumbering about with my files and notes and library books and bags of groceries and clutches of bills and lists of daily chores and notices for PTAs and cake mornings at school, into someone who treads very softly, lightly, whispering her way through rooms. For the occasion, I have kept my cotton print ballet shoes, my old silk coat circa 1932, the linen shirt I have hoarded for two years from the Trinity Charity Shop in Kensington Church Street in London, one pound ten and a soft nap to the hand-stitched collar. I will wait at the edges of his world, a presence to him as he is to me, transforming each other. If I am strident, in any way, if I tell his story to too many, he will simply disappear. He will tolerate no intruders.

An April morning with the sunlight glinting on the garnet-speckled gravel of the lawn. His childhood home, cream walls, heavy brown shutters under acres of corrugated roof. I hear my feet approach the door.

He used to play here. That pepper tree against the fence is very old, it would have been less gnarled, perhaps, but not much smaller. The red corrugated fence sends its concertina shadow down across a dusty row of cypresses. There is a little conservatory in its shade. It is empty. I know the scents of such a place, the rust-coloured spores. He might have hidden sometimes, under the cool dripping tables which held the pots of plants, in a mossy, spidery gloom. The glass panels reflect the clouds beyond my gaze at the far side of the roof of the house: refractions of light, mirror mysteries that invert the chimney pots, take up the jigsaw patterns of the trees. I stand, waiting

18

for him.

And the child who came to play.

I know it was a girl. I sense her, standing on the gravel walk. I see through her eyes, watching the porch door for him. There is he, swinging round the corner of the house, at the kitchen end, in khaki, with his shotgun. He comes towards her. Towards me. There is the iris bed between us, the gravel walk. I glance away and back – and he is gone.

Godfrey?

Standing where I am, unmoving, clod-like – how can he approach or take her with him if I insist on appropriating her myself? I must free her. But I can't until I know her little gestures and her voice, forming somewhere in my head.

I have to find her face.

I have no doubt I will. She will be there – somewhere among his letters and his photographs. We will recognise each other when the moment comes.

The archivist from the Africana Library has not arrived yet but she has arranged for me to see his family home and she is bringing the keys at eight o'clock. 'We'll have a quick nip around,' she had said on the phone. 'It's a bit of a mess at the moment because alterations are about to start. Bathrooms and kitchen. But you'll get an idea.'

I have had some correspondence with her. My thesis is the passport to all her attentions. I have said I am looking for additional material relating to Godfrey's cattle project, his correspondence with a Dr Crawford who had set up a task-group of scientists from what was then called the Department of Native Agriculture, to investigate the status of indigenous cattle in the 1940s. Though in quite another discipline, Godfrey's work on naming-practice had come to their attention. I could imagine the old biologists shaking their heads over the odd bloke collecting the indigenous colour-pattern terms of cattle for a lexicon.

–Terms?

–Must be a missionary type!

It appears that Dr Crawford had asked Godfrey to note numbers and general colour and pattern distribution of animals of Sanga-Nguni origin in the rural areas of Zululand and the Cape where his own work for the lexicon was being conducted. A happy confederacy of science and linguistics. Dr Crawford had sent a paper of his own, *Influence of Colour and Coat Cover on Adaptability of Cattle*: *My latest offering. Regards, Crawford.*

Perhaps Dr Godfrey would care to comment on what the natives themselves have to say about their herds? Breeding preference in terms of colour etc, etc, etc.
Et cetera, et cetera, et cetera . . .

19

There is no record of Godfrey's reply but there is a brief letter from Crawford, dated some months later:

Is there any reason, Dr Godfrey, for distinguishing between seven shades of red? For the purposes of our statistics, such distinctions are unnecessarily cumbersome.

There is a carbon copy of a terse and immediate report-back to Crawford and Co. No more 'quaint' differentiations:

Ndlovini District: cattle dip no 1. 51 beasts.
85% mixed stock (European breeds)
15% (Sanga-Nguni type):

48% black and white
24% red and white
12% brown and red-brown
12% red (Afrikander influence evident)
2% dun
2% white to pale dun

He would have kept *'the clouds about the moon', 'the stones of heaven', 'the stabber of the rain with the rump like a lark's egg'* to himself. Such frivolity would have annoyed the scientists: the specifics of indigenous languages are not their concern or how, in another idiom, percentages – so neat a device for quantifying – might have changed the pattern-profile of the herd entirely. There is no such thing as 'brown', Dr Crawford. There are only the nuances of mud and sunlight, mud and rain, the shade of wood smoke, the tinge of red from gall and spleen or the feathers of a Redwinged Starling.

The science is far more exact than you could believe, Dr Crawford.

But metaphor is not science. It is ephemeral. It deals in Intuition. It deals in Beauty: that inadmissible word.

I walk down the drive towards the porch. The pathway to the door is a threshold. Here, one treads softly. The house is long and low – so many shutters, so many doors, so many angles of lime-washed wall. Up on the roof, among the planes and peaks there is a little veranda room. Its railings are painted white. A staircase angles up to the portico. For a moment – just a moment – it is as if I have seen it before, as if I know it: there will be a washstand, an enamel jug and basin decorated with embossed flowers, a drift of leaves from the pepper tree shored up in a corner. I can hear my own breathing, cupped now by the still sunlight reflected off the walls.

The archivist arrives. She drives an old Austin A40 with rust on the bottom of the doors. It is a warm morning with a *bergwind* blowing but she wears a cardigan and glazed pottery beads on a leather thong. She carries a basket of files. She keeps saying 'very nice to meet you, at last'. We have had a long correspondence about this visit. About this house.

It is owned by a company of which Godfrey's father was once a director. It was sold to them by Godfrey after his father's death. He had no use for it any more. He was returning to England. As an example of colonial architecture it has few peers. It is a mixture of Godfrey's father's self-importance and eccentricity but – *quo vadis* – it reflects, now, the company's new-found awareness of 'heritage' and, having been neglected for a number of years and used only as a repository for company records, it is – according to the archivist – 'about to be revamped'. It will be used as a small conference centre. 'Intimate' is the word chosen for the brochure. A whiff of sentiment in place of the trite (and suspect) 'exclusive'. There will be a pair of suites for visiting executives, all in line with the recent rage for 'historic getaways':

Absorb the ambience of the mess tent the night before the battle of Magersfontein . . .
Experience the African night, in all its mystery, the way the early hunters knew it.
Legends like Wolhuter, Stevenson-Hamilton, Selous camped here . . .
Sleep in the room where the treason trialists held their clandestine meetings . . .

Such discretion, such carefully coordinated taste in everything. Such pastiche.

Another sort of colonisation.

The house is a labyrinth, a strangely male preserve, despite the elaborate wallpaper in the bedroom. It has the air of a 'chummery' in Patna. There is expanse and light and space in the reception rooms. The kitchen, scullery and bathroom are small, dark and spare. The billiard room is still hung about with hunting trophies. There is half a century of dust on the black wildebeest's nose. He has aged prematurely into his white-haired dewlap. Soon the clay-brick walls will fall victim to the interior designer's mania for bathroom space, will brace their unevenness for the new, paint-distressed dado rails. Duck-egg blue? Provençal sage? Tuscan terracotta?

We go from room to room and everything is carefully explained.

'Isn't this extraordinary?' says my companion, standing in the dining room with her hands on her hips. All along the walls, below the picture rail, a finely woven, deeply faded Indian cotton cloth, fine-printed in sepias and olives and rust, serves as a covering, as if it was hand-painted wallpaper. William Morris with an Afghan twist. 'Very eccentric, really,' she laughs. 'But that, I believe, was Harold Godfrey all over! I'm told that, after the old man died, our Doctor Godfrey didn't want much of the furniture. I think he kept some of the better pieces for his sons. But his wife didn't like it. He made an arrangement with the company to use what they needed and to sell the rest for him as they saw fit. Sensible really. After all, why would anyone choose to live in a mausoleum like this?'

'Our Godfrey'?

It was not proprietorially meant, it was only for distinction.

He is not mine either.

I gaze at the minute interlace of vines and peacocks on the wall. I am waiting for a sign.

She leads me through the shuttered hall. I am in the slipstream of her voice. She explains the house – not as it was or is, but as it is going to be. I hardly look. I cannot look until I am alone. I am a surveyor on a distant hill, picking out the first clear points of a geography, still to be explored.

His story begins in the nursery.

As soon as I entered it – that cobweb touch on naked skin – I knew that room. Quietly I stepped down beside the looming rank of dark-wood cupboards, the sly reflection of the mirrors and the faint stain of sun from the skylight in the roof. I knew, at once, those angled shadows, sharp as guillotines, that rind of yellow paint. I sat in the deep window recess, leaned my shoulder on the sash frame, watched the motes drift down like sediment in water. I had known this in another guise, felt its weight against my heart. As a child, in a room like this, I had first sensed death. I had brought it in myself, palms yellow with its stain.

There were lands on my uncle's farm ploughed deeply for a crop of maize. It was a bush country farm – hard, with blue horizons. The ploughing was in virgin soil. The earth was so red it seemed like innards, loosely butchered; so red, it gleamed in the hollows with its moisture, the scab of upturned soil dried to powder by the sun. All along the disturbed edges, stunted vegetation grew. There was a plant. It was spare and spiky but the fruits were firm yellow globes, strung along the branches like shaded lights. A ragged claw of stalk, spined like a lizard's foot, gripped the flattened apex of each.

It should have been a warning.

But the fruit shone and the sun touched it and I picked it to look inside its flesh. I had always had this sense – tearing with the teeth – of being the very first to see the substance on the inside of an apple or a grape. A small, but absolute discovery of purity, the pristine crystals punctured, oozing juice.

I picked a yellow fruit and the thick, satin rind rolled smoothly in my hot palm, back and forth until a stain of yellow tinged it. My father, walking just ahead, turned, saw it and dashed it from me – just a little roughly – 'Don't touch! It's very poisonous.'

In that instant, that shining morning, the world of ploughed land, of golden-globed bushes thrusting up along the margins of the furrows, were all stained by death.

In Beauty was Death. And such deception.

The rind-mark in my palm was death, cupped intimately under my folded fingers. Carbolic did not wash it away.

That night, lying in the bed in the bare veranda room of the old farm house, the ray of the paraffin lamp from the passage door for the first time malevolent, Death was drawn in the stern trajectory of the shadow of the cupboard up against the corner. It was a gallows looming on the wall while the dim lozenge of the skylight glimmered through it with a different dark. Shadow cast on shadow, it hovered, a corporeal presence, half suspended near the wall.

I would die. If not tonight, in this bleak room, by the bitter stain of the yellow fruit leaking through my skin, then in the silence of a place like this: with this dim presence and this dark.

I wept for my mother somewhere in the lively concourse of my uncle's house. I willed her with the fiercest force of will to come to me. But she remained beyond my hearing.

Only in the next room.

This dim presence and this dark.

I knew it on that autumn morning in Godfrey's nursery room as well. Not just a trick of light, not just a composition of refractions from a skylight, a shuttered window and a row of mirrors. It was another recognition, an overlap of history and of intuition, of perception and of presence.

There is an equal gravity in rooms where birth and death have taken place. Sometimes they have witnessed both. Some are sanctuaries. Others, judgement chambers.

Godfrey's room was both.

It is an autumn night when he is born. His mother does not deliver him in the bed in which he was conceived, but in the newly designated nursery. They are different worlds. She will not allow them to make association: the great ripe roses on the walls of the bedroom are decayed with the burrowing of ants behind the picture rail. Her own cell is too sanctified and spare for childbirth. She has created, instead, a nursery in an unused room. She has had it painted yellow and even if the linen cupboards with their many bevelled mirrors reflect the darker corners, the gloomy doorways, the lost interiors, the lines of linoleum, it is a hopeful colour. Her husband, Harold, has been disparaging, saying yellow is known to be full of lead and arsenic and if the child licks the walls, what then?

What then?

The windows are shuttered in dark-painted wood but, as she labours, she can see the stars through the faint ribbing of dust on the glass of the

23

skylight. The pepper trees have dropped their leaves. They eddy at the margins of the frame. Earlier, looking up, in daylight, the sky was washed a tired ochre-grey. The wind outside is dry and hot, but the flagging of the deep veranda is cold with shadow and the dustiness of flyscreens. In the long hours of labour, the change of vigil at her bedside is reflected in the pale sky deepening to mauve at dusk, the wind rising, leaves scudding at the skylight. The stars beyond. She may not have known their names, but she would have seen the clean-bladed gold of Orion's Belt, a sword drawn for his birth. Did she know it was a son, because of the constellations – the clear, aseptic wholeness of them, the sharp edge of their brightness? Did she know he would be sprung like a hunting-bow, lean as its sinew, tuned to the tapping of the stars?

There can be no reclamation of Godfrey's childhood without his mother. It is another chapter, even another century. I must coax it back, restore the boy, retrieve his life from separate spaces, give each part its register and weight. In the end, that can be my only gift to him.

I have seen the notice in the papers, tracing back through the old bound copies in the Africana Library, the smell of their pages like ashes, the leaves brittle all along the edges:

To Mr and Mrs Harold Godfrey, a son,
on 5th October, 1898.

And then, by chance, in the social columns some months later, in among reports of civic functions, society weddings and a much-vaunted (and titled) guest speaker at the City Club:

13th March 1899:
Mrs Harold Godfrey was seen in her carriage, riding out this afternoon. It is rumoured that her little son is the most beautiful boy ever seen, with fine black eyes. She is justly proud and displayed him, in his visiting bonnet.

Justly proud. Was this the start?

Ah, Mrs Harold Godfrey, you have given your heart entirely to your son and forgotten your husband. Women often do. It is unwise. The bruising is slow and insidious. Was it then that she moved to her own room, leaving the decadence of the roses behind and the chaise longue and the deeply swagged velvet at the windows? Was it then she changed it all for a demure dresser and a washstand with a plain white jug and basin and three drawers that did not run smoothly, a little crucifix and a holy water stoop?

Oh most gracious Virgin Mary,
That never was it known
That anyone who fled to thy protection,
Implored thy help or sought thy intercession
Was left unaided.
Inspired by this confidence I fly unto thee,
Oh, Virgin of Virgins, my Mother . . .

What has the Virgin Mary to do with jealousy between father and son? What has the Virgin Mary to do with Godfrey?

I do not go alone to the veranda room on the roof on that first visit. The archivist goes with me, looking about, concerned that the area has been left unswept. 'The wind is very dusty at this time of year,' she says. 'It's difficult to keep things clean. But, really, they should organise for someone to come up sometimes.' Her voice becomes, for me, the voice of Godfrey's mother, soft, a little querulous – the quiet underclucks and gurgles of a hen fussing over scraps.

I let her go up the stairs before me. She tackles them as any woman does who knows how to climb in a tight plaid skirt and lace-up shoes: she mounts sideways – I hear the brush of serviceable stockings, the little electric frictions of nylon and acrylic. It is a steep climb.

She is standing at the railing, surveying the garden, when I reach the platform.

I turn instinctively to look into the sheltered area of the porch.

There is a table with a long, slim drawer and broken handles. On top is an enamel basin and a jug. It is a pale blue-mauve, the colour of milky lavender. A spray of white flowers is embossed on it.

It is just an object, long forgotten, rusted with neglect. But it is the first sign.

Thank you, Godfrey.

The outlook is over the roof, the miniature of the conservatory, the lawn and the corrugated fencing. There are outbuildings, stables, a shed and a large enclosed section with a trough. The archivist points. 'I believe that milk cows were kept here eighty years ago. I think there used to be a commonage all the way to the railway line for people's dairy herds. Funny to think of it now with the blocks of flats and the freeway.'

A note is dropped unobtrusively in place: I recall the card (only glanced at) which I had put into the *Bute Snuff Box*, appended with '*G*' in the top right-hand margin.

umvemve [n.] – Cape wagtail (*Moticilla capensis*)
Small, feeble calf.

*Had an 'umvemve' once when I was about 7 or 8. Entrancing creature. V. upset
when it was slaughtered. Father's orders. Can't remember why.*

Still my companion is talking, pointing out the landmarks. Again she is
Godfrey's mother, with a dialogue which can only lap at the edge of my attention.
Such abundant information. Intuitively, I withdraw from her conjecture on
how many cows they might have kept, to restore the cryptic words Godfrey
had scrawled on the margin of the index card: *Had an 'umvemve' once . . .*

We go down. This time I lead. We walk across the driveway and round the
house towards the back, to the old wooden fence that encloses the calf pen and
the trough. The fragrance of dung is gone. The earth is long ago beaten flat by
rain and the relentless summer heat. A pepper tree stands in the enclosure. It
has ancient bark and knots and folded recesses of shade and light, places to sit,
from which to launch out precariously on to the edge of the corrugated boundary
wall, to give a foothold to scramble on to the milking shed roof, a high fork, a
lookout across the whole neighbourhood. It is a stronghold, a fort in the hills,
a ship in a dolphin sea, the summit of the sky.

These were not games to be played alone.

That tree, that calf-pen, that *umvemve* calf, had belonged to more than him.
He had celebrated them with someone else.

I find her back at the Africana Library that afternoon among the photos in the
albums, catalogued 'Early Days', donated by old residents, notables, from school
and club collections. There are half a dozen from the time of the South African
War, another three or four dated 1914-1918. I search among the offerings from
the first decade of the century. Again, it is a matter of recognition, of sensing
each other, knowing it is she who stood tentatively at the gate and waited for
him to come round the corner of the house, knowing it is she who sat in the
pepper tree in the calf-pen, long legs dangling, fear contracting the base of her
spine as she launched out to catch the lower, springier branch which would
bounce her up on to the edge of the fence, if she is as deft as he.

There she is. In a group. Godfrey is at its centre.

She is only a little girl, sitting on a bench with him and half a dozen other
children. She is looking at him. There is something in that look that I know,
something both diffident and rapt. He seems oblivious of her, grinning for the
world. Such black eyes, such dark hair, the contours of his face – that fine
structure – only just submerged beneath a cheek that can still be cupped by
his mother's palm. He is only eleven. The detachment is yet to come. A large
dappled rocking horse, with a wild eye, legs stretched to a gallop along the axle
mechanism, stands behind. Written underneath the picture, white ink on
black card, *Christmas Party, 1909*. Each child's name is noted.

Hers is Gertrude Hayes.

There are other girls in that album. Studio portraits with cloudy skies, a drape and a potted fern. In volumes such as these, it is only those girls of unassailably even profile – the brittleness of a tilted nose, a ridged upper lip, fine, pale hair – who may occupy a frame alone. I page past them ruefully: men always fall in love with the women that these girls become. They like the challenge of their self-absorption.

But she, she is a chip-toothed girl, squinting slightly at the sun, a hand raised to shield her eyes. She wants to be a boy, like him. It is clear in her stance. It is without a hint of display.

Her eyes are watchful as a hare's.

Gertrude. Gert. Such a little girl.

She came with the *umvemve* calf.

Such a little calf, the knuckle bone of dormant horns budding in between its silky ears.

The calf is born in spring. It is a hard spring here in the north-western drylands, not soft and budding and tender-leaved but insistent against the implacable cold, the frost – and then, a blistering wind, blowing hot air to wither buds and shoots. The earth does not slough its dry winter carapace easily. When the rain comes, the surface sucks it in and cracks, armoured like the ancient shells of mountain tortoises. There is a greed for water in this semi-desert place. The buck on the plains are thin, the crop of lambs culled by cold.

The small herd of milk cows for household needs is grazed in the pasture between the fence and the railway line. Among them they produce a threesome of calves that year. One is a 'bush' cow. It belongs to Bibleman, the gatekeeper, the 'dog-boy', wielder-of-the-smooth-wood-*kierie* with amber-coloured ear plugs in his lobes, fashioned from the horn of a long-gone ox.

It is the calf of Bibleman's cow which Godfrey loves, for its whimsy and devotion. *Umvemve*: the wagtail – as frail, as ubiquitous as the little bird. There is a recognition between child and young animal, the puzzled extension of a nose to explore and enquire.

'Look, look! He likes me!'

His mother calls it 'Rufus', with a laugh. So glib. She has not looked at its redness with any care. She has not understood its provenance. And Bibleman, deeply detached from her, does not contradict the name. To do so would invite discussion and profane the calf.

But Godfrey knows. He examines each small fold and aspect. Yes, it is red, but on its rump and head are intricate patterns of cross-hatch and stripe, of brindle and flash, red-white, white-red in mirror-pattern forms, spot to spot in perfect counterpoint, which distinguishes it from the other calves, the stolid little jersey, the cast-eyed Afrikander with its mulberry hocks. For Godfrey, the 'bush' cow's calf is a long-legged medieval knightling in a visor and embroidered cloak, a little jester-beast embossed with its own quaint heraldry. It is kin with the faun-like half-beasts of the cloth which lines the walls of the dining room, his father's dream panorama, stretched across the plaster. He knows where to find an eye hidden behind a leaf, a shape transformed – by staring – into griffin, unicorn or twilight beast, whispering along the wall.

Bibleman – eyes turned on a different Arcadia of thorny river-bank and relic hills – knows better. And tells him.

This calf is of another kind.

This was not a beast of the masters. Its authentic name – like his – could not be probed by them. They would pass by, unaware, unheeding of an ancient lineage, the long migration down the corridors of Africa between mountains, forests, deserts, and dismiss the chants in praise of cattle raised at dusk. Tender or derisive, cajoling, laughing, even simple and banal, like the small, exclusive gestures of a lover, meaning worlds.

The calf was red indeed, red as fresh blood, with a face which is the rust '*veld locust*' and a rump which is '*the eggs of the rufous-naped lark*'.

It is blood.

It is the veld locust.

It is the lark.

A trinity of being. *It is*, this metaphoric calf.

And he loves it. He loves it for its embroidered hide, for the translucence of the white, the luminosity of red, the tender little ridges of the skin at the muzzle, the wet nose, the hooves too big – 'my calf has boots' – standing poised, slightly turned out, with the cloven tips, the knees woolly. Oh, silken tail and underbelly, navel-fold and lamb-soft scrotum.

It is guileless. And trusting.

It is just like Gert.

He allows her to touch it, to put her hand into the hard-ribbing of its mouth, to let it suck. She never assumes the right. Like the calf, she looks to Godfrey for direction.

Sometimes they rope it and lead it into the kitchen where, dipping fists into the enamel sugar bin, they let it lick and pull with a fat cushion-tongue. Long-legged, large-kneed, gauche-footed, the calf knows their voices by every nuance, whisper, lift.

Sometimes, when dusk comes, they walk along the fence, balancing, arms out. Sometimes, they sit on the edge of the trough and watch Bibleman milking the dairy cows. He is swift and deft with the udder of the small calf's dam. They wait to bring the bucket to the calf, to lead – with milky fingers – to the pail, teaching it to drink.

Sometimes Godfrey runs home with Gert. They go flitting down the street, two small shadows, heads no higher than the hedges and the fences. Her house is altogether smaller, warmer, more filled with light than his. There is a tree in the middle of her lawn and the grass, because of a natural spring, is lush.

Sometimes they cut slices of bread and lard them with dripping from the jar beside the Aga stove, lie out on the lawn, press themselves against the ground, spines down, feeling the undercurrent of the earth, its slow turning. The stars are heavy here, in this semi-desert air. And bright. They seem lower, globular with liquid-light and redness. 'That's the pathway to God's cattle-kraal,' Godfrey says, inclining his head to her and pointing, so she can see along his finger.

'It's not! It's the Milky Way!' says Gert, propping herself on her elbow, almost indignant.

'Bibleman said!' Godfrey retorts.

Bibleman has said many things about the universe. She laughs then, liking it. She makes little gestures up at the sky with her arms and hands as if she is gathering up the stars with them.

I found Gert's house on the corner of intersecting streets – no mistake, consulting the old town-planner's map – behind a new concrete fence, imitating pickets. Once, it must have had a corrugated roof. It has been overlaid with cheap tiles, moulded and bent across each other to hide the erratic tinniness of their manufacture. The sash windows had been replaced by steel rectangles, lying horizontal, quite at odds with the counterpoint of tall, slanted shadow from the wooden pillars holding the veranda paling. Where the tickey creeper had once been so abundant, the owners had scrubbed the walls and decorated them with a mosaic of ochre-coloured slasto. Where the pond had been – a natural little spring in the ground, lush with kikuyu grass – a built-in-*braai* in primrose brick incorporated a fibrecrete rock and spout, passing as a 'water-feature'. Stiff papyrus, scissor-trimmed, stood erect beside it.

It was a travesty.

This was not Gert's place of light and shade and ring-necked doves and lying barebacked on the earth to count the stars at night, fat with buttermilk, calabash-candles wicked with pumpkin vine; or silent herds of white-horned cattle in the grazing lands of space, constellations linked immutably with birds and plants and flowers, a great surging pasture turning counter to the earth.

Standing at a distance, across the street, fearing to tread too closely, I notice where an old hedge shouldered the concrete wall at the corner, a path hooped the curve and the shadow of a tree scumbled blue along the roughness of gravel. The track was empty but the footprints of passers-by announced a

29

busy concourse: child feet, bare, the buds of toe-prints, long ago – the scoop of hooves – the vegetable vendor's nose-bagged horse – the pile of fragrant dung where he stood in the tree's shade on Wednesday mornings, waiting for housewives with baskets, housemaids with white enamel dishes. The path led to an open stretch of grass, a running-wild place for children from the ordered rows of houses. I felt their presence in the quiet of the early afternoon: oh, yes – they'd both been here. Often. Gert and Godfrey, hurrying down the street.

Are they really here or have I made them come? A gate clips closed; a pod falls from a tree.

It is Godfrey's father who orders the slaughter of the bush cow and its calf: rumours of foot-and-mouth disease abound. The dairy herd of prize cattle must not be affected. The indulgence of letting Bibleman – in transit – bring in a marriage beast, heavy with calf, acquired from a stock sale in the location is potentially catastrophic. Such impulsive and misplaced largesse – an irritating show of magnanimity after whisky! Oh, the little worm of conscience, made plump by drink:

–Yes, Bibleman, it can stay until you are on your way again.

So it stays, oddly marked, with its small, tight, speckled udder that produces a sort of bush-tainted elixir that has made the calf glisten. He has forgotten it was there until one Wednesday, going to the Club for luncheon, he had had a word with a senior official, passing each other through the double doors of the dining room, standing, feet placed in counterpoint to prevent their slamming closed, almost chest to chest, exchanging mild greetings, ready to pass. A grumble of complaint about having to shoot 'native cattle' on the commonage behind the mine.

–Foot-and-mouth?
Foot-and-mouth.
Godfrey's father is suddenly alert. The double doors scissor-close behind him, bounce back and forth with a heavy, low vibration.

–Damn Bibleman. Give an inch and they'll take a mile. Damn marriage cattle and making allowances for all that nonsense. Damn the whisky for allowing in a shard of generosity!

–Give an inch . . .
Whose inch?
In between the mulligatawny and the haddock he decides on forty shillings compensation. In between the haddock and the veal, on thirty. In between the oxtail and the junket, twenty. Puddings have a soothing effect on a troubled conscience. Milk puddings restore tranquillity entirely.

The dam, the little calf – cattle in honour of a marriage payment, a contract with the lineage shades in respect of a woman and her child – will have to be exterminated.

The butcher arrives on his bicycle, with an assistant.

Bibleman gets twenty shillings in compensation.

The account is closed.

Closed.

Godfrey does not understand.

I have stood in a meat-room in a bush camp with the frenzied bluebottles clinging to the outside of the flyscreen and heard the tear of the butcher's knife, dividing the fibres from the curve of flesh and the white and silver membrane of the inner hide. It is a small, consistent sound – rip-rip-rip – and there is the fresh smell of meat. Blood is clean and salty, the glaze on an eye is a little time in coming. I have seen a limp-headed rhebok ewe, skewered by a meat hook at the hock, the womb-sac with the lamb, marked as delicately, cryptically, as the nap of feathers on a bird, life so finely poised for birth, so keen and vivid in death.

So I know what Godfrey saw.

I know what he saw when he went in search of the *umvemve* calf with its red-enamelled hide and its lark-egg speckles, after school. I know what he heard – the little rip-rip-rip of the knife.

There is the *umvemve* calf, skewered at the sinew of the hind elbow, hanging in the gloom of the meat-room with its corrugated roof and its double flyscreen on the door and the hot wind shaking it.

The sheen is gone. The eyes opaque.

Godfrey stares.

He hears the flies at the screen, the regular, slow drip of blood on the concrete floor. The earth is tilting up towards him.

He backs. He runs. He runs with the sound of the gravel that he scatters, flicking up against his calves, the patter unchanged, the sting of it against his bare legs as familiar as the sting of the ache in his throat. He ducks in through a window at the back, up the stairs, across the small dark inter-leading rooms with the griffons and the beasts watching from the weaving on the wall, down the passage, past the bathroom, its mirror reflecting the white of enamel-painted walls, white enamel buckets, vast white bath. Into the nursery, the only room without the smell of gloom. Under the bed, boxed in in wood, flat-backed beneath the regiments of dust-spiralled springs. The dark is dense with his breath but he holds each one as long as he can, to keep the silence. The tears slide out, they track behind his ears.

It is Gert who finds him. Gert, running to him. She creeps down under the edge of the bed and she lies beside him, not touching because he does not move to let her in. She lies beside him with her plaits picking up the

31

lint and fluff of months, the little sobs forming.

'Why are you crying?' Godfrey says abruptly.

Stung, she does not reply. She cannot say that she is crying for him.

'It is not *your* calf.' Godfrey is fierce.

She does not contradict him. She never contradicts him.

No, it is not her calf.

She tilts her head as far back as it will go so that the tears will sink inward, but it does not help. She says then, 'I know it's safe. It's gone to Heaven.'

'Who says?'

'Everything good goes to Heaven.'

He is rigid, his face turned away from hers. He breathes the flat, dry scent of old dust, of iron bedsprings. It cauterises him – from her. From everything.

Gert weeps on.

It is shameful to weep in the face of such implacable calm. Such tears become unstoppable. They are not tears of grief or loss – but of impotence. One word would staunch them.

The word is never said. And the small embarrassed silence is more deft than a scalpel.

'Gert thinks the calf is in Heaven,' Godfrey says to his mother, half scornful, but needing her to contradict him.

'What's that, my pet?' The delicate hand caresses his head, curves at the crown, the half-conscious sensuousness of his mother's fingers outlining his ear. 'What's that, my precious pet?'

'My calf? Will it be in Heaven?'

She does not answer him directly and he has learned to suspect her ploys. She says instead, 'We will both enter Heaven one day and be together, just you and me, always,' looking at him with her vague, black, disconcerting eyes. 'But you have to be a very good boy and commit no mortal sins and go to confession every week so that your soul is always clean.'

She laughs at his grave face, takes it in both of her hands. She is sucking him into herself – through her eyes, into her core. He pulls away, wriggles from her palms and says, 'The calf didn't have a sin.'

'A calf does not know what sin is, sweetheart.'

'Well then, if it hasn't got a sin . . .'

She stands, lightly stretching. She does not deceive him – he knows she is really brisk to be gone, to deflect him. 'Get your bat and I'll throw a ball for you.'

It is manipulation to avoid the subject. She is hopeless with the ball. He

32

indulges her. When she has tossed it once or twice – duty served – she will walk away. She will laugh gaily over her shoulder, railing at her own ineptitude and ask him, coyly, for forgiveness: 'Silly old girl, when my boy is such a splendid little sportsman.' Calling her dog to her, taking it up in her arms, teasing it to exuberance, saying, 'What are we do to with him, Maisie, darling? Such a funny chap, always asking questions!'

His mother is hiding something. She is always hiding something, pretending to speak when she has no answer. – *What are we to do with him, Maisie, darling?*: dogs have their uses in awkward moments.

Instead, he asks Brother Porteous, at school, about the calf.

'Animals do not have souls,' Brother Porteous says. 'Only mortals have souls and can commit mortal sins.'

It is an odd word 'mortal', full of weight and death.

Mortal sins. Mortal wounds. Mortality.

'Animals are not mortal,' says Brother Porteous. 'They do not qualify for souls for they have no choice of good and evil. They may not strive to earn Eternal Life. They cannot go to Heaven.'

Godfrey says to Gert, 'Only people have souls.' He says it as if he wants to punish her.

'So?'

'The calf is quite dead.'

Quite dead. She looks at him. Is there death by degrees, then?

'It cannot go to Heaven.'

There is a problem here. In church, looking at the windows between her fingers with the harsh light outside and the shadow of the old, dry, misplaced palms, the saints (weren't they dead and in Heaven?) were surrounded by beasts, the bright enamel blue of their skies improbably populated by flocks of little birds. How could Brother Porteous be so misinformed when the windows were there for all to see?

'Come and look,' she says to Godfrey.

He goes, despite himself. He pretends that he is not convinced. But, next day, he asks Brother Porteous about the birds and beasts in the stained-glass Heaven. Just as guileful as Godfrey's mother, Brother Porteous tells him to pick up the papers in the playground and put them in the oil drum by the fence. Brother Porteous knows that an instruction, given in the imperative, will wither the enquiries of boys.

So he asks Bibleman. Privately.

The itinerant Bibleman tells him – quite simply – what he wants to know: the Afterlife is not conducted Above, but Below. The ancestral shades keep herds of cattle under the earth, in another country. The pasture is very good. The cattle are fat, white as *amasi*, or roan as *amabele* mixed with milk. This is where the earthly cattle go when they are dead.

Godfrey does not doubt him. Bibleman answers questions without the aid of papers and bins or bats and balls. He does not turn a distant eye on him or change the subject. How can he doubt Bibleman when the *umvemve* calf had been so beautiful? As long as it is in his memory, surely it is alive and growing with him.

And when Brother Porteous died one morning at breakfast, a mouthful of oatmeal still lodged on his tongue, Godfrey knew that he would discover the truth at last: if Brother Porteous dared enquire *why* there was a calf in the Afterlife after all, he, too, might be fobbed off with a task for asking foolish questions!

Godfrey did not mention it to Gert. He had decided to keep the triumph as his own. He excluded her from its consolation.

He did not know that he had done it.

It is by small omissions – unconsciously made – that we detach ourselves.

On his fourteenth birthday, Godfrey is given a microscope. Now he is collecting things. It is a serious pursuit. Sometimes he allows Gert to look down it. Other times, she is invited into his room to see his trays of iridescent pinned beetles and the muddy sludge taken from the *spruit* to examine on the glass slides. She does not dither at them as another girl might have done. The interest is real. She can catch *vlei*-frogs just as well as he. It is all she can offer.

His is a room full of empty corners that a girl, without brothers, might find bare. It is spare – preserved by the possessiveness of a mother, familiar with the precise, private tapestry of his possessions.

When he marries, and lives in another woman's room, his own will cease to exist. At best, it will be translated into a workshop, or a study – under threat – eviction served the moment he is gone, swept into boxes or packets: old pens, papers, cuttings, dead batteries, rusted penknives, corks (why so many corks?), labels and programmes from ancient sports days at school, tools, tubes of glue and broken screwdrivers and crumpled paintings she had not thought to praise. But this is a room that – at fourteen – belongs to him alone.

Gert sits on the edge of the upright wooden chair, avoids glancing too curiously or ingenuously at the gun-rack or the bookshelves. One ignorant word might overturn credibility: that low, insistent heat behind the ear lobes for something silly said.

He allows her in, tolerant of her harmlessness, her chip-toothed smile, no threat to greater things. He tips her plait or calls her 'young fellow' when

34

she arrives in riding breeches. He lets her take small liberties: her instinct –
finely tuned – will make her melt away at a gesture of dismissal, at a word.
She treads the edges – a creature sniffing and retreating, then bolder – alert
– bolder – then gone – fearing always the cold, swift drawing of the rifle's
bolt, taken from the gun-rack.

A heart wound is clean. Finite.

And love can never be immaculate.

In 1912, he went away to boarding school. I know the date because it is in the
School Register. Like his dictionary – every cattle term, every bird name, every
word for plant or tree or omen, sunset, sunrise, storm or calm – I read it, exploring
its cartography, tracing strands of friendship, of hostility, of loss, even of desire.
There is much to be gleaned about his school friends from a crop of entries in
that close-set volume:

'Left November17, 1914.'

Why would a boy leave a fortnight before the close of the year? Run away to
war?

Or more cryptically: *'Left September, 1912.'* The Senior Prefect in Godfrey's
newboy year? *'On Police Service, British East Africa'* (there was no more War to
run to)? Why the exile in the middle of a term?

Godfrey's own record remains unimpeachable. His school achievements
hold the promise of his later years. His entry is twice as long as others on the
page. Here, his war service is recorded, his university triumphs (academic,
sporting), his appointments, publications, honours and awards.

Godfrey-the-Golden.

I may read the entry as I will.

By small omissions we detach ourselves. By small neglects. They do not go
unrecognised, except by ourselves.

Godfrey meant to say goodbye to Gert, but he didn't. He leaves by train –
trunk packed, name painted in white letters. House. School. Town.
Province. The train is already drawing up. He had shrugged off childhood
– he gives no warning – on that final afternoon with the last prankish
gonging of the iron pipe that hung in the tree at the Bowling Club,
summoning the players to tea, ten minutes early. It has always been their
joke – secret and uproarious. She would stand on tiptoe then, poised for the
groundsman erupting from the Clubhouse in a rage – always so predictable
– and they'd run away together, knowing that he could not catch them. For
her, that bounding flight, with Godfrey, is exultant, noosing Love.

Run, Gert, run.

I think she fell. Hard. Perhaps she broke a test tube. The scald of gravelled hands, the small stones lodged grey beneath the broken skin, the smart of it, the heavy, unexpected shock of being winded. The indignity of knickers showing, the flump of breath knocked out.

Don't watch, Godfrey. Turn away.

Godfrey would never fall except in diving for a ball, rolling across a try-line. So much grace is never awkward, never gauche. One does not have to avert the eyes to hide embarrassment. One cheers his vigour.

He picks her up, sets her down, dusts her off: a sudden irritation in his fingers and his glance. No more games. He is off to long trousers and House rules. It is a serious business, becoming a man.

Gert stands, shaking, trying to laugh, facing his impatience, the shards of test tube glinting on the gravel: a fragile glass cocoon – wingless – broken round her. It is the first defeat at the hands of those tilt-nosed girls with triumphant eyes in the photo album: she knows that – just like him – they never irritate as she has irritated now, never fall – except in love (mostly with themselves), never bore, only mystify.

Such loftiness, such assurance, is unassailable. Even in bed.

It is here, on the gravel walk, that she is left behind while Godfrey goes ahead, not looking at her. The plasma at her cracked knee beads orange. It is painful to walk but there is no hint of a limp, no hint of tears. He turns at the gate of her house. 'Sure you're all right, old thing?'

It is not enough.

'When do you leave?' she says.

'Tomorrow.'

She can muster brightness and a steady voice. 'Till tomorrow.'

But he has left already. And tomorrow will become today.

She had made a present for him – *boerboon* seeds laboriously bored to string a talisman. Rebuffed, she keeps them in her drawer.

Perhaps she should have planted them instead – and let them grow.

Of course 'Gert' may not have existed in that way. What, after all, is an upturned face in a picture? It is a nanosecond caught and pinned. It only means – after all this time – what *I* decide it means. Or does it?

I know to wait for the sign. It will come.

It may take years, but it will come at last and I will expiate Gert's heart wound.

I am not impatient.

Gertrude Mary Hayes. How could she sustain a name like that?

Neither boy nor girl. The androgynous companion of his childhood afternoons. Like the *umvemve* calf, she was a victim of expedience.

I make a copy of the party photo, crop it to include only him and her. The guillotine takes care of the rest of the group. Gone, the girl with the perfect ankles. Gone, the blonde curls and oval chin. Gone, Miss Coquette with her elegant arms. I frame the enlargement and write beneath – on my own authority – '*Godfrey and Gert*'.

They exist now, in a separate space. It seems that she is satisfied. There is, after all, a little triumph in the tilt of her head.

Chapter three

Of course, none of this may be true. Scrutinised, it would not bear analysis. It is invented. I have made it up from my own experience, from innuendo in his index cards and papers, from daydream, dim remembrance – from breathing in the scent of pepper trees to junket pudding; the tug of a tongue; foetal-lamb unborn; Bibleman (where on earth did that pop up from?). These become alloyed to the tilt of a head in a picture of Godfrey – the curve of a small boy's upper lip, in light and shade: infinitely tender; a sense of his mother. Even the shadows on the corrugated walls in a tiny contact print have textures which distil, in time, to meaning. These – both real and ephemeral – experienced and seen, but mostly sensed, become the silt-bed of creation.

And yet a guiding hand lingers. The images are clear and steady. They are pictures from a magic lantern show, long ago.

'You are becoming distracted,' says the prof when I return to the Department at the start of the new term. He is irritable with the slowness of my research, not especially interested in where I have been. I have not read Derrida yet. I do not understand Derrida. I don't think I ever will. I tell him.

He cocks a brow at me. 'I really don't see the need,' he says, 'for going off in search of C J Godfrey. Get to grips with the analysis.'

I am silent.

He is exasperated. 'Frankly, bugger Godfrey,' he says.

I had someone else in mind.

'After all, the external examiner has no interest in what Godfrey eats for breakfast!' He is trying to be light-hearted.

'Coffee?' I say, parrying with the canister.

'Depends what kind.'

In twenty years his students will remember his pedantry in regard to coffee and recall nothing of his line in argument or his passion for Derrida. So much for endeavour! I shall keep – fondly – the significance of Godfrey's breakfast with me after all. He ate it from a sage-green bowl with little lines around the margin (just like I did as a child). He loved mabella porridge and brown sugar (me or him?). He liked it hot (fair guess). He drank plain Ceylon tea, not coffee (me again). He smoked trading store tobacco (I had found some duplicate cards in an empty pouch stuck at the back of a catalogue tray). He had no truck with blends in fancy tins with pleated paper to keep the moisture in.

I serve the coffee. It is as unsatisfactory as the incomplete lexicon of bovine terminology, the disarray of chapters on metaphor and symbolism, the gap where Derrida ought to be. The professor leaves his cup half full and goes to the door. He is trying to be tolerant. He believes that convent-educated girls – despite streaky hair and improbable shoes – are amenable to conscience and to rank: I promise to deliver the first three chapters of the dissertation to him by the end of the month. I will. They will be clean and spell-checked, double-spaced and properly annotated. He will take great pleasure in picking them to pieces with his forceps-mind so that my argument tumbles! As he leaves, he says again, 'You are *not* Godfrey's biographer.'

Very meek. 'No. I am not his biographer.'

If I was, I could never make the assumptions that I do and treat them as if they were facts. A novelist may – a good one – but only with restraint, disguising, always, where the 'auto' bleeds quietly into the 'biography' and never letting on. And why all these flourishes? These invented conversations? These lingering landscapes? I invent things all the time, distorting what is fragile and finely balanced, precipitating the final, inevitable loss. Reckless as a lover.

Lovers should not be trusted with biographies. But without passion, who would write one?

> . . . *if he mingles his description . . . with personal judgement and with passion he will never properly convey the actuality . . .*

Without it, there would be nothing to convey at all, Godfrey. You know that as well as I. After all, what are the comments in the margins of your index cards, if not the links which bind their words to the record of your life? What is the map you made, roughly sketched and pinned to the entry –*nala* [abundance], if not to mark some deeply felt remembrance?

It was so tentative, I did not realise what it was until I saw the symbol indicating *North*. It seemed an aide-memoire rather than a map. It was not to inform others. Conversely, it was to keep them away. There was nothing to indicate location but a small rectangle (a building?), a road or a river marked by a fine, waving line, cross-hatched for an inch or two. A bank, perhaps? A culvert or a *krantz*? A pair of ellipses. Hills? Dams? In certain places, it seemed he wished to disguise his own cipher. There was a small shaded spot and '*G*', faint enough to pose as a line in the topography. And on the back: *4/11/57: 4.34pm.*

And so to '*G*'.

I will write this in deference to a woman I have never known, pursue the story of a man I have never met. The only risk is loss of faith. She must sustain me there. It would be heresy to think that her legendary diffidence allowed belief in love to ebb away.

She saw him first through her schoolroom window. There he was, walking in the wind. He must have been a boxer once. Boxers never lose alertness, a ready counterpoint of balance. They do not have the grace of cricketers – that stride, eye set to distance, the open, undefensive boyishness, nor the bulk of rugby players, neck directing, thighs nudging. Nor the ranginess of runners. Yes, he must have been a boxer: there is tautness in his step and yet an easy roll – strong-jointed, shoulders, elbows, knees, an agile pivot serving speed. He is a deep-chested man. He wears his sleeves half rolled. His wrists are strong.

He passes the school door. His step is brisk. She hears him walking up the long veranda to the church. The children hear him too. They pause in their chanting, twenty pairs of eyes lifted to the high window. They cannot see outside, except the sky and the tilt of the bell on its wooden pole. The wind is thumping the old jute rope against its sides, a little hollow gonging.

The steps come back. They do not hesitate. Someone knocks on the door and opens it. It is not tentative, just enquiring. She turns towards him. Slowly, in surprise – petal voice – she says, 'Can I help you?'

He is a small boy, come to class, sent in his jacket, halfway to his knees. He stands, with a bag that his mother has made and all eyes are directed at it: it is not an asset for a boy. He stands in his boots and the tight, high anguish in his chest. He is only five. The teacher turns towards him. She is slim and fluted like a lily, her face among the upturned petal tips of collar, golden-clear. She comes towards him and her hand at his shoulder is cool and pale, an arum spathe, brushing his neck. He stands, face upturned, just a little past her knees: she will shower him with pollen; transfix him with the flecks of gold and green of amber eyes.
Miss Gwendoline Spender.
His first love.

'Can I help you?' she says again.

40

He still has his hand on the doorknob. He seems in arabesque – if he leans another inch, he'll pull the wall down with him and the door. A dusty knight. Prone on the floor.

She almost laughs.

He steps back, withdraws his hand slowly and is upright. 'I am looking for the minister, Mr Wilmot,' he says.

'He's out in the parish. He should be back by twelve.'

The children shift. No one ever comes to the door except Mr Wilmot. No one comes. They are poised for his words.

'Ah.'

They look at their teacher. She has her head on one side, waiting. She has tucked her hair behind her ear. 'Can I give him a message?' she says, at last.

'Well, yes.' He glances at the children. They are all attention. He looks back at her. A pause.

'A moment, children.' She steps across to the door, slips through it. He closes it behind her.

There is no subsiding, and no sound. They are straining to hear. A stranger has come, with his beard and that look! A stranger to distract her! They can see it, in the way she leaves the room. They can see it in the tilt of her head, the flush at her neck. Small boys shift, necks straight. They bristle in their chairs, make weapons with their compasses.

At break, they fight each other to the death.

She hardly notices the uproar in the playground. She drinks her flask of tea, gazing out at the *gwarri* tree by the fence. His truck had been parked there in the shade. He had backed it away, made a three-point turn.

He will come back at twelve.

Tomorrow.

It is Saturday tomorrow.

There is no school on Saturday. Doesn't he know that?

He doesn't think of it. He doesn't think of anything, except the weight of his arm against his hand at the schoolroom door, the click in his elbow, as if disengaging and her turning to him. Turning, turning, a lily opening. Miss Gwendoline Spender once again, except that he is taller now. He cannot fling his arms around her knees, waiting for unfolding hands about his head . . .

I have no idea what he thinks. How can I? No one knows what Godfrey thinks.

'*Tell G*'.

It punctuates so many of the cards. Tell her this and tell her that. Talk to

41

her. Perhaps it was the aloneness of the little house on the open *veld* and the far hills that made him go so often to see the minister, Hugh Wilmot, and, in passing down towards the church, listen to the teacher's voice flitting round the high-ceilinged room. Petal-voice: cool and soft, the echo of another which had once made him pick nasturtiums along the bank on the way to school, an offering knocked from his hand, in derision, by a bigger boy.

He had never picked flowers for anyone again.

She knew when he came, driving the old truck and parking it by the *gwarri*, leaving tyre tracks, the sign of him when he had gone. The small boys knew when he came too. Her voice went down a tone and she spoke less freely, so she could hear the steps and then race a little when they had passed, as if her words were following him – up the veranda and out of hearing, down the veranda and on to the grass. He did not open the door or interrupt a lesson.

She did not see him again for over a week until she went to the house by the store and asked him if there was anything he needed.

She has brought a coal heater and a side of mutton from a newly slaughtered sheep. She parks the Ford in the road, parallel with the pebble and concrete wall of the shop. There is a black man standing under the *afdak* with a woollen hat pulled down. His eyes are wayward. So are his teeth. He is crow-ragged, turning his shoulder this way and that to the sun. The wind is cold.

She greets him and asks for the man who has come to stay in the house. He purses his lips, tilts his head. This may be the only conversation he will have that day: he settles to it, says meditatively, 'The white man with cows?'

She does not understand. 'The one who is staying here,' she says again.

'He is the one.'

She is mystified. 'With cows?'

'With cows.'

She looks about. There are no cows. The old byre is empty. The pasture is without cows. Only a few goats browse in the bush.

The man smiles, shifts into a stance and looks about the pasture too, conjuring up something. He says, 'They are in the many boxes that he brought.' He laughs. She laughs too. What else is there to do? A little laugh of incomprehension.

'If a man has no cattle in his byre, he must carry them in his head.' He knows, only too well. He does it himself: a whole pantomime of cattle that he will never own.

She waits.

'He is down in the shed,' the man says, pointing.

She turns and takes the path.

42

Our blood anticipates us, gathers itself, prepares us for that moment of acute recognition: a person or a place. It happens seldom – once in a lifetime, twice at most.

Such a moment: it is absolute prayer.

She walks down the path scooped to smoothness between the stones and tussocks, sees the bush willows far off at the dry river-bed and the seam of a little *krantz* in clear relief, the two ironstone koppies which reflect each other in their ancient symmetry. She steps across the wire of a fence, goes down towards the shearing shed. It is a long, whitewashed building, with a faded iron roof. The great double doors are closed. The paint is folded into longitudinal flutes from the dryness and the old wood is worn to grey.

The door is heavy. It sticks. She sets her shoulder to it, eases it and slips inside.

There is a great green gloom, the quiet underlight of the trees reflected up against the high walls, into the lifting rafters. The floor is cobbled with river stones. They are uneven under thin shoes. They were laid for a farmer's boots or the bare feet of stockmen, cupping the arch, lending purchase to the toes. It is an art to walk on them.

There is a desk and a chair. It is a 'captain's' chair, marooned in this old shed so far from the sea. Here the ledgers are filled in, next to the yellowwood baling bin, smoothed on the inside with the lanolin of decades of clip. Empty tins, upended on the sneezewood palings of each pen are for the tally of the shearers, reckoned in *boerbone*. One bean: one sheep sheared.

She walks along the row of sorting tables, down the step of river stones into the storeroom beyond. He is standing in the slant of sun coming through the small window, smoking his pipe. He has a ledger in one hand, his shoulder is propped comfortably to the wall. The shadow of a sweet-thorn outside takes him up and lets him go.

He turns, looks across at her, surprised.

'Dr Godfrey?' she says.

'Mrs Wilmot?'

'My name is Grace,' she says. 'I was directed here.' She smiles. 'I was told you are the man with cows.'

He half laughs. 'Apt enough.'

He moves nearer, puts out his hand. She shakes it. Her own is cool-fingered, long-fingered, thin-skinned. It withdraws.

Cool-fingered, long-fingered, thin-skinned: I would have put my own hand behind my back, before he had taken it. My hands are sweaty when I am afraid. They are squat hands, rather like a boy's. The knuckles are crinkly. I once wished to have woman-hands that were sleek, that flirted with each other in a

43

half repose, that could touch a forehead like a breath. Mine would stick like caterpillar feet to a leaf: he would recoil from them. To make a virtue of them, I scrub things, dig things, have no use for hand cream, scorn rubber gloves for washing up.

I know how low mine score in male memory. But not Grace's. Grace has fingers to soothe and to restore.

'Hugh, my brother-in-law, is sorry he couldn't come with me but he's busy with a funeral on a farm. He says he'd like to drive across another time. I have brought you some mutton,' she says. 'Also a jar of quince jelly.' She laughs. 'I'm sorry it's not mint but I can't grow it. It always dries up.'

On such words – in half apology – lives turn: something small and prosaic when the air is lifting for flight. Sensing it, she steadies herself, says, 'Tell me why you are "the man with cows"?'

'Ah,' he smiles. 'You must have been speaking to the storeman, Wilton.' He knocks his pipe against the window ledge. 'It's the research I'm doing,' he says. 'Colour-pattern terminology in indigenous cattle. I'm compiling a dictionary in Zulu. Making comparisons with Xhosa. Among other things.'

She waits for him to continue.

'In fact, I wanted to talk to you about it. Your brother-in-law told me, in passing, that you're something of a linguist, that you were brought up in the rural areas and speak very good Xhosa.'

She inclines her head.

She does. It was her first language. In many ways, it still is.

'There's a cattle survey going on countrywide at the moment. A chap called Crawford with the Department of Native Agriculture is looking into the status of indigenous animals.' He glances at her, walking at his side.

At his look, she tucks her hair behind her ear. It is a gesture of diffidence.

'Since being in touch with him a couple of years ago,' he continues, 'I've been working on Zulu cattle terms, going through old archival stuff and working in the field in Natal. I've wanted to do comparative work among the Xhosas for some time.'

'Do you know both languages?' asks Grace.

'Yes,' says Godfrey, 'but only in an academic sort of way. I suppose that's why I might be useful to Crawford. Quite recently, he set up a team from his department to survey all the reserves. They talk to cattle-owners, take counts at Government dips and are trying to sort out the proportions of exotic and indigenous animals in herds in African areas. It's a difficult job and there aren't really enough people to look at the phenomenon comprehensively.'

They have reached the great double doors of the shed. They are heavy and Godfrey steps back to let her through the gap. She brushes him, turning her shoulder deftly, slipping past. He watches her walk a few steps ahead.

44

She is very slight.

He takes his pipe from his pocket and catches up with her. He says, 'It looks as though I'll be here for some time. Crawford's roped me in to help and I need to be in one spot long enough to record changes over a season or two. Suits us both. From here, I get out to even more remote districts and do the odd colour-count for him. At the same time I can collect current Xhosa terms and compare them with the Zulu. Gives one a good idea of which are shared and which have fallen away in one language or the other. Until I arrived here, I have only had the old Xhosa dictionaries to go by.'

'Why here?' she says. 'It hardly seems ideal so far from your own field and not really in the heart of tribal lands.'

'There's a farmer called De Waal,' he says. 'Know him?'

She nods and gives a half laugh. 'He's a funny old character. Everyone knows him. I play tennis at the Club with his wife. I also know his daughter Dulcie, but not that well. She's a bit younger than me.'

'Have you heard that Herman de Waal is doing some innovative cross-breeding with Nguni cattle?'

She shakes her head.

'I contacted him as a first step in getting to know something about the husbandry and genetics,' he says. 'He suggested I stay with him but I prefer to be independent, so he said I could rent the empty house next to the store. He owns both – and the storekeeper doesn't seem to mind my being around. I hardly ever see him – unless I want something from the shop.' He puts his pipe in his pocket. 'No intrusion,' he says. 'It's better that way.'

She hesitates, another apology forming.

'From other considerations,' he says, with a quick smile.

Other considerations.

She retreats, saying lightly, 'No one will intrude on you.'

The absence of intrusion.

He had written in a letter to a colleague:

Need to go away to work, to be in the field again. It is impossible to get to grips with the material here in the Department. There are too many intrusions on time and concentration.

But that was not the truth entirely.

They reach the house. She says, 'Let me just get the things from the car.'

She is searching for her keys. 'Do you like mutton?' The boot is open. She has the meat in a basket. She hands it to him. 'Oh, and I brought this funny old heater. It's ancient but it works wonderfully. I know your rooms

45

must be very cold.'

He takes the heater from her. It is funnelled with a little window in its belly. The insides are black with a century of burning. The legs are squat and moulded. When he sets it down, he stands back and looks at it and laughs. 'This will be something of a companion. I like it very much.'

He goes down the path and opens the door of the house. He jostles the bolt. He puts the heater in a corner.

'Now, I think I shall have someone to talk to,' he says.

'I hope it will be sociable!' She pats it. 'It looks an old curmudgeon to me!'

'Where did you get it?'

'It's from a mission that my grandfather used to visit. When it was closed, he bought up some things. My school desk was from there and our dining room table.' She tucks her hair behind her ear again – it is a familiar gesture now. 'It opens out in leaves. Very ingenious. The carpenter's signature is carved into the frame. The chairs too. They're sneezewood – rather too small for a man to sit on but I love them. They have knots in the seat like eyes that look out at you. And spindles that are inclined to scatter when someone heavy sits on them.' She stops herself. She is talking too fast and the room is very quiet. The white of the walls is milk-blue in the corners. 'Have you somewhere I can put the mutton?'

She follows him to the kitchen. The meat chest stands on legs. The flyscreening in the frame has been neatly repaired. It is empty. 'I think you should cook this soon,' she says. 'Perhaps I should have done it for you.'

The old Aga is unlit. He has been using a primus.

He is searching for matches. He lights the little stove and fills the kettle. 'Tea?' he says.

'I don't want to disturb you.'

The glance is swift. 'Tea.' Quite simple.

She stands at the window.

I see what she is watching. I know because I am looking through her eyes. She is watching him move about the room and there is a lightness in her which is unexpected.

And unwise.

While the kettle boils she follows him to the living room and she says, 'May I ask about the cattle?' She keeps her voice neutral. The excitement is guarded. She will not let him know – not yet, not until she tests him – that the world he is explaining, with such care, is as familiar to her as it is to him. And, to him, at present, she is just a primary school teacher from a small rural school, bringing gifts in hospitality. Her history is unrevealed. She smiles as he turns to his table and draws a box towards him. It is full of photographs. They are small and the monochrome of the printing can never show the colours of the animals, the tones of red and dun and brown. But she knows their shades. She has seen them often, jolting down familiar tracks with her grandfather in the old Ford, from rural school to rural school, on his rounds of inspection. She has written poems in the back of exercise books, on scraps of paper, precariously balanced on her knee, to red-flanked cattle, to oxen in the yoke, to a small clay bull she had made out of ochre mud and left to dry, its horns slowly drooping till – at last – they cracked and fell. Her grandfather had kept what she had written, bound into a folder. He had never corrected the vagaries of her spelling or criticised the large untidy writing.

She had not talked about these things since her grandfather's death.

Unwittingly, Dr Godfrey is re-revealing her world.

Godfrey lays the photos out and his voice gathers up the names. He explains, without parade, but his delight in them is evident. They are a poetry to him. She listens, entranced. It is like an old song, half remembered, the words forming again in her mind.

He makes tea. He sets the cups. He spoons the leaves into the enamel pot. He is telling her about trips to Matabeleland where the animals have horns which are particularly well developed. He tells her about the cattle of the Kaokoveld – most pure – and the Ovambo cattle and the Landim cattle in Portuguese East Africa and the herds of the Masai in East Africa which are different but which have names that echo – from an earlier time – the links of long migration and shared origins. The tray is set on a little table and still he talks and absently spoons sugar into her cup, stirs his own; takes his up and drinks. He pulls a face.

'*You* take the sugar,' she smiles. 'I don't.'

He is not a man to be sheepish, laughs easily at himself. 'Let me get you a fresh cup.'

'No,' she says. 'Yours is fine.' She takes it from him. She has no need to avoid the rim where he has sipped. She is bold, light-hearted: on the slopes of Kilimanjaro, across the dust roads of East Africa, the drylands of Bechuanaland, she is there. She strikes camp on the banks of a river. She can feel the current running out between the sandbars, the turning of the stars. Such vistas. The sky lifts and flares.

Restraint reasserts itself.

So – I will not laugh at her. She will retreat if I do – and take him out of reach. I cannot afford to make a rival of her even if I cannot see her face, nor protect him from his own foolishness by denying her existence. Without her, there would be no story – only the words of the lexicon and the well-annotated notes and C J Godfrey, the scholar.

The man would disappear.

I must allow her – and be generous.

It is dusk when she leaves. The teacups are long cold, the pictures have been spread out on the floor of the room, on the grass matting, the oil lamp lit. She rises at last and he walks her to the cár, opens the door.

'Goodnight, Grace,' he says.

'Goodnight.' She does not use a name. She has no idea of what to call him.

It is an evening of green light and pale green stars. A *bergwind* evening. She drives the same curve of hill that I do now but there is no leguaan in the road. Only the light drifting into mauve, land black with shadow but warm with wind and a nightbird hawking on the wing. Her eyes follow the swift trajectory of flight.

And he?

Perhaps he stands and watches the car drive away. Perhaps he simply goes inside and pours a drink. Perhaps he sits at the desk and opens his ledger and enters something in a column. Perhaps he writes a letter to his wife.

No one knows.

In this place, now, there is a desolation in the poverty of settlements of shacks around the drift, degenerate cattle, donkeys, the empty faces staring back as I ride by in my truck, Delekile's ubiquitous persistence, so many abandoned farms. Thomas Baines, the artist, explorer and adventurer, painted this landscape a hundred years ago. It is a glowing picture – gracious in its composition – and recognisable, even now. There is little that can change the outline of the mountain to the west, its flat crown, the wisp of cloud that drifts across its summit in the heat. There is a grandeur in his landscape, in the white-faced houses of a farm, an Attic dignity and grace in tableau figures garlanding the foreground of the canvas. He may have sanitised his landscape, orchestrating vistas of grand adventure and endeavour. If, even then, the detritus of hovels in the bushes was still there, he did not choose to see it. He punctuates the sky with the epic motion of a transport rider's whip. His *voorloper*, though in rags, walks a charmed track before the *span*, a jester and a king. Coming here now, I recognise the essential features, but the gloss is gone: rising to the surface, bred over a century, the implacable desolation is un-avoidable. Even the train line that ran here once, across this thriving valley, has rusted back into the earth. The sleepers have been carried away and the bridge that once vaulted – easily – the chasm of a gorge, is peeled of layers by wind so that only a gaunt skeleton remains, a crumbling fretwork where no one dares to walk. The wind tunnelling the *kloof* is the echo of the trains long gone. The little station building stands forlorn. I went there once, surmising that Godfrey might have sometimes come by train, alighting on the sunlit platform, the fire buckets shining and newly painted, a small garden of alyssum and cannas and irises tended by a man in overalls. I have conjured it – Grace waiting in a linen frock, her foot poised on the running board of the black car, a hat perhaps, a double felt terai – a gesture to his African endeavours.

There is nothing left.

Even the fireplace in the waiting room has been ripped from its moorings and, above the hole, someone has scrawled obscenities. The shopkeeper has screwed a metal sign, crucified against the mellow panels of his door, which features – in grim black silhouette – a combat rifle, a snarling dog with saliva flying from its jaw, a skull and crossbones. *DANGER. INGOZI.* Do not enter here. It is a different era.

Godfrey's time spanned the two – Baines' frontier vista and these present empty backlands. He sensed the moment of transition for he wrote:

The great desolation will overtake us here. A great despondency. Drought and more. I have seen the last real spring.

He was writing of a place.

He was writing of himself.

It seems that she became his assistant in the holidays. He needed someone to sort the cards and to check them. She was competent. She spoke the language well, she understood the orthography, learnt his methods and his codes, was meticulous. She had the primary school teacher's neat writing and thoroughness. She did not misfile cards. She made lists and scratched each task through when it was done.

Did she? Was it really like that?

Maybe I am wrong – maybe she was not in any way a neat, primary school teacher, despite being the minister's sister-in-law. Perhaps she was eccentric, vivid, feisty, wild – made turbans out of loud print, wore French silk knickers in shell-pink with tea-coloured lace. Perhaps she had had a butterfly tattooed on the upward curve of her bottom, in the secret place at the 'neck of the pear' – between the dimple at the base of her spine and the curve of the cheek, smoked Turkish cigarettes, painted interesting pictures, wrote verse, varnished her toenails almost plum-mauve, ate cloves, pierced her ears.

Perhaps she made an art of paradoxes, a virtue of overturning taste.

No, she was not that either. Not Grace. That was another of his lovers – the one I found in the trunk – a cross between The King's Road undercover market and Lady Ottoline Morrell: pressed purple pansies; scarab beetles set in silver;

antique Chinese silk; a collector of louche young men. Blood-Red in every way.

All wrong.

Grace was not exotic or intriguing, she was not an episode from his European wanderings. Neither fire nor flame.

And yet – most straightforward of all – for months, I simply could not see her face. I have searched his archive for it, his albums, his boxes. There are so many photographs of women – in family snaps, in group shots, all over the place – but no one who might be Grace. Perhaps he did not need – or want – a photograph. In the end, he may have wished to expunge her. 'Life goes on' and all that.

It is such an empty platitude.

Even those who say it, don't believe it, knowing it is second-rate.

In all the months of my research, I suppose I could have found her family, but I have avoided it. I have looked up the name in the phone book wherever I have been, seen 'Wilmot' listed in suburban-sounding streets: Tenth Avenue, Galway Road, Escombe Street. If I had intruded, I might have found remembrance of a grandmother or an aunt, some vague smile – *why should she be interesting?* – ending in an Old Age Home with formica tables and the sticky scab of spilled soup on vinyl-covered chairs; beige sunfilter curtains at the window; a donated picture in the foyer of a Chinese junk at sunset, memorial benches under dusty casuarinas.

I would not do it to her.

This could not be Grace. This is not the keen beauty of the *inala* cow noosed by Godfrey's arm, a shadow at his feet. So much passion does not end in this.

'I cannot pay you much to help me with the dictionary,' he says. His voice is well modulated, but detached. It is the scholar talking. 'The grant is small – but the help is greatly appreciated.'

The formalities over, he does not have to think of money again. She is here because she wants to be. The payment is to legitimise her presence in his study. His tone changes then, becomes more engaging. 'Would you like an introduction to the field by coming with me to watch oxen being trained for the plough?'

'Where?'

'Over the hills and far away.' Then he laughs. 'To Mr Herman de Waal, who owns the store and who is my landlord. He has an interesting herd on a farm up the valley.'

'When?'

'Tomorrow.' Then he says, 'Are you a photographer?'

'No.'

50

'I'll teach you. I need pictures for the record.'

That is why, in the contact prints in his catalogue boxes, there is sometimes a shadow in the foreground, the suggestion of a figure, a slim, insubstantial shadow reaching out towards his feet. It is all I have to go on. Just a shadow and the intensity of Godfrey's gaze, looking back towards the lens, the quality of light. To take it further is intrusion. But I know – I *know* – that when Godfrey comes to fetch her in his truck and she goes out to him in the early morning wind, the basket she has prepared for the journey in her hand, the clouds are already turning in unaccountable parade, the shadows of the valley lemon-blue and breathing heat. I know, for her, it is a pilgrim day.

> Grace takes charge of the camera. It is pleasantly heavy in her lap. She can see Godfrey's thumb print on the lens. She touches her finger to the spot. The minute cross-hatch of her print overlays his. She settles into herself, gazing straight ahead. She watches the morning stretch out with the contours of the road, unfold with the sky, the hills, the haze of dust left behind their wheels. On the back seat of the car is the prim little basket with the flask and packet of sandwiches. She has taken such care in making them. She has polished the apples to burnishing. Godfrey drives with his arm on the window and the sun flecking light on its springy down. His wrists and knuckles spark it back at her as he turns the wheel.
> As the road winds across the *nek* and on to plains beyond, Godfrey talks. Grace listens: the cadence of his voice; the wry, funny, slightly mocking turn of phrase. Another layer of hills lifts above the ash-soft grass. Another and another. They are blue as the heart of flame in the early morning heat. Ahead, quiet and lordly, a bustard walks the margin of the slope. They stop the truck to watch. With a slow, deep, beating of its wings, it takes to flight.

There are people who become the guardian of the secrets of others, a measure of the trust in which they are held. Grace Wilmot is one of those. So am I. Neither has the need to offer secrets in return. We know too well what may be misjudged. And yet, because of that, here I am, the curator of hers. I have sifted them from Godfrey's oblique letters and careful cards. I have divined them from her silence. I sense her presence – and this pilgrim day. I have lived with both myself.

I know the numinous in simple things – and honour it.

And Godfrey?

I am sometimes glad we never met. If he had known me, Godfrey might have burned his cards instead and closed down access to his life. Perhaps what is required is this distance and another age, before he could permit intrusion or accept his biographer's passion and commitment. In his way, he is gracious. I am all that is left to him.

And he to me.

I can stay the course – to whatever point at which he says, 'Enough.'

Chapter four

❧

Some men, it seems, were never boys. And others carry boyhood with them – in the things they keep or which they still collect, an extension of marbles or meccano, a penknife or a coin or tickets from long-forgotten train journeys. Godfrey did not appear to carry the boy in him any more. He was too urbane. The worn sophistication of the traveller to many lands hung upon him. So much scholarship. So much information. And the name! How can someone with the name 'C J Godfrey' have ever been a small boy? In his baby pictures, he is perched on the photographer's canvas, hair lightly curled. These have no connection with the man-in-the-field at cattle dips, in profile with a pipe, smoke drifting. They have no connection with the image of the soldier in combat gear, leaning on the prototypes of tanks, or with the older in his favourite tweed jacket, hair receding, beard well clipped (Grace's time) or with the picture in the University's Senate Chamber – that inner, that ascetic light behind the parchment of his lean, clean-shaven face.

No, Godfrey was not a boy.

And yet, in time, he told her. And, in telling her, he let the small boy loose. That boy, so long detached came back, alive. Both could see him running in the sun. It was a confidence which could not be withdrawn. A gift which could never be profaned. She – and I – will never turn around the unexpected tenderness of that perception and make of it a breach of faith.

There is usually a rivalry in women who have loved one man, fierce to fix him in their time and deny his history. But that is self-love, self-absorption, wishing his existence to reflect in them. They deny the separate spaces; deny him joy beyond what they can offer. But Grace was not like that. The boy was safe with her. He is safe with Gert – little chip-toothed Gert, forerunner of us

53

both, the first, fierce, small contender for his heart.

The first intimacy is to ask about the boy. The boy – more easily approached – could mediate the little awkward distances that still remained. Without looking at him, staring out at the winding, dirt track above the valley as they drove, the camera in her lap, Grace asks Godfrey where he was born, where he lived as a child. It is naive, in its way. His name, in itself, suggests dynasties. It is novel for him, at this moment, to exist without a family reputation.

He smiles. It is swift, amused.

She glances up at him. Such calm eyes. Such quiet hands.

Perhaps it is Miss Gwendoline Spender brought to mind.

'I lived in acres of house,' he says, 'with a Catholic mother and an atheist father who had been on campaign in Afghanistan.' He is briefly silent. Then he says, 'He remains on campaign. So do we all, in our different ways.'

'Are they still alive?'

'My father is,' he says. 'He lives in the old house with a retainer. He won't move. He has his telescope up in a little veranda room on the roof where I used to sleep in summer. He has it trained north, north-east.' He turns to her. 'Ever do any of Henry Newbolt's poems at school?'

'Like everyone else.'

'Well, my father's pure Newbolt – except he has subverted him. He's not looking for the "*grey little church across the park*" or "*the school Close, sunny and green*" or however it goes.' He smiles enquiringly at her. 'How does it go – do you remember?' He holds the wheel with one hand, taps his fingers gently on the outer curve, searching for a rhythm that will deliver the words to him again. ' "*He did not hear the monotonous roar that fills the ravine where the Yassin river sullenly flows; He did not see the starlight on the Laspur hills, or the far Afghan snows . . .*" Only he does. He hears and sees them all the time. They are his lost muse. Funny thing about Newbolt, with all his jingoism and his tragic heroes and honoured dead, he remains entrenched in the mindset of my father's generation.' He is searching again. She does not break into his reflectiveness. ' "*. . . Over the pass the voices one by one faded . . .*" but they don't, you know. They ensure their own immortality. So morbid. But also, so safe.' He is silent a moment, then he says, 'That little veranda room. It was a marvellous place to sleep in summer. Rather too high for mosquitoes and level with the tops of the trees. The only thing that used to bother me when I was a small chap was hearing owls. I believed that my mother, with all her pious Catholic sorcery, would be swept away under the wing of an owl one day. It seemed inevitable. By

54

the time the owl called, it would already be too late to save her.'

Of course, it was all projection, absorbed from his mother's need to bargain with God. For Life, for Death, for Absolution. Her deal with Godfrey himself, fierce to bind him: –*We will both go to Heaven one day, you and I . . .* There was no escape from her – or his need of her. She remained, another shadow, anchored at his feet.

He left the child with his mother at the station when he went away to school – his bed stripped down to the ticking mattress in his shuttered room; Bibleman herding the milk cows alone in the wire-grassed pasture by the railway line; Gert somewhere across the dusty suburb; his mother, shoulder turned away, high-collared, fingering her little parasol, somehow infusing him with unexpected guilt for going. He saw her diminish, as the train drew away, with a new confusion.

It was not the only one.

When he stood, for the first time, in the shower queue with a dozen other naked boys – small shivering bodies, hairless legs mottled blue, the sinews at the backs of their knees purple and pinched with cold – he saw: among them all, he was the only one uncircumcised.

They came to look at him, crowd round, express both wonder and disgust.

'What's wrong with your knob, Godfrey?'

It seemed to hang its head in shame, trailing its little tail like a tadpole, so tenuous it might be sloughed.

–*What's wrong with your knob?*

He had never thought there was anything wrong with it. He had nothing to compare it with. Now – a dozen specimens were available for scrutiny, presented proudly. Unripe, olive-headed, hard. Shameless. Naked.

Rude.

Perpetually rude, unlike his, which only came out of hiding – smarting and pink – when it itched. And sometimes at night. Then, he knew to say an act of contrition as his mother had taught him, hands at his side, until it shrunk away.

The other boys were not contrite. They did not seem to know what contrition was.

And none of them were Catholics.

And so is difference made. And compensation found for it: Godfrey learned to box.

He walked with that well-sprung gait of a fighter. Not belligerent, not aggressive, simply squaring up against his difference. He learned to box with skill. He boxed with guts. By the end of his third year, he was unbeaten at the school.

'I was a boxer once,' Godfrey says to Grace, glancing across at her to see how she will take it, riding lightly in the high cab of the truck with the vistas opening to left and right, the road giving way to track and corrugated stretches of sand and tussocks of grass. He reaches for his pipe from the cubbyhole under the dashboard, sucks at it. 'Well, I *was*, until I copped it from a skinny little Dutchman called Oosthuizen who'd arrived out of nowhere in the middle of the term. He beat the hell out of me! He probably had something more to prove than I did, coming to our school. I ended up in the sickbay, quite severely concussed.'

Grace is polishing an apple on her skirt, rotating it minutely.

'I think it's the one thing my father approved of – a son who could fight,' says Godfrey. 'Otherwise he didn't care much for me.'

'Why?'

Godfrey shrugs. 'He always made it clear he would have preferred daughters. Quite an odd notion, really, for a man, especially of that generation. One would think a son and heir would please him – but unaccountably, it didn't.' He laughs again. 'He didn't even bother to send me to his old school in England which he could have afforded if he'd wanted to. I suspect now it's because he was afraid I might break his long-distance record. It was a pretty creditable one, in fact. It stood for twenty years. When I began running in my third year at school, he never asked my times and I didn't tell him.'

'Were they better?'

'Does it matter?'

'It might have mattered to you then.'

'I can't recall,' he says. 'Perhaps it did.'

It had mattered very much. He had kept a carefully coded secret register of both their times, had known how hard he had to train to match and then surpass his father's schoolboy glory.

'It would have been nice to have been encouraged.' There is a small, rueful flicker at the corner of his mouth. 'In all the years I was a boarder, he never appeared though – not for a speech day or a sports day or a rugger match.'

Grace hands him the apple. It is poised within her fingers, transferred into his: a small transaction, tips touching.

'When my mother heard about the boxing, she made a tremendous fuss. You'd think I'd come out of the fight idiotic. But it seems she got herself in a state because no one, in a school like that, could have rustled up a Catholic priest in time to give me Extreme Unction if I'd died. She took the train and pitched up in the Head's office just as I was plotting a return bout with Oosthuizen. I was going to have him down and out in the first round.'

Mothers should be kept away from school. Perhaps I should have stayed away as well and got on with my thesis, pursued his scholarship and left the man alone. Instead, I went to the school and searched for the boy through the empty dormitories and locker rooms of his House: my own small, unexplained homage the only vindication for so odd a request of the housemaster in the holidays.

It was not from him that I meant to ask permission. It was from Godfrey himself.

I stepped with care through the back door, standing at the foot of the wooden-railed stairs. Even in its emptiness, there was the presence of boys. The smell of them. Their resistance to intrusion.The stairs turned against themselves in ascending.

Keep out.

The dormitory had been divided with partitions. Each boy had his cubicle – privacy, at the expense of light. It was not like that in Godfrey's time. There were two lancet windows in the wall, sanctifying space for twenty beds. From old pictures, I know that brass hooks for jackets and hats ran the width of the room.

Now, stuck up against the plaster and partitions, were posters of models, one unzipping her jeans, her belly button iridescent with gel. So much girlie-glitter. It will only just pass the housemaster's censor. These are the successors of the tilt-nosed girls. Only their names are more improbable. Some chap – cube further down the row – had not yet got to girls. He had a picture of a prize ram tacked to his bookshelf – and a tractor: state of the art, in airbrushed space.

I left quietly.

I know why Godfrey's mother made the trip. I would have made the trip myself: the invention of excuses is an art form with anxious mothers. It is said that they fool only themselves. But fear is so debilitating, it must be served – even at the cost of loss of face, dignity, whatever. It is failure of imagination in others that feeds it. One word of reassurance should not have been so dearly bought.

She comes, hearing that he has concussion and a broken nose. Her imagination at three in the morning – with the silent Virgin statue standing aloof on her little shelf – is busy with splinters of bone in the brain or the eye or the inner ear. By dawn, Godfrey is deaf and blind and mute. Before her tea is brought at seven, he is dead:

She must rescue Godfrey.

'You are making a fool of yourself,' says Harold Godfrey.

'He is ill.'

'Nonsense. The housemaster has called a doctor. It's only a broken nose and a couple of bruises. Pull yourself together.' And, in the way he says it, he implies: What sort of son is this? But more expressively, – *What sort of son are you trying to make him?*

She would not let him wither her. 'He does not need a doctor. He needs his mother.'

She has her suitcases sent down to the station. She follows with the driver, settles herself in her compartment, hangs up her travelling cape and hat on the hook by the door, quietly unpeels her gloves to write another list (that insurance against panic). Godfrey, in later years, with his different idiom, would have said – wryly – she was affected by *'isithinzi'* – a small perplexity – an inexorable little snake eating out her heart.

It is not perplexity. It is love.

In all its impossibility.

She sits very still, the train rocking, the even click of wheels a quiet novena – not for nine days, but for twenty-nine hours, repeating and repeating:

–Rescue Godfrey.

Dear Mother, nothing can rescue Godfrey. Not even your own death will relieve you of him. Nor his of you.

A mother is sitting in the Matron's room. The Head is with her. Some have seen her walking up the stairs to the sickbay. An emissary from another world, enough to send a small shiver of anxiety hovering among the younger boys. It is necessary to twitch the shoulders surreptitiously in their jackets to shrug it off.

Godfrey is called to the Matron's room. He puts on his dressing gown and slippers. A senior boy, lying with a fever in a bed by the window, eyes him. Is it envy or contempt? Godfrey's ears burn like cinders: surely someone must have died at home. He almost hopes they have. It can be the only excuse for coming here.

She is out of place even though her umbrella is so familiar. He knows the contours of her handbag, perched by her feet – in exactly which pocket

58

to find the mints, in which she keeps her powder compact, the scent of it. He is suspended at the door beyond her reach, the Headmaster implacably between them – not unkindly, but uncomprehending, simply unable to change the rules: they are too entrenched, too long-standing, far too immutable to permit more than a polite kiss. The mother – that Immaculate – can do nothing. She sits, looking across at him and his blue, distended face, her eyes wading at him, her cheeks dry. He knows what she is saying behind the small, polite twitching of her lips:

> . . . *Oh, most gracious Virgin Mary,*
> *that never was it known . . .*

The Virgin Mary had had a hard time saving Jesus.

Godfrey's mother cannot save him. There is some imperative, forbidding her intrusion. Perhaps it is God, the Father.

Perhaps it is himself. Godfrey.

She stays a few days, in the small hotel near the station. She is allowed to see Godfrey after tea in the Matron's room and the Head – a special dispensation from the doctor – gives him permission to lunch with her on Sunday, the day before he was expected to be back in class. The concession is made to the mother, not to Godfrey: mothers must be dealt with, with tact, or they become a nuisance. He offers to drive her to the station himself on Monday morning. His vigilance will ensure she feels no impulse to return.

'On reflection,' Godfrey says to Grace, 'I was most unfair to her. But what do you say in the face of such a tide of love? Drown? There was nothing I could do. She would subvert her innate dignity, purposely. It was herself she disliked so much. For some unaccountable reason' – he is wry – 'a fearful gloom descends if I am ever called to have a Sunday lunch in a hotel. It always upsets me.'

What do you talk about to your mother in an almost empty dining room with the waiters standing within earshot, ready to lift the plate as soon as the spoon or knife and fork are laid down? Here, the chicken soup – there, the little entrée of haddock. He drinks the fish down with water, trying not to taste it. Next, the soufflé. His mother eats it with her head to one side as if she is blowing feathers off her fingers.

The funny little silences and she, saying over and over, 'Now, darling, please look after yourself in future. I love you so much and I don't want anything to happen to you.'

Doesn't she know he has wars to fight and continents to cross and seas to navigate and great cities to explore? He has fights to fight and women to love and mountains to conquer and he cannot say – some trite guarantee – 'Nothing will happen to me.' He cannot take responsibility for his mother's little terrors or the wearying way she keeps her gaze middle distance, as if she has been diminished – a sulk, despite herself – because he sits clod-tongued, trying to find something to say. Instead, he watches an irritable fly land on the butter and dab at it. He is so absorbed, he does not hear – once again – 'Do you promise me?' But, as he leaves the dining room with the patter of her silky skirt brushing against her legs and the sound of her heels on the linoleum of the foyer, he feels the watery bubble of anxiety in his lower throat because, in ten minutes, she will be gone.

As she should.

As he wants her to.

But there is something in the sound of her moving down the hall and out into the street that makes him want to run after her, keep her in sight, the scent of her: the little puff of smells when her handbag is opened to extract her hanky – the imprints of her lip salve on the small starched square – the satisfying snap as it closes them in again; that skirt, even the embarrassing milliners' grapes decorating the brim of her hat, so carefully – so coquettishly – chosen.

So intrusive on his gaze – and on the gaze of others.

He had blushed for them, bobbing at the Head, every time she spoke. He walks doggedly after her. Why should such inconsequentials rack his heart and make him want to tear down walls?

He goes to the Drill Hall on his return to school and spars with Oosthuizen, even though he has been told to keep out of contact sports for the rest of the term. Oosthuizen is a good fellow, after all. He humours him without the slightest patronage: he has also seen the mother and the grapes on the brim of her hat. He lets Godfrey push him as far as he can, leaning back into him with just the right amount of resistance and weight.

Godfrey's head throbs, his swollen eye waters, but the constriction under his breastbone has slowly eased to breathing once again. By the end of prep that night, he knows the train will have drawn away from the station. He has been half listening for it, scratching out his homework in his exercise book under the prefect's eye. Then someone shuts the window to keep the wind from thumping the map of the world against the wall. It closes out the sounds of the town as well – and the train, taking the slow gradient below the hill beyond the school. He looks up, sees the lamps of the classroom reflected blindly in the window panes, opens his book again.

She is gone.

Godfrey turns north, riding a road that takes the base of a hill, leaning into the contour of the slope. They wind into rain-shadow and the vegetation changes. Here there are sweet-thorns and *dongas*, scoured where sudden storms have washed away the top soil, slabs of limestone in an empty river bed. Euphorbias and *spekboom*. Here and there a *boerboon* or a shepherd's tree, a lichened trunk, a wisp of old man's beard.

A ploughshare is nailed to a post. 'De Waal' is visible behind the scab of rust. A little track leads off across a cattle grid between the bushes. It is a poor farm, with sagging fences. Neglect hangs about the water troughs and pens.

'Old De Waal has been here many years,' says Godfrey. 'He has a small herd of Nguni cross-breeds. He's experimenting with them on harsh *veld*. He has theories about how their hardiness and fertility counterbalance their smallness and other so-called disadvantages. He also has oxen which he's trained for the single-bladed plough. He uses exactly the same method as the rural black farmer. His theory is that, in Africa, mechanisation will be a burden, something that only the rich can afford, something that will always be out of reach of the average peasant farmer. He says, perfecting the ox-drawn plough, improving it, will keep every man master of his own land. It's a different sort of progressive thinking, in its way. Most people say he's crazy, an anachronism – but, in the end, he'll prove them wrong. He has a way with cattle that is legendary.'

He stops for Grace to open a gate. She climbs from the car, not looking back. The gate is smooth and easy-running. She wants to ride on it across the scoop of earth as she had on the countless gates she had opened for her grandfather on country roads when she had travelled with him. She turns back, watches him as he drives through. She loops the link over the nail in the post. As she climbs back into the truck and closes her door, leaning to pull its weight, her other arm – in counterpoint – brushes his. She shifts away but the presence remains. It is as if he has put his hand to the back of her neck, the lightest gesture of intent. They do not speak as they drive the last hundred yards to the farmhouse. When the car has stopped, he sits, just a moment longer than is necessary, with his hands on the steering wheel.

His expression is fleeting, fixed to middle distance. Light, reflective.

She is the first to move. She closes the car door with care and leans against it.

They walk across the grass towards the house, he is at her back as they take the path between the angled bricks which mark out a bed of irises. There are roses in bloom, the banksias are heavy, long laths trailing yellow tufts. Hellebores grow with ivy against old stone walls. A bou bou shrike, unalarmed, takes himself off through a hedge.

The conversation is not between Godfrey and Herman de Waal, the farmer, even though they stand at the table and look at papers and pamphlets, gathered in a great collection over years. Herman de Waal has a Register of his own cattle, a photograph of each, bloodlines, weights, a record of birth or sale or slaughter. He stabs a finger at this and that, his voice full of rough affection. Here is Pampoenblom and Appelkoos – there, Bontrug, Rooiland and Vlek.

Colour, fruit and flowers: Pumpkin-blossom; Apricot; Speckle-back; Redland and Fleck.

Here, the bull, Ou Doringbult, named for a ridge of thorns.

But the real conversation, despite its wordlessness, is between Godfrey and Grace, a small unfolding cipher – sent, received, returned – fingerprints exploring in the air, while Herman de Waal rambles in response to Godfrey's questions.

The old man is acquainted with Grace but he does not speak to her now. He cannot imagine what she is doing here. What does she know about cattle? He calls her 'girlie'.

'I've decided the best thing to do about the problem of breeding in the right characteristics,' says Herman, 'is to bring in some Afrikander stock and use Nguni cows and Afrikander bulls. Afrikanders are also Sanga cattle after all. They come from the same origins. But what we want is the maximum milk and beef production coupled with the maximum resistance to disease which, of course, these bush cattle have.'

'But won't you lose the essential characteristics of the Ngunis over time, then,' says Godfrey. 'Wouldn't breeding with a terminal dam-line be better?'

'It depends what you want,' says Herman, prodding his finger again at a picture of one of his cows, sturdy and polled. 'We're not in this for purity. We're in this, in the end, for beef, for milk, for hardiness, for affordability. You know, if you leave an old native on his plot, he'll breed up as many cows as he can for *lobola*. He won't give a damn about the quality. It's the number that counts.'

'He's not in it for beef,' says Grace quietly. 'Cattle are only slaughtered for sacrifice. They are there for exchange. Their purpose is different.'

Herman de Waal glances at her. It is a vague glance, as if something unaccountable has ruffled his train of thought. 'I beg your pardon, my girlie?' he says. It is absent. Had she spoken? Had she asked to be excused?

Godfrey half smiles, glances down, but Grace feels his approbation. There is a small silence, then he says, 'I've an idea of getting together a few animals, as pure as I can find them and to do an experiment myself. I'd like a diversity of colour-patterns. I'm thinking of talking to Dr Crawford about it.'

Grace looks over at him. It is the first time he has mentioned this. For once, he does not look back.

Herman de Waal says – turning his shoulder to Grace in answering, just a gesture, but blocking her out, as if she is responsible, in some way, for this odd aberration – 'That's all very well for you scientists, Dr Godfrey. But, man, a bloke's got to live and for me, it's beef on the hoof. The people round here think I'm touched for bothering with bush cows at all. They'll really think you're *mal* if you start breeding up pure Ngunis just for colour-patterns. They'll be asking what for? Of course, you chaps have your reasons, but, as a farmer, I've got to watch my market and my neighbours.' Then he laughs, pulling his papers together and patting them into a pile. 'At any rate, if you start bringing in kaffir cattle from the valley, at least I won't be seen as the only *malkop* around here! But, I must warn you, no one's keen to have animals around that might not have seen a dip before.'

Godfrey lets it pass. He fills his pipe, says affably, 'Let's have a look at your steers. I'd like to see how you train them for the plough.'

They go outside into the training yard and a pair of young steers are brought in and yoked. Grace sits on the gate as they are taken through their paces round the enclosure, two stockmen in gumboots and overalls coaxing gently, every now and then the sharper note when one rams the yoke into the wooden railings. Beyond, an old shed leans its weight against a wild fig. The roots have burrowed the foundations and thrust a sucker through its walls.

'You must never shout at them,' the old man says to Godfrey, stroking his hand along the neck of the nearest ox. 'You must never make them tired beyond endurance. If they trust you, they will do whatever you say. They are not as dumb as they look' and he pats the beast affectionately on the rump. '*Kom, kom, kom, julle stout dingetjies, kom julle vuilgoedjies.*' Come, come, come, you naughty little things. Come you dirty rascals.

It is something of a love song.

Grace watches them, ready with the camera. When the young oxen rest, she follows Godfrey and the farmer into the pasture beyond the gate and up a sloping camp. There, a herd of multicoloured cattle graze. They are cross-breeds, bigger, sturdier than the cattle of her childhood, but among them are the colours, the patterns, the drifts of spots, the mottling. In a further camp a white bull stands, stout-horned, among the brush. His dewlap is a silken swag deepening to pale dun at his throat.

Grace watches Godfrey walk among the heifers with the ease of a stock-man. He inspects the red, the black, the brindled. Curious heads turn to watch him before the beasts return to grazing. These are docile creatures.

She can recognise the patterns now. She says them quietly to herself: the delicacy of the words, the fine rhythm and association. Herman de Waal calls them *bantom* and *bont* and *wolf*. But she knows differently. Among them are the '*kiewietjie* cow', named for a plover and the 'houses on the hill' and the one 'which touches the mushroom'.

They go from group to group. A small pair of calves butt and jostle. An ox turns his head, light tipping the curve of his horns. Grace, with the greatest care, watching the position of the sun at her back, takes the pictures. A cow, a heifer, the yoked oxen, the bull, Ou Doringbult, a younger bull, growing still into the weight of shoulder, scrotum, knees. He is all at angles with himself. His neck needs to thicken.

'If you're serious about getting a few cattle,' says Herman de Waal, 'there's an old packstone kraal in one of the camps near the store. I'll send over some of my boys to fix up the walls. I've got a chap who's very good with stonework. I can bring him round next week.'

'Thank you very much,' says Godfrey. 'I should think Crawford and the people at the research station in Zululand would be interested in a project. A different area – a different gene-pool. Why not give it a try?'

'Listen, Doc,' says Herman de Waal. 'Before you go running off into the *bundu* looking for bush cows, I can sell you a few heifers. They're not pure but they have the best characteristics of both. Very hardy, very well selected. There's a nice little girlie that I bought a few months ago – beautiful conformation, really good head. Unfortunately she's been polled, which is a pity, but some people's stockmen don't like working with animals with horns. You can understand it – but man, has she got a nice mirror pattern on her! Little black and white number, beautiful little hocks. And the young bull – he hasn't been tried yet, but I'd like to put him to some different cows. I know a bloke we could contact. He's got a few. Not such good stock as mine. Not so good, but not too bad either. You know, since the Government put a ban on breeding with native bulls a few years ago and started culling them, they've been very difficult to come by, but mine's a good cross. I'd be happy to let him service your cows. You could build up a beautiful little herd. A nice stock of *lobola* cattle for your sons.' And he laughs again. 'Good idea paying cattle for women,' he says. 'Keeps them in their place. No nonsense.'

Going out to the truck, Grace walks a step or two behind, holding the camera. Her notebook is untouched. She wonders if Herman de Waal has noticed. He has avoided speaking to her as much as possible. The only concession to her presence, after their tour of the camps, is that he had expected her to pour the tea. She is safe in this duty. In asking her to do it, he is circumscribing her. There is a small embarrassment in his acceptance of the cup, in the way he stirs it without looking at her. He knows quite well who she is. It is as if, in this context, he is at a loss with what to do with her. She is not the nice young teacher at the church bazaar, dispensing coconut ice. She is not the pretty young thing at the tennis club beside the tea urn. She is not the fair young woman he has seen usher the Sunday School children into the side pews in the church.

What is she doing with Dr Godfrey?

What has she to do with his cattle project?

Is she, perhaps, Dr Godfrey's *skelm*?

If she is, he must do his best to avoid any evidence that he might think it. Knowledge is complicity. *Skelm* is not his business. Godfrey is not to blame. She is.

A Good Woman knows better.

Sensing danger, men close ranks: the faintest thrashings of a fish in trouble. *–Pull yourself together, my friend.* By the hunch of a shoulder, the small dismissal of a glance, they do for their friend what he cannot do for himself. They exclude her. *–We do not want you here*. It is subtle but complete.

Wars are waged for less.

They take another route home from Herman de Waal's: the top road along the higher hills where the air is light and the temperate *ouhout* grow in pasture; where the pipings of the upland birds make a different melancholy in the late light of afternoon. This is not the call of crows in damaged places, invasive city birds clamouring under fluorescent street lamps in perpetual day. This is a high, sweet lament, lonely as the ridge and the lifting sky.

'I didn't realise you wanted to buy cattle,' says Grace.

'I didn't think I did myself, until today.'

'What happened to make you change your mind?'

'It's an investment.'

'An investment?' She smiles. 'Surely there are wiser things to invest in.'

He glances at her. 'Wiser, yes.' He hesitates. 'More valuable? We'll see.'

She says nothing. Something in his face precludes it. Then he says, 'Perhaps, to start with, I should take a few of Herman's cattle and then look around for other stock that's been isolated for some time.'

'Where will you go for them?'

'I'm not sure yet.'

'There was a place I used to visit with my grandfather long ago when he was a school inspector,' she says tentatively. 'Right away in the hills. At the back of beyond. It was very isolated and wild. I always felt I had entered another century when I went there. There was something ancient about it . . .'

In silence they look out across great spaces, deep in shadow, ridge to ridge – and then the flatlands stretching to the sea. She interlinks her fingers. Should she tell him?

Should she?

She says, 'It's a dim remembrance but I can visualise small, multicoloured

65

cattle and a very old byre. I wonder if I could find it again. It's probably gone by now.' Grace laughs then, looking away, suddenly in retreat. 'Perhaps it's all in my imagination.'

Beloved places should only be revealed with discretion. A place, intensified by love, is sacred. When love is gone, indifference changes it. Places can retreat as people do. Their detachment, though, is far more sullen, more unbending: the sky turns flat, the lifting clouds dissolve in greyness, the air is sharp and empty.

The truck edges slowly down the track, bounces between boulders. There is an intermingling of seasons in the air, that soft interchange of autumn. A little wind tracks back on itself, swirling and playful. They watch it scoop up leaves and lay them down – sudden and still – and start again, a game with an unseen watcher.

Godfrey says, 'The little wind is catching up the footprints of the dead and taking them away into the sky.'

'Why must they be taken?'

'Because, if we saw them in the sand down here, we would not believe the person had died, only gone on a journey – and soon, to prove it, there would be another set, coming back. The little wind needs to set the footsteps in the sky, so the spirit can find its familiar path.' He turns and smiles at her, half quizzical. 'You can't hunt the sky herds if you haven't any tracks, you know.'

Godfrey left his tracks. They are here in his work, in the long heritage of scholarship that rests with me, in the writings, in the face.

Grace did not.

It is as if – assiduously – she wiped them out.

Perhaps, after all, her legacy is all the more sacred – and courageous – for its silence.

They come down into the valley in the dark. Only the last flush of sunset, banked by cloud, edges the rim of hills. The beacon light in the window of Godfrey's house shines like a fisherman's lantern in a black sea.

Without explanation he turns into his yard, not taking the road round the hill and out across the flats, back to the school and the manse. The wheels of the truck rattle swiftly on the grid. The quiet eyes of the storeman's horse, standing in the home camp beside the shop, gleam briefly in the headlights. The door of the house flares, the long shadow of the fence palings arc with the sweep of headlamps. He turns into the shed. 'Let me make you supper,' he says.

'Hugh will be wondering where I am.'

66

'You can telephone.'

She follows him into the house.

She turns the handle of the telephone and waits for the exchange. Her voice is calm as she asks for her number.

'Hello, Mrs Wilmot,' says the operator, ready to chat, but someone else on the party-line cranks the handle in their ears – a small reprieve – and the operator reverts to an official voice, 'Hold on for Mr Wilmot' and gives the signal: two longs, two shorts. Two longs, two shorts.

Hugh Wilmot answers.

'Hugh?' Grace says.

'Where are you?' A touch of anxiety.

'Don't fuss, I'm fine. I'll be back in an hour or two. Don't wait up. I've got a key.'

There is a small pause. Grace glances over her shoulder. Godfrey has taken himself off to the privy in the backyard. She smiles. There is a perfectly sound bathroom in the house. 'We want to write down all the names we collected today,' she says. 'Please don't worry.' She smiles again – she had forgotten to record anything at all.

'Shall I keep your supper?'

'Supper? No. Not at all. I made too many sandwiches. I'll look after myself when I get in.'

She knows his displeasure. There is nothing she can do. He will set the phone back on its brass hook and take out his handkerchief and blow his nose and pick up the newspaper and put it down and go to his study and write his sermon. He will get up again, walk about the room, adjust a picture, making it straight. He will trim the lamp wick with his little pair of scissors and wipe the blades meticulously. He will put them in his pocket and tip on his heels to settle them. Each movement is so well known.

She feels mean for this sudden scrutiny. She feels mean for her impatience. She is supposed to be working on the *Ladies' Guild Cookery Book* for him. It is a project long planned by Hugh for the school holidays. Something they can work on in the evenings. It is dear to his heart. The money raised is to go towards the dependants of the soldiers who did not come home.

She is one of them.

It is meant to be her labour of love.

'*Favourite Recipes: tried and tested*', '*Handy Household Hints*' collected from a dozen farmers' wives and illustrated by small line drawings. Hugh has executed some himself. He is eager to sample the recipes before the final selection is made.

She has neglected the kitchen entirely since Dr Godfrey came.

She has promised milktart, made from his mother's collection, but she has mislaid the letter in which it was written.

She has mislaid everything.

Godfrey comes in, closes the back door behind him. He takes a glass from the cupboard. There is only one. He takes a mug as well. He fishes a bottle of whisky from below the sink and pours two measures. He does not ask Grace if she wants it. He simply assumes. He hands her the glass without looking at her.

'Bacon? Eggs?' he says. 'A bit of fried bread?'

He lights the primus. The flame is a small steady crown of indigo blue. He lights three candles and puts them on the kitchen table. The dripping from the tin by the stove sizzles faintly in the pan.

Of course they would have eaten bacon and eggs and fried bread – what else? No onions. Perhaps tomato. The kind that comes to the store when there is a glut, delivered in wooden-slatted boxes, tied with wire, oozing pips and plasma gently through the base where the riper fruit is squashed. Such tomatoes are cooked in stews and bredies. Their skins curl off in flutes and float in gravy. Real tomatoes, full of meat and flavour, the kind given as rations – third grade – with a pound of brisket and a bag of samp to the servants. Did Godfrey take one from the window sill and – distracted – weigh it gently in his palm? Did he slice it, cook it in lard, with a touch of sugar and a sprinkle of salt, the candle on the table guttering, the flame reflected in the window pane? Outside – nothing but the wind and the parade of stars and the hiss of the primus with the kettle on to boil?

'When I was little,' Grace says, 'I used to have our food in the kitchen – just like this. We had a table and chairs made of grass. You know the sort you used to buy on the coast, smelling of smoke and greenness?'

'And toast fingers to dip into your boiled egg,' Godfrey adds.

It does not sound silly, here in the whitewashed kitchen with the clean, iron-scent of boiling water.

'We had a cook,' says Grace, 'who used to tell stories about *uHili* and the water snake and the magical ox, Tulube. She used to turn the lamp down and pull her lids up to show the insides and caper in a strange, distorted way. It used to terrify and delight me, all at once.'

Tulube the magical ox, the water snake and the old coals shifting in the wood and anthracite stove; *dikkops* crying on the lawn; the shadows purple in the gloom of the pantry where a puffadder had once been found, slack and sinister behind the meal bin; the lamp which hissed and had a hard black and orange flame.

She laughs, a little self-consciously. 'What an odd thing to tell you . . .'

68

Her voice trails off. She turns her eyes towards the window, tugs at the end of her hair, letting him retreat, if he wants. She is thinking of the distant, the opaque '*I do not see you*' in Herman de Waal's glance.

Godfrey reaches over and takes up her glass. He pours another whisky.

She says – an adjunct to the gesture, 'Food is a funny thing. Being in the kitchen. Bacon and eggs . . .' She hesitates. 'It makes it easier to explain.'

'Explain?'

'To Hugh.' She is suddenly embarrassed. Her colour is high.

'Bacon and eggs in a kitchen is legitimate then?'

What has she said? She rests her chin in her hands, elbows on the table, hiding her burning lobes. 'Even with whisky.'

'Would he disapprove?'

'Of the whisky? Yes.' She dabs her finger at the salt that she has spilled on the table top. 'Maybe even of the bacon and eggs.'

He looks across at her. 'Have I put you in an awkward situation?'

She inclines her head. 'No, of course not.'

He smiles at her, disarming her confusion.

–*Not yet*. He does not say it. It would be precipitate.

But they both know, well enough, that it has been too late since he opened the door of the schoolroom and the small boys, sitting in their desks, scenting danger, pulled themselves alert and watched her turning to him.

Turning, turning – once Miss Gwendoline Spender – opening like a lily, following the pull of the moon.

I will leave them there, in that familiar kitchen where I cook my meals now, the little primus hissing heat into a pan of water for my tea. It is part of our understanding. Godfrey has his privacy. I guard it with my own. I will take no vicarious pleasure in intruding. As though they are waiting for me to go, I almost tiptoe to the sink, put my own empty plate and mug in the basin, leave the candle on the table – they may want the light – and quietly close the door behind me. I go so softly, I know the flame does not even dip and flutter, only wavers once, burns steady as before. There is work to do and still I sit, inventing Grace. Perhaps Godfrey invented her too – fragile and irredeemable to any but himself.

When Grace gets home, Hugh is waiting for her on the *stoep*. There is no need for him to be standing on the flags of the long veranda with a muffler on as if the autumn night is cold. He does not come forward. He must have seen her alight from Godfrey's truck and close the door quietly in the way that someone sometimes does who is aware of every movement, as if the clipping of the handle were the last part of a conversation. Godfrey, too, gets out, walks a little way with her and then, as if sensing the presence, says a quiet goodnight and turns away. Grace crosses the lawn towards the back door. Hugh sees her shadow waver along the whitewashed wall, hears the sudden click of the light on the porch and she, herself, starkly outlined at the entrance. She stands a moment, not turning to see the truck drive away but waiting, just an instant, as if she'd raised her hand. She goes inside then and the dim light is faintly pink behind the curtains.

Hugh does not go inside himself. He watches the headlights flare, now dip and dim and disappear and flare again as the truck winds slowly up the lip of the valley. The sound of the engine reaches him across the dark. Then the other sounds creep back: the heartbeat of the generator; slowly oozing grease in the shed; the crickets; far off, the shift of leaves in a wind which has not reached the leeward side, a small restless drifting in a distant stand of trees.

No truck had come before, taking her away, bringing her back, taking her away, bringing her back. And when it took her away and did not bring her back again all night – what then? What would he do then – standing in the cold with his muffler and the mocking stars?

At first, I thought Hugh Wilmot was not my business. In passing, I had seen a photo of him. It is in the vestry of the little church. He was a man with a rather disproportionately large neck. It is manly, in its way. He reminds me of a dassie, though. Ponderous, inclined to bob. He is a man who would wear a vest in all weathers. He is not the sort of man who would approve of vegetarians or socialists. He would like wide shorts and long socks in summer, don a cloth hat for gardening and take his meals at twelve and six-thirty.

His God does everything on time.

So does he.

Godfrey is not a person he would care to understand.

I decided that there was nothing I could do for Hugh Wilmot. On paper, I have every admiration. I can hear myself: –*He must have been a very good man.* Grace would have said it often, too. God would have added His approbation. What else is there to say but that? It is the highest praise.

I carry my thesis to the outhouse, work for two hours under the heavy gas camping lantern. I scan a note from the prof. He is a good man too. Very precise, very clear, just like Hugh, except that his language (self-consciously) is less polite.

–*What the hell is going on? I hope you're not still on a wild goose chase after C J G! I thought we had a meeting last Wednesday to discuss progress. Weren't you booked to take the second years for a seminar? Can't get you on that party line. Please phone.*

70

I file it carefully: *poor Prof is pissed-off*.

I trace the migration of cattle down Africa. It sounds straightforward, but it's fraught with complications and debate. I can still hear so many bearded academics yapping at a conference last June. Round and round the subject. Yap, yap, yap. Somewhere, far outside, I swear I hear beasts mooing in a pasture – and the flat, vacant thud of dung being evacuated.

There is no more satisfying sound.

Chapter five

The farm lies in a valley, backed by hills. Fifty years ago, when Grace and Godfrey came here, the road would have been dust – the fine white dust of the uplands. Now it is macadamised – but, long since, the tar has melted out into small depressions where the bones of the earth push through. There is a place, at a drift, where it curves up steeply and a small township has a toehold on the hillside. It seems to weep its sewage and its plastic into the thorn bushes that edge it. There is a little church with a cross, drunken on its plinth. The door is padlocked. Crows caper in the yard. In these parts, their cry is the sound of an empty afternoon: leached white, dry as thorns.

Sometimes, in spring, one is surprised by the abundance of small flowering plants. Little legumes with purple slipper flowers and wild pelargoniums among the *duiweltjies*. Sudden in the road, so bright, so brilliantly marked, a bee-yellow bunting and his small brown mate. The old voices persist. How much more they would have echoed when Godfrey and Grace drove here, in the truck, turning into the grass on a high slope to eat lunch and sit in the autumn sunlight, unwrapping their sandwiches from the damp cotton cloth and pouring tea from a flask.

Now, one does not stop to ponder. Any fossils – Godfrey's other passion – hidden in the rocks, must be left alone. It is too dangerous to stop: every news bulletin, the papers, bring reports of villainy. The side roads, each announced by an old black sign, alongside the marker for a cattle grid, cannot be explored by chance any more. The most familiar, most innocuous of paths, have a menace: *do not come here*.

There is a sense of dispossession in this valley, of people having gone. Farms stand empty. The sashes, where they are not knocked out like rotten teeth,

72

wink back a rusted sun. The presence that remains is immediate and faintly sinister. The ancestral shades have fled.

The track still leads past all of these, further, further into a desolation of sweet-thorn, euphorbias growing on the drier slopes of valleys, the ironstone in gulleys, red as winter aloes. I bump across a dry *spruit*, across a cattle grid and into open land. I pass a paddock at the edge of which stand the ruins of an old shed. A huge wild fig leans across the width of the foundations. Roots like grey tentacles explore the fallen masonry. Along the track, beyond the milking sheds, the original farmhouse, unchanged in more than a century, decays quietly and graciously. Further off, on a bare slope above it, a newer house stands by a cinder turning circle. It is toad-ugly with windows at the corners, a porthole by the front door, orange brick foundations and pillars, stucco plastering, a roof too small for the walls, like a Public Works or Railways house. It is a monument to post-war prudence and frugality.

Is this the place of Grace's shining day? This desolation?

Walking across a fallen tangle of fence into the backyard, I come upon a small garden. There is only a row of bean plants, earth dug for a few potatoes, the empty stalks of mealies. There is a scarecrow. It is made from an iron fork. A stick – the outstretched arms – has been lashed at right angles. It wears an overall, the head is an upturned paint tin. It leans at an angle, falling backwards, supplicating, blind beneath the rusted helmet. Its world is poised for collapse. Like Grace, I hear the bou bou shrike in the hedge. It is a morning bird, it calls without melancholy. Like her, I walk towards the house, along a path edged by bricks to mark an iris bed.

I am here to speak to Herman de Waal's daughter. Her name is Mrs Dulcie Trollip. She lives here with her husband, Arthur. Their son manages the farm from the distance of another, more prosperous property, across the valley. It is fifty years since Godfrey and Grace came here to inspect the cattle and to watch the young steers being trained for the plough. Walking towards the house, I decide that what I gaze around to absorb and know, Grace looked at too – and for the same reasons – with the same insistence on imprinting it in her mind. Except that when she came, the shutters of the older house would have stood open, the panes shone, the *stoep* gleamed with red polish, smelling of turpentine and wax. The blue shade of the pepper trees would have held the promise of sap, the water in the narrow furrow at the edge of the kitchen garden slithered over the rocks and down the gulleys, feeding cress and hyacinth.

There is no moisture on the day I go there, neither in the furrow nor the air. The windmill sails in the *bergwind* morning. There is the screech of metal on metal, a hollow dry earth beneath.

I am expected. Some weeks before, I had written:

Dear Mrs Trollip,
Please excuse the intrusion from a stranger but I am writing in connection with a
Dr C J Godfrey who did research on indigenous cattle in your district around
1946/7. I am aware, from his archive, that he corresponded regularly with a Mr
Herman de Waal, who, I believe, was your father.

Yes – the reply comes – *Herman de Waal was my father. Yes, I remember Dr*
C J Godfrey. He rented a cottage from us, next to our store. I met him, just after the
War when my husband was demobbed and we came to live on the farm. It must
have been about 1946.

Another letter from me:

I am researching indigenous cattle names and using Dr Godfrey's papers but I
am interested in Dr Godfrey himself. Do you know anything about him?

The next letter is a long time coming.

I do have some photographs. One or two of Dr Godfrey with my Dad.

Pushing my luck:

Would it be possible for you to send me copies of the photographs? I will pay all
expenses and apologise for any inconvenience this request might cause, but it is
crucial to my work.

No, I cannot send you photographs – she writes. *Copying is not possible in such*
an isolated spot. I do not get about these days. Nor can I send them, they are too
valuable. If you want to see them, you will have to come and see them here.

And so I am here. As Grace and Godfrey were. It is my own shining day.

Mrs Trollip is elderly – a strange little figurine in a new Fasco dress, a great
swathe of hennaed plaits wound about her head like an upturned basket. She
is well disposed, she is pleased to see me. She is full of news and gossip and the
importance of an interview. She is as square as the paraffin tins on the veranda,
set on bricks – a leg at each corner, just so – crowned with ferns. Meaning
business too. She, like her father before her, breeds indigenous cattle, chickens
and goats. Her brothers having both died in the war – one at Tobruk, one in
the tanks in the Western Desert – she inherited the farm. And the passion. Her
husband came along with her. He potters in the shed at the back, repairing old
machines, determined to resurrect them. The bits of scrap scattered in the

camp down at the store are waiting for attention. 'They have been waiting for attention for thirty years,' she says. I sense that he is incidental to the farming.

I learn that Mrs Trollip is an authority on Artificial Insemination, on strains in Boer goats. She still pursues the old ploughing techniques her father so loved and developed. It was their farm.

Despite what I have indicated to her about my thesis, Godfrey's work and my inheritance of it, I have not come for that. Today, I have no interest in cattle. She does not know it, though. She does not know that I have come for Godfrey and Grace. I will have to nudge her in that direction. She would much rather debate – as Godfrey often did – the merits of leaving 'bush' cows undipped.

'He was right there,' Mrs Trollip says. 'He was way ahead of his time. Even ahead of my Dad.' It is almost rueful. 'He used to say, "What is the use of 'improving' stock with imported breeds when this stock has been improving itself, by natural selection, over thousands of years. Leave it alone." He always said that the supposed defects everyone saw in bush cattle were a lot of nonsense.'

–*And culturally defined*: I recall Godfrey's notes on the subject. He had a lot to say about people 'colonising' other people: their art, music, histories and turning them around to magnify themselves, creating from the simple and the honest a pastiche of sophistication (and pretension). There may be, he said, a smugness in the collection of artefacts and their display, suggesting that the creators themselves were not aware of the intrinsic worth, another half-cocked process of 'improving stock'. I must watch that I don't colonise Delekile's work in exactly the same way. Does a piece stand alone or is its context – its display on a perspex shape, for instance, underlit at angles – the device which defines its worth? Is it the object that counts or what is chosen to enhance it?

'There was a bit of feeling among some of the farmers around here, who didn't agree with him,' Mrs Trollip is saying. 'After all, he wasn't a farmer himself. He was an expert on native customs and languages. That was really his field. People didn't want to understand him.' She takes a sip of her wine and a long draw on her cigarette. 'He wrote a paper,' she says. 'Quite a few years after he was working here.' She looks down suddenly, flicking ash off her lap. She does it busily, as if she is recalling something which – suddenly – she does not wish to share. Then she says, 'He visited from England. When was it now?' She looks up at the ceiling, tracing the outline of the hanging lampshade. 'Fifty-seven. Maybe fifty-eight' – as if saying it has triggered a reminder. 'Of course – it was October fifty-seven. He was out from England. I think it was the time when his father passed away. *Ja*' – looking across at me – 'that's it. He came here straight after the funeral and stayed in the old house by the store. He used to rent it from us in the old days when he was doing his research. He seemed to like it, being isolated and all that. It's quite a long way down the valley from here. We've always owned it.'

She stops again.

She waits, head cocked, eyes fixed middle distance. I wish I could visualise her thoughts. Then she says, 'After that he wrote a paper. *Ag*, man, what was it in?' She gently moves her lower dentures, as if searching. 'Some agricultural journal or other. He sent it to us.' She glances over at me. 'I said I'd pass it on when I'd read it, so I know I haven't got it any more or I'd show you.' She reaches for her box of cigarettes again. 'I remember that he made a lot of good points in it, but there was other stuff Dad and I couldn't follow. But I remember it was about respecting what's important to other people – you know, the natives and things. Their customs and stuff like that.'

I am sitting very still, as if listening for another voice.

Mrs Trollip pours us both a glass of Late Harvest from a flagon. She says, 'There was even a poem in it! Imagine that in a farming journal, hey?' She has a gap between her front teeth. It gives her face a particular, wry humour. 'Still, it seems that what he said offended some people.' She is more serious then. 'It was like he was bringing politics into farming and all that. They didn't like it – especially from a chap who had buggered off to England! Dad said he should have taken a less extreme line if he was going to win farmers over to breeding indigenous animals. You couldn't mix things in those days, you know. Not like now.' She puts her glass down on the cork coaster at her elbow. She says, 'He was a very clever man.' It is not intended – entirely – as a compliment.

She takes up her cigarette. The ash hangs suspended in a gentle curve. It falls into her lap again. She brushes it away. The old cushions of the couch – putty-coloured linen embroidered with hollyhocks and cottages – are full of the burn marks of stray cigarettes, left smouldering forgotten. The wine is warm and rather sweet.

'You know why I dye my hair?' she says suddenly. 'It's so the natives don't mug me when I go to town. If you've got grey hair – my God – they going to do it. You have to walk like you not going to take any shit.' The fretwork on her head glows triumphantly. She sips her wine with an equal satisfaction.

There is nothing I can say to this: I cannot react and allow her to retreat. I reach for a cigarette myself. The sun slants flat against the parquet slats of the floor.

This house, where I sit with Mrs Trollip, is her own, built soon after her marriage. The walls of the passage are lined – a little too high for scrutiny – with trophies for her cattle and her goats. *'Breeder of the Year'* – thirty years ago. The furnishings are testimony to her independence, despite the older pieces brought down from 'the big house' which fit – self-consciously – into corners. Had Grace sat on this old chintz chair, silent as I am now, simply listening? She begins to form beside me – fleetingly, in profile. Is she supplanting me – or I, her? I gaze about me at the china cabinet and ornaments. An old Victorian oil on a chain hangs side by side with a Tretchikoff print: the Chinese girl glows green over the mantel. In the hall, the Orchid sweating on the stair is flanked by a series of thin-framed photos of Herman de Waal at an agricultural show in the forties, receiving a prize from none other than the Governor General. It is suitably inscribed, formally posed. A dead fishmoth is lodged against his head. It looks like a plume in his hat.

I recall myself to my surroundings, the formica and chrome tea trolley with hoop handles settled between Mrs Trollip and me. On the backs of each chair is a crocheted antimacassar, between each seat a nest of tables set at an angle on the polished parquet. The high horizontal strips of steel window, the shallow eaves, cannot keep away the swallows that have nested here for years and years. It is a ghetto of nests, sun-seared, without the benediction of deep shade and recessed corners.

'They make such a bloody mess,' says Mrs Trollip, following my gaze to the window sill, littered with droppings. But I know she would never chase them. They are as much a part of her house as the thick, dust-laden lace curtains that keep the heat and the menace out. I guess that she waits for them in spring and, in autumn, watches their gathering for departure with anxious eyes, knowing that next year they may return to an empty house, to someone who may knock their nests down with a broom handle and sweep their careful masonry away.

We talk a long time about cattle and about goats and about the district and who is related to whom before I mention Grace. 'Did you know a Mrs Wilmot?'

She looks at me swiftly but I am all ingenuousness. 'The teacher over at Vlakfontein?' she says.

'I think so,' I say, rather vaguely.

'Yes.'

She says no more, then reaches for the wine. 'She was a very nice person . . .' – as if I might contradict her.

My hands begin to sweat, just gently. I smile at Mrs Trollip and she, glass halfway to her mouth, looks at me suddenly and shrewdly, sideways through a bifocal – it magnifies her eye, a sudden cyclops with the red palisade on her head. 'What about Mrs Wilmot?' she says.

'A Mrs Wilmot, who I believe was a school teacher, helped Dr Godfrey with his dictionary. He acknowledges her in his foreword and I wondered if there was any correspondence left behind which could throw some light on how she went about things . . .' I am rambling.

'What things?'

'In the dictionary.' I hesitate, look directly back.

I have become a consummate cheat: my expression is without personal curiosity. I am sitting on my palms so she cannot see them. 'Her entries are well organised,' I say. 'Better than his.'

'She was a good teacher,' says Mrs Trollip. It is almost prim.

'I can imagine it,' I say. 'Was she quite an elderly lady? I know she was a

77

widow. I get the impression that she was very meticulous.'

'She was hardly an elderly widow!' Mrs Trollip laughs then, as though the notion really amuses her. She looks over at me. I am scrutinised as if I were Grace herself. 'She was much younger than him. Much!'

'What happened to her husband?'

'Jack? He joined up with my brothers in thirty-nine. He was killed early in forty-four.' She turns her head towards me. Again, her eyes enlarge behind her lenses. 'Grace Wilmot stayed on to teach at the school and to be companion to her sister-in-law, Doreen, until Doreen's husband, Hugh Wilmot came back from Italy. He was our minister at the Methodist church, you know. Jack's older brother.' She pauses. 'Shame,' she taps her ash gently into the ashtray. 'Doreen Wilmot died just after Hugh got home. She was a sickly sort. Imagine – he lost his brother and his wife. Man, it was too much! Then, along comes Dr Godfrey . . .'

Her tone is at odds with the way she has spoken before, hardening up.

Her words are not for me.

She says, in a lowered voice, 'They say he was a communist.' She gives the word its full weight. 'I don't think I believe it. But if he was, I suppose it explains a lot.'

'A lot?'

'About the kind of man he was.' She gestures with her hand. It is almost brusque. It seems she wishes to convince herself. She says, 'You see, with communists . . .'

I am too intent on Godfrey to allow for Mrs Trollip's version of communists right now. The lipstick and cardigan image that I have adopted for this visit does not alert her to any leanings of my own. Instead, I interrupt – smiling – 'Did you like him?'

'Oh yes. He was a very charming man.' She smiles, half to herself. 'He really was.' She looks up. 'My father was devoted. Devoted! But, you see, that was about the cattle. Dr Godfrey started a little herd down behind the store. My father helped him set it up. He lent him a bull but, as it turned out, they didn't quite see eye to eye about cross-breeding. My Dad thought he had gone "too bush", got sentimental, if you like . . .' She ground out her cigarette and lit another. 'It was something they were going to do together. But, in the end, I think Dad was disappointed.'

I am trawling quietly. 'Disappointed?'

'By the rest.'

I wait. 'The rest . . .'

'This Dr Godfrey had a thing about the native names of cattle and about their history and poetry and whatnot, as if it was more important than the breeding and the beef. You know, very airy-fairy and always running around in the reserves talking to the natives about cattle praises and *lobola* when he should have been helping my Dad to encourage the farmers here to cross-breed in the best characteristics without getting their backs up. But, of course, we could all see what was happening . . .'

Mrs Trollip offers me the flagon. I take it. She is about to speak but a bell rings in the adjoining room. Through the open door, the cook is vigorously shaking a little bulb, a clapper caught in a round claw of brass which she sets down in an engraved cup. It is placed at the head of the table, next to the wine glass. Mrs Trollip stands abruptly.

Bells, like telephones, must be answered promptly: what might one miss by dallying?

She stubs out her cigarette rather firmly. She does not do it with the delicacy of someone who minds that their fingers stain. The ashtray is made of glass. It nests inside a miniature tractor tyre with the dealer's logo on the side. It is entirely serviceable.

We go through to the lunch table and the cook comes behind, bearing the flagon, the ashtray, the cigarettes and a box of matches. Mrs Trollip says, as she settles herself at the table, 'I have only put aside my father's pictures to show you. His cattle and whatnot. But I have got my own albums and some of my mother's. There's a picture of Grace Wilmot somewhere in one of them. District tennis tournament, I think. I didn't take them out for you. I didn't think they were relevant, you know. We can look after lunch, if you like.'

Mrs Trollip serves a plate of food for her husband and tells the cook to take it up to the shed. 'He doesn't speak,' she says, by way of explanation. 'Except to machines. He still thinks he's a tank mechanic in the war.' She spoons out potatoes and carrots, samp and gravy. The plates are laden. I wish I could approach food so honestly, with so little deceit, so little bargaining. She almost tells me to eat up. I can hear her saying, –*What are you waiting for?*

I watch her.

She is in no hurry to resume the topic or to humour me with descriptions of Godfrey. She wants to talk about congenial things. Did I know, she had bred three generations of champion bulls? 'There is nothing better . . . nothing,' she says, with meaning, 'than seeing a really beautiful bull.' She is getting off the point. She is launching into a paean of praise for desirable sires. She is an expert on genetics. She wants to linger over lunch before she gets her albums out. Besides the bulls, she wants to talk about her grandchildren. Her visitors are few. There is only her cook to talk to, a woman so startlingly like one of the figures in the *Penny Magazine – Society for the Diffusion of Useful Knowledge*, an etching from Barrow's 'Travels', circa 1830, so caricatured and steatopygic that I cannot keep my eyes from her. Her face is sunken in at the upper lip, crinkled like a dried sour-fig. Her eyes, under a sharp jut of brow, are berry-black. She is like a tuber – in colour, texture and design. She serves us slabs of meat, each with a rind of fat, bubbling with heat. Mrs Trollip says, 'If you don't eat the fat, give it to me, it's my favourite part. *Kaaiings.* Do you know *kaaiings?* Little crispy bits of mutton fat, drained and kept in a tin? Man, so delicious! When we were kids, we used to guzzle them till we got quite *naar.*' She surveys me. I suppose, in my paleness, I do not look as if I was fed on good farm food in my youth. She can sense a pernickety eater a mile off – an olive-nibbler, a Matzos-and-Marmite academic, mineral water and St John's Wort for stress – and all that bullshit. I can hear her thinking it aloud.

–Go and dig a hole and fix your head. Eat what God provided. You didn't live through The War.

No doubt she keeps every piece of string, every little cracked tongue of Lifebuoy soap, every scrap of Christmas paper, ironed flat.

She eats the fat with the greatest of relish, waving away lazy flies with one hand, lighting a cigarette before the cook has removed her plate. I hear the slow slap, slap of bare feet on the linoleum. Like the turning of the windmill in the yard, the churning thud of the separator clamped to the enamel-topped table in the kitchen, the ringing – between courses – of the little brass Benares bell, it is a lost sound: the slipping of an era.

The wind is very high outside. The tossing of the huge palm, its fronds neatly hacked up the trunk to froth above in a fountain of jade, sounds like surf, a long surging, breaking every now and then – quiet – then renewed. The clock in the hall, a 'grandmother', dating from the forties, hideous in its design, with huge round-faced weights, gongs the hour in imitation of the Westminster chimes. The sound must fill the house when no one is there with her, when she is sitting on the *stoep* alone looking out into nothing with the ferns in their paraffin tins and only the lizards and sun spiders venturing the heat of summer, Arthur Trollip marooned somewhere in his shed, among his old machines.

'I became a teacher myself,' Mrs Trollip is saying. 'In fact, I took over the school at Vlakfontein when Grace Wilmot left. It wasn't long after I finished at the Training College.' She chuckles, recalling something. 'Man, we used to have a good time as students. I was always bringing friends out to the farm at the weekends. In those days, there were eighty gates to open! It was a problem – but the chap in the dickey-seat had to do the job. We used to take turns sitting there.' She laughs, sends a drift of smoke up to the ceiling. It wreaths her head, counter to the swirl of plaits. 'Once we had a party,' she says, 'and the vicar came and my Mom made a fruit punch. She made the best punch in the district but, hell, did it *skop*! There was a new vicar and he didn't know how much hooch was in it. He got so tight he drove his car into a *donga*. He crept back and my Mom – she felt sorry, you know – she put him in a spare room and let him sleep it off and got some of the farm boys and the mules to haul the car out and hide it in the shearing shed.' She draws a breath. It wavers behind the long assault of smoke and nicotine. 'By morning the whole district knew that the new padre was drunk in our house.'

'Was it Mr Wilmot?'

'Mr Wilmot? Good grief, no! It was the C-of-E fellow, who didn't last long. Hugh Wilmot was a Methodist. You wouldn't have caught him with a drop. Very good man, only – between us – rather boring. Not like his brother, Jack.' She contemplates the zinnias in a fan-shaped green-glazed vase, angled on the sideboard. 'Jack!' she says. 'He was a marvel! Good-looking fellow. Good farmer. Rather wild also, they say. Liked his toots at the Club. Bit of a womaniser. Grace was quite a few years older than me. Let's think,' she drags a long stream of smoke into her lungs, lets it drift out of her nostrils. 'I suppose she was about twenty-seven, twenty-eight when she lost him. *Ag*, shame!'

'Did they have children?'

'Jack and Grace?' Her hesitation sounds as if she had tucked something in parenthesis. Whatever it is, it is left unsaid. 'No, they never had children.'

The shuffle feet come down the passage. The cook appears, bringing a jug of cream. From under a net cloth, edged with small conical shells, each gathered from a seaside holiday and laboriously bored and sewn, she produces a large cut glass bowl of stewed apricots and sets it in front of Mrs Trollip. They float in their syrup, furred here and there with soft mould. Mrs Trollip stares at them through her bifocals, looking askew with one, then the other. Satisfied, she scoops large helpings into faded acid-yellow bowls, the glaze netted with the finest cracks, stencilled in orange and black, some long-ago family wedding present, the height of chic from Putneys Gifts, circa 1929.

After lunch she leads me to an enclosed porch. She has laid out her father's work, his pictures of his cattle, his Register of names and breeding lines. I have seen some of it, copied into Godfrey's files. There is a folder of Herman de Waal's correspondence: letters from breeders, from Godfrey, from Dr Crawford, mauve-tinged carbon copies of his own to both. There are black and white pictures, muddled in a shoe box. I am not looking for a beast, despite the wonderful array of patterns and horn-shapes. I am searching for a face.

Mrs Trollip takes up a photo, rather small, over-exposed in a corner. 'Here's my Dad and Dr Godfrey,' she says. I almost snatch at it. Her father is centre stage – an old fellow in a hat and a jacket that was fastened across his middle, straining at the button. Godfrey is leaning on a gate, inspecting bullocks. His face is half turned. His shoulders are eloquent, the line of rolled shirt sleeve, the way the fingers tip the rim of the gate. On the back is written *5th March, 1946*.

It is Grace's writing.

There are others, too, marked with the same date and the name of the colour-pattern of the beast in question. Herman de Waal and Godfrey are in some of them, not in others. But the eye that chose each of the images, is undoubtedly Grace's. Godfrey must have sent Herman de Waal copies of his film, asked Grace to label them.

Which came first – the collection of Mrs Trollip's pictures or my construction of their visit to Herman de Waal? Did I create that day before I saw the prints? I can no longer remember. The sequence doesn't matter any more. A truth has its genesis apart from time. I have achieved the interzone which links us: I am beginning to be absorbed into their story; I am the shadow at Grace's foot.

Mrs Trollip may let me copy these. Perhaps, in the end, she will let me have them. She senses, briefly, her own power in it. She takes the picture back, turns it around and says, 'Very good-looking man . . .'

–*Except that he's a communist:* his 'leanings' – perhaps – are the reason for the thinness in his face, the faint, foreign prominence of the cheekbones. There is a vaguely Slavic look to it. No farmer with predictable antecedents, well fed on mutton fat, has a face honed to brooding like Godfrey's.

She puts the picture away, tucking it among the others. And fleetingly – incongruously – there is something almost tender in the gesture. A discretion. A small exchange.

I am allowed to look, not linger over the pictures of the cattle. I make no more comment on Godfrey or Mrs Trollip's father. I pretend that they are as incidental as Grace had tried to make them look in her pictures: beast in the foreground, Godfrey at a distance. I know the reason for the occasional lack of focus, the oddness of an angle, the cow's hooves cut off. The deference is to Godfrey's face.

Mrs Trollip sweeps the rest of the pictures together and puts them back in the shoebox. I watch it disappear: Godfrey filed and set on the bottom shelf of the cupboard with a bottle of cattle-drench, long expired. There is an urgency in me. Mrs Trollip cannot know it. I say – lightly – as she straightens up and locks the cupboard door, 'You said you might have a picture or two of Grace Wilmot . . .' She cannot be allowed to reconsider. Another day, she might be indifferent.

Or defensive.

'I'll have to go and look for my mother's albums,' she says.

I follow her down the dim passage, glancing in at the kitchen as I pass. On the high, white-painted shelves, enamelware is arranged. A ewer and basin, a soup tureen, battered by blue soap at the scrubbing board. Again, I sense the slipping of an era in these discarded artefacts, these clean, white, serviceable lines. They are curiosities now. They would fetch inflated prices in a pseudo '*Granny's Attic*'. No doubt, a drift of dust chalks out their bases. No one has moved them for years. I notice, by the canisters arranged on the counter tops, that Mrs Trollip herself – under influence of her daughter-in-law? – is devoted to Tupperware.

Perhaps it is my face, perhaps it is the silence at the far end of the house, that makes Mrs Trollip seem suddenly aware of something. She becomes quiet, almost tiptoes. It is comic to see her treading down the passage just ahead of me, tilting from side to side, in a momentum. I follow her to a dark bedroom. She opens the curtains, finds, in a bow-fronted chest, the albums she is looking for.

I sit at the window. The view beyond the glass wavers slightly at the edges, the gaunt cypresses, the pepper trees, the old decaying house on the sloping land near the river. I open the first album, going from page to page, stiff charcoal paper, the pictures labelled in white ink. So many grandmothers in long coats and large hats, so many schoolboys in junior teams, so many merinos and angoras and views of ships in Table Bay – some memorable holiday when the camera was new and atmospheric landscapes were the rage. There were the tennis parties and the tea parties and the christening parties and the Christmas parties, spanning years. And then, in a round frame, a group of four – the district tennis team – casually aligned, leaning on the back of a wicker veranda sofa. Beneath it, is written:

1943: Enid, Rosemary, Cynthia, Grace.

Grace.

There is nothing pensive or lost in her smile. There is nothing dark, nothing wounded. She laughs up – beautiful teeth – her eyes crinkle into gladness.

Yes, I have seen Grace Wilmot.

Grace.

She is well named.

Mrs Trollip wheezes as she leans down, feet firmly planted, back straight, knees flexed, to place the album in the bottom drawer again and to coax it closed. She does not want my help. She is determined to manage.

The room is furnished differently from the rest of the house. The bed is dark and heavy, well over a hundred years old. The scrolling on the wardrobe gleams. 'It was my Dad's room,' she says. 'After Mom died, we brought him up from the big house. He liked his own things around him. Also this . . .' – she points it out – 'it's my wedding photo. And my brothers.' She peers up at the group, clicks her teeth, moving the lower denture forward and back – it is a contemplative gesture – briefly unaware that I am there. She turns away from me towards the bed and pulls the satiny eiderdown straight. I step forward and look. Two young soldiers. Dead before they were twenty. The half-choked surprise of a studio shot: *–Keep your head still now, sonny. Smile. Don't move.* In the black frame next to them, Mrs Trollip, in a clinging gown with a great bushel of lilies and roses and gladioli. Mrs Trollip with a proud, deep-breasted chest, perfectly upholstered. And the hair, no different in style, but the coils of plaits gleam with health and abundance. It is a crown – quite glorious – above a handsome, even face.

There is nothing I can say. She stands in the doorway in her Fasco dress. I wish I could embrace her, tell her how little has changed. I cannot. She would despise me for the lie.

I follow her back down the passage. I leave her, as a bride, in the room with Grace and the two dead soldiers. It is right that way: I could not bear to find Grace full of old woman smells, waiting out her time – no longer measuring the seasons by the lambing of her sheep or the calving of her cattle, the progress of her sons, but by the coming and the going of the swallows, too faint-sighted to see the mould on the fruit or the burns in the cushions, keeping her faith with the past by arranging zinnias and stocks in a wedding vase stuffed with rusted threads of chicken wire to hold the stems in place, attending to an old man who no longer wants to speak.

I leave Mrs Trollip in the middle of the afternoon. It is three o'clock – that suspended time of day – echo of its predawn counterpart – that faint anguish at the emptiness of the sky, an earth without shadow. She is standing in the door of the house, haloed by the porthole. She raises a hand, standing square among the paraffin tins of ferns. It is too early for the swallows to be on the wing. She goes inside without looking up at the eaves.

I close the gate and drive away, past the rows of vegetables and the falling scarecrow, past the shed. I see an old man in overalls stooping over a lathe. I turn down a track past the the empty cattle byre. When I reach the district road, I choose another route – an upland track – turning west. I know it is the road they took, dissecting *rooigras*, shining pink and ash in the high soft light of afternoon. Perhaps I'll see a bustard, pacing the slope, breasting the pale blue horizon of the hills. Perhaps the little wind will come, taking up the footprints, brushing them away, retracing them, when evening falls, along the pathways in the sky.

It is impossible to love a person one has never met.

I do not believe that. And, if it is not love – only some bizarre obsession – why should meaning be invested in that person, so entirely – and so rashly?

It is impossible to love someone whose voice one has never heard, whose hand has never returned that first tentative touch.

I do not believe that either.

Nor that the journeys are solitary pilgrimages. I have turned often, in my work in this little house, alert, and waited for Godfrey to speak. But even if I never hear his voice, I know, the moment that I falter, he will send a sign. He always does.

It is simply a matter of recognition, an inner resonance, assurance that the grief of love is shared.

Apart, my daily life – ordered and dispassionate – moves on. Only Godfrey knows – will ever know – the hidden gesture of retreat that shields the heart. Small – perhaps prosaic: little Gert gathering the shards of glass, scattered at her feet.

The balance of regard between Godfrey and me is finely poised, one to one: through me he exists again; through him, I live beyond the commonplace. For both, it is a liberation.

But when my task is done and he goes out into the unknown in the pages of this book (his or mine?), beyond my protection – will he be appropriated by others? Will I be obliged to share – or relinquish him?

What if there is just indifference to the work?

We stand defenceless against it, he and I. It is only faith in each other – the absolute knowing (so delicate, so hard-won) – that guards us from it. Sometimes, even now, we laugh quietly together. We pretend that we are glad that there are those who do not understand.

We pretend.

What do we care for them? Their approbation would dilute this strange, fierce bond between us. We are as impetuous – and fragile – as lovers.

And – like lovers – loss is what we fear.

I hoard my treasures up against forgetting: I keep a sturdy wooden box. In it is his picture, his old birthday book, a pocket edition of *Odes of Keats* that he carried in his battledress, a stone taken from the garden of his childhood home, a chip of wood from a pew in the school chapel, his friend's dance card from a College ball at Trinity, the fibrous root of a helichrysum, prised from a grave.

I feel his presence. He is with me as I work, as certain as the beating of the blood. He is with me in the things that I have gathered from his life.

–Are you still there, Godfrey? Are you still there?

It is like asking God if He is there. Today – Silence. Tomorrow, Blazing-in-the-Sky.

Faith, like Love, is always precarious. I know that no one can sustain it.

I also know that the time will come when Godfrey will withdraw. He will say to me, quite simply, *–I am going now*.

Why now, Godfrey? Wait just a little. Just a little longer.

–It is time.

And so he'll go.

That is how – in the end – he left Grace too.

It was neither cruel, nor precipitate. It was quiet. And right.

All through the time I have been here, I have waited for something dramatic from Godfrey – for the telephone to ring, for Godfrey to say, *–Well?* It remains silent in its archaic cradle on the wall with its old woven cable cord and its brass attachments. It is an anachronism in this day and age. The storekeeper has a portable phone. He is rather proud of it. He goes about with it pushed to his ear, its aerial thrusting up, a flourish of technology in this deserted place. Next, he will have a mobile – here, where there is still no electricity and the

85

windmill is the only source of water! He is saving for one, he says. And so is Delekile, the itinerant storeman, he of the old woollen cap, pushing his *besem* round the shop floor on Tuesdays and Thursdays. What will Delekile do, conjuring voices from the sky, sending signals in the dark, when he has so little food, when, outside, three small graves mark the progress of his family?

–Hello God, this is Delekile. Can you hear me? Do you know my number, God?

Each time I return home, I take Delekile's wire creations. These are not the silver-threaded fish sold on corners, the wire candlesticks or egg baskets, so familiar now on every city street. Delekile's work is not just crafted, it is engineered: a wagon with an axle and a pair of mules with legs that move; a small stand of wood with a cow made of beaten tin and a calf running at her side. Blow on the windmill and the whole tableau is set in motion by the delicate propulsion of axle and piston. The calf runs. The cow steps out. The vane turns. Together there is a sense of speed and action. He wants me to sell them for him in the city. But I know that response will only come from the discerning eye of those who sense the intangible in his discovery of how to conjure with such simple tools. His work is not for Philistines. In the meantime, I must pay him for it and hope for returns in months – not years. His need outweighs the delicacy of an equal transaction. How easily delight can turn to irritation.

How churlish if I fall into that trap.

I pack his things with old scraps of newspaper into a carton. The contents smell of woodsmoke. The scent pervades the room. It is a presence – yet another – in this house. I feel like a curator – not so much of objects: windmill, cow and calf; trunk-loads of Godfrey's scholarship and catalogue drawers full of cards, the suitcase of photographs – but of events, still intangible, of which, despite the object of the work, I seem to be custodian. I am aware, though, that it is not just what Godfrey left behind that matters. There is something else.

I must restore them from the silence – as they restore me.

And then?

It is very simple.

I will complete the dictionary where they left off so suddenly – *umvalamlomo*: 'what closes the mouth'. I will tidy up my methodology, write my thesis and graduate. I will go on to other things. Just as they did.

Godfrey went home to his wife.

And Grace?

I don't know.

She has sent me no sign. She won't until she trusts me. Yet, here, in this house where they had worked, I sense a certain vigilance – a music suspended, held by the deftest touch, before the phrase is done. I have to find that final phrase, commit it to the page.

It will be my last task here on the day I leave this place.

Then, I will load the car and drive away.

I take a walk in the lands behind the shop, lingering at familiar places. Delekile is sitting in the sun on some bags of meal he has unloaded from the trailer. In the suspended light of this pale morning, he seems the only other living thing: two humans in a landscape with no way of approaching each other but through the barter of goods. Yet, so many times, when he has brought his work to me, I have seen his hands holding a piece – little cow and wind vane, cart and mules – and witnessed the caress in his fingers as he makes the windmill spin, the tenderness, the pride, in them – and turned away, moved.

I walk along the path at the edge of the old dam. I sit on the wall looking down into the depression. It has been dry for years and a blue-green mass of Mexican cactus has taken root. Beyond and above the sweet-thorn and the fence, the low ridge rises, bearing its armour of stone and clumps of *gwarri*. Sitting on the earth wall of the dam, I fold my arms around my knees, rest my chin, trace the *krantz* above the river-bed, the outline of two *koppies* across the miles of open *veld* behind – a perfect echo of each other – and beyond, the ribbon of the road.

Something approaches. It is ponderous. The journey towards me is punctuated with stops. The upper leaves of the grey, spiked cactus bend and shake. There is nothing furtive or inquisitive in the approach. Whatever is proceeding, proceeds with care, but without caution.

I wait.

Out of the undergrowth comes a tortoise. It is over a foot at the apex, its head rests momentarily on the golden shoehorn of its lower shell, the old legs are tick-ridden. It watches me a moment with an imponderable eye, turning its head like a lever, from side to side.

It has an ancient gaze: it has seen the birth of stars.

It was alive when Godfrey was. Small tortoise then, the ridges of its carapace ribbed like spring bark, still new with growing. Watching it minutely, I know – ruefully enough – that there is something desperate in this search of mine for continuity of time and place. It is willing Godfrey – palpably – into my world. It assures something of him, which is mine alone. It is constructing his presence. Even in a tortoise.

Godfrey would have laughed.

And yet, it creates an intimacy. These things – familiar to him, familiar to me – evolve a delicate awareness between us, an echo-step of love. It can only be sustained – *only* – if I observe a finely honed restraint. I cannot push the boundaries of this fragile, recreated world of ours. It would be like asking him – a fatal breach of our own carefully constructed trust – to tell me (betraying her) his long-gone lover's name.

Chapter six

〜○

London: February 1928.

'I have met a girl,' he says, turning his hat in his hand, glancing middle distance, down. 'She is nineteen. She is a virgin. I am in love with her.'

'Because she is nineteen? Or because she is a virgin?'

Godfrey straightens. 'You are being ridiculous,' he says.

'It was you who mentioned it, my dear. Neither fact would have occurred to me. Her particularity' – so carefully pronounced – 'seems to be that she is nineteen and that she is a virgin – not that she is a woman and that you love her.'

'You don't understand.'

'On the contrary, I understand very well.'

Godfrey's Blood-Red-Woman, she of the scarab beetle pendant and the toques and the slim cheroots. She takes his hat from him, pours him a whisky, sits him on the Turkey-weaving of her ottoman and regards him. He cannot, for the moment, meet her eye. Yes, indeed, she understands only too well. She strikes a match and lights a cigarette. She hands it to him.

He is rueful. She appears amused.

Once he had been dazzled by her.

Dazzled.

Such headlong passion. Such excess of fire and madness, extravagant with laughter – and with weeping. It was grief, let loose. Making love was the purging of death.

88

There was no end to its needs and intensities.

And then it ended. Just like that – and Godfrey came to her and said, confessing at her feet: *–I am in love. And it is not with her.*

She cannot repeat to herself the absurdity of what he has just said. He can't be serious: a motley Galahad, gone rose-white for a silken maiden, love transcendent, passion to ash. All purity.

He *is* serious.

'Well done, darling,' she says, just a touch sardonically, not enough to offend. She looks down at him, hands on his knees, head inclined away from her, the damp shadow beneath that emerging cheekbone, the angle of his jaw and she recalls his breath at her ear, his hand probing the silk of her robe, his voice:

> *'Come let us take our fill of love until the morning; Let us solace ourselves with loves, for the good man is not at home. He has gone on a long journey. He hath taken a bag of money and will come home at the day appointed.'*

She had half laughed at him, told him off for cheek, said, 'Where is that from?'

'Proverbs Seven. You don't know your Bible, my darling.'

When he was gone she had looked it up. His quote had been selective, out of context. It had left her chilled. It was then that the crystals had started to transform and the delicate blown glass of her own loving (like Gert's) to crack imperceptibly inside her.

The pieces were not on the pavement around her feet as they had been for Gert. They were in her being. With every movement she sensed their little lacerations.

> *'She was attired like a harlot and subtle of heart . . .'*

That, she was. Her wardrobe was a cornucopia of antique silks, of tapestry jackets and gipsy shawls; of sashes with pale carved ivory *netsukes* weighting them. It was all spice and attar of roses and embroidered gauze.

And subtle of heart?

It was not the subtlety implied, with its glib conceit and artifice. It was a subtlety that Godfrey might have guessed at, but had failed to read. It knew its own private weeping.

> *'With her much fair speech she caused him to yield, with the flattering of her lips she forced him.'*

'Come along, young man,' laughing at his ineptitude, his struggle with stiffly stitched buttonholes and socks, tender to the way his hair angled across his forehead in his haste for nakedness.

She had not forced him. At first, she had tried to put him off. Warned him away. Laughed at him. Admonished, scolded. Closed the door on him.

Succumbed.

She turned the Bible over in her hands. There was no woman's voice in here. It was nowhere to be found. Not even that of the dutiful wife, her worth far above rubies.

'. . . *the flattering of her lips . . .*'

What about *his*?

'*And he went to her house in the twilight, in the evening, in the black and dark night.*'

Many twilights with her lamp burning with its beaded shade drooping drops of light on to the tablecloth, red as flame, the long nights, the dense, breathless mushroom-dark of the basement room. Then, too soon, the quiet streaks of dawn. Bathing him, laying her cheek against the wetness of his back, allowing the water to trickle between them, to touch the damp of his nape with the cup of her palm, his dark head drooping in tiredness as the morning came.

So beloved.

'*Hearken unto me now, therefore, O ye children, and attend to the words of my mouth. Let not thine heart decline to her ways, go not astray in her paths. For she hath cast down many wounded; yea, many strong men have been slain by her. Her house is the way to hell, going down to the chambers of death.*'

This house? This gracious sanctuary, a way to hell? It is here, for months, that she, ten years older, has soothed the soldier in him, coaxing him back from the well of battle, the remembrance of death. With her calm, unobtrusive wisdom, she had rekindled the man.

She looks down at him, sitting on the couch. She leans her elbow on the mantelpiece. She says, 'Well then' – neither bright nor false – 'I had better send you on your way.' She examines her hands – so slim, the nails beautifully varnished: the young girl would have hands unblemished by age, without the need of paint. There would be no nicotine between the fingers, no call for whitening cream.

She has always known this moment would come. She smiles. He does not see its small rueful tremor.

90

'I think I should explain,' he says. She almost wants to laugh: he is mustering a rational approach – to keep her from hysterics.

He does not need to worry. There will be no hysterics. He has under-estimated her. She waits, as patient as if she had been his mother.

He is contrite. He talks too much, a litany of all the things he's done. He will disarm her by looking sheepish, boyish. He forgets that he should meet her eye.

She gathers up his things. There are not many. There were never any gifts.

'Happy landings, darling,' she says, giving him his hat. 'Cheer up!' She senses, in time, that her hand, once so light at his temple, might seem gauche. She takes it away.

He kisses her on the cheek, urgent to be gone.

She stands and watches him mount the stairs to the pavement above. He does not turn. She knows, by the way he takes the steps, the angle of his head, that Relief has swept him into the street. She cannot see him, but she knows that he is walking fast, cleansed, light. He does not laugh. His purpose is too grave for that.

After all, he is a man in love.

Godfrey would not have told Grace about it. It had nothing to do with her. I sense that if she'd known, she would retreat, sure of her intrusion, quietly brood on it, construct a hundred scenes in which she had no part: make him cruel and careless in a way he sometimes was, but never meant to be. Force her own dismissal.

Grace Unworthy.

He would not have told me either. But I have sat in this room and gone through the old leather suitcase of his pictures, jumbled and overturned and out of sequence and muddled in with all the others of a large, extended family. I have gathered up so many fragments of his life among these things, extracted something of him from among the dozens of Brownie snaps of the next generation. So many little dogs, so many children's parties. I sift and scratch and swoop among them, knowing – somewhere – Godfrey will allow a sign: a contact print in sepia announcing his own generation. Here are fellows at school making a human pyramid on the lawn outside the now-familiar House. Here, standing legs astride – a bivouac, somewhere in France – the officer, square-shouldered, at ease with his moustache, his pipe clamped between his teeth. There are pictures of the beach, picnics, bathing huts, six or seven street portraits: Godfrey, brisk in coat and hat. In one, he half turns to the camera, hand out, as if to ward it off. There is a woman at his side. She is very tall. Her face is slightly blurred as if she had been swift to move away. Behind, the vague facades of High Street, Kensington.

Godfrey and his Blood-Red-Woman?

And then, among another group of pictures in an old brown envelope – torn glue spots on the back – taken hastily, it seems, from an album needed for another use, there she is!

There!

Godfrey's Lover. I have no doubt.

–*Thank you, Godfrey*.

I hold her in damp fingers, tilting her to the light of the window. I almost laugh – here she is, in all her sophistication, in this small, white, monk-like room, half across the world, the *veld* outside, grey as ash, stretching away to the ironstone ridge. She has a studied face, even self-invented. The name of a London photographer is embossed on the lower right-hand corner and, in ink, diagonally across the print, in large, assertive writing, '*To C J G with love. November 1927*'. She has a fine, patrician nose, a handsome, sharp-edged lip.

Her eyes, under the painted bow of brow, are meditative.

I know those eyes: I, too, have watched and felt the fragile form disintegrate within. Nothing can repair it. Both of us will take it to the grave.

Godfrey was married in June.

–*She is nineteen. She is a virgin. I am in love with her*.

Her name was Stella. She was a barrister's daughter.

They sailed for Cape Town a month later on a mail-ship. There are pictures of the Crossing-the-Line party, of deck-quoits and tenniquoits and groups, wrapped against the Atlantic cold, holding on to a binnacle: *what a jolly time we're all having*. According to the date of his first son's birth, his bride must have been newly pregnant. Seasick and homesick all at once. There is a look of panic in her eyes, parading behind her careful glamour in the group at the Captain's table, Godfrey in evening dress – the older husband (all of thirty!), a touch suave, his dark hair perfectly groomed. It is – despite my bias – a very handsome face. He is engaging, self-aware, eager to display his possession of her. None of the wryness of later times, or the silence, is in that face. And she – she is one of the girls in his mother's album, with a perfect English bloom. Despite it, despite her charm, she is entirely at sea.

It is difficult for me to write about his wife. She was, after all, a perfectly enchanting woman. Her devotion to Godfrey was far greater than mine could ever be. If it wasn't, why would she, twenty years after he was dead, insist on being buried in his grave? He is possessed by her, even in death. Perhaps, after all, that is what he wants: –*I am bound to her, by the closest bonds, for the rest of my life*.

It was with those words that he ended it with Grace. Perfectly simple. Perfectly right.

And now, I wish that I could write this for his wife, write for her as I write for

Grace. Love her as I love the little chip-toothed Gert, squinting into the sun behind her upturned palm, such long, such very straight, brown legs. Flat-chested Gert, ready to brave the hinterland, weighed down with nets and crucibles and collecting trays and his rifle in its slim leather case; heroic little Gert, stride for stride in the interests of science, khaki-clad. Devoted. But I can't – because of them.

But mostly, because of me.

–I am bound to her by the closest bonds for the rest of my life.

And it wasn't just a matter of circumstance. Or luck. That is simply how it was.

How it is.

If I do not have a sense of Godfrey in his own house near the university, it is my own fault. I suspect it is because I do not want to find him there. I want to find him at Gert's, despite its new concrete palisade and fibrecrete water-feature. There is something of their undiluted vibrance there. I even feel him more in London, at 8 Gloucester Walk, where his lover lived, than in his own lightly landscaped garden with its soft-leaved exotics and cypress walk. Perhaps it is because it was his wife's house, more than his, purchased for them by her father, furnished with the slim, practical pieces requisite in a respectable professional family. Nothing overt. Nothing showy.

It is a house in a garden with fruit trees and a gate and a gravel drive and a shed by the fence. When the furniture was taken out and the house sold, it was simply a house, with three bedrooms and two bathrooms and a serviceable sewing room, a newly wired light-board and windows that opened and closed without having to know the knack of the hasps or where to push against the weathering.

I have been there, but he does not live there any more. Not my Godfrey. And though he does not live in Gloucester Walk either, in his lover's house, there is – at least to me – a sense of him. He is tangible in the presence that is her; in the loss, drifting with her somewhere along the iron palisades above the basement flats, in the long arcade at the station where the statue spouts dead water. Perfectly coiffed, dismissive of men's unselfconscious stares. Despite her coat and sable collar, despite her brisk, assertive stride – she is stripped of shell, her flesh snail-naked at his going. I have followed them both in this pilgrimage of mine – she, to bookshops, searching for some sign of him, some consolation, reaching for Ezra Pound – all the rage – and the newly published *Selected Poems*, rifling at random, finding first (and last):

As a bathtub lined with white porcelain,
When the hot water gives out and goes tepid,
So is the slow cooling of our chivalrous passion,
O my much praised but-not-altogether-satisfactory lady.

She had left it on a table and drawn her gloves on, tucking her fingers into the sheaths, expunging, with little jerks to settle them, the cool malevolence hidden in the pages of that elegantly lettered volume. I have followed him as well: a hurrying figure, back turned, in the arched walkway of St Mary's Abbots. I have gone with him up Kensington Church Walk or hurried another way along the back of the Franciscan Monastery. Confession times are posted on the door. He would have scorned confession then and quickened his pace. He may have stopped, instead, at the *Elephant and Castle* and had a pint, written an entry in indelible pencil in the little pocket diary. I have seen among the photos and the other bric-a-brac stuffed into the side pocket of the photo case: '*To Kensington tonight*', '*At 8 G Walk: rather brief*'. He'd have felt expansive with his pint on the counter among the colonial memorabilia and hunting prints: sahibs and rajas and elephants and waving palms. Indian, not African, but close enough to be familiar, something epic in its scenery and appointments, and – in those moments – something epic in himself as well.

And if I took a picture now – with his old Kodak camera – Gloucester Walk would echo still, in its buildings and its trees, the photo of it that I found among the '*London snaps*' in his leather suitcase. Now, there may be sports cars and four-by-fours parked at the kerb and foreign-featured au pairs bouncing babies along in modular pushchairs, but 8 Gloucester Walk still rises unchanged, floor on floor, to the sixth storey attic rooms alongside the rampart of chimney pots. The faux Dutch gable with the date inscribed, *1896*, the spine of the staircase visible behind the leaded windows, all remain untouched. I know, behind the heavy, swag-backed curtains of a new owner – an up-and-coming decorator, an architect, a stockbroker – there is still the sense of her. And if, in twilight, I walk down to the station, I will find the room where she used to wait for him, through the dim basement glass, like a tabernacle, lighted from within. I have never seen a person standing in that room. Whenever I have passed, despite the calmly lit interior, it is always still and empty.

In the road beyond, the taxis take the bend in Kensington Church Street with a certain dash, their reflections brief and swift in the windows of shops. St Mary's Abbots – once in meadows – is encased in scaffolding, the tall west window black with soot.

It is there, in *The Trinity Charity Shop*, that I saw the shell-pink knickers with the tea-coloured lace, the twenties coat with the sable collar, touched the cobweb nap of a grey silk shawl tinged green with age, embroidered, in profusion, with butterflies in oyster and teal. It is exactly what she would have owned. Perhaps, when she died, her family bundled everything up and brought it here: the pointed-toed shoes, the peignoirs with the age-bloomed ribbons drooping from their sleeves. All these things were chosen for love – and went unnoticed.

–*I have met a girl*, he'd said. –*She is nineteen. She is a virgin. I am in love with her*.

It was appalling of you, Godfrey. And uncharacteristic. You have no idea of the valour of the women who dare sacrifice integrity for love, knowing at the moment of surrender, both will be destroyed.

How naive to think that love transcends.

Even Grace knows better, existing for a time – suspended – within a brief and transient world between the rim of low hills, the plain and the steel-curved road.

It could not be sustained.

After all, he had a wife. He was hers – in law, in every other way. There is something when one shares a bed, not just for love, but for sleeping in. It is altogether different. The little intimacies – the way she turns her head in sleep, the sound of her drinking her early morning cup of tea, how she blows her nose or scratches his back – it is these, laid layer on layer over time, that decide her right to share his tombstone in the end. It has nothing to do with the seven weeks of absurd romance before the wedding, a mother-managed courtship – but the comradeship of daily living. The one who has the right to him is not the woman who has sought his soul – it is the one who knows the way he clips his nails or trims his ears. She is the one he'll want to nurse him and restore him at the end. Those things he thinks he holds so precious now, will be put away for the expedience of comfort.

It is the safety of the womb.

He will want the old familiar feel of the soles of her feet looped across his in sleep, even the daily irritations – the washing machine wheezing in the kitchen, the persistent phone, the flatulent dog, her intrusions in his thoughts.

He was never going to walk away from this.

And Grace?

Grace is the axis of a different, far more fragile world.

I have often wondered if Godfrey chose his subject to get away from home. He went on protracted field trips. Looking through his papers, it is clear that he was in the field for two, three, four months at a time. When he was on sabbatical once, he was away for a year. Godfrey in East Africa, looking at the cattle of the Masai herdsmen. Godfrey in the Northern Frontier District. Godfrey in the Kaokoveld and in Mozambique. Godfrey rescuing from oblivion, over and over, the small *umvemve* calf with its sleek enamel hide, the ghost of little Gert beside him.

As far as I know, his wife Stella never accompanied him. In the first year of their marriage, before his appointment to the university in another town, when he was trying to complete his doctoral thesis, Godfrey had worked part-time for his father's company to earn their keep. They had lived with Harold Godfrey in the acres of house with the gravel lawn. It was a strange, but expedient arrangement. A safe haven for Stella when Godfrey was obliged to go away on fieldwork. How did Stella feel – a stranger – being at the beck and call of her grim father-in-law in his embroidered Afghan cap and leather slippers? Did she resent Godfrey's absences, his strange obsessions? Or did she perpetuate, doggedly, something of his mother in her house, still too awed to rebel? Did she also visit the dressmaker, have little parties and bridge mornings? Just as I had found the piece on baby Godfrey and his mother, riding in a carriage (. . . *the most beautiful boy ever seen, with fine, black eyes*), I have come across Stella Godfrey's social engagements, reported in the local weekly's 'Woman's Page':

> '*Mrs C J Godfrey held a small party to celebrate the birthday of her little son. It was a charming entertainment with a magician and a Punch and Judy show. It was held on the lawns of Penderley, the home of Mrs Godfrey's father-in-law, Mr Harold Godfrey. Mrs Munro Mackenzie and Lady Helen Compton, the godmothers of the baby, were in attendance. A delicate rainbow cake decorated with sugared violets and accompanied by ices, delighted the guests, especially the throng of young admirers who had come to share in the festivities.*'

Poor Stella.

She was installed as homage to his mother.

Perhaps – after all – his Mother is the only woman he has ever really loved. She is also the only one who ever left him.

He was twenty-two.

When he returned from France – more than six weeks of journeying – to the wide flatlands, the November summer heat, the shimmer on the pans, the *vaal* and thorny wastes, the opencast mines, his mother had already died. She had not waited for him – as she had promised – to emerge, a man.

Godfrey stands at the gate of the house. He has walked from the station. He has not wired his father on purpose. At all other homecomings, his mother had been waiting on the platform, Bibleman behind her to carry the bags. She had always stood in the same place, under the clock, as if to announce her punctuality, as if – in waiting for the train to slide in between the iron arches and the tall leaded windows – she had the power to make it come by watching, fixedly, the great black hand vibrate as it changed from one minute to the next. It would move with a small shudder, bringing him closer. She could watch it, rapt, for half an hour or more, trusting that in the end it would deliver Godfrey up to her.

It always did.

But now, it has not delivered *her* to Godfrey.

The train is on time, almost to the minute. As his mother would have expected. As she would have willed it.

As she would have insisted.

–*Thank you, God*.

Another little penance paid off. Another set of prayers rewarded. Each letter he had received in France, ended with her love and '*mostly my prayers*'.

If *he* had prayed – would she have still been there to greet him?

Perhaps – *if* he had prayed.

He dumps his kitbag through the window. Its thud sends up a pigeon in a flurry of slate-coloured feathers. He climbs from the train and glances at the clock. No one is standing beneath it. There is a baggage trolley leaning on its elbows, waiting for a porter to load it. He allows the carriage door to thump behind him.

He peels off his jacket. He is sloughing a skin, the smell of troopship and train. The damp of France. He stands a moment in his shirt sleeves, feeling the small, warm wind, a little soughing from long ago, just at his neck, like a hand brushing it.

He sets his bag on his shoulder and walks under the clock deliberately.

It is a long way home. His head is bent against the weight of the bag. He does not look up. He watches the toes of his boots. His strides are brisk. He can hear his heels on the paving, on the tar, on the dust verges of the suburb. The rows of avenue trees begin, the little palisades of iron to hold them steady against the dry winds. He notches them up: one, two, three, four. Fourteen, fifteen, sixteen. Thirty, thirty-one, thirty-two.

He crosses the road leading to Gert's house. He does not glance down it. The sun is in his eyes. He does not need to look. It is too familiar, too often navigated over years. He passes the Synagogue. The sports club is behind him. The curve meets him now, the pavement is gravel, the familiar crunch, the familiar jerk of stones that hurrying feet send thudding up. Here, then, the sanitary lane; here, the prep school gate.

–*Good morning, Brother Porteous. Have you met my calf in Heaven?*

–*Good morning, Father Jude. Did you send a priest to my mother for Extreme Unction? She could not have died without it.*

He walks through the shadow of the seminary building, lying flat across the open road, strangely out of bounds beyond the decorative iron railings, as if it wished to break free into the open ground at the other side. He knows, without looking up, the exact hue of the bricks and the dusty green of the massive palm that stands at the corner. There will be St Joseph's lilies growing in the beds on either side of the path to the great iron-studded door. Has anyone dared knock on it long enough for the little port to open? Only for Death could one knock at that door. Only for a Catholic death. Did someone knock there – Bibleman perhaps – sent by his father to fetch a priest?

–Fetch a priest. Muttering to himself, half in fear *–Damned, bloody Papists.*

Bibleman, with the butter-gold ox-horn snuff boxes in his lobes, his feet leaving a trail in the gravel down to the seminary, would have been unalarmed by the caged eyes behind the grille of the door.

It is mid-morning when Godfrey arrives at the gate. The latch has the paint chipped off in the way he remembers, the bracket at the corner of the roof of the conservatory is still hanging loose. It is in the familiarity of things that the dislocation exists. Nothing has changed but him. It feels as if his flesh has re-attached itself to his bones in a different conformation. How can the world have altered so titanically when these small inconsequential things remain the same? His mother will step off the veranda and walk towards him with her particular rustle, her dark hair springing from the pale ivory of her temples, immaculate. Pearl and cream and midnight hair.

The front door is locked. The French windows into the billiard room have never been firm. The vertical bolt to hold them in place broke years ago. He can push the handle in and the lock will slip from its place.

The buck heads stare down. Are they conferring?

The minute contraction of a glass eye, a nostril: *–Here is the boy, back again.*

The dark wooden cues stand regimented in their brass clips against the wall. The linoleum under his feet has all the familiar contours and cracks. He walks softly through the house. No one comes.

He goes to her room.

Nothing has changed. If he opens the cupboards her clothes will still be there, neatly on their hangers. When he was small he could put his head in among the dresses and smell the prints as though the florals were alive: the crêpe of her evening gown, the silkiness of her housecoat, the light dusky blue of her tea-frock, the little shimmers and glosses and hidden smells of them. The gloves laid in pairs so neatly in the drawers, the smooth-grained ivory of the stretchers. He had loved ivory ever since. It came from the bones of his mothers hands, pale and slim.

He does not open the cupboard or look at the clothes.

His own photograph stands on the dressing table in a small silver frame, propped against a silver Christening mug with his name on it. It is not the one he had sent her of him in his battledress, his legs astride, arms folded – an echo of school rugby photos, cricket boys on a summer's afternoon, a boxer, triumphant in the ring. It is a picture of him as a small boy with his hair long and curled, little velvet jacket and lace collar, prim button shoes, velvet cap with a tassel on the back of his head. On the shelf above is the statue of the Virgin, hands folded, rosary beads draped in a long curve across her gown, her foot on the serpent and the enamel globe. Pearl white and cream, like his mother.

If Godfrey had wept then, it was not from loss – but from rage and its regrets.

But Godfrey does not weep. He has not wept since the *umvemve* calf was slaughtered and he lay under his bed, rigid beside Gert, tears like iron sweated from his eyes.

Perhaps he swept the picture and statue to the floor and ground them out under the heel of his boot.

Perhaps he walked away.

I think he simply closed the door on the small white bed and the prie-dieu and the washstand and the crucifix and the white muslin curtains and went down the hall and picked up the telephone and dialled his father's office.

'Dad?' Matter-of-fact. 'I'm back.'

'Good God, boy, why didn't you send a wire?'

'Sorry.'

'You should have sent a wire. You must always send a wire.'

–Why, Father, would you have been at the station?

Instead Godfrey says, 'Shall I meet you at the Club for lunch?'

'Good idea.'

Godfrey takes a long breath, tilts back on his heels and looks at the skylight high above. 'What time?' he says.

'Twelve-thirty. Shall I send the driver?'

'Not necessary. Twelve-thirty, then.'

He walks back down the hall, passes the living room, the dining room, the many-mirrored bathroom. He goes inside it, pushes up the seat of the lavatory. As he stands, he glances into the mirror on the wall. It reflects, behind his back, the bathroom door. A woman's gown hangs on the peg. Satin-pink. On the edge of the bath is a tin of talcum powder.

He pulls the chain, goes to the basin. Scented soap. Where is the Wright's coal tar?

He opens the cabinet above the basin. Two decorative hair-combs, a thin hairnet, a very small, dark blue bottle of perfume with a silver label: *Paris by Night*. There is something middle-aged in it. Ingenuous. It belongs to a lady who wears pink suspenders with rubber clasps, a lip of flesh at the tops of her stockings. He almost smiles at his father's innocence.

He does not go to his father's room. He walks out of the house, avoiding the kitchen wing and discovery by a housemaid or the cook. He takes another road to town. He does not want to pass the school again. He does not wish to cross Gert's road: he does not want to see her standing on the pavement, flat-chested, plain-faced, an unbeguiling woman in a pinafore with pockets, a stranger – she, who ran along that dusty verge in the shadow of trees, like a little buck, fleet in light and shade.

His father has not changed. His face still has the hawk-eyed droop to the lids, the sculpted nose, the lean, high-boned cheeks. In a way, a parody of Godfrey, faintly vulpine. He has gained weight about the middle though. A strange irregularity in the tall, athletic figure.

'You're looking well,' says Godfrey, a touch sardonically.

–Does she make him hearty soups, does she bake him little cakes, the tops snipped out and filled with cream, a leaf of angelica, a cherry rose, two powdery wings of sponge?

–Does she coax his sour temper with a mug of Horlicks at bedtime?

–Titbits?

–No fish on Fridays?

'What'll you drink?' His father is gruff under scrutiny.

'A beer,' says Godfrey, picking up the menu card: either he must play his father at his game, knock him off his seat or retreat beyond his reach, the way his mother had: *Oh, most gracious Virgin Mary . . .*

Instead, he lights a cigarette.

'What are your plans?' says his father.

'I would like to go to university.'

'Aren't you rather past that now? Haven't you knocked around enough?'

–I see, Father. Fighting a war is knocking around. A jolly good show. A bit of a lark.

'I need a qualification,' Godfrey's voice is even.

'I went straight from Afghanistan into Colonial Service. Then the Mines. What did I need with a university? If you ask me, a lot of scoundrels get their training there!' Godfrey reads quite clearly the intent in the sweeping glance about the dining room. The gesture is not lost. The weight of the Club, his father's place in it: the obsequiousness of the head waiter, the solemn discretion of the staff as he gives up his hat in the hall, the gold lettering of his name on the Presidential Board above the double doors.

'I would like a profession.'

Harold Godfrey inspects his wine glass. 'What sort of profession?'

'Something which suits my abilities. Nothing more.'

'The only thing that would be of any use to the firm is mining engineering. But you could get by well enough without that. The old fool in our department hasn't got the gumption to go on site most of the time.'

'I didn't have mining in mind.'

There is a silence as the soup is delivered and the wine is poured. Animation suspended. Both do it instinctively, instantaneously: one must not talk in front of the servants, no matter how inconsequential the subject.

His mother had always been very particular on that point. So precious. So condescending. Godfrey does it for her now, as though she is sitting there between them. His father does it without question.

His father turns his plate, brings it closer. 'Well?' he says.

'Humanities.'

One mouthful. Two. Then Harold Godfrey says, 'I beg your pardon?'

'I would like to try a few things. Politics. Economics. Philosophy.' Godfrey watches the fatty rim of soup bulge, blister, then burst over the edge of his father's spoon, tipped away from him, a little thread of parsley bobbing on the tide. It mesmerises him. 'In fact,' he says, refocusing his gaze. 'My real interest is in African languages.'

Godfrey's father dabs at his moustache.

—Shell shock. It must be shell shock. What else could it be?

He takes out his spectacles and scrutinises the menu. 'I wonder if the fish will be good today. It's usually deplorable. But I won't take soufflé – a lot of fluff and nonsense.'

—The hotel. Soufflé. Godfrey's mother's favourite. She, teasing its feather-lightness with her lips; he, with his bruised head: 'Will you promise to take care of yourself, my darling. Will you promise me?'

He had gone to war instead.

And she had died.

Quite unexpectedly. At home. In her room, before bed, standing at her dressing table, reaching for her rosary. His father had written that it had been an aneurysm in her brain. A haemorrhage. There was nothing to be done. A priest was called.

But Godfrey knew, the owl had taken her, under its soundless wing, despite the priest, despite the Virgin Mary standing on her little shelf. Godfrey had read the letter from his father in his barracks. He had folded it up and then torn it in two. He had put it in the bin, walked out.

After that, he had turned his back on God.

And yet, I sense that all his life, despite his urbanity, the grand agnosticism of his middle years, in consciously flouting God, he sought Him. In dismissing the Mother-of-God, he punished his own for dying on him so swiftly and so carelessly.

'If I have to find my own funding for my degree,' says Godfrey, 'I will do it.'

—Three years of war has taught me to do anything – or not to do it. That too.

'Where do you want to go?'

'Cambridge.'

'Indeed.'

'If I can't raise the funds, I will have to come home and work in the office.

Whatever can be found for me.'

'You can't do that.' His father is suddenly alarmed.

—Of course I can't, Father. What would you do with the lady with the talcum powder? You would have to evict her. Or marry her.

'Well, perhaps you have another suggestion?' He is patient.

'I shall speak to the bank after lunch,' says his father. 'See what I can arrange. Perhaps you should come with me.' He glances at his watch. 'I must make a telephone call.' He dabs his mouth with his napkin again. He has lost interest in the mutton and gravy.

'I will only be going back to the house this evening,' Godfrey says, reading his urgency, saving face for him. 'When we've been to the bank, I would like to visit Mother's grave.'

'Shall I come with you?'

'No, thank you.' It is the first time his voice takes a rough edge.

—I will fight you to the death if you follow me. She is not your business any more.

Harold Godfrey goes to his office and makes a call.

To the lady – or the bank?

Godfrey does not care. He waits in the hall and looks at the photographs, tracing minutely, with his eyes, the outline of the potted plants in brass-bound wooden bins by the boardroom door. His father emerges. He is brisk. In control again. Whatever has been said, is satisfactory. Godfrey follows him across the hall, across the geometric tiles of the floor. He does not avoid the cracks as he had as a child on the rare occasions he had visited the great man with his mother. Small boy, on tiptoe, balancing, wavering like a top, arms out, choosing which of the small decorative motifs to tread inside. They go out into the street, taking the shaded side of the pavement.

Godfrey finds the grave. It has a Celtic Cross, squared-off with a small iron palisade at the base. The lettering is in lead.

Clementine Paget Godfrey
23rd July 1869 – 3rd August 1918

The undertaker's gravel is still clean, white, glinting sunlight. The long shadows of late afternoon lean at the bases of the cypresses and cross. It is a bare grave – in its wording and its architecture. Godfrey has not brought flowers. It had seemed too predictable, too embarrassing in front of his father. He had taken a cab from outside the bank.

A dog-rose, spurred with thorns, white cups open here and there, has overgrown a child's grave beside her plot. Godfrey leans across to pick one bloom to lay at his mother's feet. The stems are tough. He has to take his pen knife from his pocket to clip it off. The bush marks a little fallen cross. Very small, rough-hewn, as if imitating wood. The rose has grown across the inscription. But he can see, still protected, '*dfrey*'. He bends further and pulls the brambles back. A thorn hooks into the skin of his wrist. He ignores it. He uses the sleeve of his shirt to rub the sand obscuring the name. It has weathered away.

dfrey
ay 9th 1913 – May 15th 1913

May 1913. He had been at school.

The winter term of his second year: –*Dear Mum, I hope you are well. Thank you for your letter . . .*

For six days he had not been an only child.

No one had told him.

And this life had been important enough for a cross and a briar rose. Next to its mother.

Their mother.

His mother.

–*We will both enter Heaven one day and be together, just you and me, always.*

But – in all this time – there had been an interloper. And she had not told him.

–*Just you and me, always*. Had she said it to the baby too?

Of course, she had.

It was just like her to believe they would excuse anything of her. Her deceits, her little circumventions of the truth, because she was their mother.

Once she had been his alone. She had always said she was. But the world had changed on a word '*dfrey*' hidden for eight years behind a briar in a dusty cemetery.

Godfrey disengages his wrist from the briar, replaces it delicately against the stone of the baby's grave. He places the dog rose he has cut on the gravel at the foot of his mother's cross.

By evening it will be withered by the dryness of the wind.

'I went to Mother's grave,' says Godfrey. They are standing on the veranda with cigars after dinner. There is no evidence of a woman in the house. Godfrey has not opened the bathroom cabinet but the dressing gown and powder have been removed. A bed has been made for him in his old room.

'You found it easily enough?' says Harold Godfrey.

'Yes.'

A pause.

'Good.'

Another pause. Then Godfrey says, 'Why didn't you tell me there was another child?'

'What do you mean?'

'The grave beside Mother's.'

His father draws on his cigar. Godfrey is impatient. At last, his father says, 'It was very premature.'

Godfrey waits.

'It was all very quietly and properly done.' It is simply said. It is not in mitigation.

'Why wasn't I told?'

'What was the point? You were away at school. There was no need to upset you.'

'Who decided that?'

'I did.'

'It might have been fair to tell me.'

'Why fair? The child died within a week. If your mother hadn't been so insistent it was christened because of some hocus-pocus about Limbo, it would have been buried in the hospital graveyard along with the rest like it and you would have known no differently.'

'It?'

'Female.'

'I thought you always wanted a daughter.'

'I did.'

Another pause.

'It wasn't a daughter.' Harold Godfrey says. 'It was an incomplete thing. Crooked.'

'What happened to Mother?'

'She bucked up after I'd organised the cross. We agreed, then, to say no more about it.'

'Was there a funeral?'

'A committal.'

'What's the difference?'

'No one knew, that's all. We carried on as normal. Your mother was still in the nursing home. It was better that way. That old Beelzebub at the seminary phoned me when it was done.'

'No one was there, then?'

'No one needed to be there.'

Another pause.

'What did he say?'

'Some nonsense about the sins of the father.'

'If the burial place was so unimportant, why did you put Mother next to her?'

'She once said, long after, that's where she would like to be.'

Harold Godfrey walks to the tray on the sideboard and pours himself a brandy. 'Drink?' he says, laying his cigar aside to slide the top from the neck of the decanter.

Godfrey says, 'Did the child have a name?'

'No.' Harold Godfrey turns with a glass of brandy, hands it to him. 'I don't think we paid attention to names after the birth. There wasn't any point.'

'There was a name on the grave but I couldn't decipher it.'

'Is there?' Mild surprise. 'I can't recall.'

'It wasn't that long ago.'

'Some notion of your mother's.'

This is the only way that I can construct what happened. I went to the graveyard myself. It is gravelled – not grassed. I called at the municipal offices on the site – small, Public Works Department, painted cream with brown windows and a red corrugated-iron roof and three fire extinguishers bracketed to the walls. There were two men inside, in safari suits. One was feeding receipts on to a spike on the desk. The other was smoking. A radio was playing. There is not much to do on a Monday afternoon in the municipal graveyard. It is not a convenient time to be buried. Outside, across the gravel flats, the cypress trees, planted a century before, were grey with mine dust, bent a little to the prevailing wind.

The inhabitants are divided by denomination. I write the name '*Godfrey*' on a scrap of paper. A large, leather-bound register is brought. I watch a man send his tufty fingers scanning up rows of entries. Behind, on the wall, a Pharmacy calendar – spring flowers in Namaqualand – is already a year old. Someone has circled particular days in green felt pen.

This man, with his pack of Lexingtons in his pocket, is dogged in his search, but detached. He is a man on the margins. He does not speak, he does not engage one. He brings to mind the creatures that I learned about from Godfrey – those ambiguous, those littoral, which mediate between us and the shadow-world beyond. Like an undertaker's assistant, he is strangely anonymous. But I see his glance, swift and down, from the side of his eyes, scanning. He writes three numbers on a card: R457, R458 (Catholic), F23 (Anglican). He comes round the counter, walks to the door, half leans out of it, gestures with his arm to the right and down towards the gate. 'R457 and 458, those two, just there – there – by the tree, the taller one, about the fifth row. Do you want me to come with?'

'I am sure I will find it.'

'The other one is at the other side. Church-of-England. You can come back and I'll show you when you finished here with the Catholics.'

I walk away.

I find Clementine Godfrey's grave. The lead letters are peeling but the ghost of the missing cipher is there. The words. Or the lack of them. It is untended. The dog rose from the tiny grave beside it has rambled across a whole row. This is an old, neglected corner. Many of the monuments have fallen, many of the marble angels have lost their heads or their wings. Clementine Godfrey's stone is upright but the tendrils of the rose have taken the cross by the throat and the little memorial to the baby can only just be seen buried in the thicket. The rose is too tangled to pry among its briars. Its engraving is lost to me.

I can't even be sure that I am right, except that I have been given the number of two separate plots; there is no way of telling, except that the dog rose inclines towards Clementine Godfrey's grave, gathering it greedily, pulling it in beyond scrutiny.

Standing there, in the stinging heat of a summer afternoon – way off, a funeral taking place, plastic lawn laid around the hole, like a surgeon's dressing – I gaze at Godfrey's mother's cross. There is a sense of suspension: she has withdrawn beyond my reach and sympathy.

Am I looking at that grave through Godfrey's eyes or through my own?

Is my detachment because I am angry with her – or because he is?

I have no right to pry. I have not lost a child at birth. How can I know what it is like?

In whose protection is that tiny, embryonic soul, if not in hers?

'You should have told me,' Godfrey says.

   'What's past is past. There is no point in dwelling on it.'
   –*The past is present, Father. It's what we are.*
   'It must be put to rest.'
   –*You cannot put to rest what is left unapprehended, Father.*

Rising, Godfrey says, 'It's such a mild night, I think I'll sleep in the veranda room.'

   'It's full of bat muck.'
   'I've slept with worse.'

Godfrey takes his camp-bed up to the roof. He had done it many times as a boy, lying with his back cradled in the curve of canvas, looking out between the railings at the stars. He had remembered these stars when he had been in France. Many times, he had tried to recall their conformation, the heavy honey-colour of their light, the orange moon, so different from the smooth translucent ice of European skies.

He can see the pepper tree that grows at the edge of the calf-pen where the *umvemve* calf had been, the branch that served as swing between the trunk and fence. How often he and Gert – dusty acrobats – had jumped, clung, bounced and landed safely on the crossbar. He can smell the crushed pepper seeds, knows the slim slither of the leaves under his fingers in swinging on a lath. He knows the sound of a springing branch, as immediate as if there had been nothing in between. No death, no war. No journeys. No subaltern strapped into puttees with a jaunty cap, awaiting final posting. No flush-cheeked fellow posing with his trio of friends for pictures to send home to their mothers. *–Look at us, we're off to France!* So much jolly camaraderie. So young – they are like junior school boys playing soldiers: eyes merry, elbows linked and locked against perpetual separation.

How many were lost?

Of the four – three. Godfrey, lungs eroded by gas, was the only one who made it.

–He fell at Arras.

–He was last seen wounded on the Menin Road. He said, 'Go on, boys, don't worry about me!'

–He died of typhoid. In a hospital bed. Raging that it hadn't been in battle.

Sometimes, they come to him in dreams. He had changed his will as each had died, crossing out, in pencil, the well-known name. Replacing it.

A guinea to the school janitor.

Five pounds to Bibleman, wherever he may be.

His camera to Gertrude Mary Hayes.

Yes, Gert, you were honoured when his comrades were gone.

He cannot find their voices any more. He cannot see their faces. They are recalled, instead, by the words of poets: *'Only, always, I could but see them – against the lamplight – pass like coloured shadows, thinner than filmy glass.'*

They are so much safer there.

And the place where they had been, is re-imagined through the memory of others: the dark compassion of Isaac Rosenberg, his *'old druid Time'*, his bleak, dead landscapes, *'. . . a blind man's dreams on the sand by dangerous tides.'*

There are no soldiers here, in the shifting dark of the veranda room. Not now. He lies, face to the night, the sounds of his childhood seeping back: the creak of the corrugated iron, the sifting of the pepper leaves in the gutters, wind on gravel.

Astride, mounted on the high palisade of railings, perilous above the fall of roof, he and Gert had laughed as they watched the puzzled explorations of the small *umvemve* calf in the pen below, searching for them, hearing their voices, unable to discover them, so far away above its head.

He can hear Gert's laugh.

He can hear his mother's voice – calling them to safety and to tea.

107

Chapter seven

Grace? Gracie?

Who are you, Grace?

I cannot write about you if I do not know you. Worse – if I want to be you. Worse still, a rival to replace you.

I remember the envy when I saw your picture in the album at Mrs Trollip's house, you smiling up at the camera. I tilted my head – I know I did – to look like you.

Do I have the generosity to let you keep him?

I have watched you – in my mind – walk with him through so many pastures, wandering among those cattle. I know the smell of them, the faint swish of hide brushing hide, the little jerky explorings of the calves, their delight in each other as they play, their admonishing dams, nudging them off, with a slow side-swing of the head, the uncertainty of heifers, too old to gambol, too young for gravity. An eager bull. There is a cow with upturned horns, dam of twelve calves, eyes dark in its sunken folds of skin, grown venerable. There is a calf butting at the udder of a young cow. I know the ache of its fullness, the blue-branched veins, the sap of life, the deep contraction in the letting down of milk. There is a bullock, barging at the heifers, full of need and anguish. There is the older bull, too magisterial to challenge yet.

I went to find her at the little school where she had taught, taking a winding road down through farmland. There was a signpost for a rail crossing, a jaunty train, a puff of smoke, hanging skew on a creosoted pole. The railway siding is broken down. The building that had served it is a skeleton beside the grass-grown rails. The sign, announcing it, name engraved in concrete, is almost illegible. There is an empty holding-pen for cattle. Beyond, in the folds and swells of slopes, are newly ploughed lands. The earth is coloured red, darkening to mauve. Across a further hill, planted pasture. Jersey cows. Frieslands. And, on a knoll, the church and the white-gabled school.

It is only a crèche now and poorer than it must have been in Grace's day. The farmers send their children into town. The little lockers in the vestibule are each marked with a symbol: a butterfly, a worm, a kite, a watering can, in brightly coloured felts. A small pair of tackies lies discarded in a corner. Through an arch is the low sweep of the hills, fence posts, old and knotted, at the entrance to the graveyard. The *gwarri* by the gate is ancient as stone.

Why can't I detach her from myself? Why can't I see her face?

As a child, it is difficult to be marked out as different, to carry around the singular – not morphologically – but in the heart.

'Grace is weird.' She had heard it more than once when, at twelve, she had gone to boarding school.

The knowledge of difference is disturbing.

Grace hides it in acquiescence. But it can't be concealed. It is in the way that adults treat her: the weight of equal regard, almost with a diffidence, as if her steady gaze unsettles them. It is not precocity. It is something attentive and grave – she has lived with them in their time, she knows them. No one has ever told her to run along and play.

It is not endearing to other children.

It makes them uneasy.

It makes them want to turn on her.

And yet, it is hard to force a fight. She is too unconfrontational, cultivates niceness to defuse them, unfolds in smiling. At school, her Mother Superior had said – just a little condescending: –*Grace is such a serene, kindly creature*.

Godfrey would have laughed to hear it. Once, he had thought so too. Until he knew her.

Grace was a warrior. She had a rapier eye.

It is not just internal difference which marks her out. It also has to do with her upbringing within the precincts of a rural Teachers' Training College, the only child of a mother grieving for a lost soldier-husband, cared for by ageing grandparents.

Grace had never known her father. The picture of him, taken in France, kept in a silver frame among the other memorials gathered on her mother's dressing table, with his cavalry moustache, his jodhpurs and his swagger stick, is no different, in essentials, from the one of Jack in Egypt, in his beret with its badge, eyes narrowed to the sun. The cut of the moustache, the

109

pose, the style of insignia, signal separate generations, but the detachment in the faces is the same, the stern retreat behind the gaze.

They are men who are no longer present to all that is familiar.

They have been gone too long – even before they were dead.

The repetition of history does not disturb Grace. Her mother insists it is a truth – even a glory – in the lives of women.

Men go to war. Most do not return.

It is inevitable.

Women who can carry loss with dignity, honour their dead. They honour God. Their acceptance declares a certain patience, an ineffable grace.

> '–*We shall go down with unreluctant tread*
> *Rose-crowned into the darkness . . .*'

And then?

She has overlooked the rest of the verse.

But she has always been selective in her texts, paring them of context, expunging the dissenting little shards of irony. She could have made a living writing epitaphs. She could fine-tune pathos. She had restraint – and perfect pitch.

She was unconcerned with the vast indifference of the world. It was very far away.

She tended a flame.

Grace's father's place was taken by her grandfather. In her earliest years he was her only male reference point. Scholarly in flannels, with a shock of grey hair, he was a gentle old man who collected birds' eggs and was writing a small monograph on bird-lore. He contributed a column to a mission magazine and, while he wrote, Grace would be allowed to inspect his trays of eggs with their beautifully scripted labels and stroke them gently with a sable brush to keep the dust away. Everything that Grandpa did, he did with gravity of thought – but not of heart. He laughed often. Not loudly, but with a lifting of the shoulders as if shaking it down into himself, a crinkling of the eyes and a chuckle in his chest.

He was an inspector of schools in the rural areas, a tireless worker, threading from district to district, in his ancient car. When she was small, and later in her holidays, he would take her with him, not speaking much, but alert to everything around him, and, by a gesture or a look, alerting her.

Grandpa's world was full of wonder. He did not live as testament to the dead, but in quiet celebration of life and its inheritances, its small living familiarities. Perhaps it was less noble – less epic – than Grace's mother's world. But it was far more generous. He delighted in the incidental. He did not battle God, outfacing Him with patience. He was not asking for rewards.

They were all around him.

In Grandma with her artist's hands, her violet eyes, the repose of her voice. In books. In birds. In work well done. In the old house in the mountains with its misty garden and the warm gloom of its kitchen, the continuity of its generations and companionships. In little Grace.

And when Grace had gone to boarding school at twelve, she had carried a landscape and a language in her head. She kept them to herself. They were hers and Grandpa's. To reveal them would undermine the comfort of their pleasure.

Weekends were spent with cousins in the same town.

She had to learn to play. In yards. In streets. On bikes and bars.

She learned to jostle and compete. She learned a different way of talking.

She learned wariness.

The first time she apprehends her difference is when her classmates tease her about Arnold Garmany.

He is a boy of thirteen. He rides a bike, pumping pedals with fat knees. He is all corned beef and blubber, ruddy, short of breath. Already, he carries the stamp of middle-age: a man in a sweaty synthetic shirt, flannels and grey shoes; a man who pursues discounts and saves up for a monthly treat in car accessories; a man with fleshy ears and terrier-eyes – a touch yellow and pale. Arnold Garmany picks fights in the school playground at lunch-breaks. The group stand around and mock, *uh . . . uh . . . Uh . . . Uh . . .* a rising, glottal goading while Arnold Garmany screws Ronald Harvey's small dark head into the concrete of the netball court. Is it because Ronald Harvey is olive-skinned (perhaps he is Jewish?), has a mole on the line of his jaw – a dark witch-mark – black eyes and a leg withered by polio?

Grace watches from the edges, her feet in puddles of damp for Ronald Harvey. Such a harmless little chap, such panic in his eyes, his Adam's apple darting in his throat: a feral cat caught by a dog. Arnold Garmany is so much bigger. He has weight and gristle. In time, he will hone it for the front rank and swagger about with a foul mouth, thighs which rub just a little too closely – and an anxious heart.

Inverting it, the class decides she has a passion for Arnold Garmany just because he – rorffing intentionally – has pushed her through a door, '*giving her one*', with the same posturing as the man, years later, '*God*' (a jerk in the voice), '*I always wanted to give her one!*' The screw-eyed intensity of a drunkard, the cocked knuckles balled in the small of the back – his own voyeur – knowing that he never could.

Never.

It is Arnold Garmany that Grace feels sorry for, not Ronald Harvey. Unlike Arnold Garmany, Ronald Harvey will never suffer the bewilderment of discovering himself to be unlovable. Knowing it for him, Grace is serene with Arnold Garmany – great uncomprehending boy, dabbling in his cage, grunting out his own small satisfactions, his little shows of scorn.

But it does her no service.

It simply throws up her oddness with the others. They lump her with him on the margins. It entrenches her aloneness.

In adolescence, she has to find a way to counter it.

She does – by being pretty. It is a matter of luck.

When Grace was nineteen, her mother died. She had taken to Christian Science, refused all treatment.

–*And killed herself,* her grandmother said simply.

She had scripted her own decline, paid no attention to a tumour in her breast. It was at the site of her heart, a place left hollow for something to invade. She would never concede that she resented her husband for dying, so she resented her own existence instead.

It was a bitter little martyrdom.

Grace went on without her.

There was Grandpa and Grandma in their house in the mountains.

Difference also lies in devotion to other gods. It may take time in flowering, deliver itself unexpectedly – be sought too late or found too soon. Time and place may be at odds, generations skewed. It may even go unrecognised.

But not by Grace.

Just as Grace – all her life – had anticipated Godfrey long before she saw him standing at the door of her classroom – as a student, when she had gone to her lectures, drifting along damp pavements between the ramparts of cream-walled buildings, she had often sensed a shadow-company, just outside her reach: they sit here too, in these rooms, walk through this door ahead of her as they once did, two decades before. They catch up with her at the corner of a street, hover on Sundays on the empty lawns of the Botanical Gardens, trooping down the gravel walk, overtaking her, drawing her in, leaving her again with only wind and the high-curdled sky. She is still too young to recognise them but their presence is substantial.

Then, she could not find their faces, just as I could not find hers when I first discovered 'G'. She did not know that they are there, within her reach, in the archives of the library, in the pictures that line the corridor walls of the old school on the rise of the road, at the dorm windows out of which present boys gazed surreptitiously as she passed.

It does not take much imagination to transform a face and transfer it to another time.

Nowadays, the watching boys 'rate' female passers-by. 'Two!' is bawled in my direction.

The schoolgirls going to class, crossing the road beneath the gaze of those same dorm windows, are too familiar with the ritual to care. Why should they?

Some charming Lothario, goaded by their indifference, hangs himself across a sill, yells, 'Gruck!': triumphs are so brief and so hard-won at fifteen.

Grace does not know – beyond her perplexity – as she walks, so often, so unwittingly, past Godfrey's old school house, that his picture in his boxing team, his arms folded – showing off his budding shoulders, the faint swell of his upper arms – has been hanging there for twenty years, just another small-boy face among the hundreds.

It will hang for another fifty before I find it for her, taking chances on a half-term, when workmen have been let in to paint the common room. I flit along the linoleum of the great high-ceilinged passage, searching for him.

Here is the swimming team: *1913*. Fellows pose in their woollen costumes, sitting on spindle-backed chairs, the kaross laid out under bare soles. Here is an Empire-man (Godfrey's senior prefect?), his arm flung up, the muscles slightly tensed – so much assurance at seventeen. When I look him up in the School Register (name, rank, academic achievements, sporting honours), I find that he died at twenty-two. All that cultivated gravity blown away.

Down the rows, on a landing on the stairs, is a shrine to boys more recently dead. One is a victim of guerrilla war, one has died of a long, debilitating illness, the rest by accident. Mortality lurks in the passages as the present boys troop by, streaming up and down the stairs to class or dining hall, a small fear lurking that they, themselves, might be called to join the little company, hung side by side, in black frames.

That afternoon, the light is pale and washed out through high windows. The old stone pines are shaking. Even in the stillness of the day in far-off places, I can recall their scent and conformation. And here in the passage, the ranks and ranks of team pictures and Godfrey with his boy neck growing to be a man's and his hair on end and his arms folded. Square knees, sensitive lip – neither too diffident, nor too self-assured. Boy face – so beloved – looking out.

Old loner.

Grace has never seen this picture. It is mine.

A sense of Death – and the company of Death – spawns difference too.

Grace had a sense of death – a fear of dying – in those student years. Not even in the jolly student parties, the processions and the festivals, did its presence quite recede. It was around her – in the memorials, the Cathedral plaques, the sweep of hill crowned with stone pines, the student who had killed himself, injecting poison, during an experiment, one night. She had hurried past to lectures the next day, under the closed window of his residence room. It was as bland and rimed with dust as the rest. There was nothing to show its difference except that – in there – the inexorable minutes had taken him away. What embrace was he seeking in the drift down into the dark? How long did it take the fear to even out into acceptance? What was it like to let life go?

No one spoke about him after that.

His brother, an affable enough chap before, carried around bewilderment and rage, as if, by his relationship, he'd had his brother's difference forced on him instead. He left before he had finished his degree. Grace never knew what happened to him. No one spoke about him either.

And one afternoon, not long after, when a handsome hero of the sports field, lounging against the counter in the bookshop in town, had looked her up and down, lingering – half warily – and said, 'You're pretty, you know, but you hang around with such odd people', she carried his words with her up the street as if she were condemned. He did not know what he had said. How could he possibly know? Just a gauche, unwitting chap. Another, who might remark, –*I'd just like to give her one* . . . Laughter. –*Just one*. A grunt of satisfaction. *Except* . . .

Except what?

It was then that she willed away her difference – and the silent company at her back.

Enough.

She walked fast, up the street, through the arch, along the path and into the cold of the quad, her shadow bobbing across the flower beds like a hare's, in flight. She had taken the residence steps two at a time, barged into a friend's room, borrowed her dress, made up her face, sat in front of the mirror and taught herself to smoke. At the next ball she had had a glass too much to drink, kissed a slobberer and gone out for tea in the Botanical Gardens with Jack Wilmot, Class-Comic, Hero-Boy.

No one was more surprised than Jack.

After that, if anyone had said, –*I'd like to give her one!* Jack Wilmot would have laid him out with a fist.

So are heroes redefined.

There could not have been more of a difference than between Jack Wilmot and his older brother, Hugh. Hugh wore expander rings up his shirtsleeves to keep his cuffs from grime when he was working at his books; Jack was always covered in tractor grease, socks pushed down, legs strong in his boots, a spanner shoved in his belt. Jack was everything Hugh was not. Except – despite the dash – Grace suspected there was a persistent

114

conventionality in Jack: it lay in his reverence for his mother's baking; his cause-and-effect religious notions and his devotion to the undercarriage of his motor car. He spent much of his time on his back, extracting bits, laying them out, tender as a lover. He was not as good at reassembling them as he was at taking them apart. He circled them, puzzled, even a little frantic. His devotion to his wife was just the same.

His father called him Jacko.

His mother called him John.

Jack Wilmot first takes Grace home for lunch one rainy Sunday. Grace walks up the path in front of him, nudged by a brief foreboding, the serviceable macintosh Jack has lent her wrung about her legs. In the warm summer rain, it is stifling. The house is square with a red-polished *stoep*. There is a bleached lawn and a bed of elephant ears, crassulas and a fig tree against a creosoted split-pole fence. There is a washline with a neat little bag of pegs hanging on the wire. A garden tap, padded with sacking, stands isolated in the middle of the lawn.

Mr Wilmot keeps his pipes in a stand decorated with a whirligig, like a weathercock, on top. He has winged eyebrows and winged hair and winged tufts in his ears. He has a chair that could recline if a little wheel is manipulated on the side. He shows Grace with evident pride, trying to amuse her. He tells her to sit in it while he lets her up and down. She is searching for suitable exclamations of astonishment when Hugh appears with his fiancée, Doreen Elliot. He comes in rubbing chapped hands, flaky-pink from the wind. His raincoat makes a trail across the parquet and Mrs Wilmot brings a mop from the cupboard near the front door. Every emergency is carefully anticipated: in a trice, the parquet is back to its dark dull gleam and the mop borne off to the kitchen to be rinsed. Hugh removes the clips on his trousers and puts them in his jacket pocket. He does not seem to notice his mother's ministrations. She offers him a cup of tea. There is a certain reverence in the way she speaks to him.

Doreen – suddenly proprietary – says, 'I'll get it, Mrs Wilmot. You sit and have a chat.' She goes through to the kitchen: clearly, she knows her way around. Already she is setting her little boundaries and preserves, extracting Hugh and remoulding him. Grace watches her disappear through the door. She is a girl in a cardigan. Very thin. Very neat. There is something surprised in the faint pencilling of her eyebrows. It is her only concession to vanity. When she returns with Hugh's cup of tea, she helps herself to a sip or two: a claim of intimacy which Hugh's mother is unable to subvert.

Mrs Wilmot purses her lips a little and says, 'Would you like a refill, Hugh, dear?'

Grace sits quietly as they discuss the sermon in church that morning.

115

Doreen fiddles with her engagement ring, winding it round and round her finger. Jack, arms resting loosely on his knees, seems embarrassed. When they go through to lunch, Mrs Wilmot tells Grace three times that Hugh is almost finished studying to be a minister. There have been Wesleyan ministers in the family for a few generations, she says.

'And where do you worship, Grace?' she asks and Grace can sense the deep glow at her lobes, plumping them.

'Well,' says Grace, feeling Jack's eyes on her. 'Nowhere really. My parents were different religions, you see. Anyway, I was sent to a convent. In senior school, that is. So, I suppose, I'm more of a Catholic than anything.'

There is a silence. And then Mrs Wilmot says, 'A little more beef?' – avoiding Grace – 'Hugh?'

Hugh does not rescue his mother by passing his plate. Nor does he rescue Grace. He says, 'Did they try to convert you?'

'The Catholics?' says Grace. 'Of course not. They don't go in for that sort of thing.' She is going to say –*They're far too exclusive* – but, darting a look at Jack, she stops herself. There is something in the way he is sitting that alerts her.

And Doreen is red.

Grace does not know if she is embarrassed *for* her – or because of her. She turns away from them, keeping her eyes on her plate.

She does not blush. She is too irritated. Then, glancing up, she catches Hugh Wilmot watching her. He is intent. He has forgotten to put the tip of his tongue away. She sees his Adam's apple rise slowly and then fall. He puts his fingers up to the knot of his plaid tie and adjusts it slightly.

After lunch, Jack and she go out on to the veranda.

'Did I say something wrong?' says Grace.

'My mother hates Catholics.' Then he laughs, telling her that his mother thought that Catholicism was dangerous, something that could be 'caught', even in the street. When he was small, he had always crossed to the other side of the road when he walked to school, to avoid pollution from the neighbours' stretch of pavement. Next door, pointing at a large stone house across the fence, lives a family with five daughters. The Hegartys.

Everyone knows the Hegartys in the town. Grace had been to school with them. They are glorious, exotic girls, ears pierced with small gold rings: something foreign, slightly menacing – like the mantillas that they wear to church on Sundays and the rosary beads they carry, rather irreverently, whirring them around on a finger, the cross whizzing like a small rotating blade. They all have long hair – another sign – parted in the middle, luxuriant and wild. Even their plaits bulge with energy. Besides extravagant hair, they have extravagant names. Josephine and Millicent and Theresa-Maria. No Methodist is ever called Theresa-Maria.

'Do you eat garlic?' says Jack suddenly.

'Why?'

'They eat it all the time.' says Jack. 'And they perm their hair.' She can hear his mother, her insidious Inquisition as she ferrets along the fence between their properties.

'So what?'

Jack looks a little hurt. She is supposed to collude, to laugh disparagingly. 'It's because their mother is French,' he says. He glances back out of the window, adds, a touch churlishly, 'The eldest's damned pretty.'

Grace remains unmoved.

She likes the Hegartys' house. There is an abundance about it: the overgrowth of the garden, the crumbling decay of the building itself. Even the drainage pipes down the tall walls bristle ferns and little clumps of stonecrop and the house is covered, right into the eaves, with Virginia creeper.

The exchange has been so trivial but the difference that it marks will remain immutable, like the small silence that hovers, in parenthesis, in any conversation between Grace and Jack's mother.

The next week, Jack overflows with the glories of cricket, detached from home and full of the half-sheepish bluster of the celebrated. Grace represses her alarm about his family and watches him score eighty-five, holds his sweater in her lap and basks in reflected interest – and respect – from his friends. It is an odd sensation, spoiled only by the sight of Hugh pedalling doggedly down towards the Commemoration Church with his books wrapped in a serviceable cloth, clipped into his carrier on the back of his bicycle, a reminder of Jack's less engaging world.

After graduation, Jack is offered a job, managing a district farm. He is allocated a large, sagging house with stained ceiling boards and an old anthracite stove. He takes Grace to see it. She helps him arrange his chair and table and moves his bed into a more cheerful room. He asks her to marry him while they are swimming in the reservoir with a high wind blowing and his voice drowned out by the squealing of the windmill's vanes thrumming round.

It is an odd, poignant moment.

Grace remembered, in after times, the expression on his face: a strangely fragile smile. Did he know, even then, that it wouldn't be forever?

Grace was twenty when she married Jack. Jack was twenty-two. Jack took Grace away to the old house on the farm, proprietor and king, and poured himself out with intense and happy relief. He seemed grateful more than anything. He even grew a inch in the first three months of their marriage – big, healthy, unremitting boy.

117

With Grace settled, Grandpa and Grandma moved to a home for the aged on the coast and watched the sea across a scrubby stretch of yellowing lawn through a screen of casuarina trees.

Grace was appalled. She knew they had done it to deliver her from responsibility for them. Grandpa forbade her to mention it, said he liked walking on the beach. She knew he couldn't swim and much preferred the mountains.

Without her garden, Grandma grew parsley in pots and made finger puppets for the church bazaar. She sewed them out of scraps, embroidering quirky faces. Unaccountably, one looked like the Bishop. Grandma liked the notion so much, she sent it to him as a present. She wouldn't hear a word from Grace about living in a cottage on the farm.

In 1939, when Grace and Jack had been married almost four years, Jack joined up and went North. He drove an armoured car and grew a neat moustache. A retired farmer came with his family to take Jack's place and Grace went to teach at the small church school where Hugh had taken his first post as minister. When he enlisted as an army chaplain, she lived in the manse with Doreen, helped her run the school, taking the younger ones for lessons and keeping her company. An assistant priest came once a month for services. Doreen played the organ, Grace taught the children their prayers and dredged up long-forgotten Catholic novenas for herself to ensure Jack's safe return.

Novenas did not help. He did not come back.

Only Hugh came home, with his ruddy face and his cockscomb of sandy hair.

Doreen Wilmot, Hugh's wife, died within a year. She had been ailing for a long time. Grace stayed to nurse her. They did the round of doctors together, Grace driving her along the interminable dirt roads into town. In the end, like Grace's mother, Doreen Wilmot decided Faith alone could cure her – but neither her Methodist prayers, nor Grace's turncoat ones, could stem the tide. It was a quiet burial.

Hugh asked Grace to stay on until another teacher could be found. She had nowhere else to go. To preserve propriety, a young ex-serviceman, Tommy Cooper, working as a learner-farmer, came to board. On and off, various Wilmot relations arrived to stay.

–Aren't the Wilmots a close-knit family? So nice for Hugh and Grace!

In the evening they all listened to the wireless and Grace prepared her lessons. In the centre of the mantelpiece stood Doreen's photo-portrait. Jack's picture, in his battledress and beret, occupied the space between the mirror and the clock. Grace dusted it often. In time, the face in the picture, confined by the frame, became all that remained of Jack: she could no longer see him walking in the lands, she had no scent of him, his voice was

118

not imprinted in her mind. He evaporated slowly, by degrees. She did not try to save him.

Nor did she try to cultivate her mother's patience. She had no desire for martyrdom. She made cardboard models for her classroom, painted posters for the walls, invented games out of boxes and bottles, buttons and cans and wrote to Grandpa and Grandma every week. At Christmas, she and Hugh drove along the coast and fetched them, taking them up to the house in the mountains. They sat in the back of the car, alert as two birds, in search of their nest.

Grandma died first. Without fuss. Without confusion.

Early one morning, just after Christmas, Grace came to their room with the customary tray of tea. She had picked a handful of stocks and put them in a little jug. She opened the door quietly, nudging it with her knee. Grandpa was sitting by the bed, a chair drawn up. His feet were bare. His shoulder bones seemed scooped, holding up the points of his pyjama jacket. Grandma was lying on her side as if she was asleep, quite peaceful, hand propped under her cheek, those long, lovely fingers curled in against it. It was just the small slackness, the slightest dislocation of her face, that made Grace know.

Grandpa did not turn. She laid the tray on the table and came to him. He raised his hand and took hers in his, letting his head rest briefly against her side as she stood over him.

The smell of stocks, their gentle fragrance and the underscent – a little sharper, a little more defined, the poignance of the bloom, its heart – recalls that quiet, morning vigil.

They will always be Grandma's flowers.

Grace did not say goodbye to her grandfather before he died. He did not say goodbye to her.

It did not matter. Their conversation was ongoing.

He was as present as if he had been somewhere in the house. There was nothing of impermanence about him. No loss.

Grandfather did not call for Grace when he was ill. He said it was a trifle. A touch of flu. He sat up in bed most of the night, to keep his chest clear. He read and dozed. Towards morning he put his specs in their case and a marker at the page which he had reached. His little book of bird-lore was on the table next to his glass of water.

Going off duty, the night sister found him. She telephoned Grace.

Grace went into the garden outside the church in the first grey light and sat quietly on the grass.

No words, no tears.

She was suspended from them all.

In time, she would perform her own small rite – learned in his world – and bring him home.

She would lead him from the bland, beige-painted walls of the institutional little room in the Home which he had once shared with Grandma, out along the district road, travelling inland and up into the mountains to the old house in its soft, mossy garden. She would do it alone, speaking to him, telling him what was flowering as she drove up the winding road of the pass. Here, the erythrinas were in bloom on the flat stretch just before they reached the slope. Here, where it was sunny, the plumbago and tecoma. Higher up, in damp ravines, were forest trees and creepers. At the summit, turning along the hillside, the sound of wind, of water – all the fragrance of the upland air. She would greet his birds for him, listen for the greywings in the morning, the wood owl at dusk.

His presence was in everything she loved. It had not been withdrawn. Why should she mourn?

But, in time, she mourned.

Not his absence, but her own. A sentence left suspended, drifting into silence and regret, the slow ebb of joy, the gesture left unshared.

I know that barren time.

Then Godfrey came.

Then Godfrey came and even the footpaths winding out across the lands, the old store and house, squat behind the *garingbome* standing in the blue-grey row along the road, were different. Suddenly, they were invested with a texture and light. The truck, parked in the yard beside the store, caught the glint of the sun on its windscreen, flashed its bold, intermittent presence. Grace looked for it eagerly, the world lifting again, the sense of wonder and discovery rekindled, the substance, the depth that she had known.

Hugh Wilmot looked for it as well. And when the heliograph spark of sun on glass beamed back, his God was far away.

'I am going down into the valley tomorrow with Dr Godfrey,' says Grace at supper. 'He wants to start a small herd of indigenous cattle. He has already made plans to buy a few of Herman de Waal's animals but he needs some diversity and he's interested in Xhosa stock which might be less influenced by other blood.' She sounds brisk and official. Official enough for Hugh to look up from his plate, suddenly alert.

120

There is a little thread of cabbage at his lip. He can feel Grace's eyes and he dabs at it. He looks over at her, knife and fork placed precisely at twenty past eight. The young man, the learner-farmer, Tommy Cooper, is helping himself to more potato. He is foraging and probing. Hugh glances at him in annoyance. He does not notice. The annoyance is not for him flicking the spoon, stabbing at it with his knife to dislodge the mash – it is at what Grace has said. 'Ah,' he says. He takes up his table napkin and wipes his mouth with care. 'I thought you were working on a dictionary.'

'I am,' Grace returns.

'In the valley?'

'In the valley.' She says firmly.

Tommy Cooper cocks an eyebrow at her, swills potato and water in his mouth.

Grace looks away. She does not want him to be part of this conversation, or any conversation, of which Godfrey is the subject. He is the sort of young man who likes practical jokes. His favourite opening line at meals, is '*Have you heard the one about . . .*' It is all too tedious.

Hugh continues with his stew. He cuts the small pieces of mutton even smaller, presses his peas on to his fork, holds his knife like a dissecting instrument.

He is also tedious.

They eat in silence for a while, then Hugh says, 'Why on earth does he want bush cows?'

Again Grace is aware of the covert glance from across the table from Tommy Cooper. Now he is transferring potato on to his fork by clean-blading his knife between its prongs.

'In the end, they'll be sent to the State experimental station in Zululand. A Dr Crawford has a project.'

'They are useless, man,' interrupts Tommy, full of derision. 'They never put on weight. Doesn't he know you're not even allowed to breed with them, hey?' He hooks an elbow over the back of his chair, suddenly expansive. He is getting into his stride. His fork is still in his hand. 'In 1936 they brought in a law to stop people breeding with native bulls. In Natal, the place was just running wild with bush cattle! I mean, is the chap right in the head?'

'They are adapted to the environment much better than other breeds,' says Grace. She knows she is sounding pedantic, paraphrasing Godfrey. Awkward. 'Tick resistant, especially.' She ends it rather lamely.

'So, what's so great about that? What are dips for?'

'It's to obviate the need for dips.'

Tommy Cooper does not understand the word but he says, 'What's the problem with dips?'

121

'In the rural areas people don't have access to them. It's better to have tick-resistant herds.'

Hugh is still staring middle distance with his chin resting on the bridge of his linked knuckles. He is the picture of rectitude.

'Listen,' says Tommy Cooper, 'in the rural areas there are too many bloody cows anyway and erosion and useless stock. The natives don't know what they're doing when it comes to breeding . . .'

'They have been stockmen for thousands of years,' says Grace.

'And look how much good it's done them!' Tommy is triumphant. He turns to Hugh. 'There's this joke about the native boy who had three cows. And his *umfazi* says to him, "Listen, Witbooi, I want you to *slag* one for my old grandfather's spook". And Witbooi says . . .'

'Do you mind, Tom,' says Hugh. He rises. His chair scrapes back against the mat and wrinkles it up on the floor boards. 'Grace, a word.'

She glances at him. Stands. 'Excuse me, Tommy,' she says.

Hugh has already left the room.

'I was only trying to help.' Tommy's ears are red.

'Well, don't.' She sounds sharp. She regrets it. It is not his fault. It is not his fault that bush cows are bush cows and that his world is inhabited by Witbooi and his *umfazi*. Or is it?

One word, and what is sacred – or, what is simple and blameless in others – can be so diminished. She can hear him, turning Witbooi and his *umfazi* around and reapplying them – full of derision – to Godfrey and herself, ridiculing what is delicate and apt, overturning it.

–*Where will you keep the cattle?* Grace had said.

–*I wanted to show you*. Godfrey had been almost secretive. She had followed him into the *veld*, ready to skip, ready to sing.

Above a hollow, seamed at the south by a screen of vegetation, the remnants of an old stone cattle byre had lain in the grass. A *kannabos* grew against a fallen gate. It was a place of shade, plumbago-blue as the bush that leaned in around it.

–*It is so quiet here*. Grace's voice had been hushed.

–*Holy*, Godfrey had said.

He had pushed the gate in across the tussocks of grass and the little wiry bushes that had grown up. She had not followed him inside. She knew that a cattle byre was the preserve of patrilineal shades. She had stood at the threshold, watching him. Away in the bush, a bokmakierie had called, its ringing territorial note encircled them. Godfrey had cocked his head, listening. –*Well, that's a sign!*

–*A sign?*

–*The place where a bokmakierie calls is always good for a cattle byre. It is a direct intimation that it would be propitious!*

122

Grace leaves Tommy Cooper alone with his potato and gravy and follows Hugh to his study. She can feel herself irrationally angry for the intrusion of them both, angry with herself for having precipitated it. She would never be so foolish as to mention Godfrey in their company again.

Hugh has switched on the overhead light. His face looks beige. He is beige all over. He turns to her as she comes into the room. He says, 'Grace?' He has his pastoral voice. 'I don't know if you quite understand what is happening here.'

She looks at him. She knows very much better than him what is happening. And it has nothing to do with him.

'I don't want you to be hurt.'

'Hurt?'

'Yes.' He sits in his chair behind his desk. 'My dear,' he says. 'A man like Dr Godfrey . . .'

She wants to laugh. 'Hugh, you quite misinterpret things.'

'Do I, Grace?'

'Certainly, you do.'

'I'm a man of the world, Grace.'

–*You a man of the world, Hugh! You, with your bicycle and your trouser clips? You, with your standard sermon – 'My dear brothers and sisters'?*

She looks back at him, in silence: –*Don't touch it, Hugh.*

'It's the way others might view it.' He is taking the moral high-ground in the gentlest – and most irritating – of voices.

'Others?'

–*What others, Hugh? There are no others here but you and Thomas Cooper.*

'We live in a small community, Grace. I don't want people misjudging this . . .'

–*The children in the school? Their interpretation is so much clearer than yours, Hugh*: the little offerings of flowers, wrapped in a scrap of newspaper or precarious in an empty fishpaste jar, put on Teacher's desk.

From Harry.

From George.

I love you in the world, Mrs Wilmot, from Desmond.

The parents?

She had laughed: last week's composition, '*My Teacher*'.

'*My teacher is Mrs Wilmot. She is a prity lady with yellow hair.*
She is a little bit yung she is sometimes sad. She is sad bikos
her husbind is died. She plays games with us on the swiings.
My mom says what is the biznis with the cow man. Why cows? He has got a
beyid. My mom sed mans with beyids are all bad. God has gort a beyid.'

Grace almost smiles. 'All men with beards are bad,' she says.

'I beg your pardon?' Hugh is peering at her through his specs. It is not a hot night but his forehead is damp at the winged edges of his cockscomb.

'People will interpret things the way they want to. There's not much you can do. Grow a beard, Hugh, and see what happens.'

She does not bother to explain. She is too angry. She says, 'It is Saturday tomorrow, Hugh. It is my free time.'

'What about the cookery book for the Ladies' Guild? You haven't done anything on it for weeks. I've been looking forward to working on it with you.' He is almost peevish: Jack looms between them.

'I will attend to the cookery book. I have told you that before – but I have been employed by Dr Godfrey and there is a time constraint. I have a commitment to his work which I cannot change until it is done.'

'Is that all?'

–You mean – is that all it is?

She says, 'Yes. That's all.'

Hugh goes to the window and draws the curtain. The brass rings squeal on the rod.

Grace walks away down the passage to her room, dragging her marking off the table in the hall as she passes.

You don't want me to want to get into Godfrey's bed, Hugh. You want me to want to get into yours.

There.

It has been said.

Her own chaste bed is pushed against the wall. The cat is lying on it. He turns over, luxuriating, regards her with one agate eye, curves his paw against his brow, yawns.

It Has Been Said.

Chapter eight

So often, the sign rests in something inconsequential – God's unobtrusive footnote to be taken up or passed over. It is only later that the interlinking pattern emerges and makes persistent sense of something trivial: a date, a number, the constant little *déjà-vus*, chance and coincidence.

The intended.

Just as I had come across Godfrey's folder in the university library, Godfrey, as an undergraduate, had found the first reference to the mythology of cattle names himself. Ostensibly searching for information on the development of the Mahdist State in the Sudan, deeply indifferent to both Muhammad Ahmed and General Gordon, he had become distracted in the byways of related material. He knows he is trawling for something else – a Land of Punt, a dream-city in a mind-map. He is not sure what he is searching for.

But I know.

He is here to assuage loss. Like me, he is casting for a word, a phrase, an image to restore some half-remembered grace.

He finds it among the volumes carried to his reading desk. It has been left there for him, just as his work has been left for me.

It is a slim navy book, a traveller's memoir of a journey through the southern Sudan, circa 1874. And if, as Godfrey opens it, there was no shrike calling away in the *bergwind* morning to alert him to the moment, as there was for me, the harmony of words on the printed page is as vivid, as immediate, as a sudden voice in that ancient lofty room. It is Bibleman speaking the name of the *umvemve* calf, rounding the weight of its significance with a lightness and inflection which mimics the delicacy of the little bird itself, its fragile step, its tenderness.

The pages are uncut. This book, in all the years of standing in the shelves, has never been referred to before. He takes it to the librarian's desk. The man views the volume sceptically. 'I will have to ask permission to cut it.'

'Surely,' Godfrey says, 'it is here to be read.'

'Of course.' The librarian hesitates, glances up. What could be more reasonable?

What indeed.

He fetches a paper knife. He takes the book to a corner, almost furtive, as though he is about to desecrate something. One by one the pages are revealed. The bleached edges where the blade has passed seem cauterised.

Godfrey bears the book away. Each leaf is a revelation. No eyes have seen the bound print of this volume before. It is as if he is exploring an uncharted stretch of country. And there – there, towards the end – a plate of cattle figures, one dozen of them stylised in profile, carefully etched, each with lyre horns, with a distinctive pattern and beneath, a name, explained in a footnote:

The Crowned crane.

The Grey goshawk.

The white egg of Mijok.

And here, one with a visor on its face, as if it had been painted on its skin like ancient heraldry.

Godfrey's palm rests on the page, across the drawings of the cattle, as if he wishes no one to see them and exclaim, diluting his excitement. Around him is the airiness of columns, of teak book racks, the detachment of centuries, individuality incidental to the accumulative weight of scholarship. But instead – immediate – is his distant home pasture by the corrugated fence, the smell of the pepper tree, the feel of its shade shifting across the skin like fingers exploring, the exact sting of the sun on the tips of his ears, its warmth and weight on closed and upturned lids.

So exact a smell of cattle dung.

So exact a sound of the wind across the gravel of the yard.

So exact the voice of Bibleman.

God's footnote.

It was stored a long time, like one of the catalogue cards I had put in the Bute Snuff Box with '*G*' written on it: the essential Godfrey, waiting for me to finish my other tasks first. And he, in that desolate post-war year, anonymous among the depleted numbers of young men at the university, trench-weary, lung-damaged, filed away his notes and drawings on the colour-patterns of the cattle of the Sudan and finished his paper on the Mahdist State.

He did not forget his sheaf of notes, or where he had put them. He must have sensed, even then, that – in some way – it was a sacred thing.

It is years before he comes across an article about a Dr Crawford and his work on the indigenous cattle of southern Africa, and – rummaging through old files, suitcases and boxes – finds the notes that he had written, takes them to his study in Harold Godfrey's house, his door shut against the sounds of intrusion, and reads them under the flame of a small paraffin lamp.

The Grey goshawk, the Crowned crane.

He telephones the exchange to enquire for Dr Crawford's number, standing at the window and gazing out across the lawn. He can see Stella in the driveway saying goodbye to a group of friends. In the late light their afternoon frocks are pale. They seem to flock, lifting and settling, restless to be gone, not knowing how to go. A last goodbye, another snatch of conversation, another light embrace. He turns from them back to the twilight of the study, takes up a pencil and writes the number at the top of a clean page.

And that is how, at last, he began this pilgrimage. With his files, his boxes of catalogue cards, his dictionaries and camera – snatching at every university vacation, his first sabbatical – he wandered Zululand, the Kaokoveld, Mashonaland in the late thirties, gathering comparative material for his lexicon. Even when he laid it aside at the outbreak of war to take an instructor's post in the Air Force, at the navigation school, even then (his maps, his skies, his strange topographies), he is still in search of a mythic place.

To assuage some loss.

The journey leads, inexorably, in 1946, to this leached and ancient valley.

This packstone cattle byre.

To the *inala* cow.

To Grace.

And then to me.

Throughout my research, throughout my explorations, it is the picture of the *inala* cow that has beguiled me. It is the cipher which reveals the season, the time of day, the place, a moment of resonance. On the back of the print is written, in indelible pencil, *3.03 pm 19/08/46*. For some reason, the time is as significant as the day and month and year. And through this careful recording of the time, I know that this picture and Godfrey's map are somehow linked, though the dates on each have no connection and are spaced ten years apart. They hold an equal weight in remembrance: it seems essential to be able to recall, in each, where the sun stood and if the day was cool, clear – in twilight, at its zenith.

It is this little picture – no more than a contact print – which is the leitmotiv on which my story hangs. The truth of this is something I must take on faith. I do not believe that I have been misled. There is something too particular about the man, about the planes of his face – that fine, extraordinary, ascetic face – the glance that apprehends a presence at the point from which I gaze. At this moment, I am Grace, framing him with the lens. He sees me. I do not doubt it. And there, in the print, is the shadow of a woman – the suggestion of a figure, slim and insubstantial – reaching out, across the ground, towards his feet. Like the picture of Gert and Godfrey as children, I have had a copy made. The *inala* cow is grainy in her sudden enlargement. The lines of Godfrey's face are slightly blurred but enhanced by a quality of airiness and light. Behind the group is the clear curve of the post at the entrance to the cattle byre and the withered husks of the aloe that grows in the packstone wall. I can see by the dryness of the flower head that it is long past its winter blooming.

Grace makes enquiries. She searches her grandfather's papers, telephones the school board, trying to recall the name of the man who had owned the cattle and her grandfather's dealings with him. She had been young. The turns in the road, the signposts had not been her concern, only the excitement of peering over the side of a causeway as the car edged across in rainy weather. She is afraid of making a mistake. She is afraid that the place she has described to Godfrey, woven out of perceptions of childhood and its wonder, will fall short, that the light of the afternoon on which she had last seen it, the cattle and the sound of their hooves, that sky, the feel of the wind, its playfulness, her contentment in being tucked beside her grandfather, will deliver something unremarkable and empty now.

She is able to find the old man's name in her grandfather's files: *Mr M Xaba*. She telephones enquiries and is a given the number of the trader in the district. It takes three days for her to raise a voice. The trader is away, the address is vague.

'Mr Xaba? There are many people called Xaba around here.'

'The very old man?'

'The very old, old man?'

'The very old man, Mr Xaba, lives at the house just at the other side of the road, where it turns down to Enseleni.'

Grace gleans an address of sorts. She writes to Mr Xaba, care of the trader, awaits a reply. None comes. She and Godfrey set out anyway. It does not really matter any more that they have no appointment and are not sure of where they are going. It is simply something that they have to do, the start of a journey which is theirs alone. The specific, the scientific have given way to the mythopoeic, the search for some aesthetic and its secret language. It is a pilgrimage to map a landscape of their own. Their sacred place to which they might return in after years – separately – knowing that their individual joy in it will remain invested with the presence of the other.

I know. I have been on that road myself, turning down a pass among low hills, clad with the black-green vegetation of an ancient time. The *kiepersols*, the euphorbias and the deeper, damper *kloofs*, the great trees, the quiet river. I know the lightness that brought them here. I know the lifting of the heart and the feel of the wind: that soft, dry breath of hinterland, that singing space.

Holding the image of the sacred, I have made the journey.

I find the chopped-out stands of trees.

The ash-heaps.

The leached *dongas*.

Plastic bags crucified on falling fences.

Houses have burgeoned. So has the ubiquitous turquoise paint of the eighties. The sun glints roughly on unpainted iron roofs, the graveyards of abandoned cars, the limping power lines, stripped for miles of copper wire. There is so much poverty.

In a settlement – the worst of government buildings, asbestos and prefab boards, soulless steel windows, broken glass – the poverty has less to do with empty fields than the surrender of hope. It is a sullen place. Its history has been undone, man's connection with its essence squandered. It is no longer a place where one might wish – with reverence – to bury the dead.

All day they take the stony track along the base of the valley. It is the time of doves, the mid-afternoon sound of them. They drive slowly, windows down, winding further and further, as the day lengthens out along the ridges and the slopes. At the base of the escarpment they come to a store and the trader's house. On a slope above it is the homestead they are looking for. It is there – suddenly – its conformation exactly as Grace remembers but facing in a direction that she does not recall.

So our mind-maps test us. Like a face – familiar, beloved – whose cartography will dim or transform itself in memory, until it can no longer be restored with truth. Or with justice.

She knows it, though, by the stand of mimosas and the aloes that grow thickly among the stones of the wall. And by the far valley and the river and the spur of hill. Xaba, the headman lived here in her grandfather's time. He was a deacon in the church, a teacher, a community man. He also had a large herd of cattle. Grace recalls the sound of hooves, the quiet rhythmic brushing of them in the dust, the patience of an eye turned briefly to her, her face pressed against the window of her grandfather's car.

She remembers the headman's homestead – the collection of silver-thatched rondavels, the beaten yard and the packstone byre over which the ancient clumps of kraal aloe grew, the earth inside churned and soft with the smell, the sleep, the drowsing of cattle. On the slope below is the tall, square house of the trader with its dark veranda and dormer windows, closed into a clump of gums, in a deep perpetual shade, at odds with the generous curves of hillside and river and road.

They bump up the track to the homestead of huts. An old man comes to greet them. He is bent double. He is like a stake in his byre gate, gnarled over with age and now with withering. Grace goes forward, puts her hand in his. It is warm and dry as an aloe husk. She says her name, her grandfather's name, asks if he has received her letter.

The old man nods, looks into her face, searching it and then he sets his gaze beyond her, head cocked up, animating something in the air, smiling: he has his own recollections of her grandfather. 'And you,' he says, looking at Grace, 'were such a little girl,' indicating height with his hand. 'Such a very little girl. Your grandfather,' he continues, 'was a friend to me. He was a friend of all the people, of the children in the schools. He was a friend of God.'

Grace turns to Godfrey. 'This is Dr Godfrey. He is' – she nearly says, *the man with cows* – brings him forward, 'from the university.'

'He has come about the cattle,' the old man says, touches his eyes. 'In these days it is difficult for me to write.'

Godfrey steps forward and shakes his hand. 'Mr Xaba,' he says.

The old man appraises him calmly, kindly: he knows a man of substance. He is one himself.

Chairs are brought by a grandson, placed in a semicircle in the afternoon sun. Mr Xaba sits facing them, his eyes rheumy blue. A rooster, spurred like a warrior, struts the yard.

Tea is brought, the milk thick with cream, spiked with the flavour and smell of the pasture. Together he and Godfrey have a pipe and talk of drought and ticks and milk production, of the number of young bulls born, the dearth of heifers in that year's calving. Grace sits quietly with the camera in her lap, watching.

'I wish to buy three heifers,' Godfrey says.

'Three heifers,' the old man repeats. He purses his lips and smiles then, a slight shake of the head: Godfrey will be wrenching them from him. It is like bargaining for a member of the family. He runs his hand down his face as if picking off cobwebs from his beard. Three heifers. Which will he choose?

'Only if you agree, Mr Xaba,' Godfrey says. 'There is this place I want to take them, my own byre.' He gestures up towards the low escarpment. 'I

have other cattle there. But I want only this kind, not those *Kwabelungu* –
in the place of whites.'

The old man is sceptical. Godfrey, after all, is white. He regards him
shrewdly.

Across the *veld*, far off still, there is the sound of the herd returning. The
sharp whistle of herdsmen, a voice raised in chant, a laugh, the jostle of
beasts.

'They are coming,' Xaba says, turning his head and cocking it sideways
to see up and out of his bentness.

Grace does not approach the byre, not with the old man there. It is a
sacred place which a woman may not enter. She would like to take a
photograph, but there is something remote in its long still shadows and the
small wind of late afternoon, spiralling out the dust of hooves, behind the
line of beasts. There are swifts hawking, the sign of evening coming down.

She recalls their name from Godfrey's cards: the harbinger of herds,
isacel'izapholo, 'that which asks a little milk'. The birds turn on the wing
against the drift of midges caught in the motes of light, knowing that the
time for milking has arrived. And above, in a pale sky – soon, soon, when
evening comes – the first faint star, named too, if she remembers, 'that
which asks a little milk', linking dusk with bird and byre.

The old man in his bentness, beckoning his lyre-horned beasts, points
out a small dark cow. 'There is this *inzimakazi*,' he says. 'You must have a
good black cow.'

Godfrey, pulling on his pipe, watches the animal sniff at the earth of the
byre, the moist sponge of nostrils and the quick alertness of its eye.

One of the little calves is the colour of sea sand. The old man laughs at its
butting its head against the flank of the wrong dam. It is sheepish in retreat.
And another, brindled in tan and black and yellow. Grace knows: it is
named for the puffadder.

And another, pale as buds: *that which touches the mushroom.*

And a bullock, dun-grey with milk-white legs and the lazy lapping line
marking out the dark from the light, *ebafazi bewela:* women crossing the
stream. Such a name for a bullock, associated always with a concourse of
wading women! No wonder it seems bewildered, standing splay-legged at
the gate, neither going forward, nor retreating, until roughly nudged from
behind.

Godfrey stops, separating a small animal from the rest of the herd.

It is a cow. She has the *inala* pattern.

She gazes at him, head down, then turning from him, nosing for a way
through. She is white-faced, dark-eyed, scattered with the faintest rust,
glistening along the flank. She regards him gravely, with a still attention.
He says coaxing things. She lowers and tentatively extends her head, sniffs

131

again, reaching out her nose to him. She is diffident of him. She is diffident of all. She knows nothing of the pattern of her flanks and how the curve of her rump arouses such admiration. The herders stand about and grin: they know all her small coquetries. She tosses her head – it is almost coy – as Godfrey puts his arm across her neck. She settles into the noose of his embrace.

Treading softly closer, Grace prepares the camera, checks the direction of the sun, steps forward and takes a picture. Her shadow reaches out across the ground towards Godfrey's feet. He gazes back at her. Right into the lens.

She lowers the camera slowly, not looking at him. Her shadow remains at his feet. She does not wish to step away with it.

In time, the old man lets them buy three heifers. The black, the 'mushroom' and the *inala* cow. They have to be driven up to the lip of the valley, to where the road dissects the hillside and then turns south and west again. Here, Godfrey and Wilton Mayekiso, the storeman, meet the herdsmen with the truck and coax the cows with songs and scolding, up a makeshift ramp into the back of the vehicle. They are tethered to the struts and the storeman stands among them, steadying them, his woollen cap set at the back of his head, gleaming with exertion, gap-toothed and cajoling, big-chested with exultation at the prize.

And Grace and Godfrey?

The exultation is no different. It is as if they have recaptured, in its clarity, its directness, the world of Bibleman and the *umvemve* calf. Together they are creating a universe, making it 'allowed', in its beauty and intent, not only weaving it from old histories, poems and stories; names, metaphors and images but creating a herd that grazes, slumbers, fattens, reproduces, thrives and grows. Yes, that is what they do.

Love and Beauty *are* admissible.

Against the odds. Against what other men advise.

They tend their herd. They attend to their lexicon. They are alone, except for the old stockman with the woollen cap. Their lives become the late afternoon when school is over and when Grace can leave and go with Godfrey in the truck, even driving a little recklessly to get to the house, taking the curve of the road above the valley where the store lies, sending up the edge of gravel with their wheels like a small curling wave.

Their lives are all the entries in their colour lexicon: the shining and the shimmering, the iridescent, glimmering, the pepper bright:

    —makhwifikhwifi
    —makwangukhwangu
    —manangunangu

—mampilimpili

There is something in dabbling with such words: they make their own rhymes and poems. Godfrey and Grace toss them between each other in laughter. It is a secret language, a secret joke, summoned – even in public places – love words in metaphor, as cryptic as the language of the cattle names.

From Herman de Waal's comes the bull. It is the young bull, unproven in its siring, unproven in its temperament, not yet a midlife bull. Grace loves its colour. It is a grey roan, the white and black hair of the hide so evenly interspersed, it is translucent, like daylight within shadow. Herman de Waal says that its name is *Bitchaan Shiki* – 'Somewhat Cheeky' – but the stockman, in deference to its colour, knows it by its pattern and the shape of its horns. He calls it '*Intulo elizotha elisomi ebafazi baphik' icala*': lizard of a sober colour, like the Redwinged starling, which is the women saying 'we have had enough, we repudiate the case', because he has horns that tip backwards like a woman throwing up her hands in resignation and despair.

Godfrey and Grace stand and watch the cattle when they are driven into the byre, each exploring the ground in its strangeness, the cows from the valley bunched together at the far end of the stockade, the animals from Herman de Waal's standing round the bull.

The stockman watches too, his pipe bubbling plumes like the smoke from a train, gathering energy and heat and pumping it out. He laughs to see the De Waal cows squaring up against the smaller and more delicate valley cows, the bull, blowing at the newcomers, drawing the essence of them into himself. All that weight in his outstretched neck, all that energy, the power of creation sprung in him! Grace and Godfrey watch him circling the heifers, the thrust of his shoulders, the swag of dewlap at his throat.

The *inala* cow stands her ground, watching him, shifting her weight round delicately so that she remains protected, at a distance, face to face. She regards him with steady, thoughtful eyes.

The bull advances, the little cow retreats.

Advance. Retreat.

Advance. Retreat.

Then suddenly she stands – unabashed, provocative – and takes a small step forward. The young bull is confused. He lowers his head and extends his lip, tasting the air between them. He is awkward and exposed.

The *inala* cow, pivots, with a touch of disdain, turns her back on him and trots away.

Godfrey looks over at Grace, suddenly laughs. 'She reminds me of you,' he says.

She reminds me of you.

Did he say that?

For me, it is beyond supposition. Now, if I look at the picture of the *inala* cow, the rust-speckled heifer with the white face and the dark eyes outlined, I know that the quality of Grace – as he perceived it – resides here more surely than if someone had written her history, more than if they had said she was charming or unusual or pretty. Or inconspicuous, or innocuous, or drab. Again, it is a matter of recognition. This unassuming little heifer is connected, immutably, with Grace – and in it, through it, with Godfrey's mythopoeic world, the essence of his understanding: the hills are ancient skulls, afternoon cumulus are baobabs that crown the upper blue, great-branched, flowered with open ivory cups; dew is the tears that have washed the face of the moon; flat, low rain clouds – hunting jackals scouring the sky-plains; the shadows of the early evening are hyenas, haunting the low depressions in the valleys, skirting the rocks of ridges. The red planet of summer nights is the *Aardvark-of-the-Sky* which calls out the flying ants after rain with its ancient, coaxing song.

This mythic world is Godfrey's.

It is Grace's.

It is mine.

Through them, I am initiated into a new cosmology. And neither past nor future exist in linear form. They are here, now. They reflect and affirm the present. That is why I do not document a finite Godfrey, 1898-1963, with a Beginning and a Middle and an End.

Grace closes her eyes to feel the last benediction of the setting sun on lids, its warmth in the hollow of her throat, the pulse-point of her heart, its long caress. There is the scent about her of the ironstone, the cream clematis clambering the walls, the pasture grass and dung, fragrant and fresh, the damp of shadow. And Godfrey.

They stand in the quiet light of evening and hear the milk being driven to the pail by the stockman, the deep rhythmic thud of it hitting the sides, the faint shifting of the tethered cow.

Godfrey says, recalling the poetry of milking, his voice light, 'It does not go *tso tso tso!* It does not go *gwci-gwci-gcwi!*' Then his words deepen down, 'It goes *klwa-klwa-klwa* in its abundance!'

She smiles, mimics him.

They return to the house in the dusk. She walks ahead of him.

Like the *inala*, she is shimmering, she is beckoning, turning her head – ingenuous – but knowing she beguiles. To see her go, so light and yet so confident, brings to mind the praises of the dappled cow:

'. . . *she never walks, she never runs.*
but proudly, deliberately, boastfully she walks.'

That is how Grace Wilmot walked before Godfrey into his house that day, stepping over her own diffidence, deferring guilt. And he followed her and closed the door behind him and stood a moment in the blue-white gloom of his room, the clock at ten to six on the table by his bed.

He crossed to her and laid his coat on a chair. Quiet – and almost formal – he placed her hand, flat-palmed between his palms. She looked up, resting her gaze within his. It was neither truce nor contract, but a pledge. Reverent and clean.

He led her then, turning her to him: that most intimate touch of chest on chest, of breast curving to the hollow of the sternum, the coincidence of breath, of breathing. And then, the slow-flowering grace, the first unfolding, stretching out behind closed lids – the long-compelling pull, up, up towards the open upland, far above the fall of space.

She went with him, her fingers locked in his.

There is no poisonous yellow paint in the room of their loving. No kei-apple rind seeping into the milk-blue shadows of the walls. It is a place of pilgrims, transcending ownership. I have stood at its threshold like an intruder, furnishing it in my mind with the things he might have had – a spindle-backed chair, a table, his wooden boxes of cards, a microscope, brass-buffed and heavy; a rod set across a corner on which to hang his clothes; a trunk; a leather suitcase. Perhaps he used his army stretcher as a bed.

The furnishing, now – the worst of Bellview Stores – cannot intrude. I hardly notice the imitation Parker Knoll in red and grey Dralon, the pink candlewick cover on the bed, a plywood and veneer pedestal topped with a wrought-iron lamp with a fringed shade, burned through where the satin pleats have leaned too closely to the bulb. The only piece he might have known is a chest of drawers, painted grey. Opening it, I examine the joinery. It is beautifully dovetailed. An exploration of the top shows – by the width of the wood – that it is cut from yellowwood. Such a soft and venerable grain covered over with layers and layers of gloss enamel paint. And yet, despite its paltry contents, this little room retains a purity, a light, a spacious whiteness at the angles of its high-hipped ceiling.

It is still a sanctuary.

I am here to restore it. Not to another period – there will be no need for reconstruction of its contents – but to him. To them.

Love-as-Restoration.

And when the restoration is complete? What then? Will the loving – so cleanly, so clearly circumscribed – feed on its own intensity and be destroyed?

–*Don't leave me, Godfrey.*

How many times I have said that, afraid he might turn silent, stop the cards – no more conversation, no more clues, no more signs.

Go dead.

How many times had Grace said it? Amid the laughter and the business of cattle, the catalogue, the teasing and the 'work', that little anguished cry: –*Don't leave me, Godfrey*, knowing, in the end, that he must turn his face away, leaving her to her catastrophic guilt and self-disdain. She feared, not only the loss of his presence – the man, standing at her shoulder, pointing out the errors, reshuffling the cards – but protection from her shame, her right to remembrance. Her dread had always been his swift or sudden censure, his cool withdrawal. In her mind, his regard remained forever fragile and easy to subvert: *I have no claim*.

Would they learn to scorn each other in their guilt?

What did Godfrey think? What did he want?

I have no idea. I am too afraid to ask.

I am not a man of the world who has managed the loss of lovers. Nor am I shrewd enough (or beautiful enough) to know. Like Grace, I simply sense the pull of the tide. –*Don't leave me, Godfrey. Don't leave me.*

The herd thrived. That spring, three calves were born.

Except to the *inala* cow.

She was so small, so different from the rest, the bull, in covering her, seemed coupled with another species: a wild antelope, mythic as the *umvemve* calf had been. She could not be apprehended.

'Perhaps she is still too young,' says Godfrey, running his hand along her back. 'She is very slim in the flanks. Very unbovine. She needs a bush-bull. A smaller chap than ours.'

Grace leans her arms along the spine. 'I think we should make her our ancestral cow,' she says. 'Our *inkomo yeminyanya*, so she can talk to our shades and make things right.'

Godfrey glances at her. 'What kind of right?'

'Whatever kind of right is the truth,' she says.

'For her or us?'

'Both.'

He moves his hand along the heifer's flank and murmurs to her, nudging a reaction from her to make them laugh, turn skittish: he mistrusts pensive words, when he has no answer to them. *Whatever kind of right is the truth:* truth and right may sometimes serve a different god. 'The ancestral cow is supposed to be a great producer of calves and milk. To be robust,' he says. 'Herman's *bantom* might be a better bet.'

'No,' returns Grace evenly. 'I want only this one.'

'Why?'

'She belongs to us.'

136

'Basically, she belongs to Dr Crawford.' He is dry. Purposely.

'If I thought that, I would never have taken you down into the valley or allowed you to buy her.' She is fierce but he laughs, puts his hand to the back of her neck and shakes it very gently. 'Gracie,' he says, 'no need for lamentations.' It is all caress. He is learning to defuse her. 'You can have whatever ancestral beast you want.'

The storeman, Wilton Mayekiso, tells them what to do. He brings the helichrysum from a top camp, dries it over his own fire, puts it in an enamel *beker* and gives it to them. A beast of the ancestors, the intermediary between the living and the dead, must be treated with the leaves and flowers of the everlasting plant, have it rubbed along the back, 'Making it nice,' he says, 'so the ancestors can feel this thing that belongs to them, bringing this cow to them and making them glad.'

Grace, standing outside the byre, watches them smooth the powdered plant along the spine of the *inala* cow. They are anointing her. There is no other word for their action or for the way the *inala* cow accepts them with a still detachment, with neither triumph nor reproach. The two men stand back from their handiwork and appraise her. Grace walks away – from them, from the sound of the old storeman's voice raised in a new, declamatory praise to *inkomo yeminyanya*. What has she done? To the *inala* cow? To herself?

Both – she knows – are sacrificial now.

It is at the moment at which something is created – born into beauty – that its end is enjoined as well. It carries with it the template for its own death.

Chapter nine

∽◦⌣

At Christmas, all through the time of their childhood and adolescence, Stella and Godfrey had taken their sons to join Harold at his holiday house at the Cape. Except for during the war, when Godfrey doubled at the navigation school and kept the university department alive, giving all the lectures in his own discipline and helping out in Economics and in Classics, it had become an annual expedition. It was the only time they saw his father now, unless, on a whim, Harold decided to pack himself up for a month or two in winter and come and stay. He would ensconce himself on the sun-porch with his books and his pipe. Stella encouraged him to play bridge with a collection of old cronies once a week. They sat in the living room, silent as damp crows, snatching at points.

But it was different in the Cape. There, Harold was in his own home, directed things, wore a silk bow tie and was imperious with the servants. Stella cajoled him into walking on the beach. Clean sea, the white and blue of sky and sand, the houses at St James on the slopes above the winding coastal road, the smell of stone pines in the early morning, the heat of the metal of the railway line at noon.

Godfrey is affable on holiday. Loose-limbed, he smokes his pipe less intensely, lopes about instead of striding. His projects are out of doors. He is planting an indigenous garden behind the house. He builds a rockery and takes his sons plant-collecting. He is not pedantic about their ignorance of flower names. They will absorb them if they want to. He is more tolerant, more expansive than at home. He teaches the younger how to drive. He is patient but precise. He lends his car to the elder, without too many strictures on where he might go and when he should return, reminding himself that, at the same age, he'd fought in the trenches and commanded a platoon, been called 'sir' by men twice his age.

Stella has a sunny wardrobe and a new bathing suit.

Their company is sought by everyone they know. They are a perfect couple: pleasant dinners at the Club, twilight picnics on the beach, luncheons in airy houses or under the oaks on estates surrounded by vineyards and the scent of lavender. No show, no pretension – the restrained and gracious leisure of the educated class. Stella's beauty is diaphanous: such pure skin, such a soothing presence, floating between serenity and the lilt of laughter; her education and refinement neither overwhelming nor chilly; the perfect ease of good manners. She remains just beyond the reach of intimacy.

Harold, without his embroidered cap, sits in a chair on the deep veranda with its great panorama of the bay, a travelling rug about his knees, his book at his elbow. He dozes, his bad leg resting on a cushion on a stool. Stella has put a little bell on the table beside him so he may summon her if he should need anything. At twelve and six she brings him a gin and tonic, the lemon wafer-thin, one piece of ice. She always serves it in the same glass. One that rests comfortably in his hand, carefully weighted. She has an eye for the smallest detail, expects the meticulous in return.

Twice a week they play bridge with friends: a judge, an advocate, a university colleague and their wives. Over dinner they discuss books, politics, the disappointing stand of the Communist Party on the matter of the unions. 'Growling away without teeth, far too ambivalent,' says Godfrey. They talk about the rise of Afrikaner nationalism.

'It's all rot, of course,' says Harold Godfrey. 'Smuts won't let it happen! Not after the war. A lot of rot.' He is off on campaign again, unaware that the subject hangs on other things.

No one contradicts him. The conversation eddies round him, continues uninterrupted.

'Have a fig, Harold,' says Stella, rescuing him – rescuing herself – from offering a fatuous opinion. 'They're perfectly chilled and beautifully sweet.'

Oh yes, Godfrey and his dynasty. He observed it wryly in its familiarity, its ease. He had raged against it once. Anonymous in student bars and workers' eating houses in London and Birmingham, his voice had not betrayed him. His face was lean enough, his eyes dark enough, his accent just different enough, to set him apart. His zeal was holy.

In middle age, he had regained his sense of humour, watched his comrades slide into half-apologetic self-indulgence. Those who haven't are a bit of a pain-in-the-arse. Self-righteous, like their wives. The inconsistencies of his life did not seem to matter so much any more. He was getting older, he was tired of being on campaign – he had contributed to the African version of the Atlantic Charter, rallied protest against the handling of the 1946 miners' strike, outlined demands for the abolition of discrimination. At the university, he had been accused of seditious notions in the senior common room when he had invited a trade unionist to address a number of interested colleagues. His preoccupation with Pass Laws in 1943 might have been seen as an aberration at the time, especially with the Union's soldiers at the front, but his MC from the Great War, his work in training navigators and his deeply damaged lungs, obviated the suspicion that he could have been 'a shirker'. He was amused by the small absurdities and let them ride: his beliefs remained the same, his work proceeded. He pursued it passionately – without parade. Whenever Stella's world began to lap at his inner calm and his need to retreat became insistent – to go in search of his old mythologies, his sky-gods, his Land of Punt – he arranged a field trip and went away. His chop-box and catalogue, his stretcher and his primus were always ready.

He lived in an age when such things were possible. And expected.

He did not discuss his work with Stella. It did not really interest her but she had a reverence for the idea of it – for him – as he, when she was nineteen, had had a reverence for her. She is still safe in being beautiful and competent and charming. Their world is graceful and polite. It is a refinement on his mother's – as predictable – but with more sense and less perplexity. The only icons Stella gathers round her are her silver-topped scent bottles and the pictures of her family and their English home. She had glanced over Godfrey's mother's prie-dieu and the statue of the Virgin when she had first seen them and there had been a little trimming of her mouth. It had been brief, even unobtrusive, but he had wanted, suddenly – fiercely – to defend them against her cool, her unimpeachable Englishness.

She was a marvel with Harold. She talked to him, walked with him, sometimes read to him, chatted over tea, never allowing his irritability to ruffle her, brought him little treats when she went shopping, took him for the occasional drive around the coast. They were the greatest of chums on holiday. Her patience – and forbearance – were astonishing. It was a strange alignment, serving mutual need. Neither could grasp Godfrey's work. Together, both were safe enough to indulge a sense of self-complacency – of shared English origins – to shield each other from Godfrey's detachment and his holiday pre-occupations.

'Of course, it's having been educated here. And his mother,' Harold had sometimes said, just breaching his own 'good form' in saying it, not needing to explain further. Stella would slip him a small glance. They understood each other perfectly. It was a little private confidence between them. Besides – their awe of him was shared: Stella's guileless, Harold's grudging.

His approbation was all they wanted. It was expedience – not love – which made them allies. The prize was Godfrey. Not for both of them. For one of them.

The holidays are long. Godfrey has his building and his reading but he has left the lexicon with Grace. For the first time, he has not packed it in a box to set up on his desk in the sun-porch of their holiday home, to dawdle over sometimes during a long morning. The lexicon does not belong there. In the last year it has been transformed. It is something private, something only he may touch. He does not want a housemaid dusting the boxes any more or Stella moving them when she decides on a little sewing, just 'popping them out of harm's way'. For the first time, he has purposely divided his world. Here, in his domestic life, the other is suspended. It does not – cannot – exist. He can be ruthless with himself. He knows, by a gesture, how to cauterise it. Only, sometimes, it catches him. A scent, a sound, a little unexpected reckoning.

There is a dance on New Year's Eve. His sons and Harold are waiting on the stairs. Godfrey is late. He has been out on the mountains, plant-collecting. He has left his clothes all about the bathroom and the bedroom floor. Stella hurries him into his dress suit, has to go on tiptoe, despite her high-heeled sandals, to reach up and tie his black dress tie. She steadies herself briefly with one hand against his chest. It is an unintentionally intimate gesture, not one she usually makes. It is Grace. So far away.

He pulls the tie straight abruptly, tells her to stop fussing. He propels her down the stairs, his hand at her elbow to both urge and steady her, closes her, Harold and his sons into the car, takes the wheel and drives out, the gravel of the driveway loud under the sudden pressure of the tyres.

'Slow down, darling,' Stella says quietly. 'It's only a dance.'

New Year, for the Wilmots, has often been spent at Grace's family's cottage in the mountains. Since her grandparents' deaths it has been jointly owned by her and her uncles and aunts, used by various branches of a large, extended family, up to third cousins. Depending on who had been there last, there will be a note propped against grandfather's tobacco pot in the centre of the long refectory table, detailing whether the water pump needs attention or if the gutter has been fixed, or how many bass have been caught in the dam or whether Aunty Flo has planted a bed of herbs and won't somebody please water them if somebody would remember. For years, December and January have brought Grace here. Since her marriage to Jack, his family – Hugh's – have always been welcome. Sometimes Hugh even takes a Christmas service under the trees at the edge of the lawn, the various young nieces, nephews and cousins holding candles inside brown paper bags to shield them from the wind. Everyone has a chance to choose a favourite carol.

Two large rondavels connected by a spacious living room and kitchen constitute the main house. A series of rondavels, picturesquely tucked among the old shrubs of the garden, complete the whole. The lavatory is a longdrop, half hidden by vegetation. It is situated on a slope commanding a view of the valley below. There are no passers-by except cattle grazing commonage.

The family gathers in the kitchen in the evenings, when it's cold. The table is as ancient as the house, long, wide, scrubbed into hollows. The stove burns wood and anthracite. The cast iron pot on it dispenses, on cold evenings, lamb stew and potatoes and in the early mornings, oatmeal or mealie meal for the range of small children lined up on the bench at the table. It is a room of lamplight and soft morning gloom. It is warm. Sometimes it is sweet with the smell of cooking quinces. Grace and Hugh have gathered basketfuls of fruit from the hedge, scrubbed them, laid them out, pared and peeled them. They have been happy in this task. Both share the satisfaction of seeing the red-gold of strained quince jelly in a jar against the light: it is a memory they resurrect each year. Hugh welcomes her to the kitchen, aglow with steam and stickiness. He is running his finger round the rim of the pot. The cooling residue is the consistency of toffee. To eat it is part of the ritual. He approaches his finger to Grace's mouth, 'Here,' he says. She has no choice. The happy, rather childish camaraderie of the kitchen, the ritual of the summer quinces, will be spoiled if she turns away.

She does not. She sucks the tip of his finger briefly, laughing still, playful in retreat. She is like a fish, swimming backwards. He puts his finger in his own mouth then.

She moves around the table, out of reach, picks up an armful of empty jars and takes them outside to wash under the garden tap.

Hugh turns back to the stove. He drags the heavy kettle on to the iron plate.

'Let's have tea,' he says, his voice following her. 'Ask if any of the others want it.'

She does not ask. She washes the jars, turns them upside down on the grass. By the tap, mint grows luxuriantly.

—I'm sorry it's not mint but I can't grow it. It always dries up.

It was almost the first thing she had ever said to Godfrey, not knowing what else to say. She tears a leaf off the stem, places it on her tongue, flattens it against the roof of her mouth. She knows it is a sacrificial gesture. And she knows that it is only by such gestures – their restraint, their iron intent – that each hour can proceed with certainty. It is all she has: a strategy to mark the time.

She hears Hugh come on to the veranda, glances over her shoulder. He is bearing a laden tray. His mother is sitting on the bench, crocheting. His nieces and nephews come trailing up the drive. His sister has been reclining in the sun, pouches of flesh at her armpits turning pale pink at the rim of her costume where the cotton straps are too tight. Her hair is flat blonde, going grey, a little crown of limp curls. She is perspiring gently. 'Gracie,' she calls. 'Bring me a cup of tea, won't you? I don't want to smear the lotion on my legs.'

Grace walks across the grass towards them.

Why should Godfrey be so overwhelming a presence at this moment, in a place where he has never been, among people he does not know? It is the very familiarity of the patterned cups, the way Hugh's mother uses a cake fork – as Hugh does – as if it were a dissecting instrument, the way the children swill Oros and swing their legs back and forth on the bench or her sister-in-law saying, 'One sugar and six grains, thanks' and holding out her hand for her cup, which underscore her own bewildering displacement.

This place, so connected with her grandparents and the last peaceful years of their lives, which she had always loved for its age, its smells of woodsmoke and black pot, of damp thatch, of winter mist, of the warm underscents of cut summer grass, by its very familiarity, its promise of old comfort, only sharpens – unbearably – a sense of loss. To be displaced among what is most loved, most familiar, is the greater exile always.

She almost hated Godfrey then.

And Godfrey?

I defend Godfrey first, because I love him most. I defend him, because I need him to love me best. Making sense of what Godfrey does, may reveal what Godfrey feels.

Or not.

He is, after all, a man.

He has warned me off before for intruding.

Perhaps he did not miss Grace at all. Perhaps he put her out of his mind and cast a cool appraising eye over the many women that he met at luncheons and dinners and parties and picnics. Perhaps he had a mild, amusing flirtation with an artist, sat for her to draw his face in crayon: Godfrey at his most urbane. Perhaps he paid Stella and his sons the attention they deserved. Perhaps he had laid the lexicon aside, relieved to be parted from it for a while.

In separation is relief.

Sometimes.

Sometimes, when it is clear that an impatient word, a moment left unclaimed, a call unanswered or unmade, indicate desire to retreat.

If Grace was not ready to apprehend the signs, I must do it for her, knowing

143

them too well myself.

One day, he will simply walk away, as if he were going out to collect fossils, or take the truck to the garage, or buy supplies in town. That is how he left his Blood-Red-Woman, watching in her peignoir as he mounted the stairs to Gloucester Walk. That is how he left little Gert standing in the road, laughing, saying, 'until tomorrow'; little Gert, the graze oozing at her knee and her face puckered with the laughter that is weeping. And even as Grace says – guileless and unwitting – 'Have another cup of tea', and he replies, 'Not now, I have a lot to do', he will be setting her down too, just as he set Gert down – precisely – at her door.

–*Until tomorrow*, Gert had said.

'Until tomorrow': Grace.

A heart wound is finite. It is clean. It should never be mistaken.

In denial, it always is.

Stella Godfrey has organised a luncheon. She loves company, she loves Godfrey's wry, throw-away brilliance at the table. He never appropriates the conversation, but his wit – informed, funny, without a hint of condescension – complements her own particular flair for occasion. They have sophistication – and simplicity: it is a beguiling combination.

'What are you working on at the moment, darling?' says the artist, her wine glass poised at her lip. She is all attention to Godfrey's every breath.

'Cattle.'

'Very wonderful cattle,' says Stella, her eye darting between Godfrey and their guest.

'You would find them intriguing,' says Godfrey. 'Aesthetically, they are remarkably beautiful. They have a great diversity of pattern. In terms of colour, they range from white through every combination of dun, red – even mauve – to black. They have metaphoric names which are like small imagist poems in themselves.'

'I'd adore to paint them. Simply adore it. When can I come and see them?'

'They're a very long way away,' says Godfrey, refilling her glass, 'and in rather rough terrain.'

'I love painting *in situ*. To get the atmosphere, the sense of them. And surely, you can't revel in all that poetry with a lot of farmers and rural peasants.' She is trying to keep her words within her grasp but they are errant, slipping out of reach every now and then. Taking a wavering breath, she says, 'And who translates for you?'

'I manage very well.'

'There's a farmer who helps him,' says Stella.

'But for the subtleties, surely . . .'

'I have a salaried assistant,' says Godfrey. His 's's' are more precise, less sibilant than hers.

'From the university?' She tilts her chin. 'One of your adoring students?'

'No,' drily. 'Not one of my adoring students.'

'One should always have an adoring student at a time like that. Lionel had a handful of adoring students, didn't you, Lionel?' – turning to her husband. He has retreated into his jowls with a mouthful of cheese. 'They were always running about for him, collecting samples from ponds so he didn't have to get his feet wet. They'd flop about in frogspawn for him,' she gestures with her hand, upsetting a peach from its perch in the centrepiece, laughs, replaces it imprecisely. 'Whatever he wanted. Didn't they, Lionel?'

'I am in no danger of getting my feet wet, in my line of research,' says Godfrey. 'All I need is someone who knows if "b" follows "a" or the other way round.'

'Surely' – as if she would suck Godfrey up with the wine: it is mesmerising the way she draws it into her mouth – 'you don't need anyone so extraordinarily clever for that?'

'I need someone who understands Xhosa orthography or there would be a hopeless mess.'

'Is your assistant black?'

'No. But she is a competent linguist.'

'*She?*'

He chooses his words with care. They will be accurate: their interpretation is not his responsibility. 'Mrs Wilmot is the teacher at the local primary school,' he says. 'The Reverend Hugh Wilmot is the Methodist minister. They live in the manse and supply me with a side of mutton every now and then. One of these days I will oblige by going to service on Sunday.'

He stands to take the wine bottle away, as if it were empty, but it is not. It signifies retreat. Discomfort. He wishes to end the conversation. Now.

Stella knows it. It is too old a gesture for her to misinterpret. He is defensive. What would normally have been turned to amusement and raillery, to a cameo sketch of the good Reverend Wilmot, his wife and his Sunday sermon, parrying wit on his 'lower deck' connections, is checked brusquely and uncharacteristically. She is at a loss for an instant, then she takes up the conversation smoothly, a little laugh on frogspawn, touching Lionel on the sleeve – and the awkwardness has passed.

After lunch, when their guests have gone, she says – treading deftly – 'Were you really thinking of going to church?'

'No.' He is abrupt. 'Of course not.'

'Then why did you say it?'

'To shut the silly woman up.'

'Oh, come on' – Stella's riposte, too light to offend – 'you *simply adore* flirting with her, you know you do.'

'She'd had too much wine.'

'So had you.'

'Well then. Leave it at that.'

Stella watches him. It is a thoughtful appraisal.

Nettled, Godfrey says, 'What now?'

'I am wondering why you are not looking at me when you speak to me.'

'For God's sake, Stella!' He picks up a book and puts it under his arm. 'You're blowing a perfectly silly conversation out of all proportion.'

'Not me, Clem. You.'

'Clem': its weight is precisely pitched.

It would be perilous to answer.

They are standing in their room in the old house above the sea with the white stucco walls and the curtains breathing in and out in the breath of wind, Stella in her sundress with a faint gleam of moisture on her bare shoulders in the close pearly warmth of a late summer afternoon, clouds like shell across the line of mountains on the far shore.

That is when my computer crashed unaccountably. It simply took the file away, erasing the chapter. On the screen, the little template with the red warning icon, *Fatal error*, could not be mistaken.

Fatal error.

I had overstepped the mark. It is not for me to invent Godfrey's conversations with his wife. Just as I may not walk into the room he shares with her. She, after all, did not ask for this biography. She would have turned her cool gaze on me, the faintest lift of an eyebrow: what can I know of him?

What indeed.

We do not even concur on his name. I can hear her clear ironic laugh: it has a world of derision in it.

'Look at them!' Hugh is delighted. 'Aren't they fantastic!'

The bottles of quince jelly send refractions of light across the kitchen table. They stain the wood with rose-hip red. They are limpid, varnished. The leaves of a tree outside the window lays a shadow across them, the light shifts and glimmers, the patterns are alive. They are the faint rust and translucent red of colour-patterned flanks, an abundance of dappling. Grace and Godfrey have a word for it. Even here, in the kitchen, amidst the triumph of Hugh's jam, Godfrey intrudes!

'Now!' – Hugh orchestrating with the wooden spoon – 'We must make bread! Where's that recipe, Grace? The one Dulcie Trollip sent for the wholewheat with buttermilk? We haven't tested that yet and she says, specifically, that it's easier and more reliable than yeast bread.' He is making his own selections for the *Ladies' Guild Cookery Book*. He has been writing the introduction all week. He has taken a lesser-known verse from Lawrence Binyon as a frontispiece and said some fulsome things about Grace which are quite untrue and which she has made him cross out. She did not help him in the way she should, she has not been martyred by the Aga stove or Jack. He has written it because he wishes that she had been. He has been sketching the old kettle and a bowl of quinces to decorate the section on preserves and jams. He keeps asking her to come and see. He is far – far – from sermons and the old beige upholstery of his pastoral chair in his study at home where the light is always flat and people come at five o'clock for his counsel, the door discreetly closed, the afternoon fading quietly outside.

   –*Do sit down, Tommy Cooper, and tell me the burdens of your heart.*

   –*Yes, I know you desire Grace Wilmot. I know you lie awake at night and fantasise about her. So do I. So do I. It is a beastly business. Let us pray, Tommy Cooper, let us pray.*

It is the familiar, shared over time, that forges intimacy – affection for an object, place, habit, the idiosyncrasies of humour and remembrance: the day the calf fell into the water tank and Grandma – who couldn't swim – held on to its leg and was tipped in herself; the sight of a neighbour chased by geese, their commotion and uproar; nostalgia in the smell of stocks in spring or the deep honey scent of the Pride of Madeira, weighted with pollen-booted bees, near the front door; Grandfather with his thick white hair and the way he thoughtfully touched the tips of his middle fingers to his tongue, dabbing at them, when he was preoccupied with reading or writing, his profile, once so handsome and manly, now softened and venerable, his voice, with its unsteady laughter, its little catch in his throat.

   Within the business of living – with generosity – there is surprise at the variety, the resilience of love.

Grace and Hugh make bread together. When it is done, Hugh takes the crust off and butters it, dropping a teaspoonful of quince jelly on to it. He puts the slice on a plate in the middle of the kitchen table between Grace and himself and cuts it into quarters. No one else is there, just the two of them. The others have all gone on a *trek* along the ridge above the tree line. They will be back at dusk.

   Afternoon rain in summer, an olive thrush runs low-headed along the lawn – fat man – scudding leaves and shaking them over with his feet. They watch him through the door, laughing quietly at his preoccupations and eat the bread, drifting steam across their noses, the butter and jelly oozing on to their fingers, a drop running down Grace's wrist along the pale inside of her forearm. Hugh watches its progress. He wants to lean over and counter-run his tongue along its trail, slowly, eyes closed, up towards – and into – the palm of her hand.

Grace glances at him, turns and drags a dishcloth from the rail of the stove and wipes the mess away. Hugh takes off his spectacles and polishes the lenses on a corner of his shirt. He cuts another slice of bread.

–*Oh Grace*.

He does not say it, turns his eyes from her face, lit by the underglow of pink, reflected from the jars on the table.

Godfrey returns in March. It has been three months. Grace knows it by the sight of the truck parked in its familiar place at the front door of the house. She listens for the phone, but it is silent.

She does not go to the store to bump into him. She does not dare. Her diffidence is firmly in place: he has been far away, among people she does not know, a world that is unfamiliar to her.

She has an image of it.

It is cool and lotus-green. An imagined fragrance. Spacious. Still. There is no place in it for the grim ironstone of this thorny stretch of valley.

He sends a note by post: *Where are you?*

That is all.

The morning is endless. The small boys (do they sense him?) are tedious. It is a day for spilling sticky things and getting grit in the eye or – mouth open – breathing laborious bubbles of snot: *–Desmond, go and get some lavatory paper and wipe your nose.*

When, at last, school is over, she sweeps the car keys from the hall table and hurries out. She backs carelessly over the edge of Hugh's flower bed, crushing a little clump of crassulas.

'Where's Grace gone with the car?' Hugh says to Tommy Cooper when he comes in for lunch.

'I don't know,' says Tommy Cooper, 'but she buggered up the flowers when she drove out.'

Hugh frowns and pours himself a glass of water. 'Did she say she wouldn't be here for lunch?'

'I didn't talk to her.'

Hugh spoons cottage pie on to Tommy Cooper's plate. 'Did you manage to repair the tractor you were talking about?'

'Almost. I must go along to the store later and collect a part that was sent up from town.' He stabs at the crust of potato. 'Do you want anything while I'm down there?'

Hugh tucks his napkin over his knee. 'Not that I can think of. I'll let you know.'

Not looking at him, Tommy Cooper says, 'I believe Dr Godfrey's back.'

Hugh does not reply. He pours another glass of water. He uses the prong of his fork to unblock the hole on the top of the salt cellar. He glances up at the clock on the wall. 'Got to rush.'

It is only half past twelve.

Tommy Cooper is noisy with his cutlery. Hugh puts his plate on the sideboard, excuses himself and leaves Tommy Cooper to guavas and custard.

When Tommy Cooper calls down the passage, quarter of an hour later, 'Sure you don't want anything from the store, Mr Wilmot?' Hugh opens his study door and says, 'Don't worry. I'll go later myself.'

'But Mrs Wilmot has the car.'

'Of course.'

'You can come with me, if you like.'

Hugh hesitates. He runs his palm over the cockscomb of hair, shifts his shoulder. 'No. Thanks very much, it's not important. I'll go when she gets back.'

'It might be too late.'

'Yes.' He wants to shout obscenities at Tommy, standing immovable in the passage, his big boots on the parquet. 'Perhaps.' He withdraws and quietly closes his door.

There is heat at the root of his tongue.

He hears Tommy Cooper's truck: he has gone to the store, not just for a tractor part but to nose her out. He can see him, craning in the cab of the truck, ducking past the rear-view mirror and the windscreen wipers, mouth agape. He will come back and say – conspiring – 'Saw the car at the store, but didn't see Mrs Wilmot. I wonder where she could have been?'

He cannot bear to think of Tommy Cooper's crass imaginings. They would be vile.

Grace parks outside Godfrey's door.

He is not in the house. He is down at the cattle byre.

She lets herself out at the back, almost tiptoeing along the path between the sweet-thorns. She walks into open pasture.

He is standing by the wall, his pipe in his mouth.

She is hesitant.

He turns, seeing her. He puts his pipe in his pocket and holds his arms wide, striding up towards her. Already he is laughing. Her extraordinary constructions of aloofness, of distance, of detachment, are overturned.

It is all so simple, after all.

She runs, laughing too.

'Where have you been?' He rocks her to and fro, then leans back, pulling her head away from him, gently at the nape. 'Let me look at you,' he says. 'Let me look.'

'I thought . . .' she says.

'Whatever you thought, was a load of crap.'

'What did I think?' She is laughing again.

'That I wasn't coming back.'

Her arms are round his neck.

He says, 'That heifer of yours has just turned her nose up at me,' glancing back at the byre. 'She didn't give me the time of day. Just flounced off as though she didn't know me and didn't care to. I thought, Grace will do exactly the same. All prim and school-marmish: –*Who are you?*'

'That cow has more sense than me,' she says. 'Much more.'

Hugh draws the curtains of his study. It is always a decisive gesture. He has heard Tommy Cooper's truck return. Now, Tommy Cooper is whistling in the bathroom – the noise of the taps, the thrashings in the bath, the thud of the chain of the lavatory.

He takes his Bible down and opens it and sets it on his desk. He pulls the typed pages of the cookery book towards him and flips through them: Karoo *fynvleis*, jugged venison. Among '*Miscellaneous*', *Useful Xhosa Phrases*: *serve the tea, wash the floor, polish the silver, roast the meat.* Grace had said they should not be in the imperative. It was rude. Her own versions (Dr Godfrey's?) were far too complicated for the average housewife. He had pointed out that all phrase books dealt in the imperative.

–*Haven't you seen the ones from the mines?* he had said. –*After all, it's the tone of voice that counts.*

–*It's arrogant to command or patronise.*

Godfrey again?

–*Since when have I patronised?*

–*In here!* And she had pointed at the pages.

He lays them aside as well, walks to the window and lifts the edge of the curtain. It is not quite dark outside. The garage is still empty.

The telephone rings. It *will* be Grace. He walks briskly into the hall, ready with his pastoral voice. She will be telling him she is not returning for dinner. He has something to say to her.

It is not Grace. It is his mother. 'Is that you, dear?'

'Yes, Mom.'

'I want to come for the weekend, dear, and I wonder if I caught the train on Friday morning, if you or Grace could fetch me from the station.'

'This Friday.'

'Yes, dear.'

'I don't think so, Mom.'

There is a sudden silence. 'Why?' The little tremor in her voice is instant: she has a way of making it sorrowful. It is worse than whining.

'Grace is away.'

'Away?'

'Yes.'

'Where?'

'I have absolutely no idea.'

'Don't be ridiculous, Hugh. You must know where she is.'

'Why should I know?'

'Because you live in the same house. You always know where she is.'

'I'm not her husband.'

'Is something wrong?'

'No.'

'Is she safe?'

'I doubt it. I think she is in great peril.'

'Hugh! What on earth has happened?'

'I am being facetious,' he says.

'Well, don't, Hugh. It's not nice in pastors. It gives a wrong impression. It's most unlike you.' A silence. Then she says, 'You have really upset me, Hugh. You make me feel very unwelcome. You have never done that before. I'll speak to Grace.'

'She is not here.' He is patient. 'I will tell her to phone you if she ever comes back.'

'You are being most peculiar. It's not fair of you.'

'I am not always a fair man,' he says. 'And I have a meeting in three and a half minutes. I must go.'

He puts the receiver down and stalks back to his study. He looks at the clock. He looks at the manuscript on his desk. He adjusts the angle of his lamp.

Tommy Cooper comes to the door. He says, half whistling through his teeth. 'I managed to get the part for the tractor.'

'Good.'

'I saw the car, but I didn't see Mrs Wilmot.'

Hugh sits, his fingers peaked tip to tip.

'I left a note on the windscreen to say you wanted the car. I hope it was the right thing to do?'

Hugh does not reply.

Oh yes, he can see Tommy Cooper going down to the Ford parked by Dr Godfrey's door, darting his eyes here and there. Listening. Breathing in between.

He can hear him talking to the storeman and to people in the shop: – *Have you heard the one about . . .?* Some smut to do with the bloke who fancied the vicar's wife.

'I saw old Herman de Waal at the store,' says Tommy Cooper, keeping

151

his eyes on the square of carpet on the floor. 'He was there getting paraffin for his boys. I asked him if he'd called on Dr Godfrey. He said, no, he'd call on him when it was more convenient for Dr Godfrey because he didn't believe it was convenient right now. And then I said, "Well, his truck's there. He must be home" and Mr de Waal said, "Mind your own business, young man".'

'Well, perhaps you should,' said Hugh.

'I was only trying to help.'

'So are we all.'

Grace comes in at five to seven. Just in time to serve the dinner. She is carrying an armful of files and a box of cards. 'Sorry I'm so late,' she says. 'Dr Godfrey's back and I had masses to explain to him.' She turns to Tommy – 'I got your note' – back to Hugh – 'I should have checked if you wanted the car but I thought you had a meeting in the church here.'

Hugh does not look up from his paper.

Grace puts her things on the hall table. She comes into the living room. Tommy does not meet her eye. 'I tried to phone but the line was engaged so long, I gave up. Are you ready for supper?'

Hugh says. 'Mom wants to come on Friday but I put her off.'

'Why?'

'I told her you were away.'

'Why on earth did you say that?'

'Because you are.'

Tommy Cooper gets up and goes through to the dining room, bumping the standing lamp as he passes.

Grace says, quite coolly, 'I'll phone her after dinner. And tell her I'm back.'

–Have you heard the one about Witbooi and his umfazi?

–Have you heard the one about the vicar's wife?

Have you heard?

Like Hugh, I can see Tommy Cooper, ungainly in his stealth and haste, thrusting the note under the windscreen wiper of the car, all alert in his deceit and greed to see them and remember. Tommy Cooper – like the leguaan – testing the air with his tongue, melting away into camouflage behind the old machines crouched in the pasture round the house. Tommy Cooper in the guise of probity. Stinking with deceit.

–God, I'd like to give her one . . .

Going through the cards, I find again Godfrey's entry which I had placed in the Bute Snuff box:

[*–qolo* (*u(lu)qolo* n.)

152

i) Ridge. *Uqolo lwezimpungutye:* the ridge of the jackals i.e. in a lonely place; a place of weeping, lamentation.]

The ridge of jackals. A lonely place to be.

The destruction of what is transcendent for one – a shrine, a pilgrim place – is so easily, so thoughtlessly achieved.

Others – and their fatal words, their perfidy. Their profound incomprehension.

Chapter ten

I have seen a jackal on a bare ridge at dusk. It is not cunning that saves it from the snares of farmers, it is wisdom. It knows how to adapt to the slow encroachment on its world. I have seen it stand, frozen in its colouring against the background of rock-shadow, earth, the angle of the ashy grass. The eyes, even in their stillness, are the only thing that might betray its presence. That still observance, always poised. Man denigrates it for its scavenging, its killing of lambs, its ranging into what man has claimed for himself.

–*Shoot the vermin.*

It will survive: it has its own pitiless integrity.

It is not denigrating Delekile to compare him with a jackal. There is no shame in scavenging when the world he occupies had been leached long before he entered it. He stands at the side of the road and tries to sell his wire creations. No one travels by besides the odd truck, a farmer on his rounds. What would the farmer want with a wagon and oxen made of wire snipped from one of his own fences? He is more likely to give Delekile a thrashing or to call the police. He has never learned the principles of Delekile's form of survival, just as he will never understand the jackal's. He never wants to. That is his tragedy. And Delekile's tragedy as well.

So Delekile – thin, tubercular, a little tuft of spare moustache – comes and gives his work to me and I take it away to town and try to find a market for it in some bogus theme complex, announcing itself '*A Theatre of Shopping*', with a mark-up that will make the little that I bring to him an insult to his artistry. I have no choice – there is nowhere else to go. I cannot bear the supercilious picking-over by the shop assistant of his work, the flat 'leave it with me and I'll

154

see if I can sell it', returning every month and finding the little sculptures standing forlorn, the scabs of rust beginning, sent, finally, to the sale table, half-price, until I take them away. And when I come back to the valley, he is waiting – an unobtrusive figure – his eyes alert. If he does not take his chance he will not eat. It is as simple as that.

I hover between shame and resentment. I don't know what to do. I wish he would go away.

He does not go away. Why should he? At the moment – for the moment – I am one of the few resources that he has. When I am gone, he will have to find another. It is my problem if I indulge in sentiment. He cannot.

His need is far more urgent than that. And if, sometimes, I fear him – his sullenness – it is myself, my vacillation, that I fear as much.

Fear may sometimes be a self-indulgence too, an excuse for a lack of generosity. It is easy to say (that old lie), 'I mustn't get involved' and then believe it.

When I am gone, he will remain, washed up among the stones – and so will this ridge, this high, dark ridge against the bleached sky. I have never climbed it. It was burned a few years back. It has not restored itself. There has been too little rain to replenish bushes and the flame-singed aloes stand, a company of bone.

–*We will meet at last on the ridge of the jackals, i.e. a lonely place to be; a place of weeping, lamentation.*

Weeping, lamentation.

Such words anticipate response. But what if there is none? In the old mythologies, the jackal's voice is solitary, distant. It is only apprehended in the language of the stars. That I learned from Godfrey too: the stars, the hunting-jackals of the sky, call *tsa-tsa-tsa-tsa*, echoing the hunting-jackal of the plains. It is their own lament. It invites no consolation.

Delekile knows that.

Godfrey knew it too.

So did Grace.

Perhaps, unlike me, they had often climbed that ridge, tackled the barren slope behind the store, reaching the place where the grass napped the upland, cooler and more temperate, where their cattle grazed, stood silent, listening to the tug of the grass and the slow swish of tails, flicking at the flies. Perhaps they had walked to the edge of a fold, where *kiepersols* grow grey-plumed and softly scaled among the other ancient vegetation.

I have often imagined it.

155

They go there on the day that Hugh and Tommy Cooper went to town. Hugh had a Synod meeting and Tommy had business with the bank, an appointment with the dentist and a need to see his girl.

Hugh, fretting, had tried to persuade Grace to come with them. She had declined. She could not leave her pupils until one o'clock. They had a games day. She could find no one to replace her at such short notice.

'Shall I keep dinner for you both?' she says to Hugh.

'No,' Hugh replies. 'I said I'd eat with Mom and fetch Tommy at his girlfriend's on the way back?'

'Why don't you stay the night and leave early in the morning? It would be much more sensible.'

'That is perfectly unnecessary,' says Hugh. 'I don't like you being here alone and I can't condone Tommy spending the night in a young woman's lodgings.'

'I'm sure Tommy would be delighted.'

'Loose talk, Grace. Don't be flippant,' says Hugh austerely.

She needs to hide her jubilation. She says, turning away. 'What time will you be back.'

'About half past ten, eleven. Don't wait up for us.'

'Oh, I might.'

She almost skips from the room. Hugh watches her, feeling the fleeting energy in her. The upsurge. Later, in his study, he hears her go to the telephone in the hall.

The conversation is brief.

When she brings him tea, he says, without looking at her, 'Who were you talking to?'

'Desmond's mother.'

He knows that she is lying. Her face, for all its calm, is alight.

He takes his tea and turns away.

I wish I could have walked with Godfrey on that ridge, in his real presence, as Grace had done that afternoon, heard his footfall on ironstone and earth, coming to a place where rocks fitted into one another like the carapace of the tortoise I had seen. Trying to trace their lives, I scan their place for their geography – my geography – searching for the cipher in the little map that Godfrey drew, trying to divine what each, or both, held dear and in remembrance.

The *inala* cow has wandered off. They do not see her with the others in the pasture.

'Where's our cow?' says Godfrey, shading his eyes against the slanting sun and looking about.

Grace follows his gaze. 'I hope she hasn't got herself stuck in the ravine.'

They are high above it, looking down on the crowns of trees and the tumble of rocks in its fold.

'Come,' says Godfrey, turning to take her hand and lead her over the edge, down the scree and into the shadow of trees.

They walk along the base of a *krantz*, fluted by water. Against the grey of an implacable cliff face, a small flower hangs by a hair-thread of root, the tendrils of petal opened to the light. Within the gloom, like motes of light, bees move in drowsy parabolas, coming and going from a crevice in the rock. There is the scent of honey. Looking up, the concentric crowns of trees, the tips of branches, leaves, lap the high clean sky. They stand silent, Grace's back leaning, rested, to the curve of Godfrey's chest, listening: the voice of bees, of water, wind, the faint easing of the rock face, its softer echoes.

The *krantz* curves away to the left and the trees thin. The gloom is paler, a soft green translucence and the wind reaches in among the underbrush, coming up the valley. It is a warm wind. Dry. They find their cow just within the last trees, at the margin of the thorn scrub where the *krantz*, unprotected by vegetation, rises flinty and bald towards an empty sky. She is no longer a rust-red and white *inala* cow, a flicker of colour across her flank. Under the margin of shadow, she is transformed into bolder, darker patterns.

'*Ematsh'ehlathi*,' says Godfrey softly against Grace's temple. 'That which is the stones of the forest.'

'*Ezikhala zemithi*,' smiles Grace. 'That which is the gaps between the branches of the trees silhouetted against the sky.'

The cow moves out into the sunlight and the shadows shift. Again, she glimmers with the faint translucence of rust and cream.

'*Enala!*' they say together. 'That which is abundance!'

The heifer turns to them, with her small solemn face, her dark eyes, her ears tipped with light.

She is not just abundance.

She is a radiance as well.

It is a word that Grace will associate with Godfrey all her life. It is not just the word for the *inala* cow, standing serene in the late light of afternoon, watching them – *inkomo yeminyanya*, cow of the ancestral shades. It rests in other moments.

Radiance.

For her, it is a sacred word.

It is his word for love.

They drive the cattle down themselves, the *inala* going before, turning her head now and then as if she is beckoning them, as if she knows that she

157

must lead them to the byre. Grace walks at her side, Godfrey behind, pipe in his mouth, striding, keeping them to the path. They walk in lightness, down to milking. Behind, the ridge is darkening. It rears, stark, against the violet of the evening sky.

Later, it rains. It drums on the corrugated roof, filling the *dongas*, sheening the leaves of the *garingbome*, leaning to the wind. They lie and listen in the early dusk, cocooned in the shadow of the room, a light, cool dampness at the window. They hear the sighing of the sky, sense the vastness of the moving clouds – way beyond the ridge of jackals and the iron road. Godfrey seems to be asleep. Grace can feel the length of him, turns slowly, curling in against his side. She cannot see his face in profile, but she knows its lines, its stillness in repose.

I am under your rib, in the shelter of your heart.

I breathe with you – breath of my breath – in striving or in quietness.

I lay my face to yours, my shadow to your shadow.

I lie against your back, articulated to your spine, my arm beneath your arm, elbow cupped to elbow, hand to hand, ebbing with the quiet tide of sleep.

I do not dream: I am not searching for you here.

You are in my blood, which cannot be divided.

He stirs, searches for her hand, laying her palm within his palm, enfolding it.

'Say a poem for me,' she says.

It is his voice she will remember. Its quiet comfort. He gives each word its weight.

Its radiance.

Of all things, it is most beloved.

At nine, the telephone rings, waking them.

Grace is instantly alert. 'Oh my God! What's the time? It'll be Hugh.'

Godfrey turns on the light. He peers at his watch, gets out of bed and walks, naked, down the passage to the phone.

It is Herman de Waal. 'Dr Godfrey?'

Godfrey can hold the telephone receiver away from his ear to hear him. When he speaks, it is as if he is calling to a stockman in a distant camp. The voice must carry, after all, over such a distance. 'Can you hear me?' Herman shouts.

'Mr de Waal?' says Godfrey. 'News travels fast in this place. How did you know I was here? I only came back a few days ago.'

'Ah.' Herman de Waal betrays nothing.

'How are you?' says Godfrey. 'Did you have an enjoyable Festive Season? How's the family?'

'In the pink,' says Herman de Waal. 'In the pink.'

'Good show.'

'There's a stock sale early tomorrow morning,' yells Herman. 'Can you make it?'

'Where?'

'Stock pens in town. I've been hoping you'd be back. I need some support on the Nguni business. I'm having a bit of difficulty in being allowed to market them with other cattle and I want to get rid of a few steers. The auctioneer is giving me the runaround. You'd think I was trying to sell buffaloes. I'll pick you up if you like. Sorry to give you so little warning. I hope you're not busy.'

'When?'

'Seven-thirty tomorrow morning.'

'Right. Seven-thirty.'

Godfrey returns to the room.

Grace is already dressed. She is pulling on her shoes. She looks up at him, sideways through her tousled hair. 'Hugh and Tommy will be back by half past ten. Hugh will be wild if I'm not there.'

She goes to him as he pulls on his trousers, puts her arms about his neck. 'I just want to be allowed one night until morning. Only one.'

'So do I.'

He kisses her on the forehead. 'Get your things and I'll bring the truck round.'

As he goes out of the back door, letting it swing closed behind him, the telephone rings again. Without thinking, Grace starts down the passage and answers it.

It will be Hugh. Suspicious and frantic. Frantic herself, she must stop him from phoning around, looking for her.

What will she say?

—*Mind your own business, Hugh?*

—*Go to hell, Hugh?*

—*Sorry, so sorry, Hugh?*

'Hello,' she says, ready for battle.

'Good evening.'

It is not Hugh. She does not recognise the voice. It is a man's. It sounds elderly.

'I hope I have the right number?' By the tone – brisk, almost familiar – it is Grace who feels the intruder. 'Is Dr Godfrey there?'

'He is out just at the moment. I can get him to call you back. He should be here in about half an hour. I can leave a message?'

159

'To whom am I speaking?'

The hesitation is brief. 'His assistant.'

'Could you ask him to return my call. It is his father.'

'Certainly, Mr Godfrey.'

'Thank you.' He rings off.

It has been Godfrey's voice. Without the warmth. Without the charm.

Grace replaces the receiver. She is shaking. Her palms are damp. She presses them against her thighs. Oh God, why had she answered the phone? What if it had been his wife? And what is 'his assistant' doing there at this time of night?

She runs out to the car. 'I've just done the most idiotic thing,' she says. 'I'm so sorry. I didn't think.'

'What's the matter?'

'I answered the phone. And it was your father.'

Godfrey says nothing.

'I'm terribly sorry. I was in a panic. I was sure it was Hugh.'

'We were working late.' Godfrey is glib.

It sounds appalling.

It is appalling.

She thinks, then, of Tommy Cooper's note, a few days before:

Mr Wilmot said I should say he needs the car.

Didn't want to disturb you.

Voices closing in. People watching. Someone listening on the party-line?

What did Herman de Waal know? What had he sensed?

What, Wilton Mayekiso?

What, the storekeeper?

And Desmond's mother? What if Hugh bumped into her? What if she looked back at him and frowned and said *–Mrs Wilmot didn't phone me about Desmond.*

And now, in the darkness, with the rain slanting down, she is pinned by the headlights of the car.

–Is Dr Godfrey there?

That cool, patrician voice.

'Your father has never phoned before,' she says, searching for excuses. 'I thought you hardly ever spoke to him.'

'No,' says Godfrey tersely. 'He never does. He only phones when he wants to come and stay. It's a ploy to get me to turn it into an invitation from my wife.'

'Do you think something's wrong?' Grace can feel her heart in her throat. Godfrey does not reply.

–Is Dr Godfrey there?

Is Dr Godfrey there?

Godfrey drives fast. His hair, usually so smooth, is sticking up. She cannot reach across and touch it. He would recoil as if she had released a spring. His face is set in profile.

'I thought it was Hugh,' she says again.

'It's not your fault.'

—It is my fault. All of this is my fault.

All of it.

An owl lifts from the dust of the road. Godfrey swerves to avoid it. The headlights catch the eyes of a hare. It wheels, sharp on its haunch and is gone, put to flight. At other times, they would have slowed and wound the windows down, letting in the soft dust of dusk and searched for the footprints in the sand. Now, there is only the jarring of the wheels on the corrugations and Godfrey's small curses under his breath when he has to brake.

Long before they reach the house they can see the lights. The car is in the garage.

Grace says, 'They're home earlier than they said. Leave me at the gate.'

Godfrey slows, leans over and opens the door for her. She turns to him, her cheek against his beard. He puts his hand briefly, firmly, to the nape of her neck. 'It's all right,' he says.

But it is not.

She is out of the car and hurrying along the drive. She turns and sees Godfrey's face flare into light, a beam reflecting back from the bush in the rear-view mirror. It is a strange, spinning image, distorting him.

Grace lets herself into the kitchen. She kicks off her wet shoes. She walks down the passage to Hugh's study and knocks. She goes in before he has answered.

He is not there.

She sits in his pastoral chair and waits for him.

She hears the front door open and his step in the porch. She is suddenly – unassailably – calm.

She listens.

Hugh has a way of closing that door as if he is performing some small ritual, leaving something of himself outside on the steps. The priest, perhaps – the carefully modulated language (*—my dear brothers and sisters);* the particular back tilt of his head?

He will hang his keys on the hook by the umbrella stand, letting them dangle on the decorative brass key rack. He will go to the dining room and take a piece of fruit from the bowl. If he chooses an apple he will extract his penknife from his pocket and pare it in a perfectly controlled spiral. If it is an orange, he will cut the rind from the ends, score the skin deftly in sections and pull each off. He will come to his study bearing a tiny starched napkin and the fruit on one of the small square plates his wife had prized so much.

He opens the door and is halfway across the room before he sees Grace sitting in his chair. He simply looks at her and takes another seat. He opens his knife and begins to peel his apple. She has never seen his face like this before. She has never seen any face so unaligned to its usual calm.

She wants to kneel at his feet, put her hands in his lap and say, 'I am so sorry, Hugh,' not because she has wronged him but because the deconstruction of everything believable to him, is happening as she watches him. His fingers are steady in paring but the knife slips and the peel is sliced through before he reaches the base of the fruit. It falls to the floor. He bends down to pick it up. The blood is high in his forehead and in his neck. He is sweating.

All her self-justification is nothing, not in the face of this collapse. She does not know what to say.

At last Hugh speaks, clearing his throat. He does not have his pastoral voice. He simply says, 'It is your life, Grace. You are not beholden to anyone.' She expects him to say, 'except to God' but he does not. Then he says, 'But Dr Godfrey is.'

'Yes.'

'And?'

'I haven't had the guts to think about that.'

He waits.

'I have never been betrayed, so I can't comprehend it,' she says.

'Does that justify it?'

'Of course not. It is terrible of me.'

The apple is untouched. Its flesh is white, shining where the skin has been peeled away.

'What are you going to do?' he says.

'I don't know, Hugh.'

'Neither do I.'

He could be talking about himself. He moves as if his flesh has been singed away, leaving him as exposed as she. It is almost a complicity. He says, 'I'm so sorry, Grace. About all of it.'

'Why should you be sorry, Hugh?'

'About Jack. About Dr Godfrey. Me. So sorry.'

She goes to him and sits on the arm of the chair, half facing him. Her hand encircles his head, draws it down. 'It's my own fault,' she says – echoing him – 'about Jack. About Godfrey. About you.'

'You couldn't help Jack's dying.'

Her hand is gentle at his temple. 'No. I couldn't help Jack's dying.'

162

Then she says, quite simply, 'And if you'd been Jack, this conversation would have been the same, Hugh. It would have made no difference.'

He does not recoil as she thought he would.

He knows.

For Grace, Godfrey is beyond explanation. Beyond reason.

It is something that he understands as well as she.

She releases him, stands, walks quietly to the door. Hugh lets her go. There is nothing more to say.

As he drives, Herman de Waal is full of news, full of breeding programmes. He does not draw breath. He mentions nothing personal. He is more garrulous than usual. His daughter, Dulcie Trollip, sits between him and Godfrey in the front of the truck. She is going with her father to the sale. She is learning about stock. Her husband Arthur, bewildered by the war, is staying behind to see to the dipping of the goats. He will stand with his arms crooked over the bars of the dip, shoulder height, like a man in stocks, supporting his weight. He no longer has strength in his legs. He would rather hang by the nape of his neck.

Dulcie is a sturdy girl. She has sturdy legs. Her hair is wound in a lustrous chestnut plait about her head. She has a gap between her front teeth which is beguiling. She sits very straight between her father and Dr Godfrey. She turns her head every now and then to see if the steers, tethered in the back of the truck, are secure.

'How's my young bull doing?' says Herman. 'Have your cows knocked the cheek out of him yet?'

'He's very fond of the heifers you sold me,' says Godfrey. 'But he's not so keen on the ones I got from Xaba.'

'Who's Xaba?' says Dulcie.

'An old man who lives near Enseleni.'

'That's *doer* and gone, man. How did you get on to him?'

'Heard about him from my assistant.'

'That old *skelm*, Wilton, at the store?' says Dulcie.

'No,' says Godfrey. 'Grace Wilmot's grandfather knew him and she remembered that he had a big herd. So, I thought it might be a good lead to follow. Getting in some diversity, you know.'

There is a small silence. Herman de Waal is looking for something to say. Dulcie Trollip turns to check on the steers again. Her ear lobes are aglow. Godfrey, suddenly alert to their discomfort, says, 'If I come back with you, you can have a look at them and see what you think. They are really very nice indeed. Two of yours are pregnant already. Two of Xaba's are a bit young still. Only one, that I expected to take, won't have anything to do with the bull. I'm a bit concerned about it. She doesn't seem to fancy

163

him.'

Herman laughs. 'Can't please them all.'

'She is particularly beautiful. I want to breed with her, if I can.'

'Beauty is never the best criterion in judging a good heifer,' says Herman de Waal. It sounds like an admonishment. Did he also mean –*Beauty is never the best criterion in judging a Good Woman?*

'I haven't given up hope yet.'

Indeed.

Herman de Waal shifts gears rather awkwardly and the steers in the back jerk and clatter. He slows for them to restore their balance.

'If a heifer doesn't take the first time, you usually have a problem,' says Herman. 'Ask Dulcie.'

'You'll have to cull her, Doctor,' says Dulcie Trollip.

'I don't know that I could do that. I'm particularly fond of her.'

Dulcie Trollip laughs a little gruff snort of a laugh, not unkind. 'You can't be sentimental about them, you know. They're not people. It doesn't help in the long run. It only gets you into big, big trouble.'

Godfrey is silent.

It is a motley lot of cattle in the pens at the stockfair. They mill about, the stockmen standing, leaning on the poles that divide the pens. The auctioneer is on the podium drinking tea, pushing a *vetkoek* into the steam, talking to the manager. There is an urn on a trestle table and an array of white cups. A woman is taking payment for refreshments. Dulcie Trollip joins her, bringing a large tin of sandwiches. They count out change, are ragged by the farmers. Dulcie stands with her hands on her hips, head tilted back in laughter. The stockmen and herders gather at a distance. There is no tea for them. Someone passes round a tin *beker* of thick, cold sour porridge. It goes from hand to hand.

Tommy Cooper is sitting on the raked seats, his socks around his ankles, his teaspoon standing upright in his cup. 'Hello, Oom Herman,' he says, rising, shaking the old man's hand.

'Tommy.'

'Good morning, Dr Godfrey,' says Tommy Cooper.

Godfrey has never met him before. He shakes his hand.

'Don't you know Tommy Cooper, Doc?' says Herman de Waal. 'He's managing the farm at Vlakfontein, over near the school.'

'How do you do,' says Godfrey formally.

So this is Tommy Cooper. Grace's impertinent, infuriating Tommy Cooper.

–*Mr Wilmot said I should say he needs the car. Didn't want to disturb you.*

Godfrey searches his pocket for his pipe. It seems the best thing to do.

Tommy Cooper's neck is hot and his voice is loud. He is like a big dog who has just flushed out a snake. He doesn't know whether to bark or run.

The stands fill up. The auctioneer is impatient. It is time to begin. He is flexing his voice. People drift away from the tea table.

A tall, stooping man walks in, gazes about vaguely, skirts the perimeter of the seats. Godfrey looks across at him, says to Herman de Waal, 'There's Humphreys from the Veterinary Department.'

Herman follows his gaze. 'That's him. Good bloke. Know him?'

'We went to school together. Played cricket in the same team. Very good bloke.'

The man is about to pass them to find an empty seat. Godfrey touches his arm. 'Humph?'

He glances back. A smile creases up around his eyes. This is a man who has spent his days out of doors. He is bleached below the eyebrows. His throat and his forearms are burned deeply to the cut of khaki collar and sleeve. 'Godfrey.'

Godfrey shakes his hand, other palm to his forearm, a gesture of affection. 'Have you come to check up on us all?'

'Policeman Humphreys,' says the man. 'Quick stock check, health check, check on shady characters like you!'

Tommy Cooper makes a small grimace, just a flicker. Godfrey does not introduce him. 'Have a seat.'

'Why're you here?' says Humphreys. 'You're the last fellow I expected to see. I was talking to some chaps at an old boys do and wondered where you were this year. Someone said you were in Zululand, writing dictionaries.'

'Still am. It's a lexicon of cattle terms. I'm finishing it off here by doing comparative work with Xhosa. I'm devoted to the local herds.'

Again – just a little too obtrusively – Tommy Cooper shifts his legs.

'Mr de Waal and I have a project with Ngunis,' says Godfrey. 'Cross-breeds and trying for a purer strain as well. I'm working with Crawford too. He roped me in when he heard that I was in the field. I must say, I've found it so fascinating, I have started a small herd myself.'

'Once you're bitten by the bug – man, there's nothing you can do. It's like falling in love . . .' says Herman.

A nicker from Tommy.

'The only problem,' continues Herman, 'is keeping the doc from over-enthusiasm in the reserves. There I go, offering introductions to any bloke within a hundred square miles who's been converted – nice, well-inoculated animals, tick-free, papers, the lot – and he runs off and brings a *trop* of bush cows up from Enseleni which, mind you, only moo in Xhosa and turn their noses up at my bull! What's the world coming to?' He is still laughing as he says it, gives Godfrey a small friendly shove. 'But listen,' he says, forearms on his knees, hands linked, talking more confidentially, 'I get worried about the attitude of other folk. They're very conservative, they don't like the old patterns interfered with. We've got a lot of work to do to convince them about the advantages of indigenous animals.'

'What advantages?' says Tommy Cooper.

Herman de Waal ignores him.

Humphreys says, glancing at Tommy Cooper, 'Oh, there are advantages, believe me. I'll be very interested to see the results of Crawford's work twenty years down the road. I think these animals will surprise us all.'

The first cow is brought in, calf following. Startled, she barges into the paling, lets fly a barrage of loose dung, half slips in circling round. The auctioneer's, 'Whoops-a-daisy', brings a laugh. She frets at the barrier, bewildered, stricken, as the auctioneer starts his patter. In retreat, she blunders through the open gate, cannot find her way out along the narrow passage to the holding pens beyond. She is trying to turn in too small a space to see if her calf is following. Panic makes her graceless.

'Are you serious about breeding?' Humphreys says to Godfrey.

'It's early days still. But there's something intriguing about them. Somehow, they're a metaphor for something elusive, rather more important than we're aware of. I'm still trying to work it out.'

There is a small silence. Humphreys seems a little at a loss. Sensing it, Godfrey says lightly, 'Look, I know I'm only a play-play farmer in comparison with my friend here,' turning to Herman de Waal. 'But I think I understand the constraints he's dealing with.'

'And there are quite a few,' says Herman. 'I have to make a living, but I'm in agreement with the doc about the need to experiment. I've been doing it for years against the opinions of others. But I've always believed we have to make the best of what we've got. There's also a vast number of people in rural areas who are also stockmen. These blokes haven't got the resources, they have to plough their own land, they have to have animals which will cope with the pasture available. This nonsense about only breeding with European bulls in the native areas which you blokes brought in in the thirties, is pretty short-sighted.'

'I'm starting to agree with you,' says Humphreys, 'but it originated in the idea that "improving" things was necessary and only European stock "improves". That was the thinking then. I suppose it still is.'

Godfrey gives a small snort. 'And a wealth of indigenous characteristics bred in over millennia is lost along with traditional African wisdom and experience – not to mention the wider damage done to society by such monumental condescension!'

'It all comes down to money,' butts in Tommy Cooper. 'And farmers deal in pounds, shillings and pence. There's no play-play about it. That's what counts.'

'What an unfortunate world it would be if we all felt the same,' Godfrey says drily.

'Why must we behave like natives?' retorts Tommy Cooper.

Godfrey's gaze is slight, ironic.

Tommy Cooper says again, persisting, 'Why must we behave like them . . .' – the pause is brief – 'with cattle . . .' – he dares it – 'or with women, keeping one for home and one for work?'

Tommy Cooper is triumphant. He is running his hand over his head. There now! He has put that Dr Godfrey in his place and said what everyone else knows and is too *poeperig* to say because he is a professor or whatever. He glances up to find someone to grin at. No one is looking at him. They are watching a set of three young steers jostling, bewildered, in the ring.

Godfrey flashes him a glance. His contempt is magisterial.

'Very poor quality,' says Herman de Waal peremptorily, gesturing abruptly towards the steers. 'Can't see why this lot should be "an improvement".' He turns his shoulder on Tommy Cooper.

Humphreys, the vet, glances from one to the other, vaguely bewildered – *What was that about?* – and returns his attention discreetly to the ring. 'These must be yours now,' he says to Herman de Waal as a pair of young patterned animals trot in. They are delicately sprung, like painted rocking horses. They are white with black stippling on the flanks. 'Nice conformation at the withers,' he says. 'Very nice.'

No one bids for them.

'See what I mean?' says Herman de Waal. 'I don't know how we're going to get past this notion of "bush cows". It's a bloody losing battle.'

Dulcie Trollip comes along the stand and squeezes in beside her father. 'Sorry, Pa,' she says. Her plait is slipping down to her nape. She pins it up with quick, deft fingers. 'We're just not going to give up on this, see? But maybe we'll have to breed in more beef to make them heavier. Get a bit more Afrikander into them.'

'People don't like them because they look scruffy,' Tommy Cooper says to her. 'They like things to be nice and even, like you expect them. Not *bont*. It's confusing, man.'

After the sale, the farmers gather at the tea table again. The auctioneer joins them. He has a stock of auctioneering jokes. He swills his tea and grins at his own wit. Tommy Cooper says, 'Hey, I must tell you the one about Witbooi and his *umfazi* and his father's spook . . .'

Perhaps it is unfair to denigrate Tommy Cooper. He is, after all, a young man who went to war. He fought bravely through the Western desert. Perhaps, then, his closest link to normality – to sanity – was his repertoire of jokes.

167

When implacable forces are moving against one, perhaps the only respite is in the ridiculous. –*Listen, God, have you heard the one about the vicar's wife? You'll like this one, God, it's really quite a hoot.* Else he might panic at the vastness of the desert, its relentless silence, the menace of an unknown enemy. If Tommy Cooper had ever ventured beyond the perimeters of the camp, its little man-made margin of detritus marking out his place, if his mind could have comprehended such a thing, what would he have said, if – by chance – he had stumbled upon a cave with paintings – a grave, stately pantomime of cattle, thousands of years old, linked by the harmony of horn and hoof. Could he have said – dared – in this still sanctuary, celebrating the diversity of colour and of pattern, so ancient, so reverend, –*They are scruffy,* –*They are bont?*

Such a speculation is unnecessary: Tommy Cooper would not have ventured there at all. He would have waited for the end of daily duty, patient as an ox, eager for a pack of smokes, for a letter from his girl at home, stirred up the ashes of his fire with a friend and leaned his back more comfortably against the wheel of their armoured car. The logic in their laughter – and perhaps their tears – would be lodged in news from home.

–*Hey, have you heard? Listen here, man. This is what Reggie's popsie did when he was sent up North.*

–*Holy shit! Read it out again!*

–*You won't believe it! Reminds me of the one-eyed chap trying to look through the keyhole to see if his wife was getting up to something . . .*

Light another smoke and fall about with laughter. The little point of fire in the fingers, passed between them, is the only light on which they can rely.

Dulcie Trollip brings a tray of tea across to her father, Godfrey and Dr Humphreys, still sitting on the raked seats after the sale has finished. She has brought, too, a mound of polony sandwiches, cut thick with a leaf of garden lettuce in between. She says, 'One of the cattle boys wants to buy a *tollie*, Pa. He just came and asked me if he could speak to you.'

'See,' says Herman de Waal. '*Now* the blokes are going to laugh at me! The only person who wants to buy one of my animals is a native boy! Only thing is, it shows he's got more sense than anyone else. And *now* the problem comes about how is he going to pay for it!'

Godfrey does not remark: it is a tired assumption. He chooses a sandwich. Herman goes with Dulcie, following her out to the stock pens at the back.

Humphreys follows them with his eyes, smiles. 'Handsome girl,' he says.

'Very knowledgeable about cattle,' says Godfrey, absently. 'She's a valuable assistant in the whole operation.'

Humphreys watches her a moment longer, turns back to Godfrey. 'Keep me up to date with progress on this project. You know where to find me. I'm back in the office in town a few weeks each month. I often drop in to the university to see a chap in the lab who's very helpful with blood analysis for my tick research. I visit him quite regularly. If you let me know when you're back in harness, I'll come by. Only thing, if you're bringing cattle up from the valley, I must confess I'm concerned about whether they've been dipped.'

'Crawford has his reservations about dipping.'

'That's all very well in a closed herd but you have a lot of other susceptible cattle around here and the last thing you want to do is antagonise the locals. They won't be sympathetic. It won't help the cause.'

'Of course.' Godfrey relights his pipe. He is silent a moment. Then he says, 'If you had a particularly good specimen of a young cow and she wouldn't take the bull, what would you do?' He is busy with coaxing a glow. He does not look at the vet. 'Any suggestions?'

'Cull her.'

'I was hoping you wouldn't say that. It seems a harsh thing to do when she is really such a beautiful animal.'

'No use being beautiful without being able to reproduce.'

'That's what Dulcie said to me this morning,' Godfrey is rueful, half laughing, 'and she's a woman herself. She said I couldn't afford to be sentimental.'

'Dulcie?'

Godfrey looks up. Dulcie Trollip and her father are coming towards them again. A slight indication of the chin, 'Dulcie,' says Godfrey.

'Ah.' Humphreys stands as they approach. 'Good advice,' he says. He watches Dulcie Trollip for a moment, then he says, 'Come on, Godfrey. You're a scientist too. I don't need to tell you what to do. You know the score.'

'Sold,' says Herman de Waal. 'But not on the "never-never". I put my foot down at that.'

'These chaps really love their cattle,' says Dulcie Trollip. 'You should have seen the grin! But we've got to take them home again until he can scrape up the money and come and fetch one. He says it's for *lobola* so you can imagine how long it's all going to take. It's such a palaver and how the hell is he going to transport it? All the other nigs were standing round, chaffing him. Couldn't you hear the racket? *Bonga-ing* away as if he'd got a whole herd. It was sweet, man, seeing him so happy.'

Dulcie is pinning up her hair again. —*It was sweet, man, seeing him so happy.* She grins up at Godfrey. She is so artless, so without guile, it would be churlish not to grin back. He carries the tray for her, returning it to the table. She walks ahead, chatting easily over her shoulder to him. Herman de Waal and Humphreys follow.

Little incidents, misconstrued. Reinterpreted. Walking with someone, seen by someone else – a whole series of stories emerge which have no foundation.

–Aha, Dr Godfrey, I saw you sitting in the university grounds with a young woman.
–Only my student.
–Indeed?

Grist for someone else's fiction, floating here and there, to be taken up, at random – or to lie dormant and unnoticed, sometimes for weeks, even months.

'Wouldn't mind doing research in Godfrey's neck of the woods,' says Humphreys to his colleague, poring over a microscope together in the lab. An assistant brings them coffee, the professor, at the next bench, is casting his eye over a list of results.

'Why? Where's he working?'

'The other side of Vlakfontein. Very barren stretch of country. Nothing for miles. He's started a herd of cross-bred Ngunis with a chap who's been interested in them for years. The old fellow's doing nice work. Quite pioneering, really.'

'I'd hate to be stuck out there. No pubs. No girls.'

'It has its attractions, believe me.' Humphreys laughs. 'It seems his daughter is Godders' assistant. What a handsome little wench she is, with a fine head of plaits, handy with stock!'

'I wonder if she's handy with anything else,' says his friend, jokingly. He is a hearty young man, preoccupied with conquests which he always hopes to make. 'Some blokes have all the luck!'

'Good reason to apply for sabbatical,' says Humphreys, humouring him.

'Is that what they call it these days?'

The professor looks up, alert, lays his papers down. Idle talk is one thing – but idle talk about a colleague, as senior as himself, is very bad form.

He fulminates about it to the Dean. It is an illustration of the very thing he has been talking about for months: the serious lack of discipline among junior staff, the laxness since the war. The lack of decorum. He has a particular reverence for reputation. He expects others to have the same.

'But, whenever there's trouble,' he says ominously to the Dean, *'cherchez la femme!'*

'Not Godfrey,' replies the Dean mildly.

'No smoke without a fire,' says the professor, stoking the fire himself. He could have chosen something less banal – but he is a scientist and wit is not his forte.

The Dean laughs about it with a colleague of Godfrey's. The butt of the joke is the fulminating professor, not Godfrey. The point – the parochial preoccupations of the self-important. 'The picture of Cromwellian rectitude,' the Dean remarks wryly. 'Poor old Godfrey!'

Weeks later, at a bridge evening organised by Stella in honour of Harold's visit (always diligent in finding things to entertain him and to keep him occupied), Godfrey's colleague, searching for small talk, mentions – rather tactlessly – in Harold's presence, what the old professor had said, mimicking, with exaggerated gravity, ' "*Cherchez la femme*"!'

Harold snorts. *Cherchez la femme*, indeed! What a lot of bollocks. He takes himself off irritably.

It nags at him all evening.

He recalls his telephone call – all that time ago – and a young woman's voice, rather breathless, even a little fierce:

–He is out just at the moment. I can get him to call you back. He should be here in about half an hour. I can leave a message . . .

She had been perfectly professional, perfectly correct.

And Godfrey had returned his call: *–My assistant told me that you'd phoned*, mentioning her, without the slightest hint of consciousness.

Harold Godfrey had put it out of his mind then.

Rather firmly.

But now, on this chance remark, this rather vacuous comment – '*cherchez la femme*' – the woman's voice is very clear.

In its diffidence, its hesitation, it had conjured youth and grace.

And something of anxiety.

It had been nine o'clock at night.

What was a woman doing there at nine o'clock at night?

–Working late, indeed!

When the guests have gone, he says to Stella, rather brusquely – and too suddenly – 'I think it's time Clem came home.'

'He's still busy in the field. He'll be there for ages yet.'

'This running about with cows is ridiculous. He should have a proper job.'

'He has got a proper job,' says Stella, frowning slightly.

'At home.'

'At home.'

'Get him back.'

Stella looks at him, suddenly attentive.

She does not push the point. She knows him – and the code – far too well for that: by saying nothing, honour and discretion have been served. She must interpret this as he intends.

Stella would not have said, blustering –*There's no smoke without a fire!* She is far too fastidious with words, with thought, for that. But an ember of anxiety, –*Are you really going to church?* has been rekindled.

Mrs Trollip, with her basketwork of thinning plaits, the stiff folds of her Fasco dress, all her treasures carefully displayed about her living room, waiting out her time with the coming and the going of the swallows, her ashtray and her box of cigarettes handy on the nest of tables by her easy chair – what would she have thought, if she had heard that chance remark: –*What a handsome little wench she is!* and known how fateful to Godfrey and to Grace it had proved to be?

In all its innocence.

Despite her gruffness, her asperity in loneliness and age, I know – now – that Dulcie Trollip, peering through the greenish magnifying lenses of her specs at the picture of herself in her wedding dress, her brothers, touching with bent fingers the stiff pages of her mother's photo album, understood, even if she never found a way to say it, that Love – even Beauty – is admissible.

They had even been admissible in her. So long ago.

Chapter eleven

'Perhaps I'll have to cull her,' Godfrey says.

Grace turns from the desk and stares at him. The set of cards she is working on is poised in her hand. She lays them down.

'When I went to the stock fair, I was talking to Herman de Waal and a chap from the Veterinary Department called Humphreys.'

Still, she is silent.

'I didn't want to mention it to you at the time. I couldn't contemplate it for myself. It seemed impossible.'

'What did they say?'

'If a heifer doesn't take, you have to accept she's not going to be a breeder.'

'Perhaps it's the bull.'

'The other cows are pregnant.'

She turns towards the window then. She can see the cattle in the pasture. Wilton Mayekiso is with them, leaning on his stick, absorbed: the age-old harmony of stockman and beast. He is no longer a man with cows which he carries only in imagination. She hears him, speaking to them, conjuring their praises.

'It's a simple matter of expedience, Grace,' Godfrey is saying. 'We both accepted it when we went into it. We understood the risks. We jumped together, knowing that.'

Together, yes.

'And now?' she says.

'And now, we have to deal with the consequences.'

'So you are going to ship her to the abattoir.'

'If she is barren we can't send her to Crawford's station in Zululand. He won't want her. If she can't reproduce, she's of no use.'

'Intrinsically?'

'I don't know, Grace.'

'Yes, you do.'

Oh, yes, you do, Godfrey.

'What do you want me to say, Gracie?'

She wants to remind him that the *inala* cow, the ancestral beast, can never be culled or sold. She is symbolic, proof of transcendence – in existence and for them. She cannot be sacrificed to science.

And Grace knows he cannot say it. Just as he cannot say that anything between them is too important to override expedience.

Perhaps, after all, their reverence for the shades, their delight at the quirks of synchronicity, of sign and pattern – the reawakening of wonder – have been only a game between them. In the end, the aesthetic, the spiritual, are all a self-indulgence. A little joke. An excuse to give weight to something rather ordinary – even paltry: –*Have you heard the one about the vicar's wife?*

She picks up the cards, tapping them together, gently, on the desk.

He comes to her and leans her in against his shoulder. 'It's just bad luck,' he says. 'We must be practical, Gracie. We have commitments to Crawford and to others. We have expenses. In the end, it's the right thing to do.'

She says – as she had said before – 'We must do whatever kind of right is the truth. That's our commitment.'

'To who?'

'To God.'

'And if there is no God?'

She draws away from him. 'Then to Crawford.' Her voice is flat. 'And if we do that,' she says quietly, 'nothing has been sacred.'

It is put aside – as anything is put aside that is impossible. Neither wishes to think about it. Neither dares. And the little *inala* heifer grazes in the pasture, tugging at the grass, flicking her tail – its slim long elegance, such perfect conformation, so much more gazelle than cow.

The other cows calve. The byre is a nursery. Grace and Godfrey watch them grow into their knees and skins. They are all moist nose, little polished hooves.

–*My calf has boots!:* Godfrey recalling what he had said to his mother as a small boy, watching the *umvemve* calf poised beneath its dam's side, butting for a teat.

In the quiet of the afternoon they work at the dictionary. The summer pasture is flattening out to dryness. The early flowers have disappeared.

'We're nearly at the end,' says Godfrey, surveying the boxes of catalogue cards.

Briefly, he meets Grace's eyes.

'I will miss it,' she says, turning away.

They work at their usual pace, Grace sitting with the cards, Godfrey checking them, looking over his reading glasses at her, half humorous, sometimes grave. He types at the kitchen table – reports, a paper, a letter to Crawford. She knows that he is making arrangements for the transportation of the herd from the railway siding. Soon the cattle will be gone and the stone byre they have reconstructed will stand empty, settling back under the encroaching bush, the sweet-thorns, the *gwarri*, the kraal aloes clambering among the ironstone.

Partings are usually anticipated, planned: conversations, gestures, what will be said – by one and then the other. It is carefully rehearsed – and turns out quite differently. I have followed Godfrey from the moment of his birth, heard his voice before I committed words to the page, listened for his tread. I have *seen* him. Here – he is standing at the window holding negatives up to the pane. The light and the empty sky beyond give them clarity. He is labelling each. Grace is not there yet. She will come, after school. He will listen for her step on the flagging of the back veranda, hear her light, quick call from the kitchen, turn and see her in the doorway – and her face, as if she thought – believed – that he was gone: her relief in finding him, her little laugh of gladness.

The telephone rings and Godfrey lays aside the negative he is labelling and walks down the passage to the hall. 'Godfrey,' he says.

'Clem.' It is Stella.

He is cheerful. 'I didn't expect you to phone until this evening. Is everything all right?'

'I don't know. Perhaps you can tell me that.'

'What do you mean?'

'Harold says you should come home.'

'Is he ill?'

'No, he's fine. He just wants you to come home.'

'Why on earth should I come home if he says so?'

There is a pause. 'Clem – *I* want you to come home.'

'Is something wrong?' He is gentler then.

'I don't know, Clem. Just come home.'

'It's very difficult to simply leave. I'm nearly finished the dictionary. I have to arrange for the cattle to be railed to Zululand. It's not that easy at the moment. But, of course, I'll come if you need me. Just tell me what it is. Is it the boys?'

'No, they're well. I telephoned each of them last night. Perhaps you should speak to them yourself some time.' The sentence is too long. Her voice wavers.

'Stella?'

'It's not Harold. It's not the boys. It's you, Clem.'

He hunches a shoulder against the phone box, bends his head in, keeping her voice contained within a small space.

'Clem.' She is in command again. Now there is an edge to how she speaks. It is no longer supplicating. 'I'll expect you by this evening.'

'This evening?' He is about to laugh her out of it.

'This evening,' she says.

I do not want to imagine how Stella feels. I only sense the slow creeping fear she might have felt, like an infusion in the blood, numbing it, that finer instinct, sensing his preoccupation: his face, turned from her, an unawareness of her presence when he works, knowing he is somewhere else, that he has been somewhere else for a long time. No specifics – just an absence in his eyes.

Harold says, looking up from his paper, 'Is he coming?'

'Yes,' says Stella crisply. 'Tonight.'

'About time.' Harold shakes the paper slightly and continues scanning it. He is not reading, though: he is sitting in the Club at the lunch table on a hot day in February, almost thirty years ago. His son looks back at him, those deep-set eyes – like the mother's – slightly haughty. Dark. He says, – *I would like to visit Mother's grave.* There is something monklike in the thinness of that fine-boned face. A forbidding purity. Harold is afraid of him.

–Shall I come with you?

–*No thank you.* A glance: the cold dismissal of the one betrayed.

The absolute barrier. The implacable distance.

Harold knows, too well, the dread of a betrayer, the poison of deceit.

Now, his son knows it too.

It should arouse his compassion, even a small ironic humour. Instead, he feels a chilly little indignation. A scorn.

At himself.

And the wish to maim, because of it.

Partings must be planned. The time to say the right words, to remember a caress, to return it, to mark, with a touch, what is intimate and loved: an ear lobe, a knee, the temple, the little hollow where the sternum ends, the veins of the inner wrist, lids closed against the comfort of a cheek. The whole cartography of love must be secured.

176

But sometimes parting is not planned. No sign. No mark. Only afterwards, the headlong grief. And then, in retrospect, the small unnoticed intimations are recalled, the signs, rising to the surface: Gert, standing among the shards of glass, laughing out of fear; Godfrey's Blood-Red-Woman, examining the stain on her fingers as she hands Godfrey his hat and sends him out into the street, glancing up, knowing that his face is already turned away.

Grace walks into Godfrey's house with a basket of vegetables, the carrots and turnips still covered in soil, ready to be pared and cooked with a dab of butter for supper, when they have finished the afternoon's work and walked down to see the milking in the byre. She puts the basket on the table and goes to find him. He is in the bedroom throwing clothes into his suitcase.

'Where are you going?'

His smile gives no alarm. He says, cheerfully, 'A summons from town. I'll be back in a day. Two at the most. Let's have a quick cup of tea.' He reaches for her and gives her a kiss in passing. She picks up his shoes from the corner, pushes down the lid of the suitcase for him to fasten it.

They stand together for a moment, linked – this inviolable little room – then he goes out quietly. She draws the calico curtain across the row of clothes, takes up the paraffin lamp to refill it and to trim the wick. Fleetingly, there is a sense of sanctuary, a closing calm: she has performed a valedictory rite.

Godfrey is out at the truck as she sets the cups on the table and boils the kettle. He comes in, puts an arm about her neck, noosing her. It is the gesture that he used to coax the cow when they had found her at the byre at Enseleni. It is the gesture that he knew, so long ago – boy, heads butting, playful – when he led the small *umvemve* calf into the house with Gert.

'Is something wrong at home?' she says.

'Nothing to worry about.' He does not mention his conversation with Stella.

They seldom speak of their domestic lives. It is a matter of honour, of discretion towards others, to keep it circumscribed. The longer they have worked together, the more they have created a separation from the outside world and this retreat. Identity, for each of them, remains within the precincts of this place. They do not wish to imagine another. They do not dare. Nothing must intrude. Even the lexicon stands in its wooden boxes with the little polished brass handles on the desk, no longer carried back and forth from the university when Godfrey has to go: it belongs with Grace.

'Will you phone and tell me when you're coming back?' Grace says.

'Of course.' He takes her hand and chafes it gently.

'I'll see you in a day or two, then. I'll just carry on with the work.'

177

'How far are you?'

'Almost at "*V*".'

He makes no comment: he knows what the first entry will be, recalls the notes he made years ago.

Imvalamlomo: what closes the mouth.

He reaches for his cup, draws it within his fist, warming his palm. Despite the calm with which he sits at the table with her, he can feel the slow-kindling ember in his gut, betraying him. He looks across at her and smiles, puts his hand to her cheek. She leans her head into the caress. It is tender, calm.

He glances at his watch. 'I must be off,' he says and stands briskly. He may not linger. He scoops up his keys. The embrace is brief. He is handing her away before she is ready to let him go.

–*Don't leave me, Godfrey.*

She watches from the door. She notices, as he drives away, that he does not look back, with a wave, a grin. He does not turn his head. He is too intent.

Something is amiss.

As the truck takes the curve of the hill, she lets her eyes lift to the iron ridge, the long line of it, the bald *krantz* and behind, the pair of equidistant hills, the faint wavering line of the dry river-bed.

She goes into the house and washes the cups and dries them and sets them on the tray, as if for his return. The constriction in her throat is the start of tears – with no reason – when his hand is still so warm against her cheek.

I am afraid to follow Godfrey home. I have always been afraid to go with him. I cannot construct his conversations with Stella. I know nothing of their intimacy. Or their laughter. Stella will not allow it. Why should she?

She does not want to know about the work.

She does not care about the cattle.

She tolerates no intruders.

I do not blame her. I am also a wife. I cannot have another snatch at intimacies that belong to me. I would be outraged.

So, preoccupied with penance, I return to Grace, as afraid to leave this sanctuary as she.

I want to justify it for her – and I can't.

I want to tell her that she has her own integrity: I can't.

I want to tell her I believe – like her – that Love and Beauty are admissible. I can't.

It is late when Godfrey arrives at his front gate. He parks the truck in the street. Harold's car has taken his place in the garage. It leaks a slow patch of black-green oil. The stain has been covered with sawdust. Godfrey's protracted absence has given him rights.

Godfrey looks at it a little sourly.

Harold is standing on the veranda. He is wearing his Afghan cap. His small round spectacles flash discs of light. He is upright, hands clasped behind his back: he is on campaign.

'Dad.' Godfrey comes up the steps, sets his suitcase down, puts out his hand. The exchange is brief. 'Is Stella in bed already?'

'I think so,' says Harold. 'She went upstairs straight after supper. Want a drink?'

A drink is defence against anything unpleasant.

'No thanks,' says Godfrey.

They go inside. Godfrey leaves his suitcase in the hall. Harold is at the sideboard. He pours a whisky. Godfrey looks directly at his father. 'Why have you called me back?'

'We can talk about it in the morning,' says Harold. He glances tentatively at the door.

Godfrey closes it. 'Now,' he says.

'Then I'll come to the point.' Harold's lip quivers at the edge of the glass, slightly prehensile, seeking out the liquid. 'It's about your assistant,' he says.

'Yes?'

Harold gives him a look. He knows it well. Once again, small boy, he stands accused – bewildered – between his mother's distractions and his father's iron will.

'Well?' Godfrey's voice is cold.

'It's been intimated to me,' says Harold. He takes a sip, 'Just to me' – he takes another. 'There is talk – no doubt it's loose talk, but talk nonetheless' – he puts his glass on the sideboard – 'of a liaison.'

'Talk?'

'A colleague of yours. Humphreys.'

Godfrey's blood is beating behind his eyes. 'Humphreys?'

'His remarks were relayed to me.'

'Humphreys?' says Godfrey again, incredulous.

'He saw her with you,' says Harold.

'Oh, good God!' Godfrey turns from him, walks to the mantelpiece, faces him. 'That was Herman de Waal's daughter! She breeds cattle with him. They took me to a sale.'

'She is not your assistant?'

'No. She is not my assistant.'

Harold is standing, his head tilted back, as if scenting evasion. Godfrey does not pour himself a drink. He will display no relief. Only a man without honour would have felt it. And how could he, when the truth – in so preposterous a guise – has been so nearly spoken?

'This man, Humphreys, has not met your assistant?'

'No. Humphreys has never met my assistant.'

'Then he is wrong?'

'He is wrong.'

'I am relieved to hear it.'

Godfrey has an inclination to knock him down. He knows exactly with what care his father is selecting 'facts': in time, he may relay them, without compromise to himself. He hates him for it. He hates himself for having learned so well – so deftly – how to do the same. They do not fool each other.

'Does Stella know anything about this?'

'No,' Harold takes up his drink again. 'But I sense she is uneasy.'

'Because you made her.'

'Because, for good reason, I felt the need to protect her.'

'That's my job.'

'I would have thought so.' Harold looks at him directly, says deliberately, 'Don't play with fire, Clem. I'm not a fool.'

Fleetingly – this once, just this once – Godfrey cannot hold his gaze. 'I'll go to Stella now,' he says.

'There will never be a reason to mention this between us again,' says Harold. There is a hint of triumph.

'No.' Godfrey turns from him: it is the drawing of a blade. 'There will never be a reason.' There is nothing acquiescent in his tone.

The children are drawing. Grace has taken the crayons from the wooden locker and placed a handful on each desk. In the heat she walks along the rows. Small heads are bent, the little shiftings of shoes and scuffings of heels. She goes to the window and looks out across the playground to the house. The old bell'ombre tree seems to grow from hunched shoulders, leaning to the stone wall around the vegetable garden. The windmill creaks its morning sound, easing its joints. Hugh is standing on the back veranda talking to the gardener, showing him where to trim the creeper on the wire pergola beyond the kitchen door. She can hear a laugh, a small exchange, Hugh's hand on the man's shoulder. Hugh walks away then, glances over at the school. He does not see her but his face, for an instant, is exposed – clenched – as it had been when she had sat on the arm of his chair, facing him. –*I'm so sorry, Hugh*.

There is nothing of Jack in the way he walks, in his build, in the colour of his hair. Jack did not have sloping shoulders or tread with his feet turned out, but there is something in the face, its expression, the slight bewilderment

180

that she knew from long ago: she had upset the certainties, the order of his world. For Jack, love had been perplexing. It is so for Hugh as well.

Hugh stops, looks up at the sky, at his watch, then stands with his head bent, slightly cocked, as if he is talking to someone. It is not Hugh at prayer. It is Hugh battling Hugh. It is fierce and private.

She backs slowly from the window, turns. Little Desmond is looking up at her, his hair askew from how he had slept and counter to the way it usually grows. Only one of his front teeth has come through. He says, very solemnly, 'Who are you talking to, Mrs Wilmot?'

'Was I talking?'

'Yes.'

'What did I say?'

'I'm so sorry you . . .'

The others have put their crayons down. 'What a silly thing to say.' She laughs.

It catches in her chest: a faint drift of nausea, trembling in her throat. Mimicking her, the little hiccup in her voice, the children laugh as well. Except Desmond. He has the same expression of perplexity as Hugh, as Jack. He has seen her face: a certainty – an absolute – has been disturbed.

I go back to the university rather wearily. I hate the start of term and all the disruption. The first year students are strangers, the seconds intent on new alliances. They choose their seats in tutorials. It is all so predictable. The pecking order – its odd convolution – establishes itself instantly. I can tell within five minutes who will colonise a seat for the rest of the year and who will not. Those who don't are either diffident, dithering at the door, or they are the sort who are eager for disruption and parade. Like Grace's little boys, both can be very tedious at times. It will take a week or two to settle down into the old complacence, the sloppiness, the mid-term spread of grubby T-shirts, sockless sports shoes and dingy skin.

I am feeling disconsolate. The prof was in the States in the vac, delivering a paper. He has returned affable and rather fat. He has a throwaway worldliness which will last until the first batch of essays comes in and he has to sit down to mark them. At every tea break he has a new slant on Americans, on academia, on coffee shops, on the press. He a great authority on everything, drops names which he knows will go unrecognised by me: I have long accepted how parochial I am. Oddly, my lack of information makes him indulgent, if a little lofty. He seems quite pleased to see me.

Pleased enough *not* to ask me what I have been doing: he has far too much to tell.

I am glad to be spared. I am a perfect audience, a perfect repertoire of –*Really? –Fantastic! –Tell me more*. I would not let a word about Godfrey or Grace or

181

even the cattle out of my grasp. Like Godfrey, leaving his catalogue boxes in Grace's keeping, my preoccupations are not for anyone's scrutiny. I will guard them fiercely. But I wander about with an odd, persistent little melancholy. It asserts itself at mid-afternoon. I take it with me to my daughters' ballet classes, sitting in the car outside the scout hall, listening to the piano. The tunes for the barre exercises have never changed, the teacher's voice, over generations, – *One, two AND, pum-pum-pum,* clapping in time. *–And one and two AND* . . . Beyond its pitch – softer, greater, is the sound of the wind in the stone pines. A small desolate lament for whatever is lost, wherever, however. *–And one and two and relevé.*

And one and two.

I take that little melancholy with me in the afternoons, to the quiet corners of our garden, away from the persistent sound of the phone or into the research library where I turn over the old volumes and search for his name, obsessed with signs, inventing them when none are to be found. Going to the car-park I take the long way round, crossing the quad, skirting the fountain. I glance at the door of the Senate chamber. He is in there with his faint amusement and his pipe and his still, ascetic face.

–I see you, Godfrey.

The melancholy lodges. A quiet little grief.

I cook the supper with it.

I weep in the bath because it has sunk itself in me.

An *isithinzi* – a small perplexity – like his mother's, gnawing from the inside: that persistent little yearning, that secret search for grace. It seems so assuageable.

And sometimes on a *bergwind* afternoon, surreptitiously, pretending business elsewhere, I take the road past the house where Godfrey and Stella once lived or linger outside Godfrey's school. That fleeting boy – Godfrey with his grave face, his tender lip, his straight, dark hair. There is a benediction in the deep shadow of high stone walls. I have ventured on to the secluded lawn outside its oldest building (holy turf) where the sports teams pose for pictures. It is too damp and sunless for the grass to grow. Instead, a kind of small, flat, shining pennyroyal is thick on the ground and the old Virginia creeper is branched across the masonry like veins on a strong man's arm. I have stood and imbibed the smell of pines – dust and resin – as he must have done, I know the scent of wet blue jacaranda flowers, popping slightly as they fall on damp tar roads.

I am Grace, alert to him, even in the turning of my own head, knowing he has walked where the roots of trees have pushed up the paving, past this low stone building, past this high whitewashed wall. But there is the prof sitting in a coffee shop reading the *Mail & Guardian* and waving it at me to join him.

'I must describe to you this place I visited in Boston . . .' he begins before I have had a chance to tell him I can't stay.

And Godfrey retreats.

I am no longer Grace.

I am a colleague. 'Got to dash. Have to fetch the kids from dancing.'

I can see him purse his lips. It is amusing to him that I am so middle class. *The kids*. When he has children of his own, he will suddenly find, against every inclination, that they (if they are girls) will want to go to ballet too. They will desire – more than life – a tutu and a paste tiara and fairy wings. It will not please him. All his present discourse has not been brought to bear on the deep, the primal need for a pink vinyl handbag with a snappy bobble clip, a Barbie doll with glitter shoes, a turquoise pony with the satisfying scent of moulded plastic. I tried to dress my daughters up in *jalimani* dungarees with applique and bright red buttons. They were scorned, very early, for cerise and turquoise Ts embossed with plastic comic characters which melted in the tumble-dryer. His hand-crafted wooden train, his puzzle blocks, his array of Edu-toys and Edu-books, will never have the same appeal.

I hurry off, telling him, for the third time, how much I admire his paper. There is nothing more that I can say which will not sound repetitive. I even have a new insight on Derrida. I take it away with me and record it on one of the cards I have bought to imitate Godfrey's. I have written in pencil at the bottom – *What do you think of this, Dr G?* Who was your god when you came back from leave? How many times did you stride about the corridors of the London School of Economics and sit at the feet of the great Malinowski, make excursion to Oxford to listen – awed – to the frosty Radcliffe-Brown, return to set an essay, posing the question, *'Is Social Anthropology a Science or an Art?'* in deference to the sensibilities of both.

Such imponderables. No one has resolved them yet.

And how did you feel about the students who said it was a Science? *QED*. And those who said it was an Art? *Maybe/ Perhaps/ Not sure*.

And how many times did you set that question, Dr Godfrey, before you had to make the choice yourself?

Ten years, Godfrey.

Ten years.

Did anyone ever suspect how your allegiance shifted?

And why?

I wonder.

Godfrey listens to Stella as she speaks, saying little. She is formal, clipped, retreating to the nuance of phrase and gesture familiar to the world from which he had rescued her so long ago.

She is in her English place.

There is no ironstone or aloe. No mythology of stars.

Her meanings are clear. She is precise.

–Is there a reason for his protracted absences beyond the demands of fieldwork?

–Is there any need to stay away to write up his records?

–Can't they be completed at the university?

She is a woman of unimpeachable honour and intelligence. There is right and there is wrong. To betray her quiet integrity, her order, is reprehensible.

To dishonour her, unthinkable.

She is loyal to the fact of him, the principle of him.

He is her husband.

She does not deal in ambiguities. The present is her concern, his restoration – *now* – to his family and home. His private ambitions and beliefs – his old griefs, the histories that cling to him – are secondary to the family good, the family name, the order and restraint for which both of them are so well known.

He hears the sound of her gown as she moves about the room, swift to barricade him in, reclaim him – from this moment on. Nothing unpleasant will be surmised. Nothing unpleasant will be said. She is dealing with the present – and with how it will proceed. She has no patience with imponderables: no child exists in her understanding of him. No boy. Why should they? His distant past – his need to seek its restoration – does not concern her. She had no part in it. He is an adjunct of herself, born at their meeting, augmented on their wedding day. She has long been impatient with the notion of his mother, her melancholy, her neurosis, her search for absolution: the muddle of it all. And yet – so often, so unwittingly – secure in the custody of him, she becomes his mother, standing underneath the station clock, watching the inexorable minute hand, waiting to reclaim him.

Hearing her, watching her, he stands amazed – as he once had stood amazed, in youth and ardour – at her quiet force, her presence. It is cool and Virgin blue.

He is reverent to its beauty, its fatal calm.

In silence, he listens and allows his own brisk subjugation. He capitulates – wearily – to the sanction implicit in her voice, to her rightness. Not his soul, not his laughter, not the tide of life in him – but his word.

And whatever he has done – however silent now, however fierce and unregretful he may be – that word will bind him.

It is almost a relief.

He will never overturn her world.

And, knowing that, what did Godfrey do? Did he take her in his arms to assuage her fears, make recompense, do whatever was expected to restore her equilibrium? Or, respecting her restraint – and permitted to withdraw – did he go to his study, close the door, turn on the reading light, sit at his desk and take up his mail, opening his letters with the paper knife she once had given him, slitting them cleanly along the upper margin, laying the accounts in one pile, the correspondence in another.

Neutral.

Unemotional.

Unmoved.

I can imagine nothing which might be authentic. I can invent no words for him which could be plausible. Domestic-Godfrey – Stella's Clem – is an unimaginable stranger. No doubt, between them, they have their language and their rituals, their laughters and their irritations; their silences; their intimacies. Perhaps, after all, that is the authentic Clement Godfrey. And this Godfrey, *my* Godfrey – my Godfrey of the little building by the store, my Godfrey of the ironstone hills and the aloes and the cattle byre – so beloved – is only a shadow-man.

An invention.

Not just for me – but for Grace as well.

In the morning Stella goes out at ten.

'I'll be an hour, Clem. Have you seen – there are cards from the boys and a letter from Cambridge?'

She takes Harold with her, leaving Godfrey with his correspondence and his tray of tea. Such discretion, such self-restraint: she allows him time to do whatever must be done. She knows, when she returns, the task will be complete. She will not pry. Any indiscretion on Godfrey's part is his own failing. She will indulge him – but only so far. He is well aware of the rules. He will follow them.

How can one be human in the face of such restraint? How can one be human if sin is not the thing indulged in – and regretted – but the shame of being tempted in the first place?

Godfrey hears the car drive away and puts his cup aside, untouched. He stands. He arranges the articles on his desk. He pulls the blotter straight, aligning it. He takes the pencils from the pewter mug in which they stand, dividing them from the pens. He picks up the paper weight and tests it in his palm. He replaces it on the surface of the desk. The sound of it is heavy and sharp – a footfall in the room. He can see his face distorted in the round glass surface, prism-ed with the indigo and scarlet of the pattern in its heart.

He goes to the door. Opens it. Walks down the passage to the telephone in the hall. Takes up the receiver and dials the exchange. Above him, the morning laps at the ceiling through the fretwork of the fanlight over the front door. He traces its pattern with his eyes, back and forth, back and forth.

I wonder what it's like to lose – precipitately – the right to intimacy. To know, by the sudden turn of a shoulder, the swift set of a face in profile, a word, that the end has come.

Just like that.

The implacable anguish of that moment.

Or to lose a spouse one has loved and lived with for many years – *flesh of my flesh:* it surely must be grief which lodges, not only in the heart, but in the womb, even if it is long past childbearing. The womb feels first, in the deep foundation of its flesh, its blood, the ebbing of life, the presence of its own death, as it once – in joy – sensed fecundity. Hands are boneless then, cannot echo any more, palm to palm, the unity of bodies, striving for creation, either in their reaching, or in fingers fiercely locked. It is defeat without the honour of a fight, a slow attrition, without the hope of resurrection.

Oh yes, the womb knows the grief of loss. It knows death, long before life has gone.

It is a cool morning, pewter-grey with streaks of sunlight on the hill. The *kiepersols* are pewtered too, the shadows in the folds teal-blue, softening to green. On the lawn in front of the church, a wagtail steps through the grass, its tail finely sprung.

The phone rings. Grace had known it would. She goes to it before Hugh can come from his study.

It is Godfrey.

'Grace?' An enquiry. Then he says, 'Can you speak?' It is gentle, alerting her.

She will know, by his tone, that he has something to say to her which should not be overheard. He is asking her to listen.

'Yes.'

'Are you all right?'

'Are you?' She has not answered him.

'My father knows.'

'Only your father?'

'Stella guesses.'

'I see.'

'From now on, it's up to me.'

'Of course.'

–I am bound to her by the closest bonds for the rest of my life.

186

'I have given my word.'

There is nothing she can say.

'I will be back next week to make final arrangements for the transpor-tation of some of the cattle to Crawford's station in Zululand. The others will have to go to the stock sale. Could you tell Wilton? I will let Herman de Waal know, so we can return the bull.'

–And the inala cow? But she does not trust her voice.

'I'm so sorry, Grace.'

Yes. She knows those words. She has said them herself.

She leans her head against the rough, whitewashed wall. The day before, he had noosed her neck caressingly, as he had noosed the neck of the small *inala* cow, alert to its diffidence, afraid to rebuff the trusting little thrust of its head against his side, its foolish, its ingenuous display of love. She too had stood – unwitting – within that calm, that immutable protection.

'Gracie?' It is like his hand on her cheek: when it has really mattered, he has never let her down. There will be no need to trim their words to match a mood. Now, he is saying, very simply, what both have always known must be said at last: *–the time has come*.

'Here it is then,' he says.

'Yes. Here it is.'

She steadies herself with her hand, lays it flat against the window ledge, as if she is resting it once more between his palms, her cheek against his cheek, her chest against his chest, her shadow on his shadow, giving herself into his keeping.

Godfrey is gentle. 'All of it was wonderful, Grace. All of it.'

–Ah, my dear love, that is generous of you.

'Distance can't destroy it.'

–If I could lean my head, just once, against your heart.

'And nothing will change it.'

But she knows it must transform in time, retreat by fractions. His essential presence will recede. His familiarity. The life of him, within this place. His blue shirt will be given away, his old shoes will finally be discarded. Someone along the road will wear them into another history. She will have no right to shelter him, to seek him out. She will listen for the telephone but the intervals will become longer and longer and, one day, there will be nothing more to say beyond the trite and obvious. He will be beyond her reach. People will talk of him with the proprietary brashness of friendship or relationship from which she is excluded, a stranger to a passing con-versation. And if she were to meet him in a street, what would she say – what *could* she say about their daily doings which did not sound fatuous? It would be worse – much worse – than silence.

–And when you die? How will I know when you die?

187

But she does not say it. Perhaps it will not matter then. For death is now. It is immediate. She knows, as well as he, that when she puts the telephone down, the intimacy will end abruptly.

She feels each second fall away, voices sliding gently – and inexorably – out of reach. Together, they are disengaging something fragile, releasing it to freedom.

'I love you,' she says.

'And I love you.'

She replaces the receiver. Her fingers are steady.

She goes to the kitchen and pulls the kettle on to the hottest plate of the Aga.

The wind is vagrant in the tree outside. She keeps her breath from being vagrant too, steadies herself against the rail of the stove. The evening before she had put a white geranium in a small glass vase on the kitchen table. The white candles in the white enamel candlesticks, the flower, the white enamel jug send their shadows up against the whitewashed wall. She sits in the cool, airy gloom of the kitchen and examines them. Her calm is absolute. The wireless is standing on the kitchen table. She turns it on. An adagio: a cello and a flute. The reception is not good but the flute recalls the sound of the upland birds that they had heard under a great white sky on the edge of the escarpment the day they had driven out to Xaba's homestead to see his herd. The lament of the flute leads the cello on to its own weeping. Flute to cello, cello to flute, echoing each other.

Grace does not weep.

She examines the shadow of the geranium head against the kitchen wall, the reflected flakes of petal, grey-blue on white, translucent as pearl. She knows that – soon – the tumult will come. She knows that she will say, in anger and in anguish – he, back to the university, the debates, the paper he is writing, his investments, his old companions, his garden and his trees, his house, his dog, his music, his wife: –*I wish that it may break your heart*.

It is her own she wants to bludgeon out of life.

From this moment, she must begin to expunge him. She must learn to cauterise the wound the way that he – a man – has always understood. Without complaint. Without the slightest show of sentiment.

He will expect it of her. He expects it of himself.

She will force herself to put his things away, sacred as the relics of a saint: the picture of the *inala* cow, the photo of the small boy, the tender upper lip, the airy shadow of a garden tree across his face, the poems he loved. She may not look at them again.

She smiles (Gert laughing while the shards of glass blister and wink on the gravel at her feet): how can she forget the pitch of his voice on the night that they had lain together, the rain drifting at the panes, the slow turning

188

of the words about her? He was bringing to her something of his life from long ago, almost before she was born: his half-forgotten childhood, his lost comrades. As he spoke, she had watched the steady profile of his face.

> *There are waves blown by changing winds to laughter*
> *And lit by the rich skies, all day, And after . . .*

It was the way he said 'And after': an ineffable calm, descending quietly:
–*And after . . .*

> *Frost, with a gesture, stays the waves that dance*
> *And wandering loveliness . . .*

She had curled into his side, tucked down to breathe him in –

> *. . . He leaves a white*
> *Unbroken glory, a gathered radiance,*
> *A width, a shining peace, under the night.*

A white, unbroken glory, a gathered radiance, a width, a shining peace, under the night.

What if she should lose the sound of the words? What if they should be transposed into another voice? What if – in time – she could not recall his phrasing? Or his room: the moon-white walls, the mirror above the dresser giving back the reflection of cloud and space beyond the window.

What if she could not recall the shining peace?

The Radiance.

Under the night.

189

Chapter twelve

Grace takes the car without asking and goes to Godfrey's house. She unlocks the door, walking through the kitchen and into the living room. The lexicon is laid out on the desk. She opens the drawer and removes her carefully sharpened pencils. She picks up the small pile of catalogue cards on which she had been working. She arranges them in the box, takes a new shoulder-card and writes 'V' on it. She glances at Godfrey's notes pinned together in her folder, the ruler marking the place where she had finished the day before.

She reads the next entry.

–*valamlomo (imvalamlomo / izimvalamlomo)* n. [<*vala* (close) + *umlomo* (the mouth): lit., close the mouth.]
i) beast presented by a suitor to intended bride's father.

She writes the words on the card with care, checking the punctuation three times as she has always done. No brackets will escape her. She does not put the card in its place in the catalogue box. She props it up against the other empty cards. She slips her pencils into her bag.

She will not linger in the room. Even if she stands in here with him again, it cannot be the same. From now, it can only be an ordinary space, with an ugly floral couch, a desk, bookshelves and a small, squat coal-burning heater. She takes the heater to the car, heaves it into the boot. She returns, goes from room to room, running her eye over surfaces to check if anything that might be hers is left. She sees the tray that she had laid with cups on the kitchen table. She takes the second cup away and stores it in the dresser, dropping the teaspoon into the top drawer beside the stove. When he walks in, there must be nothing to betray her presence.

He may not come alone.

She even puts up the seat of the lavatory, restoring the bathroom to male occupancy and neglect.

She locks the back door behind her, the smell of the old iron key on her fingers, its smooth shaft, cool in her palm. She walks towards the store. The sand on the path is stinging hot, even through the soles of her sandals. Her shadow is short at her feet.

The shop is dark. She stands a moment, resting her eyes in the gloom. There is the smell of the German print in bolts, of indigo and starch. She knows the soft imprint of the colour on exploring fingers, she knows the feel of it held against a cheek. She does not look at it, nor at the columns of enamel buckets, stacked one within the other, the flat, saucer-sized ginger biscuits on the counter, the boxes of Lennons medicines, the case of penknives and mouth organs.

There are no customers. Even the seamstress who sometimes sits on the veranda with an old treadle Singer making pinafores, is somewhere else today.

Wilton Mayekiso is behind the counter and she says to him, in Xhosa, 'Here are the keys, Father. Please give them to Dr Godfrey when he comes.' She reaches the door, about to step into the sunlight when she turns and she says, 'You can never slaughter the ancestral cow, *inkomo yeminyanya,* can you?'

'You can never slaughter it.'

'A person does not sell such a cow?'

'A person does not sell it.'

'It should not be exchanged?'

'No. It should not be exchanged.'

She stands then, looking up towards the ridge. Today, it is bright with colour – with the red of ironstone and the blue-plumed sage of *kiepersols.* The *krantz,* gleaming, seams and dips towards the west.

'Do you know the way to Enseleni?' Grace says.

'I know the way.' Wilton is standing with the keys in his hand, watching her.

'Will you come there with me?'

He looks at her, head slightly cocked. 'Yes,' he says.

'I will bring a truck.'

Imvalamlomo: What closes the mouth.

It was in those catalogue cards, arranged alphabetically in the box, that I had first sensed a presence and a conversation. It was the faintly pencilled marks that had alerted me: '*G – look at this!*', '*Tell G*'.

Godfrey to Grace. Grace to Godfrey.

I had collected those cards together and laid them out, knowing the writing of each, following the alphabet. They had recorded their own mythology, their own history, on the margins of their lexicon. It was their cosmos. There, I found the secret words of trees, the *izibongo* of cattle, the singing of the stars; the lion-eye in the heart of the baobab flower, the smoke of *impepho*, the dew that hangs on the tip of a gazania leaf to announce the coming of the rain. But the shadow of lament and loss was also there, its desolation: the secret scent of the python, the breath of the owl, the envy of the moon, the grieving hare imprinted on its face, the solitary jackal on the ridge.

Godfrey to Grace: Grace to Godfrey.

Voice to voice. In anguish and in joy.

In the old leaves of this neglected set of cards, Grace and Godfrey touch each other still – that most tender, that most intimate of gestures, the union of hands, of fingers, interleaved.

It is Beauty. It is Love.

And here, it is admissible.

But I know, too – as instantly as if the sudden silence had been mine as well – that the last handwritten card – *imvalamlomo*: what closes the mouth – is where the conversation ends. It is not only an ending. It is a pledge.

Nothing will betray: each other; God; the shades.

And yet – by that courageous, steady hand – the words declare the heart-wound.

It is finite.

Clean.

It cannot be mistaken.

Returning home, Grace goes in search of Hugh. He is not in his study. She finds him in the church. She hesitates. She does not like to intrude when Hugh is in the church alone. Hugh – so often inept, even gauche – has a simplicity in his devotion, a quiet decency. She waits in the porch for him.

He comes out. 'Grace?' He glances at her face. 'What is it, Grace?' He waits for her to speak, checks the old habit of listing his requirements for the polishing of the silver, the buffing of the pews, even the final proof-reading of the recipe book.

'I need to ask a favour.'

'Yes?'

She does not look at him – the faint sweatiness about his neck, his glasses slipping down his nose. He shoves them up with a middle finger, back to the bridge.

'Do you think that you could persuade Tommy to lend you his truck tomorrow afternoon without allowing him to offer to drive it?'

'What for?'

'I need a truck to transport an animal.'

He looks bewildered, but senses that if he asks too much, she will retreat.

'Where to?' he says.

'A place called Enseleni.'

'I don't know it.'

'It's a long drive.'

'Is it necessary?'

'Yes.'

'I'll try.'

—You can never slaughter inkomo yeminyanya, can you?

—You can never slaughter it.

Where, then, does such a cow go when it dies?

Where do any cattle go?

In flight from the carcass of the *umvemve* calf, hanging hideless by a hock in the meat-room – membrane and sinew and soft infant flesh – Godfrey had asked that question all those years before.

—Animals do not have souls, Brother Porteous had said. *—Only mortals have souls and can commit mortal sins. Animals do not qualify for souls for they have no choice of good and evil. They may not strive to earn Eternal Life. They cannot go to Heaven.*

But Bibleman had known differently. The *umvemve* calf, Bibleman had said, had gone to another country, below the earth where the pasture was abundant and the herds were fat and their hides were incandescent with the light of the moon and stars. The *umvemve* calf and its mystical dam could transcend death. They were the intermediaries between the lives of men and the presence of the shades.

It is there – written in the cards. In Godfrey's hand. An article of faith. Something Grace and Godfrey both believed.

There is no doubt.

Believing it myself – for them, through them – I have asked informants in the field. Stockmen. Farmers. Herdsmen.

—Where do cattle go . . .?

I have asked Delekile too. I can see his face, the swift rearrangement of his mouth – he is wondering how I can ask such a foolish question.

'Where do the cattle go, Delekile?'

His answer, like the answer of all the others, is simple and straightforward.

'To the butcher,' he says.

'I will drive,' says Hugh. 'You can direct me.'

He is very clear. He is calm. He is not even sweating. His hands are not tentative in steering over bumps. Although he is a man who rides an upright bicycle with a carrier for books, drives a motor car with his hands equidistant on the wheel, he commandeers this truck of Tommy Cooper's with a strange authority and deftness, just as he had asked for it. Tommy had begun to enquire why he needed the truck – thought better of it and withdrew the question. Hugh offered him the use of the car to take to town for the afternoon.

Tommy left before Hugh and Grace, driving with the window wound down and his elbow on the edge of the door, his finger on the wheel, his shoulder hunched to the frame as if he were squiring a girl on a date and needed his other hand free to slip along the back of her seat. He had slicked his hair straight back from his forehead, exposing the pale line where his felt hat usually protected his face from the sun.

As he rattled away across the cattle grid, Hugh had glanced at his watch, taken the truck keys from his pocket, flicked them into his open palm. 'Come, Grace,' he had said, going swiftly out to the driveway, opening the truck's passenger door for her, swinging himself into the driver's seat.

Grace can never hear the sound of gravel under tyres, its swift unravelling and the ringing of the cattle grid, without recalling that journey, its fierce *bergwind*, its ash-grey ridges, a livid sky, building to the north.

On the back of the truck, Wilton Mayekiso is bowed in against the flank of the *inala* cow, protecting himself from the flying dust. And she? Today, she is simply a *vaal*, shanky bush-heifer, standing, head lowered, moisture drooping in little strands from her nose on to the floor of the truck. She half raises her head and lows once, as if dragging the cry into her chest. A small, perplexed lament, breaking up inside her throat.

Hugh drives with implacable competence and calm.

Hugh Wilmot does not understand the conversation. It is between the old man, Xaba and Wilton Mayekiso, the storeman. The old man's English, when he first greets them, is courtly, measured, but whatever is to be discussed now, is to be said in Xhosa. It is the language of the cattle and of stockmen. It is not done to exclude Hugh, it is simply right this way. Grace stands, head slightly tilted. The old man, turning the hat in his fingers, the imprint of tips on felt, tilts his head as well, as if, between them, they are circumscribing and embracing something fragile.

Hugh cannot know what is being said, nor could he conceive of it, even if all the words were familiar tools in his hands. He does not apprehend the idea of the shades, the ancestral cow, the process of its preparation for that office, the aggregation of memory that supports its choice or the means of its inheritance. Nor could he ever understand that this small, inconspicuous cow, horns too young to have curved yet, hocks like a gazelle, standing dispirited and stressed, is a symbol of something both ancient and immutable and that her transfer into Xaba's keeping, is a necessary act.

An act of faith.

—Without it, nothing has been sacred.

The old man listens. The storeman, Wilton, speaks. Grace completes the circle.

—An inkomo yeminyanya cannot be slaughtered.

—It cannot be sold.

—It cannot be exchanged.

But, it can be restored to its provenance. There, it may – symbolically – regain its state before its consecration, exist, interjacent in the herd, neither secular nor sacred. A partial cenobite, returned, like a failed novice, into the keeping of those who reared it and who will care enough to pity it discreetly. The stockman will not treat it with the reverence which is owed to *inkomo yeminyanya* but nor will he rejoice in it, humour it, flatter it, as he does in the fat, the fecund, the comical, the strong – the working cows and oxen in the herd.

She will always be marginal, despite her perfect little head, her perfect little pasterns.

She is flawed.

She carries the moment of her deconsecration like a small, unhealed wound.

She will not belong.

No money is given, no papers signed. The transfer is by word. By word, Xaba will protect the small *inala* cow that had been born into his herd. She will not be slaughtered, she will not be sold. If she is sacrificial in the end, it will be in a *lobola* payment: an exchange between the lineage shades. Perhaps, most apt of all, she will become '*imvalamlomo*', the last beast paid in a marriage transaction. What closes the mouth.

The final gift.

Hugh Wilmot watches as the *inala* cow turns from them towards the byre. She hesitates a moment, alert, sensing a familiarity. She turns her head and looks back at them. By that gesture – the twist of her head, the shadow of its silhouette dipping back and lifting across her neck – it seems she has saluted them. She draws away, then. The flush of red on her sides, the speckling of white along her flanks, her groin, her neck, the outline of her head, the little points of horn, are cryptic against the dusk of the packstone byre wall.

She keeps the curve of the kraal, disappears from view.

Grace does not move. She remains poised, hands folded in against each other, her shadow steady at her feet.

Enseleni is a place I had conjured in my mind, given a geography, a landscape. I had taken it up from the word on the foot of the card marked '—nala (inala / izinala) n. abundance' where 'Heifer from M.Xaba, Enseleni' is written in pencil.

Enseleni exists. It is not marked on a regular map. Only on a survey map. It is recorded on the lowest curve of contours of a folded hill. I went there with Delekile. He knows it well enough. For him, there is nothing mystical about it. It is simply a neighbourhood on a hillside. He can direct me without difficulty. He has relations. He knows of the family of Xaba. They have lived there always. He does not pore over maps. He orchestrates no skies, no winds. His reading of the ancient and romantic cattle byre that we pass, is that it's high time someone repaired the gate. The poetry of aloe hedges is not remarked, it is simply fixed within the matrix of his language. He does not need to analyse the metaphors – he thinks in them, as a matter of course.

'Here is Enseleni,' he says. He knows it by whatever curve in the road alerts him, as surely as if we had turned into a signposted street. It is simply a sweep of hillside, a swathe of sky, scattered homesteads, the new community of ploughed allotments, scruffy, half-breed cattle, grazing on a slope.

Once a trading store stood beside the track. The tall gums, their trunks in rags, grow in a protective half square. The dry, spiny bush of arid country has pushed up among the toppled earth bricks. Further along the road there is a new store with an ugly angled parapet and a large warped sign. Beside it, a blue-painted container, marooned at the edge of a *donga*, serves as a cellphone shop. Somewhere, beyond the ridge, the ubiquitous red and white beacon will stand within a nest of wires, protecting it from vandals. We cannot live without that little signal any more, its comfort and security – *'you have active diverts'* – to keep our fear at bay. Why should we want God's intercession in our need when there is the recorded voice of the service provider? It is so much more reliable.

Beyond the foundations of the old store, protected, too, by gums, there is a house.

Its core is very old. It must have been the trader's in Grace and Godfrey's time, but it has changed.

Round the original bungalow with its deep veranda and its high corrugated-iron roof, inset with three turquoise-painted dormer windows, is built a collection of pole and dagga buttresses, roofed with thatch, set with plate glass windows, monster eyes. It is a strangely ribald house, even menacing. The smallest plume of smoke, a drunken breath, comes from its turquoise chimney.

Delekile, perched beside me in the car, says, 'This is the house of Xaba.'

'Are you sure?'

'I am sure.'

'Isn't it the trader's house?'

'Yes,' he says. 'Xaba is the trader.'

Delekile and I leave the car in the road. I lock it carefully. We stand at the gate. There is a dog tethered in the yard. I do not trust the chain. It bounces and strains as the dog jerks itself at us. It is howling hard enough to bring someone from the house.

No one comes.

There is a woman walking in the road. We ask if she has seen Mr Xaba. She nods. Mr Xaba will be in his shop.

So we go there, Delekile and I, into the breeze-block interior with its barred, horizontal steel windows and its formica-topped counters. There is a display counter with fried fish, scotch eggs, chilli chicken and curried beans. There are sacks of bloated orange cheese snacks skewered on a spike. There is a life-sized laminated cut-out of last year's soccer hero, grinning his approbation of a line in energy drinks. Divine Love condoms, easily dispensed in rip-off sachets hang on a card, pinned to the shelf behind the teller. They do not seem to be a popular brand. Under a plastic dome by the till are rows of coconut snowball cakes, pink with cochineal. Mr Xaba is talking on his mobile on the back porch of the shop. His 4x4, standing in the sun, is packed with crates of soft drinks.

We introduce ourselves.

Mr Norrence Xaba is young. He is affable. He is a man in a hurry. He is on his way to town and needs to make deliveries at his other shops. He also has a plane to catch.

'We are looking for the home of a Mr M Xaba who lived here in the 1940s,' I say. I do not add, *'He is a man with cows.'* I say instead, 'Apparently he had a large herd of indigenous cattle from which a Dr Godfrey bought a number for research purposes.'

'Mr M Xaba was my grandfather's brother,' says Norrence Xaba. 'He passed away many, many years ago. I did not know him. His family has moved to town. They are still there.'

'I do not need to contact his family,' I say. 'I have come to see the site of his cattle byre.'

It seems such an odd request. Mr Norrence Xaba is taken aback but his commitments are too pressing to enquire why, with his cellphone carolling in his pocket and the crates of soft drinks perspiring in the van. Someone is calling from an inner office that the other phone is ringing too. We wait while he juggles the landline and the cell tucked between his copious shoulder and his ear. Somewhere, in the yard outside the shop, is the thump-thump-thump of a taxi wired for beat. The vibrations from its speakers come through the floor. I can still feel it in the concrete, under the soles of my feet, after the taxi has driven away.

He returns to us, armed now with his briefcase. He says that a lad from the shop will take us up behind his house. 'The old buildings that belonged to

197

Xaba are still there,' he waves vaguely with a hand. He adds that some have fallen in. Other people are staying there now. He is not sure about the original house. He thinks it was a traditional hut. He does not go up there. He is too busy. There is still an old cattle byre. He knows it well. He remembers it from when he was boy. Yes. A very old one. It seems as if he needs to convince himself of its existence on our behalf. If he is insistent enough, perhaps we will find it – or imagine it to our satisfaction.

'I am sorry. I am very, very busy.'

We understand.

'I do not go up there. I am very busy. Really.'

Yes, we understand.

We do not detain him any longer. He is gone with a cheery wave, two passengers squeezing in beside him on the front seat. He takes the bumps in the road with practised ease. He is round the curve and over the rise before Delekile and I have managed to ascertain which lad will be our guide.

He sidles up.

He is a boy of about fourteen. He is silent, just indicating with his hand where we must follow, concentrating on pulling at trailing pieces of grass as he walks, twisting them about in his hands. He has an inscrutable wariness. He leads us past the turquoise house. The chained dog wrenches at its leash, barking insanely. The boy pays no attention. Delekile half laughs. Something amuses him. He is probably visualising what I would do if the dog got free. I write in my notebook, *'Mr Norrence Xaba's house. African Baroque'*, a reminder to add a description later. Delekile and the boy are patient while I take a quick photograph, eye on the dog.

We proceed up the hill.

I do not think the boy that Mr Xaba allotted to us has any clue of what we are looking for or why he had been chosen to lead us. He looks about vaguely, still twisting the grass heads. Delekile asks him if there is a byre near here.

His reply is barely audible. 'I don't know.'

We reach the perimeter of another homestead. It is unkempt, but there are chickens in the yard. Walls have been patched with fertiliser bags. The only new thing is a JoJo watertank sprouting a pipe leading from a lean-to roof. There is a remnant of an old fruit tree. There is a scrap of a plumbago and tecoma hedge. The roots are muddled and half trampled. To the left and down, there is a dense clump of kraal aloes still entangled with the flat ironstone building blocks of a packstone wall. Whatever else might have stood here has been carried away. The earth is tussocked with clumps of grass and bush. Something oozes like an old oil stain with a filmy mirror of rainbow on its surface. A corrugated-iron privy, leaning to the prevailing wind, is hunched against what must have been a gatepost: an old sneezewood column and a place where an iron bracket might have been embedded in the wood to hang a gate.

In this bland and empty place, without shadow in the midday wind, the horizon is sunk in dregs of khaki dust. It is as if all the earth has grown a scab on it, a crust of pus in colour and in smell.

I cannot recreate Grace's sacred place from this.

Nor does it seem appropriate. What is the anachronistic little story of a woman and a heifer and her unresolved cosmology in the face of the struggle being eked out here? The present is what should concern me – *must* concern me: Delekile with his thin legs, his ravaged lungs, the hopeless boy. It is a tale I do not have the energy to write – just as the lad who led us to this place hardly has the energy to look about him: need is too relentless – and expectation too eroded and too tenuous.

Back at the shop I buy him some food. I give him money. As we drive away I glance in the rear-view mirror. The boy is not watching us. Nor is he eating the food. He is simply standing in the empty yard. He is disengaged in every way.

And here I am, intent on my own small resurrections, pounding life into what has already died.

For what?

Why don't I care as much about the living any more?

Godfrey comes back to the valley. He comes alone. Harold has offered to accompany him. Godfrey refuses. He telephones Herman de Waal and arranges to meet him on Tuesday. He contacts the Railways about transporting his cattle. He puts two empty suitcases in the truck and a selection of cartons.

Only Wilton Mayekiso is at the store when he arrives. The shopkeeper is doing deliveries. Wilton has the keys. He does not follow Godfrey to the house but he sees him turn aside and walk down to the byre. A little later he comes into the shop and he says, 'Where is the *inala* cow?'

'It has gone to Enseleni.'

'Who took it.'

'The *umfundisi* and the teacher.'

'How did they take it?'

'In Basie Cooper's truck.'

'I see.' He takes his pipe from his trousers pocket and fills it. Then he says, 'Did Cooper go too?'

'No.'

'Just the *umfundisi* and Mrs Wilmot?'

'And me.'

'Did you take it to Mr Xaba?'

'Yes.'

'And what did he say?'

'He said he would look after it.'

'Did he pay them for it?'

Wilton Mayekiso is silent. Godfrey looks across at him. 'You do not sell *inkomo yeminyanya*,' Wilton says.

'It was an expensive heifer.'

But he knows, in saying it, he is mocking himself: a bitter little mockery, a bitter little tale.

He goes to the house and unlocks the door. He walks into the kitchen. He notices everything. The diminished tray, the lavatory seat, the prim covering on the bed, the curtain drawn across his clothes, the card propped against the catalogue boxes: *'imvalamlomo'*: what closes the mouth.

I do not know what Godfrey felt. I cannot imagine it: I am not a man. I would like to think he wept for her. I would like to think he raged and howled like a dog, felt the tumult of all that was lost, was wrenched with aloneness and regret. But I think – deferring it – he went to the telephone and opened the book on the Government pages and gave the operator the number of the Railways and asked what time the cattle truck would come. What else could he do? What can any man do but just 'get on' when he does not think that grief – no matter how implacable – is owed him?

Grace knows he is back. She knows that just beyond her own rim of hills, where the road curves round and the store stands below the slope facing the ridge and the line of the empty river, his truck will be parked by the house. She can see him and what he is doing as surely as if she had been with him. She is aware of him in every movement that she makes and in her breathing. She knows he is aware of her.

Just beyond the ridge.

And yet, he has never been so far away. There is nothing she can do to reach him – unless he chooses it himself.

And he cannot choose it.

She teaches the children calmly, stands in the playground during break while they play. She glances once at the *gwarri* by the church fence under which he had always parked his truck. The sky is a pale blue, ribbed with light cloud.

–I am the whey from the milk pail, I am the lightest streaks of cloud.

She will have to stop seeing the world in terms of cattle-colours. To survive she will have to lay these metaphors aside, their shared cosmology.

She turns away and walks to the swings. Desmond is hanging upside down on the gym bar suspended between the forks of two small trees, bony little knees giving purchase, arms hanging loose.

'The sky is the earth. The earth is the sky,' he says and half twists his head to look up at her.

Once she might have answered, 'Of course – as Bibleman says . . .'

Now she says, 'Are you sure, Desmond?' – and hates herself for it.

Herman de Waal has come with his daughter, Dulcie Trollip, and his truck. Godfrey makes them tea. He is a little careless of the cups when they have finished. He breaks one as he slides them off the tray into the sink. Dulcie clicks her tongue in sympathy, takes the pieces in her hand and puts them into the bin. Godfrey pays no attention to it. He leads them down to the byre in silence.

'Well, I wonder what this young bull of mine will say about my taking all his girlies away from him,' laughs Herman, trying to lighten the silence.

As he suspects, the young bull is reluctant.

'What a fuss!' says Dulcie, slapping him on the rump.

It takes several attempts to heave him up the ramp into the truck. His complaints are not mournful. This is no lament. He is laying charges – stamping his feet and filling the back of the truck with dung. They pay no attention to his bluster. When new cows are presented to him, he will forget this small harem. He is a male: the privilege of choice is his. He will get over it soon enough.

When the De Waals have gone, the young bull tethered, a stockman steadying him, Godfrey tells Wilton to drive the rest of the herd down to the station and into the holding pen.

He opens the gate of the byre, looking at each cow as she leaves, counting her off in his notebook. He has his pipe rooted to his lower lip. Two of the calves are still young but they follow surely enough. Wilton directs them with low, gentle whistles. He glances at Godfrey. Like him – for a while – he too was a man with cows. He understands why nothing can be said as the byre gate is closed behind the herd and why a man may take his pipe from his mouth and probe the ember with a twig for a minute at a time, not looking up.

Not long ago, I drove to the station in the valley. Delekile did not come with me. I did not need him. And anyway, I knew which road to take. The platform was overgrown. There had been no vehicles taking stock or milk or wool down to the station for many years. The building stood with the panes of glass in its windows broken. Those that were not, reflected the encroaching thorn bush which had pushed up the rails in places. Someone had taken away some of the sleepers. The dog pins had been flung aside. Small dry patches of charcoal and dead ember in the building were evidence of vagrants. In the waiting room there was a gaping hole in the wall where a slow combustion stove must have stood. '*Fuck the ANC*' was scrawled above the hole: by whom or when, I cannot

201

tell. Someone disgruntled, someone's inept little fist-shake against change. There was an old Coke can flung in a corner, rat droppings along the skirting. The holding pen for stock was still there, the poles too sturdy to fall into decay as the building had. I climbed on to the struts and sat with my face turned up to the sky. There was no sound but the faint contracting of the rails and, a hundred metres down the track, the plaintive piping of the wind in the girders of the bridge that spanned the empty river-bed. There was no fragrance of dung, no rich growth in the pen, evidence of generations of stock having passed that way before.

Looking down the platform I could see, here and there among the weeds, the corner of an angled brick demarcating a flower bed. Beyond was the gravel yard. Did Grace come here in the car to fetch him sometimes? Did he alight on this platform, his bag slung over his shoulder – that ardent, that ascetic face, eager for her. Perhaps he knocked her hat off, lifting her a little, laughing. Spontaneous joy. Instant and uncontrived.

Oh, I see you, Godfrey. I see you, Grace. Your radiance is mine.

And then, one day, the cattle truck drew up and the ramp was rattled down on to the cinders on the track and the small procession of cows, the little calves, mounted into the gloom of the car, to be barricaded in, Godfrey and Wilton standing on the platform with the Railways official, exchanging papers.

Now, it is an empty, sullen little sidetrack, a bleak, deserted line.

It is all too long ago. There is evidence of nothing – except for those who can imagine it.

All afternoon, Grace waits for his call or the sight of his truck parked under the *gwarri* by the fence.

–I have sent the cattle away.

–Yes.

–I believe you took the inala cow back to Enseleni.

–Yes.

–Thank you for cleaning up the house and leaving the papers the way you did. I could not fail to notice the last entry.

–Yes.

And then – what could he say?

He could say nothing.

He could not repeat the words he had said when he had last phoned.

Not in a vacuum.

Not with the cattle truck drawing away beyond their reach. *'I love you'* needs a context, even when it is beating loudly – and inexorably – in the blood.

Even if he comes, it is futile to speak.

Forcing herself, then, she leaves the house and walks out beyond the graveyard, taking a little path between the bushes, skirting the school along the contour of the hill.

It is here that the railway line passes across the flats, a kilometre away. It is here the line glints in the fierce sun in summer between the green-grey thickets of prickly pear and *spekboom*. Now, the line is silent. No trains run here any more.

Grace walks along that path, sometimes catching her foot under a root in the sand, noticing the spider tracks of small passing creatures – a shrew, a tortoise, the little three-clawed imprint of a bird. She sits a long time on the crown of the hill, eyes scanning the railway line. Two trains pass. It is the second that is slower, without many cars, some open. There is a cattle truck. At that distance – so far away – it is insubstantial, without shadow, without sound. A small brown presence creeping across the plain.
    She watches until it is no longer distinguishable.

> *I could have wept and howled*
> *To see the bridal cattle pass;*
> *Not for me, but for the beautiful ones,*
> *For Thathalasi and suchlike,*
> *Lovely, with a high-bridged nose.*

She had known that poem all her life – a fragment waiting for its context: *for Thathalasi and suchlike*. Grace rests her forehead briefly on her folded forearms, breathing quietly. She has never seen Stella Godfrey, but that is how she knows her. *Lovely, with a high-bridged nose.*
    When she gets home at dusk, Hugh is standing in the living room, alone. He says, without looking at her, 'Dr Godfrey came about an hour ago. He couldn't stay. He was sorry to miss you.'
    Still, he does not look at her.
    She says, 'Anything else?'
    'I suppose he came to say goodbye.'
    She turns away. 'He has already said goodbye.'

Chapter thirteen

❧

And so the conversation is at an end.

I sit with the catalogue box on the table in front of me in the little kitchen of the house. The cards are foxed with the lightest rust, a rash of small uneven spots across them. They are no longer white. They are fifty years old and for fifty years they have been lying unfinished, quietly waiting for someone to complete the work.

Here I am, then, holding them in my hand, looking for the notes that Godfrey made and which Grace had left, neatly stacked on the work table with a ruler marking the last entry that she wrote.

I will use parts of it as an appendix to my dissertation:

'*A Dictionary of Cattle Terms*'
(*after C J Godfrey*)

'*This lexicon was compiled by Dr C J Godfrey between 1933 and 1947 during fieldwork in various parts of South Africa. It is an important record of a particular branch of indigenous knowledge and should prove a valuable resource to any student of African languages. An additional set of terms, collected during the 1990s, is listed in Appendix IV, which reflects a recent shift of emphasis . . .*'
etc. etc. etc . . .

I will complete the lexicon – '*v*' to '*z*' – and see if the University Press might be interested in publishing it as a handbook on its own. It is a significant piece of work. I will write an introduction and acknowledgements on Godfrey's behalf. Having inspected his papers, his articles and books, I will phrase my words in the same formal, dispassionate way as Godfrey always did. He would applaud the vision and scientific rigour of Dr Crawford, the dedication of the team of scientists at the experimental station in Zululand. I notice, from his other work, that he is never effusive. '*Grateful thanks are due to . . .*' a Miss A, a Mrs B, '*for help received in the preparation of the MS for the press*'. So much for the secretarial assistance.

–*Grateful thanks are due to Mrs G Wilmot for assistance received . . .*

Is that all, Godfrey?

Surely you could have chosen a less retiring phrase?

She is, after all, the keeper of memory, its devoted custodian, witness to the restoration of the small *umvemve* calf, of Gert – vivid little Gert, flitting along in the shadow of the hedge with you, lying on the grass to see the great parade of stars. She is witness, Godfrey, to the boy-fight at school so long ago, the spring and balance, the strong, slim suppleness of knees, the budding shoulders, boy-fists ready, head tucked in. She knows the veranda room, nestled high among the acres of corrugated roof, with its washstand, its basin and its jug, the stretcher bed, the silhouette of the pepper tree against the night. She harvests the poetry, learned, once, in anguish by the soldier, brought home to the silent house in the empty post-war days, repeated over and over into remembrance. She knows the student – serious, absorbed, softly pronouncing into the lofty cavern of the library reading room at Cambridge, the melody of Dinka ox names: –*I am the grey goshawk, I am the silver sand fish, my bellow is the roar of the great river, my breath the wind of the desert . . .*

Oh yes. She knows.

Intuitively, she even knows the Blood-Red-Woman, has walked her own imagined pavements outside the empty rows of basement windows of a Gloucester Walk, seen the draughty arcade with its little marble fountain where his lover passed, her sable collar turned against her cheek, indifferent to the stares of men. She knows that Blood-Red-Woman's loss. It is as fierce as hers. Fiercer, in its old, predictable regrets.

And yes, she knows your mother – ivory and pearl – inventing herself (–*O most gracious Virgin Mary . . .*), her Afterlife (–*We will both enter Heaven one day and be together, just you and me, always . . .*), to assuage the loneliness, its perplexing little griefs. Her terror of death.

And – different from your mother's (freer, less exacting) – she has evolved an Afterlife with you as well. Subverting loss. Excluding Death. Bibleman says . . .

–*Grateful thanks are due . . .*

She does not want grateful thanks, Godfrey. She wants to run with the boy, laugh, shout, leap. She wants to stride the world with the man: the energy of love is boundless in her. Its exultation. Its sheer soaring madness.

There is nowhere you may go, Godfrey, where we do not apprehend you.

—If you were in my flesh I would tear you out, but – kusegazini – you are in my blood, which cannot be divided.

Godfrey retreats to other things. I cannot even find a letter acknowledging the arrival of his little band of cows in Zululand. In despatching them, releasing them for scientific scrutiny, something of their essence disappears. They are tagged and catalogued and sent. He signs the papers and he walks away.

From Grace. From me.

Godfrey writes a series of papers on *'Function and Structure'*: homage to Radcliffe-Brown. His research changes direction. The aesthetic, the symbolic, the spiritual, are left to other scholars. He concentrates on economies, systems of exchange and political theory. He is invited to Cambridge as a visiting lecturer. The timing is perfect. His sons have both chosen to pursue their studies in England. Stella has encouraged it. She has always been determined in cultivating Englishness: it is something she can claim for them and for herself. They can all go together in the summer, before the start of term, explore the countryside at the weekends, spend time in London, acclimatise.

Stella rejoices.

Perhaps they will never have to come back again. They can buy a small house, somewhere on the outskirts of Cambridge, perhaps a flat in London. She has her inheritance and her investments – and who knows what offer might be made to Godfrey at the university. At any university.

The slight archness which Stella has always endeavoured to repress – forbearance of their parochial life in a small colonial town – transforms itself into briskness. She can plan – *at last* – a return to an older and more gracious world. She is a little neglectful of her friends, a little supercilious. She has others to anticipate – *at home* – who understand the nuance in what she says, whose sensibility – and information – do not need coaxing, whose sophistication is so much less tenuous – and trying. She packs Harold off, writes lists of instructions for him to deliver to his housekeeper, promises to write every week, and arranges his luggage with the precision of a general's batman.

When Harold has gone – looking suddenly old, a little shabby, wispy haired and sour – she telephones the shipping line and books their passage, quietly insisting on the cabin she prefers. She books for their sons as well, requesting a berth just enough removed from theirs, for privacy. 'We'll meet the boys in Cape Town, Clem. It's going to be heavenly all being at sea together after that. Absolutely heavenly.'

All I have to go on are some pictures. Godfrey and his sons, standing like cadets at ease in tropical kit, Stella in a new-look bathing suit with a sweetheart neckline and a pair of sunglasses and a scarf knotted in her hair. Stella in evening dress at the Captain's table. One of those party pictures with a full ashtray in the foreground and the blank face of a steward behind and everyone round the table leaning in towards each other with that exclusive shipboard intimacy, a studied carelessness, a little prowling lust.

Absolutely heavenly.

There is also a snapshot of Godfrey. I wonder who took it? Certainly, he was unaware. Perhaps it was one of his sons, coming up beside him on a deserted deck. He is hunched in his coat against the cold – the heavy swell of northern seas, a swollen sky. It is a picture full of wind and cloud. His eyes are half closed against it and he stands in profile. He is clean-shaven, his dark straight hair is blown across his forehead. I have traced that brow over and over, those fine-hinged cheekbones and the faint angled line from inner eye to jaw that gives his face both its humour and its lean ascetic grace.

What is this expression, this grim fist holding his coat closed at his throat? There is something inexorable in it.

Something, I know, that Grace has never seen.

This is where he says 'Enough' to me.

It, too, is finite. It is clean. It cannot be mistaken.

He has turned his face away from me as well.

Sitting here, with the remnants of Grace and Godfrey's story, I struggle to proceed. There is nothing to prepare me for the sudden nothingness, the lack of resolution. I could say – *So what? What can you expect of an ill-considered love affair?* – and get on with the thesis. The prof would be delighted. It would free me up to keep the first years off his back.

Besides – this story has been written countless times before. It is hardly new. It is repeated over and over. The first storyteller, by a gesture – pre-empting the resonance of words – wove his tale out of his own longing, his desire, his shame, his loss. His aloneness.

And his expedience. (Why he? If there is loss – it is as likely to be hers.)

And that is why I should not have been surprised that – in the end – Grace agreed to marry Hugh.

Grace knocks on Hugh's study door and opens it without waiting. Tommy Cooper is sitting in the extra chair. Hugh leans back in his, fingertips touching. Tommy turns swiftly to her, face flushed.

'Sorry,' says Grace, backing. She closes the door gently. The voices inside do not resume. Clearly Hugh and Tommy are waiting to hear the sound of her retreat. She walks away down the passage and sits on the sofa in the

207

living room. She looks up at the picture on the mantelpiece of Doreen Wilmot, Hugh's wife, with the brooch at her throat and her hair carefully permed, a little fingerling of curl across her forehead, too high – emphasising the pencilled arch of her brows. Despite the pose, the exact tilt of the chin, it is a strangely inattentive face.

Grace looks at Jack, in the matching frame.

It is all so long ago – in perception more than time – that it is difficult to re-imagine Jack, her own strange detachment and his happy, boyish relish of her. They had been children playing at romance and weddings. If he was here, he would be a farmer now, struggling with an overdraft, preoccupied with the weather forecasts and the level of the water in the wells and she would have been helping with the dairy or supplying the Co-op with vegetables. She would – in thrift – have recycled curtains, made anti-macassars for the chairs (on her mother-in-law's instruction) to hide the worn places in their backs, played tennis more regularly at the tennis club with Dulcie Trollip and her mother, with Enid and Rosemary and organised the church fête for Hugh, having him for supper every Tuesday evening (cottage pie and peas) and for a roast on Sunday, after church. She would fret about his need of a wife and be over-anxious on his birthday in case he felt bleak. And for herself and Jack, there would have been two or three small children. A little Jacko with dark hair and sturdy legs. Perhaps a small Hugh. Or a girl. Like Jack and Hugh's mother – or like Doreen Wilmot, the colour of oatmeal.

Grace opens the veranda door and goes into the garden, leaving Jack to his soldier's smile and his puzzlement. She walks the edges of a bed where she has planted stocks – a reminder of her grandfather and the high fragrant patches at the Christmas cottage in the mist.

She hears Hugh open the porch door and Tommy Cooper's trudge as he crosses the gravel to his truck. She does not turn. She picks a dead head off the flowers and bends down to lift a small snail from a leaf. She holds it on her finger: the translucence of its young shell, the faintness of its form inside, the little inter-turning glove fingers of its horns. So tentative, so fragile. She restores it to a wilder part of the garden where it will do no harm. She will not crush it underfoot as she has seen Tommy Cooper do so many times.

Hugh walks across to her. She turns to him. 'Sorry to have interrupted you and Tommy,' she says. 'Is something wrong?'

Hugh sighs. He thrusts his hands in his pockets, rocks slightly on his heels. 'Tommy came for advice, that's all. And I don't think he wants to hear the advice I had to give.'

'What about?'

'He's obliged to get married.'

Grace does not look at him. 'No one is obliged to get married,' she says.

Perhaps, after that, it was the last time she dared believe it. The last time – defiant – that she said it, knowing its futility. Hugh's words – spoken with concern but with a conscious piety (–*we are all sinners, my dear brothers and sisters*) – had evoked a sharply repressed retort in her. She had recoiled from his certainty.

He is so unequivocal.

He says, 'He's got a girl into trouble.'

–*Naughty Tommy!:* Again, she wants to challenge his priggishness:

'What kind of trouble, Hugh,' she says, intending to provoke him, but he does not sense derision.

He peers at her a moment. 'The unfortunate girl is in the family way.'

'I know that, for God's sake.'

'Did I say something to offend you?' He is bewildered. The colour draining into the angle of his jaw is somehow embarrassing. She cannot look at him. There is a kind of nakedness in Hugh when he speaks to her, a covert exposure that she does not wish to see. She knows he cannot help it.

'She may not be the only one.'

To say it – so glib, so flat – and to have it linked forever with Tommy Cooper and with Hugh's prim cliché, is absurd. Without Hugh's words, without the need to defend, she would not have spoken at all.

She can hear the walls of the citadel falling in, the dull thudding of it in her blood.

Hugh is oddly exultant. 'Oh my God!'

It is not an oath.

Hugh Wilmot does not move. He does not move as Grace walks away from him towards the house. This is a moment for his pastoral calm. The benediction of wisdom, the quiet word – directed at himself – which he has so often offered others in their need.

–*Well, Tommy, this child may be a blessing. Fatherhood is sacred, Tommy. Marriage is a sacrament. Sometimes – unwisely, even sinfully – these things happen but we learn to turn them around for the greater good. It can be an opportunity to glorify God.*

And Tommy had mumbled, 'Yes, Father Hugh,' and gazed at the floor an inch from the toecaps of his boots. –*Except, Father Hugh, I was only looking for a quick fuck.*

Hugh goes to his study and closes the door. He sits at his desk. There is a little ornament which he keeps to weight his papers. It is made of plaster of Paris, from a mould. A Scottie dog, head on one side, a paw raised. Doreen had given it to him before they were married. She had said that Jack had helped her choose it. One Saturday morning, at a bazaar, Jack jollying her along. He turns it around in his fingers. He is not sure if he keeps it for Jack or for Doreen. It does not matter. It has stayed on his desk, a small reminder of an older world and its security. It is dusty but he does not wipe it. He is afraid that he will rub the paint away.

He goes in search of Grace.

She is in the kitchen. He stands at the door. He says, 'Would you like a cup of tea?'

'Thank you, Hugh.'

He puts his arm briefly about her shoulder. It is not an unfamiliar gesture. 'I'm so sorry, Grace.'

Nor is it an unfamiliar phrase.

The deconstruction of belief. Piece by piece.

The only way to manage loss is to withdraw, thought by thought, giving the retreat a framework and a purpose. A set of rites. A clear recessional. Leaving the sanctuary intact.

Only objects are left, perhaps small rituals: the way the table is laid, the special grace reserved for Sundays, the making of the jam. Things circumscribed by a certain time, its music, its companions. Hugh's Scottie dog. The pictures on the mantelpiece, the little vase Desmond had given Grace at the end of the term: *'Mrs Wilmot, with hugs and kisses from Desmond'*. There is work to be done in the garden. There are new seedlings to plant.

The house beyond the ridge, beside the store, remains unoccupied. Already, untended, little sprigs of thorn have grown up into the cracks in the concrete of the front step. The tap on the water tank drips unheeded. It holds no expectation any more. It is empty. There is something sullen in the squat construction of its walls.

'Have you told him?' says Hugh.

'No.'

'Wouldn't that be wise?'

'No.'

'It's a shared responsibility. I trust he would see it like that.'

'Of course he would.'

'Well?'

'I don't choose to tell him.'

'Can I ask why?'

'No.'

The only regret she will allow Godfrey is that they are lost to each other. Not that he had met her. Not that he had known her. Not that he had loved her. She would not be the source of his self-recrimination. She would not let him deconstruct her out of anger at himself, making of her memory a burden and a guilt.

The kettle is boiling and Hugh makes the tea. He does not speak until he has set her cup on the kitchen table. 'I will help you in any way I can, Grace.'

'I know.'

He does not move: she will either weep for the relief of confession or she will withdraw into an implacable silence.

He waits quietly, the steam from his cup drifting slowly up about the folded edges of his hands.

With relief, he senses the tremor in her, the slow gathering of breath, its drawing in.

Grace weeps.

It is not just for the loss of Godfrey. It is mostly for herself.

Once I had this dream. Quite simple, really. Quite clear. Godfrey and Grace on a hillside. It was not the ridge of jackals or the ironstone and aloe. It was sparse but it was temperate. Below the slope there was a town. Godfrey was walking just ahead. His presence was a consolation, an absolute. But he turned away down the hill and Grace could not follow him. Even though he went without her, drawn away from her to that mysterious place below, there was no sense of discord or repudiation.

She let him go.

They had been pelagic wanderers, blown, for a time, into kinder waters.

But only for a time.

Now the lifting wind has come – a greater force – reclaiming each.

Grace walks on alone along the contour of the hill: the underharmonies of upland birds, the cello calling to the flute, the flute in answer; that wind; the vaulting sky.

It has radiance.

I wake with radiance as well.

Hugh lets her weep.

'I'm so sorry, Hugh.'

He does not move. He does not speak. When she is quiet at last, he says, 'I will marry you, Grace. I will expect nothing of you, nor hold anything against you. I will simply love you.'

She does not answer him. She sits in the stillness of the kitchen, her cup before her as she had sat in the kitchen in the Christmas cottage in the silence, with the sun coming through the window, making the quince jelly in the jars they had filled refract a scarlet glow all across the table. There is

211

no sunlight now, no fragrance of warm quince, just the sudden rumble of the fridge, turning its engine over, settling back into sameness.

–If you were in my flesh, I could tear you out, but you are in my blood which cannot be divided.

It is the same with this baby, an existence which she could not have anticipated after all the years of childlessness with Jack. Unobtrusive, still unknown – impossible – it had gathered up her blood, making it its own.

Disbelieving – oh, but knowing – she had denied its existence until, one morning in the classroom, she had felt a flutter, fragile as an insect wing brushing skin, and turned alert, seeking the movement outside herself. It had come again. A little thump, a tremor. She had stood – poised – with a terror and an exultation.

She remembered the silence around her, the children writing far away, and hearing, only, the surging in her ears, the murmur, carrying weight and substance: *you are in my blood, which cannot be divided.*

Again, the flutter and tug, so faint, so small.

So living.

Not once had Grace and Godfrey exchanged anything at all. No gifts and no mementoes. Their autonomy was absolute. They had never even shared wine from a single glass.

There was nothing that they owned together. Nothing they had chosen in a shop. They were always deferential, offering each other – still enquiringly – sugar for their tea.

It was love without a record.

A bond without the possibility of history.

It would remain that way.

It is Grace on the hillside in my dream, allowing Godfrey to turn away, down into the town, into its fullness and its welcome – and walking on alone.

It is the right thing to do.

It is the only thing to do.

It is not the same for Tommy Cooper. It is not the same for Tommy Cooper's girl.

She had phoned that morning.

Hugh had answered.

'Is Mr Cooper there?' A little shrill, a little breathless, close to hysteria. Hugh had recognised the kind of girl behind the voice.

'Tommy is out on the farm,' he had said. 'He should be back at lunch time. I will tell him to contact you.'

'It's very urgent.'

Underlined.

'Can I give him a message?'

'No, thank you. Just tell him to phone the minute he comes in.'

'Certainly. Will you give me your number?'

He did not ask for her name.

When he returned, Hugh had given Tommy the slip of paper on which he had written the number. Tom had put it in his pocket and eaten his lunch, seemingly unconcerned. He had talked about the roadworks down at the drift and given his opinion that the causeway would not be high enough, if a good rain fell. 'But then, good rain never falls,' he had said and laughed.

As Hugh left the table, he had said, 'The young woman insisted that you telephone as soon as possible. It seemed to be urgent.'

Tommy Cooper took the slip of paper from his pocket and glanced at it again. Hugh went to his study and closed the door. He had heard Tommy Cooper cranking the handle of the telephone and the sound of his voice, at a distance, asking the exchange for the number.

Ten minutes later, Tom had knocked.

He had come into Hugh's study, standing just inside the threshold.

Hugh had glanced up from his book.

Tom's gaze had darted about the room, unable to settle.

A blow to the solar plexus, breath fragmented?

'Sit down, Tom,' Hugh Wilmot had said.

Tom had seemed to wade towards a chair.

For Hugh, it has been a tumultuous day.

He waits, suspended, his gestures slow, only his breath swift and pulsing in his throat: a strange ebullience, close to panic. No one can see it. His cleric's collar remains implacably starched. His neck is damp at the back. He wipes his forehead with his hanky, pats his cockscomb with his hand.

He had watched Tommy Cooper take his fear off, out of the room and into the lands. No doubt, he would expiate it by driving his workforce hard, exhaust it by shouting expletives across a camp, snatching at mastery.

And, an hour or two later – a player in a pantomime – Hugh had sat across the kitchen table and heard Grace weep as Tommy Cooper might have wept, if he had understood the real mystery of love.

Without meditating it – even without a guiding prayer – Hugh had said to Grace, quietly – very simply: –*I will marry you.*

It is neither absurd nor spurious.

His need – in all its contradiction – is as great as hers.

213

At five, Hugh goes out, called to an old man, to attend his dying. 'Expect me when you see me,' he says to Grace. 'I doubt that I'll be back for supper.'

'I'll keep some aside.'

She returns to the kitchen to prepare the meal. She stands, staring into the grocery cupboard, her hands limp at her side.

The deep weariness after tears. The suspension of emotion or regret.

She cannot think – right now – of what Hugh has said.

She is moving in silence.

She hears Tommy Cooper coming back, bucking his vehicle across the corrugations.

The slam of the truck's door.

Tom shouldering his way in down the passage, the keys being flung into the bowl on the hall table.

He comes to the kitchen

'Would you like a beer, Tom?' says Grace, without turning.

He almost stumbles. 'Sorry?'

'It's been hot today. Would you like a beer?'

'A beer? In Mr Wilmot's house?'

'Why don't we share one, then?'

'Hey, you're only joking, aren't you?'

'Why should I be joking?'

'Okay,' he says, uncertainly. 'I didn't know you kept beer.'

'It's left over from Christmas. It's probably rather old.'

'Beer's beer.'

She fetches it and two glasses and sits down at the table with him. She says, without preamble, 'Hugh tells me you are getting married.'

Tommy's face is a beacon. He glances at her. Her eyes are grave and quiet. She is not going to recite to him a homily on sin. '*Ja*,' he says.

'Are you happy about it?'

He takes a sip of the beer and wipes the back of his hand across his mouth. 'People are always happy to be getting married.'

'People get married for all sorts of different reasons, Tom. Sometimes, I think happiness is a side issue. A matter of luck.'

He says nothing, looks at his glass, dabs his finger at a drop of foam. He does not look at her. He says, 'Why did you get married?'

'Jack was a good fellow, Tommy, but we married very young. If he'd lived, we'd have grown up together.' She looks across at him. 'We got married' – she searches for a word – 'by surprise!' She turns her glass around in careful fingers. 'I suppose this is the same for you.'

'I'll say it's a bloody surprise,' says Tommy, little flags of damp and heat forming along his temples. He looks at her sideways, not knowing how to react. He drains his glass.

She has seen that expression before, both bewildered and belligerent.

Then Tommy Cooper says, 'I think she caught me, on purpose. That's what some girls do, you know. They catch you out.'

'No they don't, Tom. There are times when no one thinks. Not her. Not you.'

'But it's different for blokes.'

'Who says it's different for them?'

He says, 'You're not a bloke, Mrs Wilmot.' *–Let me tell you one about the vicar's wife; –Have you heard the one about this popsie in a bar . . .*

Grace wants to laugh: yes, of course – everyone knows the guile of women. Their cunning and mendacity. Meretricious – all of them. But Tommy Cooper would not understand those words, so there is no use saying them.

–Women are full of shit. That's how he'd explain it. *–Catching blokes. Pinning them down.*

'Females just want babies,' Tommy Cooper says. 'And that's okay, that's fine . . .' Reasonable Tom, emphasising what he says by a gesture, laying out a principle. 'It's how they go about it.'

'No, Tom. They don't just want babies.'

'What do they want then?' He folds his arms and looks at her. 'Tell me.' He is defiant. 'What do they want?'

–Belief, Tom.

Instead, Grace says, 'Consistency.'

'Consistency!' He puckers his face. *'Women want consistency!'* He is starting to laugh. 'The bloody cheek of it!'

Grace laughs too – but for a different reason.

Then Tommy says – suddenly – his colour high, sweat blistering on his upper lip, 'It was hard in the war, but maybe being a soldier was best. Maybe it would have been better if I hadn't come back.'

She looks across at Tommy, struggling to defend himself against the sudden crumpling of his face.

Grace goes around the table.

–Maybe it would have been better if I hadn't come back.

It is slow motion – a rite deferred – reaching back through time. She kneels down beside him, linking her arms about his neck, stroking his shoulder gently, rocking him. 'I'm so sorry, Tommy. I'm, so, so sorry.'

It is Jack she holds. Jack who is clenched against her. Jack's dry weeping.

It is not Tommy Cooper's fault that his world is circumscribed so brutally. He is ruled by fear. He fights his bewilderment with teeth and fists. They are the only things he has. In war, no wonder he did not leave the shadow of his tank, the strict triangle of his tent, to explore the hills and stand – tranced – by a

215

pantomime of painted figures in a cave. Perhaps it's just as well he never went. He might have scrawled his name and date across the ancient frieze: *'Tommy Cooper was here'*.

I know where Tommy Cooper comes from. It is unfair to despise him. Standing in a shop one day – linens displayed at discount prices, execrable turquoise duvet covers, cellophaned in bags, row on row – a little boy, spike-haired, large eared (small Tommy Cooper) – was wheeling round with out-stretched arms, wavering counter to the whirr and dip of the ceiling fan, laughing with the gurgle and pause, the chuckle and rise of unconscious, uncomplicated glee.

He is a fan, a whirligig of wind.

A helicopter hovering.

A spaceship spinning just above the racks of shop-soiled towels and cut-price face cloths.

His grandmother – square-hipped in Bermudas, a beach shop ensemble, matching earrings, her reading glasses on a beaded chain – brayed, 'Jarryd, if you don't stop that now, Nana will tell the lady standing over there to phone the police. She's got the policeman's number, I can promise you.'

Small boy, frozen – no possibility of an escape – had turned to look at me, his glee curdling to a whimper.

In time, he will learn to disregard his grandmother (–*Silly old bitch*) – but the dread remains. He will grow up as Tommy Cooper did, with his clutch of clichés and his dictums, his smutty jokes, his bitter little homilies by which to live. –*If you don't behave, spiders, snakes and goggas* (nasty ones) *will get you*. The bogeyman. The communists and Jew-boys. The police. The kaffirs (*munts, boegs, houts*), and terrorists and hijackers. Don't forget the *moffies*. Don't forget the Devil.

And Women.

With a grandmother like that, perhaps it's not surprising he mistrusts them. No wonder he is maimed.

I have seen photos of Tommy Cooper's wedding. They were not difficult to discover. His family still farms here. The house, in a dip below the lands and pasture, is surrounded by trees and smaller camps of kikuyu grass. There is a pond in the garden with a concrete frog on a toadstool. It is not offensive. There are ferns growing round it, a haunt of dragonflies, a clump of arums, lush and strong. There is a little text on a wooden sign, words in praise of gardens, decorated with pink painted flowers, a present from a child. It is an uncom-plicated, happy place. There is a guava tree in the backyard, starched guest towels in the bathroom and a bag of knitting on a chair on the veranda.

Tommy Cooper's daughter-in-law serves me tea and banana loaf. We talk about growing herbs. She tells me she is very fond of golden cypress trees. She has ordered half a dozen from a catalogue. She will plant them round the rock garden. There is no dissembling in what I ask her. I am not looking for a sign or feeling my way into Grace and Godfrey's story as I did, so long ago, at Mrs Trollip's house. Nor am I Grace, revisiting a sacred place. There is no sense of synchronicity in the calling of the birds in the garden. I do not even notice them today.

I tell her I am looking for the Wilmot family. Hugh Wilmot was the minister at the Methodist church nearby. Her father-in-law once boarded with him when he was a young, unmarried man, just after the war.

She knows nothing of that. She knows nothing of the Wilmots. But she has some old photos. She refers to Tommy Cooper as 'Pa'.

'He passed away last year,' she says. 'He had bad emphysema. He was a great smoker all his life. And a bit of a drinker, but nothing terrible. Mom is still alive. She stays with my sister-in-law in Roodepoort now.'

'How many children did they have?'

'My husband's elder brother, Tom. My husband, Mike' – she looks across at me, enumerating on her fingers – 'and their sister in Roodepoort. She's the oldest.'

'Born?'

'Let's see. She's over fifty now. Nineteen forty-seven – somewhere around there.'

'Was Mr Cooper farming here then?'

'Yes, I think so. You'll have to ask my husband, Mike. I think, maybe, he and Mom were on another farm when they got married. He didn't inherit this farm or anything. He leased it. I'm not sure when he bought it. I think he got it cheap in the drought. When was that? About 'sixty-eight. Mike will remember. I wasn't around then.'

'It doesn't matter.'

She brings the photos. There are not many of them. She rifles through a pile of snapshots, finds the older prints, hands me a wedding picture.

So – this is Tommy Cooper.

He is tall. He is thin. He is a young man who has been to war. A young man with large ears and a grin. He stands outside the magistrate's office with the sun full on his face, bleaching out his features. His bride is in a summer frock with a little hat and the ubiquitous bouquet. She is pert, she is sassy.

'Mike's Mom has a great sense of humour,' says Tommy Cooper's daughter-in-law. 'She's quite a character. She kept Pa in his place, even when he had a drop too much and got argumentative. Now we pass her around between us.' She laughs. 'She comes to Tom and his wife or Mike and me when Mary-Grace has had enough. Or rather Mary-Grace's husband.'

Mary-Grace.

It is a sign after all.

'That's an unusual name,' I say, going underground.

'*Ja*, I suppose so. Pa apparently insisted, from when she was small, on the whole thing. "Mary-Grace." No nicknames. It was just some fancy of his. I once said, –*Why Mary-Grace?* And he said Mary was for his own Mom and Grace was how he'd like her to be. He didn't say why.'

I make no comment – look out over the lawn towards the rim of bush before the pasture starts, place my teacup carefully in its saucer: –*Little boy wheels round and round with the lift and dip of the fan, intent, searching after wonder, unravelling imagination.* Tommy Cooper, searching after wonder too, groping for it, sensing it is there – as insubstantial as a rumour, flowering in a place he cannot reach – had named his daughter Mary-Grace.

Chapter fourteen

Grace and Godfrey are withdrawing from each other – and from me. They have left me in a place which is hollow, even ominous. Leaving the farm where Tommy Cooper's family lives, I turn into the road, passing again, on the way up the long incline, the driveway winding through bush to the church, the house and Grace's little school. The landscape flattens out. It is deserted. It feels damaged, full of stands of scruffy wattle trees. I am aware again of the crude white letters which had been painted on the roofs of farmhouses during the State of Emergency, with their security numbers, starker now in contrast to the faded flaking reds and greens of corrugated iron; of workers' houses – the flotsam of farm construction – unchanged over decades. The insanity and contradiction still remain. The poverty. The barricading in (I passed a boom an hour ago) the barricading out (the hillside nearer town has spawned small breeze block houses kept at bay from farmlands by a razorwire fence). No one is secure: neither the barricading nor the barricaded. I read in the paper a week ago that a storekeeper had been shot at Enseleni. No name is given but I know that it is Mr Xaba with his juggling phones, in the wrong place, at the tail end of chance. All that energy, that resolution – gone: *–I am really very busy*. Blown away – for a watch or a cellphone or his 4x4 with its cargo of cooldrinks. Or maybe not. Maybe for something more sinister: the strange, disjointed drift of smoke from the chimney of the turquoise house, the surreptitious windows, the dog baying hectically, anticipating threat.

Welcome to Enseleni. It is a prosperous place. There is a money lender, *Quik-Cash Supa-Loans*. Xaba's store has changed hands and there is a new funeral parlour, *Rest Assured with Chitibungu Funeral Directors*. Disease and death has become opportunity, nourishment. And, of course, the cellphone

219

shop in the painted container donated by a shipping line, decorated with an *Aids Awareness* logo, dragged up here on the back of a truck, has settled into the forlorn grass at the edge of the *donga*, a strange new detritus from the sea. It will never rot. It will never rust. It will squat at Enseleni –

–*till the cows come home!* says Prof. He thinks he is amusing.

I am looking for signs. Without them, no one can write any kind of story about this place and its sudden inner silence. It would be plotless, flouting the rules: *Conflict* (through each carefully constructed phase) to *Resolution*. Very simple. Very clear. Without those rules, there can be no framework.

–*Good,* the prof would say, –*you must learn to deconstruct things. Authorial intention is always suspect.*

Indeed.

I tell him that's bullshit. He says it's not. But he doesn't know the hidden structure of the signs. He can't discern their pattern or their sequence. He does not know a shrike's call from a mynah's. He is oblivious of the spare translucence – and the shape – of my empty landscapes. And because he does not understand the signs, he does not have devotion for the little things: their humour and their consolation. He has no god to bargain with. He sees no sense in writing this at all.

If I do as he says, I will start to lose belief, to disassemble things as Grace did, in the weeks after Godfrey left. Like her, I will demolish sentences, words, gestures, phrases, courting chaos.

Don't do it, Grace. It is unfair to Godfrey.

But I see her face briefly – the angry flash, her brow lifting: how rarely she has held my eye or challenged me.

What do I know? I have not been left by Godfrey.

She has.

For me, he is a face in a portrait. He is words on a page. He is a eulogy in an old newspaper, comments on a catalogue card, the presence in a room. He will, in time, be contained between the pages of a book.

My Godfrey.

Mine.

The way I want to see him. The way I want him to be seen.

What have I to lose?

I have never stood against him, poised by a breath, perfectly pitched to the current of his touch. Indivisible. Immaculate.

Or destroyed.

Kusegazini – you are in my blood which cannot be divided.

Oh yes, that it true. But for Grace, it is different.

It is she who *knows* his blood. Its substance. Its weight. Its smell. Its heat. The thin blue tracery at wrists, at groin, at temple, in his neck, the hollow of his throat. She knows its tumult and its steady, quiet tide. Its rest. In sleep, she has laid a fingertip against his pulse, left a breath against his lids, imprinting her touch in it, sending it to anchor in against his heart.

Now, the only way to bear the loss of him is to deconstruct him. To deconstruct herself for what she did.

Grace is ruthless, even brutal on herself.

For not having loved Jack enough.

For not being able to love Hugh in the way he wants her to.

For having loved Godfrey at all.

For so great a sin.

The judges are as grim as hangmen.

Godfrey has gone.

She will not follow him.

She has no place in Godfrey's house. She does not know his sons. She has not met his friends. Godfrey, the professor – so urbane, so invulnerable – is not the Godfrey that she knows. Without his mythologies, his place in the ironstone valley below the ridge, Godfrey is a stranger.

Most intimate of all, most beloved, he will always be a stranger.

Intimacy ebbs and then corrupts. One retreats to a carapace of stone, the other – shell-less – feels the peeling back of skin, nerves left raw and unconnected. Intimacy, betrayed, it is a dangerous thing. Once ardent, self-absorbed, it transmogrifies, becomes the enemy within.

–Don't leave me, Godfrey.

But he has.

All his small omissions rise to the surface, air through mud. She misinterprets him, over-analyses, is ungenerous, unjust. Jealous. And painfully astute – an underwater creature feeling the faintest traces in the tide. Once she made allowance, but that allowance is re-examined now. Piece by piece, right from the start.

–Hello? Godfrey's voice on the party-line, long ago, the whirring of the handle under someone else's impatient fingers, rapping in Grace's ears.

–I'm missing you, she says.

–I won't be able to come down next week. He is brisk. *–Too much on here. Visiting lecturers. A good old friend is coming from England. Wonderfully stimulating company.*

–Who?

He says the name. She conveys delight for him. He has told her about his friend before. So many anecdotes. Now, she senses he is irritated with her familiarity, her intrusion. She withdraws, just in time. *–Shall I parcel up what I have done and send it?* She waits for a reply.

221

–Perhaps. He is already having lunch in the hotel dining room, intellectual sparring with a group, pipes after coffee, the old fan in the ceiling revolving the smoke with each rotation.

She has only offered to send it to provoke his assurance that he will come for it himself. A year ago he would – there would have been no question of excuse. He would have come for it and stood behind her and leaned in quietly to catch – not just the words on the page – but the warmth of her shoulder.

–Send it registered. He uses a pet name, as an afterthought.

Its intimacy, intended to disarm – even to console – does not reassure. He is moving on.

Is he?

Perhaps, when she put down the phone, he had whistled off to town, amused by her. Had she sounded like an official from the post office, buttoned to the chin, starchy and prim?

–The counter closes at twelve-thirty, sir. Please fill out the form before you come to the desk. Next!

Silly Grace: she did not know how ridiculous she'd sounded – not chilly, but like a wasp, a little high, thin-edged and poised to sting.

And he had been – at best – avuncular.

–Hello, Gracie?

Once, Godfrey from the university.

She makes her voice glad. *–How are you?*

–Annoyed.

His being annoyed neatly precludes her from saying what she needs to say. Subconsciously, he knows it: she will rally to his being 'annoyed' so he doesn't have to hear her. She laughs at his relief. He is light-hearted at his quick reprieve (isn't he droll?), thinks of another little turn of phrase to entertain her. *–It's good to hear you sounding so cheerful*, he says.

Ah.

–My typewriter's playing up. He is back to being irritable. *–The ribbon keeps jumping out of the sprocket and the damned Dean wants a report* . . . He is full of gruff complaints. She knows he is sitting with his legs up on his desk, scratching at his pipe. *–Well, now* (noises in the background) *–we mustn't waffle on. Here's Mrs P with my tea* (his ageing secretary, a sausage of iron chignon horizontal at her nape) *–Thanks, Mrs P!* Even down the party-line Grace can hear the rattle of the teacup and the clucks and caresses of Mrs P's voice. *–Mind if I slurp in your ear?* He is absently sipping. Grace waits: he is phoning because he feels he should, not because he wants to. *–Just thought I'd keep in touch.*

He has no idea that she is holding on to the wall of the passage next to the old phone box, trying to breathe. The brightness she invents – the sunny, friendly repartee – builds a dogged and deliberate distance that he does not sense. He is talking in a vacuum far away (–*Good old Grace is really bucking up these days. Very nice to have her cheerful*).

Can't he hear?

Of course he can, but he no longer dares to listen.

He used to listen – oh, so deftly, with the delicate fine-tuning of a man who wants to be a lover. Then, he would not have said, –*Buck up, Grace*. He would have coaxed each word, each thought from her, leading her tenderly, never assuming, gently probing for the chink that would let him in.

Now, he is hammering his way out.

She knows what will come next. He does not need to say it. –*Got to dash, Gracie. I have a lecture right now* . . . She knows he has at least twenty minutes more. A year ago he would have kept her till the bell rang – and beyond. –*Lovely to hear your voice.*

–*Off you go then, or you'll be late.*

–*Good Lord, look at the time!*

Look at the time.

She puts the receiver down very carefully. She would never be so obvious as to drop it into its cradle. She watches the old woven cord wind round itself into a frayed brown spiral again. She walks away, tread very soft, as if she wished to pass unnoticed – mostly by herself.

Oh, mostly by herself.

Perhaps, for him, she exists in a certain space, contained and circumscribed. Beyond the valley and the house, that room, this lexicon, she cannot be. To let her in – even in thought – would be catastrophic. Her presence is suspended at the university, at a conference, in his own home: the quiet, high-ceilinged rooms, cut-glass with zinnias, Persian rugs past their prime, the neat, perfectly ordered precision of his family's daily round. His wife has the soul of a janitor. She lives by lists and pre-empts any inconvenience. He, in turn, is unvarying in his routine. Here, there can be no *umvemve* calf, no *inala* cow, no moon that grazes like a great white bull in the sky pastures.

Such whimsy would be scorned.

Just as I have constructed Godfrey in these pages, remoulding him from almost nothing, coaxing him back (my tenderness for him, my elegy), Grace begins, in her desolation and her self-contempt, to dismantle their world, piece by piece. In doing it, she snipes at him. It's left to me – the more detached – to vindicate him and be generous.

And yet, perhaps I'm not objective any more: I am beginning to take Grace's part. I am no longer an observer, balancing fact and probability – the fine-tuning of biography. I am no longer so dispassionate. Sometimes, I want to find him and confront him for her.

Just for once – I want to win.

I want to overturn restraint, to rise up armed, to roar my anguish out for loss of joy.

He would have been bewildered.

He will proceed and do what he does best – learned and honed since the time he let his deepest grief leak out among the dust and springs under his old box-bed at the death of the *umvemve* calf.

He just 'gets on'.

He expects Grace to do the same: his homage to her kindred soul, belief in their equality. Like him, she must survive – and find her joy in other things.

I will not contradict him: it is Godfrey who decides.

And Grace who waits, listening for the phone to ring.

It doesn't. And it won't.

And yet, for weeks, Grace remains alert, walking softly through the rooms of the house, attentive, just in case she does not hear it.

–Don't leave me, Godfrey.

But he had.

Long ago she had placed her palm on Godfrey's palm, her hand defenceless, opened-out, sheltered by his. It had seemed a simple gesture. It was not. It was complex and grave.

Now, there is nothing she can do to bring him back. She has no right.

Nor can she curl her fingers round her palm, retracting what she offered, self intact.

It is all too late. Her aloneness is implacable.

–Don't leave me, Godfrey.

It is not something that Stella would have ever said. She would never lay her naked palm between his palms, abrogating power.

She knew he wouldn't go.

On the road from the school and church, from Tommy Cooper's farm, the track leads down into a valley. It is here that the bush banks thick to the edges of the road: tecoma and plumbago, clumps of *boerboon* and milkwood, an inland echo of the coastal bush. The road dips towards a drift. It crosses a river which is full because of rain. I stop the car. It is late morning, hot, even humid, in this hollow. I am alert because – local wisdom from Mrs Cooper – one should not stop in deserted places. It is unsafe. They are right, of course, but I stop anyway because I know, by another local wisdom, that this pool is a place of *abantu bomlambo* – 'the people of the river', who inhabit the interzone of water between the earth and that other country where the pasture is rich and the

224

herds are plentiful. A place where sacrifice was made once, where sacrifice is made still – sending out into the centre of the pool *impepho* flowers, a small libation of beer in a basket. Godfrey would have known this place. So would Grace. They might have placed a stone for their dead – and for themselves – on a little cairn. They might have seen a water wagtail and smiled, knowing, by its presence, that they were known too, their rites observed.

The undergrowth is thick, hanging over a pool, backed up by a causeway. Here, the overhang is perfectly reflected in the water, each leaf in mirror, quivering minutely, each distant slant of sky – the world inverted in the surface of the pool.

–The sky is the earth, the earth is the sky.

Yes, Desmond – as Bibleman says. I will not contradict it.

As I turn away, the smell reaches me.

Floating in the dead water where the current does not reach, in the bright putrescent green of algae, is the carcass of a cow.

I remember how I ground the gears from neutral into first, jerking the car. I almost stalled, flooding the engine. *–Do not stop in deserted places.*

I drive up the slope and out, bursting into open country. I trail a parachute of dust, whipping out behind my wheels.

But the dread is not in the earth, in its cycles of life and death: its burden is in me.

In what I do with it.

I wonder, often, if there are any pictures of Grace's wedding to Hugh.

I think there might be Brownie snaps – just one or two: an insurance should their children ever ask, something to replace the album of Grace's wedding to Jack (put away discreetly among his mother's private things – the shrimp-coloured gladioli, Grace with a band of paste orange blossom holding a long, slim veil, Jack with his hair cut high above his ears and up the back of his head and Grandpa looking grave with a carnation in his buttonhole), something small that they might have framed and put on their mantelpiece. Just Hugh and Grace, in black and white, without attendants, a small posy the only hint of occasion, Grace with her head inclined, Hugh's hand at her elbow, cupping it, as if to hold her steady.

Perhaps Hugh judged a second wedding might be assumed to be the first: Grace had always been Mrs Wilmot. She would be Mrs Wilmot still. And Jack would become, again, Hugh's younger brother, killed in the war.

Long ago.

Hugh has an audience with his seniors, asks for a transfer to a parish in Rhodesia. In another country, in another home, their history would be incidental. It is quietly arranged. Hugh listens to the kindly counsel of the

Moderator, without comment. It could have been him, talking to Tommy Cooper, in his study at home.

–Sometimes, unwisely, even sinfully, these things happen.

Hugh senses his own rebellion, just as he has felt Tommy Cooper's. The good man has missed the point, as he had missed it, once, himself. For reasons Hugh would not dare to scrutinise, he does not hint at altruism on his part or mention a Dr Godfrey. Instead, he feels a vicarious little triumph – even a pleasure – in being censured for his 'sin' and a sudden sense of power over Grace, an overwhelming longing and desire.

Hugh lets the Moderator finish, and then he says – quite firmly – that marrying Grace would not be viewed as an obligation on his part. On the contrary – it is a gift from God.

Tommy Cooper takes Grace and Hugh to the station in town. He believes that they are going to a family gathering of some description, somewhere on the Reef. Grace isn't well. She is staying on for a while with a relative and Dulcie Trollip is coming to the school to take her place and teach while she is away. Mr Wilmot will be back in a week. There has been some talk of a transfer in the last few days. Mr Wilmot insists he has been wanting a transfer for some time. How could he want a transfer when he has just dug up the vegetable garden and planted it again and has been talking about painting the roof of the house green instead of red? Tommy Cooper glances at Grace in the rear-view mirror. She is unaware of him.

Grace sits in the back of the car. She runs her finger along a crack in the leather seat, over and over. They take the turn from the church out on to the district road.

What will little Desmond say when he discovers Dulcie Trollip in her place on Monday morning?

–Where is Mrs Wilmot?

–She has gone away.

–She would never go away without saying goodbye.

–She is not well and she has to work in a dry, high place, so she has gone to the Reef.

–What is the reef?

–A thing in the sea, says another child.

–She will be drowned.

Indeed.

She had asked Dulcie to take her place herself. She had not left it to Hugh. He could say what he liked to Herman de Waal – or to anyone – but Grace would not allow another woman in her post without telling her why she had appealed to her. Beyond that, what was said did not matter.

    –What happened to Grace?
    –Does anyone know where Grace went?
    –Can anyone guess?
    –Have you heard the one about the vicar's wife . . .

Dulcie Trollip answers the phone. She picks it up gingerly, wearing large workman's mits. She is mixing cattle-dip in the yard. She has left a man holding the slim copper spout on the can so it doesn't drip.

    'Dulcie? This is Grace Wilmot. I wonder if it's possible for me to come and see you this afternoon? There's something I would like to ask you.'

    Dulcie is surprised. She has never had much to do with Grace. Her other-worldliness, her pale beauty and her way of speaking has set her apart from the women of the district, even when she had been married to wild Jack. She reads books no one has heard of. She is known to have 'funny ideas about the natives'. She was certainly heading for trouble on the farm before Jack went away, talking about building a school and getting women to make things out of *jalimani* print – tablecloths and things (who'd want that stiff, smelly material on the table? The blue dye would get on everything in no time). It is in the way she speaks Xhosa, with a quietness, as if she were requesting, not commanding or even telling. It is in the way they respond to her, not keeping the proper distance as they ought. Someone at the Women's Institute said she had a barmy old Grandpa who collected Xhosa bird calls in the *gamadoelas* in the Transkei . . .

    But that is something Dulcie likes.

    It is something that she knows. It reminds her of her father and his cows, the acceptance of something else, something unexpected. Like Grace, she has been the brunt of talk herself. She knows the little fearful scorns of others too.

    –The De Waals have gone quite 'bush' over kaffir cattle.
    –Malkop Herman. Mal Dulcie.
    –Poor old Arthur Trollip! Guess who wears the pants in that family?
    –What do you expect, man? He hasn't got his 'varkies in die hok' since the war. Who's going to farm if Dulcie doesn't?
And Dr Godfrey?

I see, now, that Mrs Trollip, in her funny, fierce, loyal way – both ingenuous and brusque – had been defending Grace, searching out some consolation.

    –They say he was a Communist.
Something must be blamed for everything that happened. Something clear and unequivocal, which no one could contest. Something to deflect the urge to pry.

It takes a woman to defend a woman.

Grace asks Hugh for the car after school. She tells him where she is going. He walks out to the garage with her, opens the door and flicks a fallen leaf from the windscreen.

'Drive safely,' he says. His air is proprietorial.

'I won't be long, but I would like to ask her myself.'

Hugh hesitates, glances across at her, his eyes a little magnified behind the lenses of his specs. 'You won't say too much?' He is diffident: he does not want to annoy her. His temples are damp. He brushes away a bead of sweat.

'I will tell Dulcie Trollip what I need to tell her,' Grace says. But she touches his hand in reassurance, gives it a small pat where it rests on the edge of the car door.

She drives away. Hugh watches her. For a moment – just a moment – he imagines Godfrey sitting in the seat next to her. He has a sense of Godfrey easing his long, unselfconscious body into comfort, lighting his pipe, saying something to make her turn and laugh, leaning into him.

The unmeditated intimacy of a gesture. It is quite different from the way in which Grace had touched his hand.

When Grace arrives at the farm, Dulcie is standing in the foundations of her new house. She is wearing boots and riding breeches and is directing a man with a barrowful of wet cement.

'I've caught you at a busy time,' says Grace, walking down the path towards her.

'No, man, that's okay. I just need to get these boys laying the cement before it's dark.'

Dulcie's husband, Arthur Trollip, is hovering about over the innards of a truck hoisted up on bricks. Dulcie puts her hand to her plaits, pats them into place, glances across at him, raises her voice – a warning to him to keep away, 'I'll send you up some tea.'

He grunts, seems to peer furtively at Grace. He starts clanging at the radiator with a spanner.

'That's right, make a hole in the thing!' Dulcie says to herself and walks off briskly, leading the way.

Grace follows her down to the old house. They do not go inside where Dulcie's mother will be knitting in the living room. They sit on the grass-weave chairs on the veranda among the tins of sword ferns. Dulcie lights a cigarette and calls over her shoulder into the house for the housemaid to bring tea. 'And biscuits, Nomabini! Biscuits, hey?' Then she turns to Grace. 'Well,' she says. 'It's a surprise to see you.'

'Yes. I'm sorry and I hope this isn't going to be a huge nuisance but I have something rather particular to ask you.'

'If I can help.'

'I know you're a teacher, Dulcie. I need someone to take over my post.'

Dulcie Trollip is surprised. 'I do the farming here. Mostly for Pa because Arthur's not himself and thinks he's still fighting in the war.'

'I know.'

'The cattle take a lot of time . . .'

Cattle. The word hangs between them.

They do not need to mention Godfrey. They both know that it's because of him that Grace is here.

'I don't want to let the children down in the middle of the term but I have to go away. If you could hold the fort until a permanent teacher is appointed? I'm sure they will be able to find someone by the time the new term starts.'

'I have so many projects. The cattle. The house. I've designed it myself. I need to be on site.'

Grace does not plead. She simply says, 'I don't have a choice.'

Dulcie looks across at her. She puts out her cigarette slowly, her eyes on the camp beyond the lawn, where her cattle graze.

'Will you be coming back?'

'No.'

The tea is brought and a little plate of biscuits.

Dulcie's Peanut Biscuits. Grace has typed the recipe out for the *Ladies' Guild Cookery Book*. She has made them once herself. They are light and crumbly. Roasted nuggets, full of shortening.

'Dr Godfrey still keeps in touch with my Pa,' Dulcie says suddenly. 'He always wants to know about our herd. He phones occasionally. Not long ago he sent Pa some articles from a friend who's a vet. A chap called Humphreys. I met him at a cattle sale, once. Nice bloke.'

Grace is at a loss:

—*Where is he?*

—*What else does he say?*

Dulcie Trollip anticipates her. She says, 'Pa told me Dr Godfrey and his family are moving to England. I think he meant for good.'

Again, Grace does not speak. But Dulcie senses the attention in her repose. 'He is going to lecture. And his sons are to study there. I think Pa said his wife is English and doesn't really like it here and it's only Dr Godfrey's old father that keeps them in this country.'

Only Dr Godfrey's old father?

Oh no, Dulcie, it is not only Dr Godfrey's old father! It starts with the *umvemve* calf and Bibleman. It is the pepper tree, the corrugated roof, the old veranda room. It is the map banging on the wall in the dusk-wind at prep and the smell of boxing gloves, leather and sweat. It is the empty *veld* grazed by cattle, the red and the dun, the eland-yellow and the mushroom-pale. It is the reptile road, the aloe and the ironstone, the cow called *inala*, the ridge of jackals. It is the hot wind blowing from the interior, nudging at the window. It is the catalogue, the hidden conversation. It is the long blue shadows on the lamplit wall. And more. *And more.*

Kusegazini: you are in my blood.

Which cannot be divided.

Grace puts down her teacup.

—It is only Dr Godfrey's old father that keeps them in this country.

It is not this unborn child.

There is the taste of iron in her mouth. She remains quite still. Then she says, 'Hugh and I are getting married.'

Dulcie does not move. She does not speak. She does not know what to say.

'That is why I'm asking you to take my place at school,' says Grace. 'He will join me when he's packed up here. A month or two, maybe more.' She stops. Then she says, 'He's a very good man.'

Dulcie does not look at her. She chooses her words with care. 'You can be good about something you want very much.'

'He didn't ask for it.'

'No.' She gives a small laugh. 'But I should think he's on his knees, thanking God.'

Grace glances across at her.

'Come on, Grace, everyone knows it. Even before Doreen died. Even before Jack. Shame, poor Mr Wilmot.'

Grace can feel the blood in her neck, its painful surge.

Dulcie says, 'Where are you going?'

'Rhodesia.'

'Rhodesia?'

'No one knows any of us there.'

There is a pause. Then Dulcie says, 'How long have you got to go?'

'Long enough.'

'What shall I say?'

'That I was offered a teaching post in a city. I had to take it up as soon as I could or I would have lost it. I *will* take a post. If what you say is true, I suppose no one will be surprised if Hugh follows me.'

Dulcie opens her box of cigarettes and chooses carefully, as if there is a great variety inside. She picks one up, puts it down, takes another. 'I think that people will be pleased.' She lights the cigarette and adds, 'For him.'

'For him.' Grace's expression is a little wry, self-judging.

Then Dulcie says, 'I'm sorry you couldn't have what you wanted. Women very seldom do.'

She takes another drag, sends the smoke up, is silent. Grace knows she is speaking of herself. Dulcie stands and leans against the parapet of the veranda, her back to Grace. 'I'll take your post,' she says. 'I haven't much experience, but I'll do my best.'

They walk up the path together. Dulcie points out the foundations of her house. The yellow brick is stacked, waiting for cement. 'I always wanted to build a house,' she says. 'Even when I was little.' Her laugh is gruff, a little harsh, directed at herself. 'I decided to have something that was mine. Exactly the way I liked it. I didn't want to redo my Mom's house one day and feel that her spook was giving me hell for moving a room around. I've had that all my life. When the folks have gone, I'll turn the old dump into a cow shed or a workshop or something. I'm going to make a nice garden at the new house and have a bird bath. Man, there's nothing better than birds in the garden. That's what I'm going to do, bugger the rest.'

Grace opens the car door, puts her foot on the running board, half turns to Dulcie. In the garage, off to her left, she can sense Dulcie's husband watching them again, a spanner in his hand.

He calls, 'I thought you were sending up some tea.'

'*Ja*, in a minute,' Dulcie says. 'Patience is a virtue.'

Grace does not hear the muttered retort.

If Dulcie does, she does not care.

Grace climbs into the car. 'Well . . .' she is a little awkward. 'Look after yourself. And thank you.' She puts out her hand and touches Dulcie's strong fingers resting on the window's edge. Dulcie grips them briefly, not looking at her, her voice unsteady just a moment. 'I suppose there are other things besides love.'

'Yes,' says Grace quietly.

Half rueful, even shy, Dulcie says, suddenly, 'He's one hell of a man!'

Grace glances up at her. 'Hugh?'

'Dr Godfrey.'

They both laugh then. It is the only way to stall emotion.

'I'll be thinking of you,' Dulcie says.

As Grace drives away she sees Dulcie Trollip in her rear-view mirror, standing on the foundation wall of her house, neither triumphant, nor forlorn. Just standing quietly, surveying it.

–*I suppose there are other things besides love.*

And other ways to honour it.

231

Tommy Cooper drives sedately, as if he is part of a procession. Hugh, beside him in the front, hat on his lap, does not speak. Without looking up, Grace knows each turn, each camber where the wheels take the curve, slotting into long-run ruts, touching with an outer edge, the little bank of sand along its margin. Here is the place where the track is steel-grey over corrugations, the ironstone coming through the backbone of the earth, curving the hill, and far below, the little house and store in the empty plain.

She keeps her eyes on the inside of the car. Only the reflection of light, of hill or wall, is cast back flat against the glass of the closed windows. The colours flicker across her face, her hands resting in her lap.

They are turning west and south. She hears the ringing of a cattle grid. She knows that to her right, rising up from the plain, unremarkable and bare, is the ridge where the herd once grazed. It is gaunt and jackal-backed against an empty sky.

Uqolo lwezimpungutye.

Ridge of Jackals. A lonely place to be.

Chapter fifteen

Hugh and Grace are married by a fellow minister, a man who had been an army chaplain with Hugh, who had gone 'up north' with him and served in the desert. He is an earnest, kindly man. He does not labour them with homilies. He does not talk about 'adversity making one strong' or 'taking the good with the bad' or any of those pedestrian little platitudes designed to disguise a failure of imagination. Besides, he knows that Hugh has already had an interview with the Moderator and there is nothing more to say.

Hugh has asked to be married in his church.

In the sight of God.

The vows – both his and Grace's – cannot be given in a registry office in front of an official. It would make a mockery of everything that Hugh believes, expose the underside of motive which he will not own, its little jealousies and triumphs. This will not be an arrangement. It will be a pledge.

The witnesses are the verger and the vicar's secretary.

There are no hymns, no sermon, and the only flowers are in the posy bought by Hugh from a florist's bucket in a store on the other side of the street. Hugh has brought his Brownie camera. The minister takes a few hasty pictures, trying to cajole them out of awkwardness.

After the ceremony Hugh and Grace and the minister walk across to the hotel and order tea. Then Hugh goes to the post office and sends his mother a telegram.

Grace and I were married at 3.00 this afternoon in Krugersdorp.

In haste is guilt.

He hopes she will assume it, believe the obvious when the child arrives: he and Grace have lived too long in the same house. They are human, after all.

She knows nothing of a Doctor Godfrey. She never will.

He walks back down the street to the hotel. He can see Grace sitting on her chair, half twisted in to face the minister. She is very still, in exact repose, the flowers in her lap. The minister is talking. No doubt, in his mild, serious way, he is telling Grace about their army days. What else can he say to fill the time without intruding?

It seems to him, if he should speak too loudly or move his hand or lean towards her, he would startle her away.

Hugh comes up the steps, puts his hat on a chair. 'Well,' he says, cheerfully. 'That's done.'

The minister rises. 'I should be getting along. Ladies' Guild at five.'

–Ah, the Ladies' Guild. Hugh laughs: a little in-joke between comrades.

Rain starts to fall. They all turn to watch it. Big, irregular drops splash into the sand of the pavement, indenting gravel.

'Jolly good luck to have rain on your wedding. I always tell my brides that – but you have to be brought up in a dry place to believe it,' says the minister. He turns to Grace, 'Cheerio, then, and God bless.' He takes Hugh's hand, looks him in the face. It is an exchange – God's soldiers. 'Keep in touch,' he says. 'Let me know where they send you.'

Grace watches him go, Hugh at her side.

It is four-thirty. The light beyond the rain lights the roofs of houses and a mine dump, shimmering the thin, turning leaves of gums grouped around a patch of open ground. There is the sigh of tyres on the street, the whip of a bicycle spinning by, the single heavy thud of drops dripping from a drain.

'Shall we go upstairs?' says Hugh.

She inclines her head.

The grain of the wallpaper on the landing, a sad pastiche of fleur-de-lis plastered across an earlier stucco surface, is rough to the touch of trailing fingers. There is a cuckoo clock, hung too high, the brass weights, shaped like Christmas fir cones, hanging on their chains.

At five-thirty Hugh comes down to the lobby, taking the stairs with care, as if he is afraid of causing a disturbance. He almost tiptoes to the desk, asks discreetly for a tray of tea to be sent to Room 15, on the second floor, stands a minute, quiet and reverential, looking through the front door at the rain.

So events and places in each other's lives become unknown to Grace and Godfrey. Dates do not share a meaning, the coincidence in daily thought drifts quietly apart. The routines of their days are unconnected. Familiar clothes have disappeared: his dear blue shirt, his camel cardigan, the shoes which are moulded so exactly to the shape of his feet, with the wrong-coloured laces. Familiar books with little tags to mark important places. A piece of music is forgotten, the words of a song which seemed so apt. Anniversaries – of whatever kind – are uncommemorated by the other. Godfrey knows nothing of the day that Grace had married Hugh. He feels no intimation of it, packing up the files in his study on an autumn afternoon, pasting labels on the boxes that he stores them in. Grace knows nothing of the day that Godfrey sails for England. She has no apprehension of him standing, surrounded by luggage at the foot of a gangplank, the high wind sending the harbour water sucking in a deep long swell between the liner and the quay. She has never been to sea, or watched, from the stern, the coil and thrust of the churning wake. She has never been to England. She has no reference in her mind, no notion of a house, a garden or a landscape. She has never seen his wife or sons. She only knows he will not drive a truck any more, or carry a knapsack for the bits of this and that he picks up in the *veld*. He will not look to distance – gauging space by miles and miles – with a navigator's eye.

There is no distance where he is going.

And she? She floats in his subconscious in the context in which he knew her, the features of her face fixed against a period, a time. She is the dim glow of a paraffin lamp, the sound of *dikkops* crying moonlight in the open lands, the *bergwind* breathing in the early hours just before the dawn. But there are no reminders where he is. No thorn, no *dongas*, no ironstone, no endless sky. All that remains is a snapshot tucked into the back of his catalogue box in an envelope, a shadow stretching out towards his feet as he stands, arm linked about the neck of an *inala* cow: *3.03pm, 19th August, 1946.*

It becomes, suddenly, a long, long time ago.

A place may be the source of intimacy. It compensates for loss. Intrinsically, it can't betray.

It can be built – and even shared.

It can be beloved.

I have traced, through the Methodist Church Register, some of the parishes that were served by Hugh Wilmot and there is one where he was incumbent for almost eighteen years. I have the address and the name of the parish. I know it stands in one of those unremarkable streets in a new suburb of a new town. I sense it is built frugally. No architect has dreamed it up. It is the work of a practical builder, taking his chance on returning soldiers and the post-war housing boom: three bedrooms, one bathroom, kitchen, lounge-dining room combined, carport, servants' quarters (shower over the hole which serves as a lavatory), quarter acre of grass, edged with poinsettias with a thatched fence, in front, to screen the house from the road, cannily woven, whispering with white ants.

There is a gum tree at the gate. It is a double column of silky grey and white and mauve-green bark. It is a landmark for miles around. Driving in, Grace looks up at it, its high crown against a sunny sky.

The house is drowned in bougainvillaea.

There has been a craze for multicoloured walls and the builder has used all his ingenuity. The dining room is terracotta, the bedroom pastel blue and buttercup (two walls each), the bathroom pink, with pink bath and tiles, edged with a row of black, the kitchen – 'hospital green' in high gloss finish.

Grace is dismayed.

She paints the house herself. White from end to end. Outside and in. Windows, doors, pillars. There is nothing she can do about the dull mottled institution-shade of the low asbestos roof. She encourages the scarlet bougainvillaea, allowing it to wander.

And here is Hugh, always ready with the tool box. He is a great repairer of things. He is a man who can build trellises and make furrows and trench vegetable seedbeds. He wears his cloth hat and his shorts and his long socks held up by elastic garters and he pops on camphor cream to soothe the sunspots on his arms. His glasses come unhinged and he binds the bridge across the nose with cellotape.

Grace digs flower beds into the deep red soil and plants zinnias and marigolds. They are not her favourite flowers – too brash, too bright – but they thrive under the blast of a tropical sun. In spring, the garden is ablaze, not with the plants of her grandparents' Christmas cottage, not with stocks and ivy and jasmine and plumbago, but with banks of colour and excess. On summer afternoons it is luminous against a sky, building purple storms. But in the early morning, before the light has unsheathed itself and the shadow is still deep, she walks along the beds, inspecting them, feeling the baby, as if it is stretching for the new day too. It is starting to turn.

And Godfrey seeps back.

Gone are the recriminations, gone the strange distortions of the things he said – gruffly perhaps, or in irritation (man things) – which she has wilfully misconstrued.

–It is.

He had said it once.

And why should he repeat it, when the truth of it is simple and immutable?

–It is.

Steady as a distant lodestar.

Sometimes she sits in the dew, in the quiet time of day, disturbing the little catapulting grass insects with her outstretched legs. Sometimes she lies flat

236

on her back, feeling the pull of the ground beneath her, taking her into the earth, the weight of the sky pressing down.

–Where are you?

The arch of sky above is unimaginably wide.

But she is not alone in listening and her breath seems greater than herself. It is as if a hand cups the nape of her neck: that first intent. So tentative, so tender.

–If you were in my flesh I could tear you out, but – kusegazini – you are in my blood, which cannot be divided.

She places her hands together on her tummy. A small benediction. She had never thought of tearing this child out of her flesh.

It is hers. And it is his.

It is their blood, which cannot be divided.

–Oh, my love.

She goes in when the sun breaks through the shrubbery. Morning is sudden. And the mystery is gone. Hugh will be in the dining room, at the table, doing his Bible reading for the day. She must muster-up for a thousand things after she has brought him tea. She runs the church with him as if she were his fellow minister, his right hand. She is driven, meticulous, competent. The only task she has ever abandoned was the *Ladies' Guild Recipe Book*. She had stuffed it into an old envelope (the bright, thick, orange-yellow OHMS with a brass flange to keep it closed) and posted it to Dulcie Trollip. Somehow, she could not look at the entry for quince jelly with its jaunty sketch of fruit and leaf. It brought a strange sharp sting to the base of her throat: the remembrance of sun slanting through the clear amber liquid in a jar, the faint rustling of the olive thrush scavenging in the leaves under a bush, some inexorable turning point – Hugh's intent gaze, circling her – and she, shaken by a sudden sense of loss, in words recalled:

–You need jelly with your roast. I'm sorry it's not mint, but I can't grow it. It always dries up.

Here, any recipe books will be left to the ingenuity of the ladies in the choir while Grace keeps the records and writes the letters as she had for Godfrey. There is not a minute of the day which she does not fill. It leaves no time for introspection.

Or for God.

She is glad of it. She does not wish to confront Him about Godfrey. Or ask why love was such a sin. For, if it was, why did it remain so absolute, so numinous?

So indestructible?

Here, I must try and think with Grace and understand her choices and her

237

acquiescence. But I am bewildered, not knowing what I would have done. There is a strange blankness in my mind. An incomprehension. Perhaps the difference between us is that, in 1947, she had no choice at all: the baby's rights over her own would not have been debated. For Grace, it was simple. She would ensure the best for the living child – at whatever cost. *Her* desires, her freedom and her needs were put aside. And how can I judge her choice out of the context of her time? Who knows what Right is the Truth – or cares, as Grace did then?

And how can I judge her when I have never thought to make commitment to a man I did not choose, fulfilling obligation, knowing always that the sin, like a little stillborn corpse would lie between, considered with the final word. The unspoken backstop to argument, to anger, even to inheritance.

Except, Grace – and I – reckoned without Hugh.

Hugh is shown into the recovery ward in the maternity home. He stands at the door, his hat in his hand. He comes forward to the bed, his face half grave, half rapt. He is awed, as if he has come to a holy place.

Grace looks up at him, her pale hair is still damp about her face. She has that other-world detachment and stillness, the dignity and distance of momentous striving. She is luminous, the baby is in her arms, bathed and wrapped.

'Come,' Grace says. It is the first word that she has spoken and her voice dips and cracks as if she has broken through a great silence. Again. 'Come.' She lifts the baby and offers it to Hugh.

The child is put in Hugh's arms. He looks down at it.

Hugh Wilmot – who had cradled a hundred babies in their Christening robes – holds the child and weeps. It is very simple. It is without awkwardness.

'I want you to name her,' Grace says.

Hugh looks across at her, his lips forming words that cannot come. He rests his eyes on the baby. 'Thank you,' he says.

It is the child to whom he speaks.

It is homage.

Hugh chooses 'Ruth' without hesitation. He wants a name with dignity. He wants it to reflect, for him, the inheritance her coming has secured, the consolation they might give each other – mutually – throughout their lives.

He knows (Grace will never be called on to admit it – he is not a fool) that both exist in default. Both were unintended. It will be his bond with Ruth, their shared triumph, binding Grace to them.

Hugh says, bringing the baby to Grace, 'You know, she looks exactly like you in every way.'

'Does she?'

'Oh yes.'

Grace puts out her hand and takes up the small fingers of the baby, uncurling them delicately against her own.

Hugh is watching her, but she simply strokes the fingers, fragile as tiny growing shoots. 'Ruth is a lovely name,' she says.

The room is very still, lapped by sunlight at the window. Grace can hear another voice, something of the cadence and the pause, the breath drawn, a hand turning hers to his, palm to palm, a snatch of an old verse – the things they had learned at school, almost two decades apart, laughing at the clarity of recall. Ballads and sonnets and odes – searching for them, taking turns. She had had to follow him, her words shadowing his. *'The voice I hear this passing night was heard in ancient days by emperor and clown . . .'* – and then, more gravely, conjuring the figure in a landscape (and Grace suddenly silent and listening), *'Perhaps the self-same song that found a path through the sad heart of Ruth, when, sick for home, she stood in tears amid the alien corn'*.

How could she have known the portent in those words, not just in the name, but in all of them?

Grace and Godfrey do not need a mediator any more. They have gone their ways. Suddenly, their lives, disconnected from each other, disconnect from mine as well. I share their limbo and trudge back to my office at the university. I can hear the prof in his room, talking on the phone. When he is finished, I will dump my chapters on his table and hope that he will read them – this week, next week, maybe not at all.

I deliver them (and their secret history) a little dismissively, with something of spite: if Godfrey had been my supervisor, he would have called me to his office within a day, offered me a chair and pushed the manuscript across to me, the margins filled with his small, careful writing. Arrows, diagrams, questions posed, nice little ticks where he approves of what I wrote – enough for encouragement. So meticulous.

He would have looked at me, appraising me thoughtfully – and with the quiet respect he gave instinctively, his innate courtesy, his tact – and asked me how I felt the work was getting on. There – I can see him consulting the bowl of his pipe, putting a question to me about methodology, not making it sound like a reproof or some clever postmodern conundrum for which someone as ignorant as I could not possibly have the answer. No small triumphant little snorts, needling out my inadequacies – but simple questions, simply put.

–Have you got a ground plan?

Godfrey always had a ground plan. Perhaps it was his time in the Navigation School that decided how he worked, charting his way with skill and economy, making a diagram, working it round (even turning the paper upside down), linking things up, sure of the signs – as sure as I have been in writing this.

–*Right!* a direct gaze, ready to go – pipe poised – inviting me to take the challenge with him. Godfrey would never have thought to send me scampering for coffee or pontificate on theories while I clattered about with cups. We would be comrades of the same campaign.

He would ask me what I knew.

Suggest what I might consider reading.

Make three forward appointments for us to discuss what had been written the week before. There would be no time to lag behind or be distracted from the task.

He would listen before directing. If he thought I was off the mark, he would tell me, without preamble or apology.

And we would get the job done, without a waste of time, of energy or ego. Yes.

Knowing that, I lay my papers out. I go through each notebook and file. I make a chart, finding the loose ends, checking the footnotes, double-checking the references. Godfrey would have told me that the first and most important job in doing research is to record sources accurately, never having to go back to check date, publisher or page. To do it right first time and put it in the proper place. No mistakes. It is not the same as Prof, despite all his scholarship and all the papers he has published, the endless conferences he has been to. Go and ask him for a reference and he will spend an hour flinging piles of notes around, scratching like a demented rooster, being waylaid by something he has written – hardly to the point – darting at it, 'Ah, have a look at this! What do you think?', then settling into his chair, leaning back, feet up on a half opened drawer and flipping through the paragraphs, me hovering, desperate to escape. All I wanted was a page number and a date.

Prof: 'How far are you?'

'Pretty far.'

'Sounds ambiguous.'

'It is.'

'Well?'

'I have one last bit from Godfrey's archive that needs sewing up. Something missing.'

'What?'

'The final word.'

'About what?'

'The meaning of cows.'

'I'm not interested in *his* last word on the meaning of cows – whatever that means! I'm interested in yours.'

Fair enough. But I insist. 'I can't hazard one till I've seen his.'

240

'Bugger his,' Prof says. 'Frankly ' – (ah, his favourite word) – 'I mean, what is this? An African Languages dissertation or a report for the Department of Agriculture?'

The Department of Agriculture?

'Focus!' he says rather peremptorily.

–*Thank you, darling Prof!* I might have flung my arms around him – but I desist.

I sail away, out of his room, along the corridor, down the stairs, past the long rows of photos in the passage outside the Vice Chancellor's office. The bronze heads of the founding fathers gaze right through me with their Empire-eyes. I stride – despite the danger of big shoes – half skipping past the fountain in the courtyard, trickling away, the happy waterlilies lying torpid in their pool, past the gum tree, up the wide steps and into the library.

Instead of pounding up the stairs to the first floor I turn right, barge through the double doors and enter the Science Library. The librarian looks up from the desk. Her appraisal is swift and uninviting. No – she does not approve of my big shoes or my bright pink tights. I do not care at all. No doubt she is enchanted by formulae, thrives on statistics, will sniff me out as an imposter. I know that she would not approve of moons and stars like cattle either. She would not approve of ambiguous leguaans, balancing notions of *reality: unreality; truth:deceit.*

Nothing is ambiguous in her science library, except my presence in it.

I go to the catalogue and open the drawers – '*Ga-Gu*' – leaving small damp prints on the old cards. It would be easier to look on the computer, but I don't. I want to see the writing of the person who catalogued things long ago, its personality before it was transformed into sterile information on the screen – before it became ephemeral, sometimes stalling or disappearing behind a prompt – <*Quit*> – or some other imperious command.

I hasten through the dozens of cards, the little brass rod holding them in place, rubbing against the backwood of the drawer like an oar easing itself in rowlocks. I am searching for something Dulcie Trollip had said to me, so long ago, about a paper he had sent. The words are vagrant in my mind –

–*There was even a poem in it! Imagine that in a farming journal, hey?*

I sense the librarian's aggravation behind my back. She doesn't realise that if I went to the computer now, all that sudden energy and impatience would probably bring on another '*Fatal Error*' icon.

There!

Only one entry.

Only one.

In the *Journal of Agricultural Research / Landbounavorsing. Department of Agricultural Technical Services.*

I am restless, waiting for the librarian to fetch the file. The benches are full of students. I find a little space and wait, turning my pencil through my fingers and dropping it. A glance of irritation from my neighbour who leans to pick it up from where it has rolled under his feet. The fellow on the other side is an incurable sniffer. He seems unaware of everything but the set of diagrams before him. I start to count the seconds between sniffs.

The file is brought. The librarian puts it in front of me, without a glance. There are a number of journals inside. I go hastily to the common index. Finding the entry I want seems interminable. I wish the chap beside me would blow his nose or go away.

Up and down the columns, over the page. And the next.

I settle myself closer to the edge of the table, leaning in.

And then, there it is.

I let out a whoop. I know it sounds like the crow of a child discovering its voice – that sudden, that exultant glee.

Everyone looks up. I do not care, I hunch across the journal, shielding it, a miser keeping Godfrey from the scrutiny of those who do not care. I will not let him dissipate in here.

I put my finger on his name. I am marking him.

The Nomenclature of Indigenous Cattle: an aesthetic appreciation
4th November 1957.

Why here? Why not in a language journal? Why not in those which dealt in metaphor and poetry and oral inheritance?

Ah. Practical Godfrey.

He has sent it to the journal so that scientists and farmers would see it – not men with words, but men 'with cows': Herman de Waal; Dulcie Trollip; Humphreys. Dr Crawford. They must take it up, incorporate it, make it an adjunct to the understanding of milk production and feed-lots and fat percentages in beef.

Used.

Passed on.

My Messianic Godfrey, seeing the whole of things.

But, suddenly, Grace turns to confront me.

No.

It was Grace who had seen the whole of things: – *We must do whatever kind of right is the truth.*

Without that nothing is sacred.

She had not sacrificed truth for expedience. Not then. Not ever.

And he, knowing it, has vindicated her. Here. In this article. Too late, perhaps, but in the most public place that he could choose – open to censure, indifference – even to derision from his scientific brothers.

He has written this for Grace.
–*Whatever kind of Right is the Truth*.

To start with, there is an abstract and acknowledgements. In his precise, dispassionate way, Godfrey thanks Crawford for including him in the original survey. He acknowledges Mr M Xaba of Enseleni, his own stockman, Mr Wilton Mayekiso; Herman de Waal and his daughter, Dulcie Trollip.

> *While working in the field collecting the terminology for colour-patterns of indigenous cattle among the Zulu and the Xhosa-speaking people in South Africa, I was invited by Dr H K D Crawford to participate in his ground-breaking survey of indigenous cattle. Although my discipline is Social Anthropology and my particular interest the Nguni languages, I was struck, as Crawford and his team from the Department of Agriculture were, by the necessity and the wisdom of according the indigenous cattle of the subcontinent the status and attention they deserve and which has been so assiduously ignored and neglected by Government, scientists and farmers alike. These cattle have, after all, adapted to the conditions of Africa over millennia. To dismiss their importance and denigrate their astonishing qualities is not only shortsighted, but arrogant.*

I want to laugh. I can see him – sprung – orchestrating thoughts with his pipe, scratching away with his fountain pen, chucking it down every now and then, half talking to himself – his hair, in its straightness, flopping over an eyebrow to be swept back with an impatient hand. Those intense, deep-set eyes.
    Nicely sardonic.
    Give it to them, Godfrey!

> *A group of scientists and interested volunteers,* he continues, *working in various disciplines, contributed to the research, much of which was carried out in isolated rural areas, mostly at Government dips at the times when local stock owners gathered with their cattle. On such occasions, data regarding the number, purity, colour and conformation of the animals of a particular district could be fairly reliably gathered. Other information was collected from owners regarding fertility, milk production, longevity and cross-breeding. This work highlighted the urgent need to establish a centre where indigenous cattle could be observed and bred in a scientifically controlled environment. Personally, I established a small herd which could be monitored over a specific time period. Unfortunately, the stock was not as pure-bred as would have been desirable, due to the lack of suitable animals in the area. It was a start however, and interesting data emerged from the experiment. When the experiment ceased, the cows and their progeny were sent to the breeding station in Zululand to be incorporated into Dr Crawford's control herd.*

The rest of the text is concise and clear. Pure science. Godfrey details the necessity of diversifying the gene pool, of dealing with disease, of breeding in characteristics which would enhance milk and beef production without jeopardising the purity of the strain. He has charts and diagrams. He has statistics. He has a grid of figures which I do not understand. But I do not want to finish reading. I know, ten pages on, his voice will stop and there will be no more.

I count the pages and see the columns of endnotes, set in smaller type and written in italics. As an undergraduate, I never read endnotes. It was too much like hard work. I know now that in endnotes may often lie the hidden cipher to a life's work, the writer behind the words, his or her personal experience of the research, despite the dispassionate argument in the body of the text.

In the endnotes, an incidental sentence (the whoop which I have just let out in the silence of the science library) may be the germ of new directions, new works launched.

I know to search them for the signs. I am never disappointed.

And, in going through them, one by one, it is as if I have discovered, once again, the secret conversation on the cards in Grace and Godfrey's catalogue.

The endnotes are addressed to Grace.

A confessional. An act of love.

End note 3: **umvemve:** *small, weak calf; Cape Wagtail (Moticilla capensis). This term (both Xhosa and Zulu) applies to an unweaned calf which is particularly delicate. The name links it metaphorically to the Cape wagtail, commonly found in byres and pasture, specifically associated with cattle and believed to bring luck to stock owners. If a wagtail is killed accidentally, it should be buried with two white beads to atone to the ancestral shades. The killing of the trusting 'umvemve' is viewed as an outrage of very serious dimensions, something that could blight, forever, both the owner and the herd.*

The rip-rip-rip of the knife; the flies in frenzy outside the wire walls of the meat-room. The clean metallic smell of newly butchered meat, its taut blue sinew within the sheath of membrane, skewered at the hock.

The first sacrifice to expedience.

*Endnote 13: '***Bitchaan Shiki***'. The individual name given to a young bull in my herd with a pattern which was described in complex terms, indicating the great accuracy, the humour and penetration with which a classification is often chosen.* **'Inkunzi entulo elizotha elisomi ebafazi baphik' icala'.'**

Old Wilton Mayekiso with his angled face – the leanness of perpetual hunger and physical work, his wayward eye, his one good tooth indenting his lower lip

– a pirouette of laughter, crying out suddenly, 'I am the bull which is the lizard of a sober colour and the Redwinged Starling with horns which are the women saying, *"Oh, we have had enough! We repudiate this matter!"* ' And in imitation of the slant of the back-tipped horns, flinging up his hands, the posturing of women as they mock at men. And Grace and Godfrey standing at the edge of the byre and laughing while the bull tastes the air, alert for the smell of oestrus, bunching himself – those great battering shoulders – while his horns (the ribaldry of women) parody his self-importance.

The note continues:

> *This particular beast was a fertile sire but proved to be unsatisfactory when put to a purely indigenous heifer. Impatience for breeding results compromised wisdom. If such results are to be achieved, sensitivity, discrimination and delicacy of handling, are essential. The failure, in this case, was purely personal.*

I smile. Did you hear that, Grace? Did you?

> *Endnote 23:* **Inkomo yeminyanya:** *beast of the ancestors. This is an animal that may never be slaughtered, or sold or exchanged. In doing so lies the greatest sanction. The beast of the ancestors is chosen as a sacred trust. Its covenant is binding through life until death. No expedience – financial or scientific – should interfere with its status.*

The *inkomo yeminyanya*, prepared with the rubbing of *impepho* along her back, the words of praise, of dedication, is the second sacrifice offered to expedience.

The note sits square at the bottom of the page as if it were underlining all that has gone before. Keeping my finger there, marking it, I return to the body of the text and continue reading.

The sniffer in the bench beside me has gone. I did not notice him rise and walk away. The student who had retrieved my pencil has also gone. His place has been taken by someone else. I do not even look up in idle curiosity to see who is there.

I marvel at Godfrey, at the integrated universe that he creates. His writing, even in explaining diagrams and graphs is unrepetitive and elegant. But it is only in the last few paragraphs that he reveals himself: he turns his attention from science and posits another argument. The intellectual, the historical, the political. He attacks prejudice and narrow thinking, scorns the legislation forbidding the use of indigenous bulls. He is concise – and satirical. His argument is way ahead of its time.

> *In the study of these cattle, during which I was able to observe my own herd in a circumscribed setting and at close quarters, it became evident to me that it is not*

only the scientific approach to the study of these animals which is significant but that, in the search for understanding, the aesthetic and spiritual dimensions, which have always been at play in the perceptions of cattle-owners in Africa, cannot be ignored or sacrificed to purely commercial expedience. In owning Sanga-Nguni cattle, I had to acknowledge that this aesthetic and spiritual importance could not – and should not – be assessed in isolation – as a thing apart. Our present disequilibrium, I believe, is due to the outrunning in scale of the spiritual and intellectual by the material elements of society. I have suffered from – and for – that disequilibrium myself. In assessing the role of cattle in indigenous society, it must be remembered that they are not simply commodities. Their success as a breed, within the context of this country, their wider significance, rests not only in their present or future economic status but also in their legacy as part of an older cosmology in which they were treated with reverence and care: a time when love and beauty were admissible.

There is a strange urgency now in the tone, as if, somehow, Godfrey was working against a tide.

Time is running out.

I know his handwriting – how it must, in the original, have accelerated across the page: those long drag marks of the pen linking words, those imperious stabs of the pen, dotting the '*i*'s'.

In many ways the history of the indigenous cattle of South Africa is reflected in the history of their traditional owners, whose rights, dignity and worth as human beings has been so arrogantly disregarded. It is at the peril of administrators and of Government to ignore the glaring inconsistencies in its attitude to all that is indigenous to this country – its natural resources, its livestock, and, most especially, the people who – from time immemorial – have husbanded the land.

We ignore this at our peril.

And then Godfrey launches into the names, as if astounded at their aptness, their poignancy, their microcosmic landscapes: *I am the beast which is the houses scattered on the hillsides; I am the cow which is the branches of the trees silhouetted against the sky.*

Oh yes!

Here are no more pasterns and jaws and the characteristics of polls. Here is the beast who stretches himself like the star-of-the-morning; here is the white bull whose voice is the thundering of the rain or the wind echoing in the empty gourd; here is the dove-cow tethered to the clouds.

He forgets restraint.

Here is Beauty.

Here is Love.

They are admissible.

His paper is a song of praise.

It is all art.

Beneath it is written, *4th November 1957*, and the name of the little shop in the ironstone valley.

This paper had been written for Grace. As clearly as if he had inscribed her name across the top of the paper in bold print, italicised, for everyone to see.

I am about to close the journal but I glance again at the endnotes, lingering with them.

Inkomo yeminyanya: ancestral beast.

It is not the last endnote.

I see there is another and I turn the page.

Endnote 24: **inala** – *abundance. An extraordinarily beautiful and delicate pattern; faint red and white spots subtly blended.*

And then, in brackets below:

(While writing this paper I was taken to see a painting by my former stockman, Mr Wilton Mayekiso. It was a Bushman painting of fairly recent origin – executed, perhaps, within the last one hundred and fifty years. There are many examples of rock art in the area in which I was resident. This particular painting was isolated and exceptionally well-preserved although the face of the krantz on which it was painted is barely sheltered from the elements. It was a perfect representation of a cow of the inala pattern. Its discovery seemed symbolic, highlighting a hypothesis which has interested and puzzled me for the last decade – that dogma, in anything, is dangerous and that whatever governs the apprehension of the aesthetic and the spiritual, has its own laws, as immutable as those of science. I believe that it was no coincidence that I was shown this painting. Seeing it was humbling – it cautioned me against presumption and brought to mind lines from Vita Sackville-West's poem, 'The Land':
    'That nature still defeats
    The frowsty silence of the cloistered men,
    Their theory, their conceits; . . .')

I want to jump up and shout.

I am pumping with energy. 'Oh, Godfrey! Yes!'

The librarian looks across at me. I smile radiantly at her. It is not returned.

It seems the sky outside the library windows is radiant as well. Distant cumulus are thrusting up above the hills beyond the skyscape of red-tiled roofs. Across those hills – far across those hills – is that ironstone valley, those marching battalions of aloes, both the sapless and the living, flanking the ridge of jackals with its *krantz*, its dry river-bed below, its twin *koppies* with their ironstone crowns.

—*I believe that it was no coincidence that I was shown this painting.*

I know, now, that those little lines, scratched faintly on the slip of paper in Godfrey's catalogue, affixed to the card *'inala: abundance'* are not an *aide-memoire*, an idle scribble, but a map. They are river, hills, house and dam. As familiar – and obvious – as my own home in my own familiar street.

Godfrey's map. Marked *'G'*.

If I could ever find the notebook in which Godfrey had written the original of this paper, there would be a leaf, torn in half. It would match the slip of map stapled to that card.

It comes from the same source.

It is the last sign. And I have found it.

No, Godfrey – it is no coincidence indeed.

I fill out a photocopying form and put it inside the journal, to pass to the librarian. I stand a moment by the desk, my hand damp on the cover.

I know there is a presence.

The librarian tells me to come back tomorrow, takes the folder from me with her slim aseptic fingers: she has no idea of what she holds.

I leave the library very quietly then, treading softly down between the book stacks. I do not turn. I hear my footsteps. I know a shadow-company goes with me down those rows of manuscripts and texts, those books and those anthologies. I pass the rack where I had first found Godfrey's manuscript. I pause a minute. I know the space I left in taking it. The folders have sunk in, to hide its absence.

My laugh is small. It echoes in the stacks: a swift, wry response, offered back to me.

We walk on quietly. Almost solemnly. Our footsteps marking our recessional.

Reaching the great sweep of the library porch, I look up. I expect the sky to burst with music. But it is still. The door sinks back quietly behind me.

I stand outside the sanctuary, under the arching sky. The clouds above the hills are a landscape of *krantz* and ridge and hill. The empty spaces of the dusk – a late, pale green – is sky-pasture stretching out above the hollow of the town.

Earth is sky and sky is earth.

—*Of course, Desmond. So it is. As Bibleman says.*

Chapter sixteen

∽

Godfrey sits at the table in the kitchen in the little house by the store. He has lit the lamp and he has laid out a rasher or two of bacon, a tomato and a couple of eggs. He has cut a chunk of bread. He has a small flask of whisky. It is on the table in front of him. He drinks it with water from a cup. There is no ice, but it does not matter. The summer night outside is cooler now that the sun has set. There is a stillness, as if the heat of day has sunk deeply into the ground. With dusk, a quieter, cooler drift of air lifts the edge of the curtain at the kitchen window.

Godfrey has left the stable door open. Through it, he can see the ridge. And now, in silhouette, undisguised by colour or light, the slight protuberance of the two hills beyond, rising from the upland plain.

He draws a map.

Here is the line of the empty river. He draws it with care. He turns the paper round and starts it from above, as if he is walking down it, remembering how it turned to the right, opening across even ground and then to the left, butting up against the start of the *krantz*, just beyond the place where he and Grace had found the *inala* cow standing in the shade at the edge of the bush.

—I am the stones of the forest.
—I am the gaps between the branches of the trees silhouetted against the sky.
—I am abundance.

Here is the *krantz*. He draws two lines, almost parallel, but then converging. He shades the place between them at their greatest distance from each other where the rockface is higher. Here is a *witgat* tree, bark white as bone, leaves small and dark, shrunk from lack of water, growing on a river-bank where no water ever flows.

The sun had been hot. It was an unrelenting noon.

He had stood and looked about him, but Wilton Mayekiso had walked on, quite deft, just the slightest gesture of his hand, directing him.

Godfrey had followed – a place of lizard-bush, dry and scaly, without depth or shade. There is no moisture here.

Wilton had stopped, inclined his head, slowly, in silence, as if a sudden movement might startle something into flight.

Godfrey had come forward, intent.

And there – on an angle of the rockface, very slightly sheltered from the sun, no more than four or five inches tall, the image of a cow.

Faint. Delicate. Fragile. Her head turned back.

Beckoning.

An *inala* cow.

–*Abundance*: in white and ochre-red.

She had stood there a century or more. Not triumphant. But deliberate.

Godfrey had stepped up to the rockface and gazed at her, the slight toss of her head, the poise of her hooves, the shimmer of her.

–*She reminds me of you.*

Had he said that, once, to Grace?

Oh, yes. He had said that.

Godfrey tears the sheet in the exercise book down and across, dividing the page in half. He folds the slip and puts it in his wallet. He will staple it to the card '*inala*' in the catalogue, to remind him. He has traced his journey precisely. If he should return, he would find it without hesitation.

–*I believe that it was no coincidence that I was shown this painting. Seeing it was humbling – it cautioned me against presumption . . .*

No coincidence.

It is Godfrey who had taught me, from the first, to read the signs.

He had read them himself.

And this ancient and delicate beast, created over a century before, solitary on its rockface, is a source of continuity, a relic of an older wisdom, a sign that the search for beauty – and the love with which it is created – remains irreducible. It is the nourishment that feeds the heart.

It is admissible.

Soon it will be moonrise. The star, *isandulela*, the harbinger of summer, is just above the far horizon. Higher, is Orion's Belt – the zebras of the sky-plains and *ucanzibe*, the stars of hoeing and of labour.

Godfrey leans on the edge of the open stable door. The old sounds, the

250

old smells, sink back. *Bergwind* and pepper tree, red dust, succulents and drought. He looks up into the dark. It is the old night sky of his childhood. The Milky Way is clear, abundant with stars.

–*That's the pathway to God's cattle-kraal*: Godfrey to Gert.

–*It's not! It's the Milky Way!*: Gert to Godfrey.

–*Bibleman said!*

And Gert had laughed, liking it, and making little gestures with her hands as if she gathered up the stars in her arms.

Below, dark against the translucence of moonlight, is the ridge.

It is so familiar.

How many evenings had he and Grace stood outside and watched the green light of evening darken down, leaving the jackal-spine of rock, the long line of desolate outcrop, the sharp silhouette of aloe or spur: *uqolo lwezimpungutye*.

The Ridge of Jackals. A lonely place to be.

Her cobweb presence is around him, as if she has spoken.

If, once, he had missed, intensely, the passion of her, it is the gentle stretch of her arm about his neck, her palm at his nape, the flutter of her breath at his temple and against his eyes, that he misses more. The comfort of her settling in against his side, fitting to him, skin to skin, inner wrists touching, the companionship of silence as they dozed together or as they worked, sitting side by side, close enough to lean a head against an arm, touch the back of the hand.

Where is she now?

He returns to the table, fills his cup again, picks up his fountain pen and opens his exercise book at the beginning. He smooths his palm across the page. It is a gesture of intent. Her palm within his palm.

Godfrey begins to write.

The Nomenclature of Indigenous Cattle: an aesthetic appreciation.
4th November 1957.

He pauses, takes a sip from his cup, sets it down, adds more water from the jug at his elbow.

While working in the field collecting the terminology for colour-patterns of indigenous cattle among the Zulu and the Xhosa-speaking people in South Africa, I was invited by Dr H K D Crawford to participate in his ground-breaking survey of indigenous cattle . . .

It is near midnight when he cooks his eggs and bacon on his primus stove and boils a kettle. He spoons the rough mixture of coffee and chicory

251

grounds into a pot. He adds a pinch of salt. It must be strong and invigorating. He still has a long way to go.

He has always associated this particular smell of cooking, and its comforts, with this kitchen and this house. With Grace.

—Food is a funny thing. Being in the kitchen. Bacon and eggs . . . it makes it easier to explain.

—Bacon and eggs in the kitchen is legitimate then? Even with whisky?

And they had both laughed at her embarrassment and the plump pinkness of her ear lobes.

—Ah, Gracie. We both knew then. We both knew. Even as I walked through the door of your classroom and saw you turning: a lily opening, following the pull of the moon.

All through the writing of this, I have sensed the advent of this night for him. The years between are left behind. They have their story too – but it is not the one that Godfrey gave to me. England belongs to Stella and his sons, to his other life.

To Godfrey with another name.

He does not want intrusion.

All I know is that he secured a post and turned his mind to other things, unconnected with his origins or cattle. He became involved with university administration. He spent time serving on committees. He hosted official functions.

Dozens of them.

No doubt Stella shone at all of them. Her quiet ease, her grace could always be relied on. She was never ignorant or fatuous. She was perfectly English. Their house was always full of visitors and scholars passing through, the background murmur of talk and quiet laughter.

I am sure, unobtrusively, Stella put away reminders of their colonial connection. It resided only in Godfrey's books and the odd Africana lithograph among other hand-tints grouped in the passage of their house. Their garden was formal but enchanting. It had settled into a gentle, soft abundance. It reflected Stella's own maturity: pale, restrained – as fine-boned and beautiful as when Godfrey had married her. She had saved her skin from the withering of the southern sun in time. There was a dewy fragrance about her that would not be compromised by age.

Grace, so much younger, would wear less gently. She wanted to teach again, helped Hugh raise funds for a primary school being built by volunteers for the children of workers in the peri-urban plot-land outside their town, driving the truck that brought the bricks and working daily with an old man with a wheelbarrow, a spirit level and a ball of string. She supervised the laying of the floor and chose the lino, to warm the concrete screed, cutting it herself. She wore her hair brushed back into a knot or a plait. Such simplicity enhanced the length of her neck, the poise of her face. Her arms were slim and strong, her hands tough, her nails worn to the quick.

Once Godfrey had turned her hand over in his and said, 'These strong, these beautiful, capable hands.'

He had never guessed how capable, in time, they would become.

Hugh is meticulous with figures. He keeps a ledger which he fills in every night. They take a holiday, once every two years, at the sea. They are lent a flat by a parishioner, at a nominal rate, with cream walls and brown-painted doors and old woven curtains behind which – in the off-season, undisturbed – generations of wasps have made their paper nests.

It is unremittingly drab. And the coast, with its torpid sea and its smell of estuary silted brown with summer rain, its inland detritus washed up at river mouths, is not the sea that Grace had known as a child. It is not the sea, distant and dark, beyond the dune fields, the sea that broke on long deserted beaches, where jackals sometimes scavenged, where single skeins of cormorants scudded just above the turning line of wave, a sky oyster-smooth and grey, the brindled ribs of sand left where the tide retreats and terns and waders gather.

Grace does not complain.

She leads her children down through scrub, across the railway line and on to the dirty, sloping sand of the borrowed beach and builds castles with Ruth and the boys, using discarded bottle tops for windows, an ice lolly stick as a flagpole, lays out the towels under the old umbrella and saves it, continually, from turning inside out in a capricious wind. She watches them in the waves, swims with them in the tepid water of a blind lagoon, keeps Hugh from sunburn by soothing lotion on his arms and neck.

They make the long *trek* home again, too far east for the landscape to remind her. There is nothing here to bruise the heart.

Hugh's mother comes to live with them.

With Grace at work all day, Hugh's mother moulds the house to suit her own routines and tastes. Her furniture – Father's jointed chair, the china cupboard and the sideboard – are brought in and take their place, dominating spaces which had been uncluttered and light. They have a certain smell, the same that Grace had sensed as she stood at the door of Hugh's mother's house at eighteen, Jack pressing in behind her in his old rubber-lined mac, his face damp with rain and eager and ardent and shy.

Again, Grace does not complain.

She has her school. She has her garden and her trees, with their own mythologies. She has her records – just a few – which she plays, sometimes, when there is no one in the house. Albinoni. Haydn's twenty-sixth. Dvorak's cello concerto. The flute calling. The cello in reply. Those upland birds, their high lament. And sometimes she goes out at night – late, very late – climbing through the low, open window in the heat and stands on the lawn and looks for Orion's Belt, tracing its conformation – swordsman, huntsman, zebras of the sky-pasture.

–The clean-bladed gold, sprung like a hunting-bow, lean as its sinew, tuned always to the tapping of the stars.

Oh, I see you, Godfrey.

In late October 1957, Harold Godfrey had a stroke. It was severe enough for a telegram to be sent to Godfrey advising him to come. It was signed by a person whose name he did not recognise.

M Mabb.

Someone from the company? Someone from a hospital? A doctor? An official? An acquaintance or a friend?

Stella telephoned the airlines and booked a ticket for him on a flight, promising to follow if he needed her.

'If the worst comes to the worst, darling,' she had said, 'how on earth are you going to manage to pack up the old house? There's simply mountains of stuff in it. It'll be a nightmare. And if he recovers, we'll have to make new arrangements.'

Godfrey knew that his father would not recover. Harold would make sure of that.

He would never live in the world dependent on another, without enough wit to sharpen his scorn.

'I'm sure I'll manage on my own,' said Godfrey. 'There's lots of staff to help. The biggest job will be finding work for them and making sure they're all right. As far as the furniture's concerned, I'll sell off everything. The company may want it.'

'Not everything, Clem. I don't want it, but you must think of the boys.'

'I'll think of the boys,' he had returned quietly.

But Harold's house was not the place of their boyhood, only of his. His sons did not remember it well or have attachments to its contents. Theirs was a clean, quiet, ordered world. It had never been solitary. There was no tumult of owls come to carry off their mother. There was no Gracious-Virgin-Mary to beggar passion. What did they care for a company of buck heads with sad glassy eyes and cobwebs in their ears? Or a pepper tree beside a pen and a corrugated-iron fence with jagged edges and rusty holes?

For them, their grandfather's home was recalled as something vaguely exotic, even dashing. Something they could boast about to English girls.

–My grandfather has hunting trophies all over the walls of his house and one

254

helluva elephant gun.

—There's a bloody great hyena skin on his study floor and a buffalo head over the fireplace.

Godfrey let them tell their story: at their age, full of colonial vigour and the shadow of the trenches, he had entranced his Blood-Red-Woman in Gloucester Walk, with a history of his own.

No doubt, the stories would lead each of his sons to bed – which was all that they were wanting.

In its time, it had led him too.

Godfrey had packed his bag himself.

'Surely that's not all you're taking, Clem?' said Stella, surveying the small portmanteau. 'You'd better have a suit.'

'What for?'

She did not reply.

'If I need a suit, I'll borrow one of Dad's,' Godfrey said.

Stella had turned away. The idea was slightly macabre: wearing the dead man's suit to his funeral.

Godfrey had ignored it.

In a strange way, it was a closing of ranks between Harold and himself. An act of intimacy so seldom sought. Harold would have thought it practical. —*Why drag a bloody suit about, if you don't have to? Take one of mine!*

Stella had looked at him, slightly repelled. Then she'd said, 'And you'd better not say anything controversial while you're out there. I believe the government is very touchy these days . . .'

'About people like me?'

'About people like you.' Her voice had been a little bleak.

'They probably know more about me than I do, so I won't concern myself too much. They'll have my articles and broadcasts already.' He'd looked across at her and smiled. 'I'm going to see my sick father,' he'd said. 'I'm not going to a rally.'

'As long as they know that.'

He had been affectionate then. 'Really, Stella, you see the thought-police under every bed.'

'You might be arrested.'

He'd laughed. 'Nonsense.'

'What about the piece you wrote on the Defiance Campaign?'

'So what! Lots of people wrote about the Defiance Campaign.'

'Still. They're here – not there.'

'Don't fuss.' He'd given her bottom an absent pat in passing.

It was a frivolous gesture. Quite uncharacteristic. He had a sudden, strange ebullience: he was sitting on his school trunk at the station, going

255

home, for the hols. He was looking eagerly down the line for the train, fiddling with his luggage labels, until they came unstuck.

He'd turned from Stella and opened his cupboard and reached for his camera on the top shelf, pulling it down by the strap. He'd caught it deftly. It was the same camera he had had for years.

He saw it, suddenly, in the lap of a woman, cradled in her hands and then held to her face – head slightly tilted, hair pale – as he had stood with the neck of the *inala* cow noosed by his arm. He had taken the cap from the lens, glanced at it, checking for mildew. He'd seen his face inverted, clean-shaven now, so much leaner.

Harold is paralysed down one side. His face – the old hawk – has slipped sideways as if half of it has disintegrated inside the skin. He follows Godfrey with his eyes. Godfrey walks about the room. It has the power to oppress him still: the great dusty heat of the heavy net curtains, the swags and the finials, the paper roses, their garlands and loops, masking the interior labyrinth of termite nests. The door to his mother's room is closed.

He will go there later.

The old family retainer brings a tray of drinks at six, as he has for forty years. The same decanters, the same glasses, the same presentation ice bucket, the silver dented with wear.

'I don't think you should have a drink, Dad.'

'To hell,' is what Harold seems to mutter, meaning yes.

Godfrey pours the brandy carefully, diluting it well with water.

On the 27th of October, the night nurse asks to move the patient to Godfrey's room. It is nearest the bathroom. She needs water and towels and a convenient place to wash her hands. She has laid out a small table near the basin. She has placed a white towel over everything and wiped the little cabinet where Godfrey had found the hair nets and the dark blue bottle with the silver top: *Paris by Night*.

Of course, she must do what is convenient.

'He wouldn't let me move him before,' she says.

But Harold seems no longer conscious of them. At ten in the morning he has another stroke. He lies, with a thin trail of moisture at the corner of his mouth, his eyes closed. They move him without demur.

Godfrey helps the nurse and the retainer lift Harold into a wheelchair. They push him down the passage. The thin mattress lies on Godfrey's old box bed made up with clean sheets. Above, in the roof, is the skylight. The windows are reflected in the long bevelled panels of the mirrors on the cupboard doors.

In the early hours of the morning, the nurse nods off, insubstantial in her corner, a dim white presence. Godfrey sits on an upright chair, only a distant lamp in the hall wedging light along the passage, laying shadows out at angles.

I have stood in that room, alone, since the archivist took me there with her stream of information. The first time I saw it, it was the room of Godfrey's birth: the night sky, so distant and aloof beyond the skylight, the guillotine of shadow sent up by the angle of the cupboard door, the dim lozenge of the moonlight on the wall. My own fear of yellow paint, the stain of poison from the rind of the yellow fruit, leaking through my palm.

In beauty is deceit.

–What if the child licks it? Harold had said. *–What then?*

Godfrey brings his chair closer to the bed. He turns on the night light, sees his own shadow lurch suddenly across the ceiling, gaunt-winged as a bat.

Godfrey picks up a book that had been lying in the wheelchair, something that the nurse had read to his father a few nights before. At a moment like this, Godfrey feels, he should be paging through something more appropriate, something to recite to Harold – his favourites, his Newbolt. His Laspur hills, his far Afghan snows. Or Vitai Lampada, at least: Empire going down.

Instead, the book is a P G Wodehouse (Empire still) and the marked page about a pig at a country fair.

Harold is breathing still. Godfrey reads, his ear alert. The slow push and stumble, push and stumble of his father's breath.

Death like this is so ungenerous. So glib and unfastidious.

He wants to say something. To perform a rite. A valediction. Have something to bestow, the age-old forms to mark the passage of the soul.

Anything.

He is at a loss: his father had always jeered at religion. The great battle-ground between him and his mother: grief for the unloving, empty bed.

Godfrey knew that the nurse had offered to fetch her pastor for Harold a few days before and that Harold had glowered – ireful – a look that said, 'Get rid of her.'

A *pastor*?

Godfrey had almost laughed. It wasn't the matter of an officiant – but of a word. A *pastor*? A Rector or a Dean would have given no offence. Even a bloody curate.

For his father, it was not a matter of religion, but of class.

Godfrey had thanked her, told her gently that he would deal with the spiritual journey himself.

Now, there was nothing he could say. Nothing he could read or chant or utter.

Only sit.

He did not even give him his hand.

He could have said, *I love you.*

But he didn't – because it was never said, in this room or in this house, as if to say – or feel it – was a curse.

Say it, Godfrey, before it is too late.

Say it.

But he does not say it. He can't. He does not even think of it.

He sits, powerless, as he had sat in his desk at school, hearing the map of the world thudding against the wall in the evening wind – and beyond the windows of the prep room, the sound of the train taking his mother away.

With relief.

Did you ever wonder what your mother felt, alone in the carriage, the lights of the town strung out fainter and fainter, facing – head-on – the force of her fear of losing you? Its unrelenting grip?

She had buried a child already.

You think it is courageous to 'get on'?

But, sometimes, it is not.

Sometimes, it is Full Retreat.

Godfrey cannot bear the sound of the laboured breath and he gets up quietly and goes down the passage, into the dining room where the cotton cloth which his father had stretched across the walls, droops and sags in places: the griffins and the unicorns, the peacocks and intertwining roses. Behind the leaves, the small imagined face of the *umvemve* calf.

Harold's Persian fantasy.

Godfrey goes out through the French doors on to the gravel drive and breathes night air, taking long draughts, over and over. He climbs up to the small veranda room, sets the enamel jug back in its basin on the washstand, out of which it has been tipped by the wind.

He is gone less than ten minutes. Seven at the most. As he reaches the hall he meets the nurse coming down the passage, her shadow in front of her, walking away from the light, stepping softly for a woman so large.

'Dr Godfrey?'

Godfrey stops.

'He's gone.'

'When?'

'Just a few minutes ago. No more than five.'

'Why didn't you call me back?'

'I couldn't chance it. I didn't want him to be alone.'

She does not follow him to the room. She knows, by the set of his shoulder, that he does not wish her to be there. He takes his place at the side of the bed again. Sitting very still.

He is suspended.

All he can think of – trying to push the sound away – is of lying on his back underneath this panel bed, among the fleece of dust and lint, breathing in the scent of iron springs, feeling the burn of weeping in his throat, fighting breath, holding out against his grief for the *umvemve* calf. Gert, trying to say '*I love you*' by her presence and her tears.

And his defiant – his fierce – his absolute disdain.

–*There is an equal gravity in rooms where birth and death have taken place. Sometimes they have witnessed both. Some are sanctuaries. Others, judgement chambers.*

Godfrey's room was both.

At ten in the morning, Godfrey knocks at the door of a block of flats in a side street and waits. He pats his pockets, searching for his pipe. He does not take it out. It is a habit, a security. It must be there, when he should need it.

He knocks again.

He hears footsteps. They are slow and the door is opened just a fraction, held by a chain on the inside.

A woman's face. Her lipstick, hastily applied, a little slipped from its corners, just the slightest parody.

'Mrs Mabb?' He touches his tie. 'Clement Godfrey.'

She says nothing but closes the door gently in order to undo the chain and then pulls it open again. She stands back. As he walks into the hallway, he says, 'Thank you again for sending the telegram.'

'I had to take the liberty.'

'Of course. I'm very grateful.'

'Do sit down.'

It is a small room, cluttered with furniture. A woman's room. A woman who has lived alone a long time. The little gestures – a bowl of artificial flowers with ferns tucked in between to make them fresh, a china dog perched on a mat in front of the radiator. A china cat. Substitutes for something long ago.

There is no place, in a flat so small, for animals. On a bureau are pictures of others as if they had been children. An old snap of a Persian. A Yorkshire terrier in a woman's arms.

Hers.

At fifty perhaps. Maybe older. Her hair curled up, her waist marshalled by a belt. A smile.

'Can I get you a cup of tea?'

'Thank you.'

'It's all ready. When you telephoned this morning, I hoped you would stay.'

He hears her in the kitchen. The kettle has already boiled. She comes in with a tray, meticulously laid. The cloth is starched. The pot is silver-plate. The cups are small and fine, thin as shell.

She seems to tremble as she comes towards him and he rises and takes the tray from her and sets it down on a small table.

'That's very kind of you,' she says. She puts out her hand to steady herself on the back of a chair. She does not look at him.

'Let me pour it for you,' Godfrey says.

She takes a small handkerchief from her sleeve and dabs gently at her nose.

The quiet clink of cups. The sound of traffic in the street. She says, 'It is very understanding of you to come.'

'Not at all. I think the understanding is all yours.'

She cannot reply, glances up and at the window, to gain her equilibrium. She says, 'Is your family well?'

'Quite well, thank you.'

'He was proud of his grandsons. Are they finished studying?'

'The elder is. He's just written his Bar exams and passed. The younger is at Cambridge still.'

'And Mrs Godfrey?' Her voice is not steady then. She takes a breath, starts again. 'He always said how beautiful she is.'

'Did he?' Godfrey picks up his cup. 'They had a bond.'

'I suppose it was being English.'

Yes. Both so very English.

Godfrey smiles across at her, knowing neither of them can claim that, coming from this town with the dust and thorns and great flat plains and empty pans. It is in their voices and their eyes and the under-tan of skin, burned early by a semi-desert sun.

Godfrey says, choosing his words with care, 'I would have called you earlier but I didn't know who exactly had sent the telegram until the doctor told me this morning, when he came to sign the certificate.' He turns the cup in its saucer, sets it down. 'I had assumed it was sent by an acquaintance, or the nursing service. There simply wasn't time to ask, it was all so quick – and my father wasn't always lucid, so he couldn't tell me.'

Mrs Mabb is folding her hanky systematically.

Godfrey continues, 'It was only today that the doctor said you'd engaged the nursing service yourself. I'm so grateful to you and, of course, I've told them to send the account to me. I wish you had come to the house or telephoned. I would have been very glad to see you.'

She has not touched her tea.

'I think he would have been glad too,' Godfrey says.

He does not look at her as she folds her handkerchief across her knee, over and over.

'I was there until Monday,' she says. 'I only arranged the nurses when I knew you were coming, in case you came alone and needed help. I thought it best to leave you then. I wanted to do the right thing.'

'You should not have been so diffident. You have been wonderful to him. The doctor told me.'

She does not respond. She is defensive. What does he know?

Godfrey sits as upright as his father in his chair, with this woman at his side – her soft, stocky ankles wedged into tight shoes, her hair hurriedly curled for his coming – struggling to suppress her grief, needing, more than anything, to appear acceptable. There is a spot of misplaced powder at her ear and her earring is only clinging, coming adrift.

She adjusts it.

He sits, wanting to reach out to her.

Unable.

She says, suddenly, 'You are very like your father.' She makes a small gesture with her hand. 'I think.'

Her voice breaks then. She gets up, unsteadily. 'Will you excuse me a moment.' She goes to the passage, her hand touching at the wall as if she cannot see it. He hears her in the bathroom, blowing her nose. She comes back. She has renewed her lipstick and her powder. She has dabbed it under her eyes to hide the redness.

Godfrey says, 'Shall I come and collect you for the funeral tomorrow? We can go together.'

'That is very kind of you, but I will just stay here. If you don't mind.'

'I would have liked you to sit with me.'

'He would not have wanted that.' She glances up at Godfrey then. There is a small fleeting challenge in her face.

–*Do not pity me*.

She does not say it: she only feels it. It is something that she knows will never change, as long as men have power and women give their tenderness.

However futile or misplaced.

When Godfrey leaves, he takes her hand. Her fingers tremble at his touch. He says, 'My father was a lucky man to have your friendship. It must have meant a great deal to him, through so many, many years.'

There is a mirror in the hall, Godfrey sees himself in it, looming over her

– the sag of her shoulders and the back of her head with its sparse curls, the little clasp of her pearls rolling over against the fold of her neck. She smells of talcum powder. It is a soft smell. Very unobtrusive.

Suddenly, she says, 'Did he say anything?'

Godfrey knows it has cost her dearly to ask. He wishes he could lie.

'He couldn't speak.'

'No.' She smiles and lifts her eyes up to him. They are a pale hazel-green. They are gentle eyes, even in their wariness. 'He never could.'

No. He never could.

Godfrey goes along the black-painted passageway past the rows of doors, down the stairs and through the old art deco entrance with its angles and sunbursts of bevelled glass, on to the porch. He walks to the post office, sends Stella another cable.

Delaying my return by a fortnight. Stop. Will wire new times as soon as possible. Stop. Love to all. Clem.

It is a hot morning when Harold Godfrey is buried. A wind is blowing dust about the churchyard. The undertakers stand at a distance, smoking unobtrusively, as the congregation files in. The service is brief. Godfrey speaks, saying what he has to say. Short and to the point. In that church, Harold seems absent, despite the coffin and the simple spray of lilies lying on the lid. Godfrey has the sense that his father might be taking tea with Mrs Mabb in her sitting room instead.

–Will you have a sandwich, dear?

–How about another cup of tea?

The comfort of the nursery rediscovered, Harold with his feet on a stool and his tie pulled loose. Harold, cocking a snook at them, 'for all that humbug'.

But Godfrey knows Harold even better. Despite the disparagement, Harold would expect 'good form' at his funeral.

He knows his son will deliver it.

Godfrey has given the eulogy. Godfrey has chosen the reading and the hymns. Harold would not be disappointed: *He Who Would Valiant Be* and Parry's *Jerusalem*.

Empire Hymns.

Harold on campaign – always on campaign. The Laspur Hills. The Afghan snows.

After the funeral there are drinks at the Club. Some stay for luncheon. A few cronies from the old days. Old men brought out, voyeurs to their own mortality. Sour or hearty or subdued, they shuffle into their accustomed seats at table.

Look about.

One less.

Harold gone.

There is already quite a company – a veritable Club Committee – down in 'Section A: Anglican' – in the cemetery.

Who will be next?

On the night of the funeral, Godfrey packs his bag. He leaves instructions with the staff. He will be back in a few days to arrange matters. They must carry on as usual, as if Harold had been sitting in his chair on the veranda and looking at the pepper tree across the drive. Nothing should be done until he returns. He takes a lamp and spends an hour in the garage tinkering with the car, cleaning up the engine and checking the tyres.

It is after midnight when he is ready for bed. For the first time he goes to his mother's room and opens the door. He turns on the light. The shade has gone. The bulb is bare and bright. The prie-dieu is dusty in the corner. The Virgin, with her foot on the head of the serpent, still stands on her shelf. The holy water stoop is empty. A dead fly lies in it, desiccated over years.

Had his father sat (as he had sat with him), beside the bed in which she'd died and never said a word?

–*What did he say to you, Mother?*

–*He couldn't speak.*

–*No, he never could.*

–*I love you*, would have sufficed. Nothing else is needed.

Neither one of them had had the sense to understand it.

Instead, a Catholic priest, excluded from the real meaning of those words – but more courageous, nonetheless – had given Extreme Unction and sent her off alone, a dab of holy water on her head.

For a moment, Godfrey wants to kneel on his mother's prie-dieu and say those words – so inadmissible. He wants to say 'I love you'.

To Gert.

To Bibleman.

To his Blood-Red-Woman, standing with her elbow on the mantel, his hat in her hand and looking down at him. So brave. Holding her disintegration steady until he left.

He wants to say those words to Harold, who, it seemed, had never said them in his life.

He wants to say them to his distant English sons.

To Stella, virgin-blue, beyond his reach.

He wants to say them – over and over – to his mother.

But instead he quietly takes the statue from its niche, and dusts the starry head with a finger tip.

Oh most gracious Virgin Mary,
That never was it known . . .

He replaces the Virgin on the shelf, turns, and closes the door.

Tomorrow he will take the car and drive south.

He will find Grace.

They will go together to their empty byre and admire their herd, standing side by side and echoing the colour-patterns of their cows, voice to voice.

The *umvemve* calf. The *inala* cow.

–I am abundance.

And before he walks away, he will say the words he must. He will not have expedience extort his soul. He can hear the voice of Mrs Mabb and see the wry, sad, injured knowing in her eyes.

–He couldn't speak. No, he never could.

Chapter seventeen

Godfrey knows it is the last time he will take this road.

Once, it had been so familiar. Driving it, was always going home. Each signpost, each grid. The valley of his other world. His enchanted time.

He passes the little town but does not turn left across the railway line and go in. He continues on, heading for a smaller district road and the De Waals' farm.

He had phoned the night before, from a hotel somewhere to the north, shouting down the party-line and got Dulcie Trollip.

'Hello, Dulcie? Can you hear me?'

He had told her who it was and there had been an exclamation of surprise – almost of concern. 'Good Lord, Dr Godfrey!' – Dulcie shouting back – 'What are you doing here? Where are you?'

He had told her where he was, and said, 'Is your father there?'

'He's already gone to bed. *Early to bed, early to rise* . . . You know, all that! Shame – he hasn't been too well lately. He has heart troubles.'

'I had no idea. I'm very sorry, Dulcie. Do you think he'd be able to see me tomorrow?'

'He'll be so glad,' she had said. 'He hardly gets about these days. Hell, Doc, we haven't seen you for so long. Why're you coming our way?'

'In fact, I'm out from England because I've just lost my old man. We had the funeral yesterday. I'll be here another week or so to pack up everything and sort out his affairs. But I needed a bit of a break and decided to come down to see the old place by the store and tie up some loose ends.'

'Shame, Dr Godfrey,' said Dulcie. '*Ag*, man, I'm sorry. Was your father ill a long time? Or was it sudden? Did he see you?'

'Yes, he saw me but he'd had a stroke so he wasn't really able to communicate. He knew I was there.'

There had been a small silence – and before Dulcie could flounder any more for something appropriate to say, Godfrey asked, 'Dulcie, I wonder if it's at all possible to spend tomorrow night at the house I used to rent from your father at the store? Do you still own it? I'd really be incredibly grateful if I could.'

'*Ag*, man, why stay in that old dump when you can have a comfy bed with us?' says Dulcie.

'That's very kind of you, Dulcie. But, in fact, I have a piece of work to finish which I need to do right there.'

Godfrey has no idea why he had said it – but it is the only excuse he can find for his refusal.

And it's the truth. He needs to be there.

In his old place. With Grace.

Dulcie had seemed at a loss. So was Godfrey. He could not mention Grace. Not so crassly on the phone.

He could not even ask where she was.

Perhaps she is still at the school. Perhaps nothing has changed, even her small charges: he remembered how they had looked at him, as if he were an ogre come with designs of abduction. What was the little fellow's name?

–*I love you in the world, Mrs Wilmot, from Desmond.*

Perhaps she would arrive in the old Ford with a tide of dust along the running board and walk in through the kitchen door with a basket of vegetables from the garden. A loaf of mealie bread. Some rusks. A side of lamb.

–*You must have jelly with your roast. I'm sorry it's not mint but I can't grow it. It always dries up.*

Godfrey had said, 'I hope you understand, Dulcie, I'm not turning down your very kind hospitality but there are a few things to do with my work that I need to check in the *veld*, where I was working, so to speak.'

Again, he does not know why he had said it.

He simply wants to be there, with the ridge of jackals and the *dikkops* crying.

'But if I could call in on the way past and collect the keys and, perhaps, borrow a towel and a primus and have a cup of tea with you and your father, I'd be very glad.'

'Of course,' she had said. 'I'll pack you up a box of things. It will be good to see you. Dad speaks about you a lot, telling people how the great Dr Godfrey agreed with him about indigenous cattle and all that.' She'd laughed. 'He is always glad to get news of the herd at Dr Crawford's too. It seems it's done very well.'

'We've got a lot to catch up,' Godfrey had said. 'I should be with you round about two.'

'Look forward to it.'

South and east.

There has been a drought for a number of years. Godfrey sees it in the *veld*, in the erosion. The sky has an empty scale of cloud, dry spaces without moisture or refraction. At one, he sees the signpost at the side of the road, pointing east up a valley. It has not changed. It is black-painted, fading into grey with the luminous white letters peeling off in flakes. It is hanging at an angle, tilted skywards. He turns on to dirt and rattles over a cattle grid, driving slowly, anticipating the rise of land, the faint cartography of river and empty plain, the deepening folds of hills, the outcrops of ironstone. When he reaches the second cattle grid he will see the *witgat* trees and then, when the land rises just a bit more steeply, the aloes taking the slope, the ranks of euphorbia. And, in between, the sneezewoods and the *kiepersols*, the *spekboom*, and sporadically, their little fire-tongues of blossom – foretelling drought – the *boerboon* trees with their lichened bark, small and ancient, blood in stone.

Here is Herman de Waal's gate.

The track, the windmill, the wild fig which has probed the foundations of an old shed are still there. The building leans at a greater angle than before. One day the wall will collapse, bringing the rafters down.

Here is the training yard where Herman had put his oxen through their paces, and behind, the sudden wildness of a ridge, the *veld*, simply waiting for its moment to overtake again and bring the small burrowings of man down into the earth and hide them.

And then – unexpectedly – as Godfrey edges round a clump of concealing bush – there is Dulcie's house.

As if to contradict him, Dulcie's garden has grown up around it. Her house stands shining in its square of lawn with the beds of flowers neatly laid, each outlined by a angled brick. There is a bird bath and a garden swing with a set of floral cushions. For the moment, Dulcie has won and Godfrey can hear the satisfying thump of the windmill pumping water and the squeal of the vanes whirling round.

And there is Dulcie, standing on her lawn, still in breeches but with an overshirt. She is hugely pregnant.

She greets Godfrey almost shyly, anticipating his glance: she deals in husbandry but she feels a little awkward about being the subject of the science herself. Godfrey, noticing the flush, touches on the subject lightly.

'You're looking marvellous, Dulcie. And your garden is just as blooming.'

She laughs.

He admires the bird bath and the swing and says, turning to her, 'I can think of nothing nicer than to sit and have a pipe with your father and talk about Ngunis. You know, he's always been a very innovative farmer. Way ahead of his time.'

'He thinks the same about you,' says Dulcie. She could say it straight. Herman has often remarked that he and Godfrey would be vindicated in the end, despite what others said about 'bush cows'. It was the interest that they shared. There was no need to dwell on Herman fretting over stories he had heard of Dr Godfrey's politics and the articles he sometimes wrote in newspapers. Didn't people understand that politics had nothing to do with farming?

People didn't understand.

Godfrey would have smiled at that: generous with Herman's own incomprehensions.

—They say he's a regular communist, Tommy Cooper had once said. *—And you know what that means.*

No one could explain – quite – what it meant, but no one would admit it. Whatever it was, it was bad.

—Very dodgy . . .

—Very rum . . .

Depending on who was talking.

Herman has his own views on Godfrey's politics but he isn't going to waste them on an ignoramus like Tommy Cooper who would blow them up, making as much of a monkey of himself as he tried to make of Godfrey. He had said, once, to Dulcie, '*Ag*, man, the doc's such a decent bloke – and hell, it was good to have someone to discuss cattle with, wasn't it, my girlie? A chap with an open mind about these things, even if he got a bit ahead of himself at times. Sometimes these clever blokes just aren't practical about the natives and things like that. They're not working on the ground, so to speak, so how can you expect them not to have their heads in the clouds?' Her father had laughed then, as if he had thought up something clever.

He didn't like the subject of Godfrey being discussed in company. It might lead to other things. To speculation, which he did not want to hear.

Herman has his own ideas – an intuition – at the sudden and precipitate departure of Hugh Wilmot and Grace, of Dulcie's fierce defence of her.

He would never say what he suspected. Not even to Dulcie. He would never put her on the spot, or expect her to break a confidence.

But he is a man who has lived his life in observation. He has watched stock at pasture, the little undertows, the ebb and flow of urge and preference, of season and connection. The things that grow – the things that don't. He knows the old laws of Nature. He reads them, as if they were prescribed.

He is a man himself.

He knows well enough how things begin.

And why.

'You'll find Dad rather changed,' says Dulcie. 'He's really not well at all. Come and sit on the veranda.' She takes the front steps with care. She leans in through the door and yells, 'Nomabini? *Letha iti*' – bring the tea – 'and tell the *Oubaas* that his friend is here.'

'How's your husband?' asks Godfrey, taking a seat.

'Not so good,' says Dulcie. 'He works on old machines up in the shed and won't do anything else. He was a tank mechanic in the war, you know. He sleeps very badly and makes a helluva racket, babbling away and thrashing about. I think he drives his tanks around. He's always worried they won't be ready. What for, I don't know. He can't seem to say. I thought it would have improved by now, but it hasn't. Funny how some people aren't affected and others are.'

'Oh, we're all affected,' says Godfrey. 'Some just push it deeper down. It comes to catch you at the most unexpected moments. It doesn't go away. Perhaps the baby will help. Someone to be hopeful for.'

'Perhaps.' She reaches into her pocket and pulls out a packet of cigarettes. 'I suppose people think babies don't have to worry with the past.'

'I suppose not – until they acquire one themselves.'

'I wish that was true,' says Dulcie with an odd little break in her voice, 'but they inherit things. The good and the bad. And you can't choose which.' She draws on the cigarette. 'I shouldn't smoke,' she says suddenly. 'But it's just a little pleasure that I don't want to give up yet,' and she looks at the lighted tip and does not turn her eyes to him.

He seems to be easy, looking out across the grass towards the camp below, where a flock of angoras are browsing, his legs comfortably crossed.

–*He doesn't know*. Dulcie takes another draw. –*He really doesn't know*.

They talk about cattle then. Dulcie says, 'Dad was very sorry when you went off to England and got out of the cattle business.' She taps her ash tip off against the edge of the veranda wall. 'He always said he wished you had written something or lectured to make people understand how important it is to look at indigenous breeds instead of buggering about with imported animals that get diseases and have a habit of *vrekking* in droughts. How'd he say it? "Dr Godfrey's such a clever bloke with words, he'd soon persuade them." ' Then she glances across at him, daring it, 'He said if you put as much energy into cattle as into politics, you'd have everyone running Ngunis in no time and stay right out of trouble yourself.'

Godfrey laughs out loud. He could just see Herman, ruminating and glowering and cajoling, the way he spoke to his oxen – half affection, half exasperation.

'I wish there was time to take you over to Vlakfontein to see some of my new animals,' she says. 'I've got some handsome little heifers in that herd.'

She sounds just like her father. Exactly the tone and pitch of how he would have said it, exactly the way of looking as if she were being confidential about 'nice little hocks'.

Godfrey says, 'Is Reverend Wilmot still at the church at Vlakfontein?' He hesitates. Dulcie keeps her eyes ahead, looking out in the same direction, as if they are still discussing cows. 'And his sister-in-law? I thought I'd call in on my way past.'

'They've been gone for years,' says Dulcie. Still she does not look at him but she can feel his slight shift – and of course, anticipating it, she knows he is reaching for his pipe.

'Got a match?' he says.

She passes him the box.

'Where did they go?'

'They left just after you,' she says. 'Mr Wilmot got a post in Rhodesia. In one of the smaller farming towns.'

'And her?'

His avoidance of her name gives him away. It is as if he dares not say it. He lights his pipe. He is busy with the match. 'Where did she go?' he says.

'Grace?'

'Yes.'

Dulcie is watching the goats in the camp beyond the lawn. One is pushing its head under the fence, entangling its horns. It is bleating plaintively. It is not really stuck, only foolish.

She answers, rather abruptly, 'She married Hugh Wilmot.'

Godfrey does not move: *–Jesus Christ Almighty!* Instead he says, 'Shouldn't we take that goat out of the fence?'

And Dulcie says, 'It only thinks it's stuck. When it calms down, it'll be fine.'

Godfrey sits quietly with his pipe, watching.

The goat, giving up the struggle, slips easily backwards out of the wire and Godfrey says, 'As usual, you were quite right, Dulcie,' and smiles wryly at her.

'They can be very dumb sometimes.'

'Just like humans.'

They laugh.

Godfrey hesitates – then he says, 'Do you keep in touch?'

'We used to send Christmas cards.' She stubs out her cigarette and flicks it over the wall into the flower bed. 'She doesn't write much in them. The odd bit of news. That's about all.'

She will offer nothing more. She can't, without betraying Grace.

The tea is brought and Dulcie says, 'Let me just go and see where Pa has got to.'

Godfrey is grateful to her. She is leaving him to regain his equilibrium. He sits in the chair with his pipe in his hand. He watches a dung beetle struggle across the flagging of the *stoep*, its spiky legs scratching for purchase. He gazes at it with a still intensity: a long journey that will end against a wall. It is all quite futile.

It stops as if to look about, changes direction, stops again. Godfrey stoops to pick it up and put it in the flower bed.

He hears footsteps in the hall, Dulcie saying, 'Take my arm, Pa. Mind the step.'

Herman comes out on to the veranda, fingers hooked round Dulcie's elbow, stick in his other hand. He is wearing an old brown dressing gown with a twisted cord binding. His spectacles have thumb marks on their lenses. He seems to peer round them, out of hiding.

His hand is just as strong as it always was. He wheezes when he speaks, 'Hell, Doc. It's good to see you.'

Godfrey brings a chair up and he and Dulcie lower Herman into it together, settling him. Dulcie busies herself with the tray, calls for a forgotten tea cosy.

Godfrey says, 'I'm sorry to see you're not up and about, *Oom* Herman. Dulcie will be telling you how to run your cattle in no time.'

Herman laughs. It rattles in his throat. 'She tells me how to run them, anyway,' he says. 'A real bossy breeches.'

'Nonsense, Pa,' says Dulcie, handing him a cup of tea, stirring it for him, arranging the biscuit. She is so deft in everything, Godfrey senses that there is nothing old Herman does for himself any more. He looks up at her with rough affection.

'About our Ngunis,' says Herman, suddenly. 'Man' – he stares into his cup, shifts his slippered feet – 'what a lovely little herd.' He is conjuring the past: his voice falters and steadies. 'Have you been in touch with Crawford, Doc?'

'Not for some time. I was hoping you could tell me how things are running at the experimental farm.'

'We get bulletins every now and then,' says Dulcie. 'Don't we, Pa?'

'*Ja* – but you know, it's still an uphill battle to convince people. What you need to do, Doc, is write something to explain the importance of these animals. Something that will really reach farmers and other blokes out there. You need to get it out of people's heads that these are just kaffir cattle.

No more, no less.' Herman coughs. He struggles a moment for control. The old rope-veins of his hands are full of nodules, the sun spots have deepened into liver-coloured mottling. The mark where his hat was always pulled down across his forehead is still there, the skin above pale and thin, his brush of hair in wisps. He takes off his glasses and wipes them on the corner of his sleeve, trying to get his breath. He says, 'Damn it, if I was younger, I'd write the thing myself! But you know I'm no good with words. That's your business, Doc. After all, you wrote a whole bloody dictionary. You've got to get them here ' – and he knocks his fist peremptorily against his chest – 'to get them thinking.'

The afternoon settles in and they speak of cattle and droughts, of breeding and windmills. The three of them sit, facing out at the lawn, none looking at the other, following the same things – goats in the scrub below the fence, inspecting, always, with the eyes, as farmers do. Herman says, in mid-sentence – 'you'd better see to the leak in the trough down there' – and carries on relating the history of *Bitchaan Shiki*, the young bull that Godfrey had once borrowed.

He has gone on to sire many calves.

Herman says, 'They called him *Dabul' umhlambi* in the end.' Again he coughs and laughs at once. ' "What sweeps right through the herd". He was a really eager blighter and the heifers loved him!'

Except the small *inala* cow.

So poised. So fastidious.

Godfrey puts his cup on the tray and lights his pipe again. He is having difficulty breathing evenly. —*Jesus Christ. What has she done? What, in Christ's name, has she done?*

Dulcie is watching him. He glances away. He says, 'I suppose I'd better get on, *Oom* Herman. I need to buy some supplies at the shop. I should be there before it closes.'

'If it is,' says Dulcie, 'just go and call that old chap, Wilton. He still lives behind the store. He'll open up for you.'

'Wilton?' Godfrey can hear himself, his studied cheerfulness. He is so busy with his pipe, he can look at nothing else. He keeps thinking of Mrs Mabb with her lipstick at an angle – betraying her – and her handkerchief, folding it over with unsteady fingers.

She had tried so hard.

Dulcie says, 'You remember Wilton, don't you? He's been there for donkey's years. He's such an old *skelm*. Whenever I go down for anything he tells me how his second wife is "brandy" and that he wants to divorce her and look after his other wife properly.'

'He never used to drink.'

'He does now.'

'That's a shame.'

'What else is there to do? Look at the drought! There's bugger all to plant and bugger all to eat, if you'll excuse the language.'

Bugger all indeed.

'Listen,' Dulcie leaves her chair, pushing herself up heavily. 'I got out a towel and some clean sheets and a primus stove. I baked this morning so there's bread and I've taken a few chops out of the freezer. You can cook up something nice. There's also candles and matches and soap.'

'That's very good of you, Dulcie,' Godfrey says. 'A couple of eggs was all I needed. I was going to get them at the store.'

'No, man. We've got plenty here. The eggs at the shop will be *vrot* in comparison with mine, I can promise you.'

'Don't get up, *Oom* Herman,' Godfrey says. He goes to him and gives him his hand.

Herman says, 'Next time you're here, Doc, Dulcie and I will take you over to Vlakfontein. You must come in the spring when the little calves are frisking. Man, there's nothing prettier. It's a sight to really cheer you up.'

They look at each other. There is no dissembling in the glance.

'That's a promise,' Godfrey says quietly, returning the grip.

It is a pledge of regard.

And a word of farewell.

Both know they will never see each other again.

Dulcie leads Godfrey into the kitchen where a box and a basket are already prepared. She says, 'I've gone in for bush hens, you know, just like my bush cows. Their eggs are ten times nicer than other eggs – but you should hear the fuss the local farmers' wives make about it, like I've done something mad. They were just the same to Pa about his cattle. And here's everyone breeding up fancy bantams and things which just get gobbled up by the *nywagis* in no time. My bush chooks are much too wily for them and fight like hell if something comes near the nest. You won't taste better. Either the chicken or the egg.'

Dulcie is off on a favourite subject – bush chickens and marauding genets – keeping up the flow of chatter, sensing Godfrey's distress, knowing her father will be blowing his nose like a trumpet out on the veranda. She talks fast, wily as a bush hen herself, leading him away, wishing she had words of comfort for her father, to allow his dying; to offer Godfrey, to salvage love.

Godfrey takes the box from her, balancing it under his arm. He is standing, tall and spare against the light of the window, his face in gloom, a silhouette man. Dulcie wants to turn to him and say, 'You have a daughter, Dr Godfrey. Her name is Ruth. She is nearly ten years old. Don't you think that you should know her?'

But how can she say that when Grace has chosen not to tell him and has rearranged her history.

Grace's own expedience: protecting him. Protecting Ruth.

Paying for her sin. Over and over.

–*A Good Woman knows better.*

A good woman knows.

Godfrey is walking behind Dulcie, quite close to her back. They leave the house and take the path across the kitchen garden. He says, suddenly, 'Are they happy?'

Dulcie does not turn. 'They have their obligations.'

He is at a loss.

As she reaches the gate and opens it, Dulcie says, 'I reckon, being obliged makes Hugh Wilmot very happy.' She glances back at him.

How can she describe that still, watchful face? Those eyes. She knows he wants to ask, –*And Grace*? She makes a small unconscious gesture with her arm – protective of herself, her child – infinitely brief. She says, 'It's not our business any more.'

There is no sting in her words. Her voice is calm, even gentle. But he cannot question it. He doesn't have the right.

He has abrogated it.

–*It's not our business any more.*

Dulcie had included herself when she had said it: the generosity of woman, woman-lore, allowing him no nearer, but absolving him gently – because he is a man.

And suddenly – implacably – he hears his mother's steps as she walks across the lobby of the old hotel, he trailing her, clod-footed, in his school blazer and his big shoes.

Bewildered by vexation – and by yearning.

He stands back, shaken.

Dulcie searches under the hedge, deft with her fingers, knowing the nesting places of her hens. She picks out four large eggs and lowers them gingerly into the basket. They talk about cattle again and stroll to the car. Godfrey greets Arthur Trollip as he comes from the shed, wiping his hands on a greasy rag, a strange vacant look in his face. Arthur lumbers down towards the house and Dulcie stands at the car waiting for Godfrey to put the supplies in the boot. He straightens and takes Dulcie's hand and shakes it, almost gravely. 'You take care of yourself,' he says. 'I hope all goes well with you both.'

She looks down, blushes a little – she with her gap-tooth smile and sunburned skin and her crown of plaits. 'Hope it's a big boy to help me run the farm,' she replies, gruffly.

'If it's a girl like you,' says Godfrey, 'it'll do just fine running any number of farms.'

Dulcie likes that – but she says, dismissing it, 'Didn't have much choice when my brothers went to war.'

Godfrey puts a hand on her shoulder briefly and gets into the car. He is swift to leave.

Dulcie watches him drive away.

For the first time in years, she has the urge to cry. To howl out at the sky.

For Godfrey. For Grace.

For Arthur, stuck somewhere in his tank, unable to get out.

For her father in his old brown dressing gown and his thumb-smudged glasses, planning the new calving season, seeing – already – the calves at pasture with their dams, knowing their colours and their patterns. Knowing it is all too late.

She wants to cry, for herself. 'It's those bloody hormones,' she says out loud, 'making me so bloody stupid!' She casts a derisive glance at her midriff, as if it has embarrassed her. She marches back down the path. She picks up a clod and hurls it at a rooster in her seedbed. 'And you' – she says as the baby turns in her stomach, pressing in against her liver – 'You stop kicking, you little bugger!' She stops, gazing at the moving arc made by heel or shoulder, visible under her shirt. She lays her hand on the place, tracing the movement. Practised and gentle with stock, it is a hand that soothes.

She walks into the house.

'Where's the tea?' says Arthur.

'Patience is a virtue,' she retorts. Then she says, less roughly, 'It's on the veranda. I'll bring more hot water, if you like. You and Pa can have a cup together.'

There are different memorials to those we love. Some are built and tended. Some are only carried in the heart. Brief, caught at – fixed. An image in a dream; a light-fragment in the mind, almost like a sound; a kind of fleeting warmth, subtler than a scent; music remembered on waking.

Mostly unexpected. Made concrete by imagination.

Godfrey's mother had not been present in the memorial to her in the cemetery, with its old untended plot. That is simply a point of reference. A public resting place.

To visit it – as Godfrey had done, briefly, after the mourners had left his father's graveside on the morning of the funeral – was a gesture of remembrance and respect, knowing he would not be coming back again.

He had taken a flower from his father's wreath and laid it on the grave.

He had put another on the child's.

It had seemed misplaced – even gauche – among the tangle of the dog roses which encircled and covered the pair of memorial stones, binding them together. He had bent, squatting, and settled it firmly among the branching thorns. He'd rested his forearms on his knees, his hands linked, regarding it with steady eyes.

Then he'd stood and turned away.

His mother had not been waiting there for him. He could not feel her.

Nor could he feel her when, at last, he went into her room. Not even when he took the statue of the Virgin down and wiped the crown of dust from the veiled head.

Instead, she had been alive – sudden, unexpected and exact – as he had followed Dulcie Trollip down the yard to look for eggs. By the gesture of Dulcie's arm – so slight, so alert in its protectiveness – he had known his mother's presence. She was there, as Dulcie turned him from a threshold which he could not cross.

It had been gentle. But it had been firm.

–In whose care is that embryonic soul, if not in hers?

Godfrey does not take the road past the school and church. He does not wish to see them now. He does not wish to meet another priest or to open the door of the school room.

And find what?

A teacher he has never seen?

A row of small boys looking up at him, defending?

He drives on, taking the slope up and out of the the valley, into the next, making the long curve, travelling east: the old track looping the ironstone hill.

There is a moment – just a moment – when he thinks he is on the wrong road. The *veld* is bare, stretches of bush have been cleared, exposing the earth and rock. He stops the car and climbs out, looking about.

There is an air of desolation that he has ever known before.

An emptiness.

Perhaps it is in him.

Or perhaps it is in the red earth, showing through, the soil leached where it was rich before. And he remembers writing, long ago – in a spring when the rains had been good and the pasture green and the rivers full, eleven years before:

The great desolation will overtake us here. A great despondency. Drought and more. I have seen the last real spring.

276

And he says, aloud, his voice half hoarse in the silence, 'I'm sorry, Grace. My God, I'm sorry.'

The store is closed and the house behind the pebble wall is locked. Much of the byre has been dismantled and the stone carried away. He can only see its outline and the great trailing clump of blue plumbago which had clambered on its eastern side.

He walks back to the house and goes around to the kitchen door. Leaves are shored against it. A spider web vibrates slightly in the drift of air. He turns away, taking the path to Wilton Mayekiso's house behind the store.

It is an afternoon of pale sky. The ridge is bland. The *garingbome* all along the road have yellow heads, drying out to brown. Someone had been chopping up their leaves for fodder. Some are shorn, their rims of thorn stripped off.

Wilton Mayekiso is listening to the wireless. He turns when Godfrey's shadow falls across the open doorway, gives a faint half squawk in disbelief. Then he comes forward, wiping his hand on his overall, putting it out with his other hand holding his own wrist – diffident – and Godfrey takes it firmly, *'Molo, Mayekiso.'*

They exchange greetings, over and over, as if filling up each of the years that have gone between.

The old tusk tooth has gone, the eyes are rheumy. Mayekiso has the emaciation of a man who drinks too much and eats too little. His wife is out in the yard, busy with a bucket and a pig in a corrugated iron *hok*. It is too far for her to see who is talking to Mayekiso. She turns back to her task.

'I see the old cattle byre has fallen down,' Godfrey says as they walk towards the car.

Mayekiso makes a clicking in his throat. 'The man at the store kept using stones for other things,' he says. 'He takes them here. He takes them there.' He looks up at Godfrey shrewdly, half enquiry, half anticipation. 'He is not like us. He is not a man with cows.'

'Not like us,' says Godfrey, putting a hand on Mayekiso's shoulder.

Mayekiso stops and looks ahead, chin lifted, as if – suddenly – he is seeing something in the empty camp ahead. He says, gesturing, 'You must bring them back again.' Head cocked, enquiring, ready to exult. He shows a wedge of gum, a laugh waiting. Then he turns back to his imaginary pasture, conjuring, cajoling Godfrey. 'They were everywhere! That one – *iwarolo!* And that other one – *inqilo!*' And he touches his throat for the collar of the Longclaw for which the pattern is named, making darts and flutters, to imitate the bird. And then he straightens suddenly, 'And that one, the young bull – do you remember? *UBitchaan Shiki!*' Mayekiso bunches his shoulders into an attitude of intent and says the name again, with great exaggeration.

Godfrey laughs with him.

'I am told he has a new name now,' says Godfrey. '*Udabul'umhlambi* – what sweeps right through the herd.'

So much bluster in that bull. So much male anxiety.

Wilton Mayekiso smiles and then, as if he is treading lightly on little hooves, he says in a hushed voice, '*Inala*.' Abundance. '*Inkomo yeminyanya*.' The ancestral beast.

He is thoughtful, scrutinising the pasture. He is looking for her – she has wandered somewhere, as she always did. He shakes his head, 'The teacher, the *inkosazana*, liked that little cow very much,' he says.

Indeed, she had.

Godfrey is silent too. Then he says, 'There are no cattle left. There are none where I am. None.'

'Indeed there are none,' says Wilton Mayekiso, glancing about, suddenly disdainful of the empty stretch of *veld* leading to the road. He shrugs his shoulders, shaking them off. 'Not even one!' He raises a finger, pointing at the sky, as if accusing God.

Godfrey does not contradict him.

And then Mayekiso says, 'Only on the rock.'

Godfrey looks at him. 'On the rock?'

'Where it is painted,' Mayekiso says. '*Kudaaala . . .*' Long ago. He draws out the word, giving it length and longing. He laughs then. The maudlin laugh of an inebriate, masking a fine regret.

'Where?'

Mayekiso gestures with a finger, almost dismissively. He says, 'It has always been there. *Kanti . . .*' he says, with a faint expression of surprise – *and even yet* – 'you have not seen it . . .'

'Where?'

Mayekiso looks along his own arm, as if he is taking aim, imitating – by a subtle gesture – a San hunter. '*Ngaphayaaa . . .*'Again the sing-song, conjuring, drawing the word out, stretching it to measure the distance to the place that he is indicating.

'Will you take me there?'

Mayekiso makes a wry, small cluck in his throat, as if he half regrets having mentioned it. It is a stiff walk. He would rather sit and have a pipe with the doctor and ask him if he won't return and build the byre up and buy more cows from Enseleni.

Godfrey takes his tobacco pouch from his pocket and offers it to Mayekiso. It is not a bribe, it is a gesture of friendship: a diffident request. He says, 'I will get my camera.'

He takes it from the car, slings it on his shoulder. There is a sense of ritual in the gesture.

Mayekiso leads.

They make their way through a camp towards the ridge. In the light of afternoon, its shadows are undistinguished. There is no dip or fold to show the line of the river. The *krantz* is stark and dry, the two *koppies* rising further back out of the upland, are barely visible. A finger of cloud hovers. It seems the heat will soon dissolve it.

They climb the slope and skirt a stand of trees. They are the same, in which, on that distant afternoon, Grace and Godfrey had found their small *inala* cow, grazing on her own, moving slowly through the dappled shadow of the underbrush.

Wilton Mayekiso turns sharply along the edge of the *krantz*, leaving the bush and following the line of the river. He crosses it and moves slowly over fallen boulders.

The *krantz* diminishes.

There is a place where a *witgat* tree grows. It rests against a crevice, leaning into its shelter. Its crown is frail, almost leafless against the sky. It is a tree which is suspended between living and turning into stone.

Wilton Mayekiso stops. He turns and waits for Godfrey.

Then he steps back, in deference, gesturing with his hand.

He walks away and lights his pipe and sits beside the tree.

–There is only one cow left. It is painted on the rock.

Godfrey stands before it, awed.

He does not touch his camera. He does not move.

It is an *inala* cow. Ochre-red and white.

–I am Abundance.

Its head is turned, as if to beckon him.

The light is slowly changing.

In the brightness, the colours are matt and dense with their own substance, made from the juice of plants and earth and clay. They transform as it fades with the slant of the sun – noon-ox lowering its horns – giving them translucence in shade, an undertone of coolness, an energy. Abundance is transforming from the warm speckle of a lark's egg into starlight.

The head takes a new animation.

Godfrey stands before her as the dusk brings the *inala* cow into life.

The sounds of evening settle in. The last calling of the cattle-birds. The swifts and swallows hawking, high above.

He stands and weeps.

It is unobtrusive. Simple.

It is without the bewilderment of loss that he had known as a child when he had wept for the *umvemve* calf.

Restoration is here, with the *inala* cow, beckoning from the rockface.

Love and Beauty are admissible.

It has been a long night.

Godfrey looks at his watch. It is five past six. The pale green of morning, the little streaks of cloud, dove and pink, lie along the hills. The *dikkops* have gone. They are moonlight wanderers. They have yellow eyes. They do not stay beyond the dark. Dew has freshened the ground, even in this drought.

Kusempondozankomo: dawn.

The time of the horns of the cattle, silhouetted against the lightening sky.

The sun rises and there is a brief and sudden silence.

Transition into day.

The bulbuls and the buntings call. There are fluttering among the sweet-thorns in the yard.

He has finished the paper. He has written without pausing. He has filled an exercise book. He has said everything he had to say.

He has carried a presence through the hours of work. An image.

A small cow of the *inala* pattern.

Ochre-red and white, head turned to beckon him.

Endnote 24: **inala** – *abundance. An extraordinarily beautiful and delicate pattern . . .*

Godfrey writes fluidly, the words linking. He is breasting through to the end. As he writes, he makes boxes into which he scrawls his endnotes, annotating them with stars and arrows and instructions to himself as editor.

While writing this paper I was taken to see a painting by my former stockman, Mr Wilton Mayekiso. It was a Bushman painting of unknown date – executed, perhaps, within the last one hundred and fifty years . . . I believe that it is no coincidence that I was shown this painting. Seeing it was humbling. It cautioned me against presumption . . .

He and Wilton Mayekiso had walked away in the last white light of evening. They had crossed the river-bed and set out across the flatlands, down towards the store. They had paused to fill their pipes, passing the matches between them, the flame flaring in the dusk. Godfrey had put his hand on Wilton's shoulder as they'd turned for home. He had said, 'You are right, *mfo'wam*. There have always been cattle here.'

And they had gone on together in silence, looking ahead, at the empty pasture, gathering their herd, calling it up, bringing it to byre, with laughter and in praise.

The sky is quince-skin gold. All the *veld* is quince-skin gold in the early morning sun.

Godfrey takes his bag out to the car. He hands Dulcie Trollip's box and basket to Wilton Mayekiso to give to her when she comes to the store. He has included a note written on exercise paper, thanking her for her kindness, telling her he has written the first draft of a paper – as she and her father had suggested – and that he will send it for consideration to an agricultural journal as soon as he has corrected it.

> *I will forward a copy to you and hope you will like it. Please let me know if your father approves! Please pass on information about it and its existence to anyone who you may think would have an interest. This is the only means in my power of making people understand the full importance of these cattle, not just in economic and scientific terms, but their even greater spiritual significance in the minds and hearts of men.*
>
> *It is the only message I can send.*

Dulcie will understand him.

He gives another envelope to Wilton Mayekiso, containing a gift, wrapped in a greeting, written in Xhosa. He shakes his hand and says, 'I wish that this could buy a cow in calf, so you could start our herd again. I wish it could buy many.'

'And then we would build our byre,' says Wilton.

'And we would be men with cows again,' says Godfrey.

Wilton Mayekiso looks into Godfrey's face and shakes his head and says, 'We are both old now. And our sons are already grown and have no cattle.'

'The time will come for our grandchildren to restore them.'

'Perhaps.'

'Until then, there are still cattle in the sky and under the earth. And on the rock.'

'*Kunjalo*,' says Wilton Mayekiso. 'It is so.' And then he says – half sadly – '*Kanti . . .*'

And even yet . . .

Godfrey does not look back. He turns the car into the steel road running

281

the rim of the hill. Behind, the ridge rears up towards the morning sky.

Uqolo lwezimpungutye: Ridge of jackals.

He sees the fault of the rockface. He sees the line of the dry river. He sees the *witgat* tree.

And somewhere there – somewhere – the small *inala* cow, still in slumber in the quiet shadow folded on the face of the *krantz*.

He turns north and west out of the valley, its ironstone and aloe.

The sky ahead is clear and still.

The early sun behind is radiant.

Chapter eighteen

My thesis must be handed in. I toil in the turmoil of it, with an odd inner calm. It is the work that I must do for myself. But it is also something I must do for Godfrey. What he had written in his paper, all those years ago, was also left for me.

Dogged old lexicographer.

It is his legacy – given to the student, not the writer. He expects my rational attention.

–The moment of dispassionate understanding is not complete until it has been clearly communicated to other men.

Did he write that for me – all those years ago, knowing, even then, that I needed cautioning?

–Yes, you know me, Godfrey.

But he also knew I'd see it through. His purpose is my purpose.

He has secured me my profession, my particular niche.

The other, is a journey for Godfrey and myself. Our private – and mutual – restoration.

It is done now and I must face his slow, personal withdrawal from my daily consciousness, the terrible attrition. He will be left, at last, between the pages of a book, on the third shelf from the top, my Godfrey-treasures in their wooden box, pressed down by the gatherings from a newer project.

–Don't leave me, Godfrey.

But he will.

And, in time, when others ask, who is Gert, who is Grace – what will I tell them, Godfrey? What will I say?

Oh, I can point out Gert's house. I have seen it. I know Grace's little school in the dip between the hills. I have stood in the arch and seen the old *gwarri* leaning at the fence post.

I have seen the cattle byre with its tangle of plumbago and its kraal aloes.

I know the room of Grace and Godfrey's loving. I know its shadows and its silent corners. I know the blue light at the angle of the ceiling. I know the lozenge of the mirror in reflection on the wall.

I hear his voice.

And all his poetry.

Will these things slide back into their present conformation: the mind-map – so intense – rearranged to order?

–Don't leave me, Godfrey.

If you go, Gert and Grace will go as well, dissolving back into the upturned face of a child in a print, a woman's shadow at your feet.

If you go, the *umvemve* calf and the *inala* cow will follow.

I will be left with the lexicon and Delekile's wire creations. His trotting cow, its calf, his windmill turning at my touch.

And what will I have to offer him?

How long can he survive, in so great a desolation, by conjuring these images from nothing but a length of wire and a scrap of tin?

How long can I?

The printer jams, the paper runs out, my children resent my preoccupation, our house is chaotic, the good man is phlegmatic, as he always is. He brings me tea and Marie biscuits and surveys the mess with humour. I fall asleep on the carpet in my study, the last chapter half collated in my hands. By the evening the thesis will be printed and ready for the binder, the floors will have been vacuumed. I will be home.

–A heart-wound is clean. Finite. And love can never be immaculate.

I gently slide the great pile of the final manuscript on to the prof's table.

Two volumes: dissertation; appendices and figures.

The prof peers over his reading glasses, surveying me. 'You look rather tired,' he says.

'I am.'

'Let me make you coffee.'

And he does.

We sit in his study with the coffee cups between us, the prof with his feet resting on the opened lower drawer of his desk, my script in his hands, the familiar peaks and troughs of red-tiled roofs beyond the window, laid out below us. He glances at me every now and then and smiles. 'You might look like death – but you're full of cheek today,' he says. He settles the pages and wriggles them comfortably.

'Today it's allowed,' I say.

He laughs. 'Tell me another!'

I am tired but happy.

He seems to be happy too.

He almost twinkles. 'Good feeling?'

'Good feeling.'

He settles back in his chair, reaches for his cup – the familiar little kiss across the steam – and takes a sip. 'It's a matter of eating an elephant, a teaspoonful at a time.'

'Now you tell me!'

'Bloody crazy,' says the prof. But his own dissertation – all three volumes – is resplendent in maroon on the shelf behind his head: it's a brilliant piece of work, I know.

'Bloody crazy,' I repeat.

We are comrades now. A red gown will also hang behind my door and someone will come along and remove the plate in the passage with my name, replacing the title with '*Dr*'.

'What happened to C J Godfrey?' asks the prof. 'Did you find the last word on cows?'

'I found the last word on cows,' I say. 'And Dr Godfrey went home.'

'I was getting worried that you'd become romantically distracted.'

'Were you?'

'Well, you were showing signs. And since I hardly thought it was the cattle which were a subject for romance . . .'

Like Godfrey, I also know the moment when to say, 'Enough'. I smile. My voice is light, disarming. 'I think you're wrong,' I say. 'They're a metaphor for love.'

He gives a little snort.

'It's true.'

–In the sky and under the earth.

–And on the rock.

'I'd like to see you convincing the scientists of that.'

'I don't have to,' I say. 'Dr Godfrey did it for me.'

I leave the prof settled with the thesis. He will send it to the external examiners today. I do not even wash the coffee cups. I walk through the corridors, full of exhilaration.

Punch-drunk, battle weary.

I am close to laughter, close to tears.

I wish that there was someone I could tell. Someone who will know the triumph and the love.

I need Godfrey.

I stand in the corridor, waiting for him. Perhaps he will be on the steps of the library with his pipe and his tweed jacket with its leather elbow patches, striding off somewhere, trailing a plume of smoke.

–*Godfrey? Stop. I have to tell you something.*

I dare the Senate Chamber.

I do not go right in. I stand at the threshold, at the far end of the long table, the chairs facing in, the congregation of professors looking down.

'Godfrey?'

The deep shadow on one side of his face throws into relief the lean, steady plane of his cheek, the amused line of his lip, the sense of smoky gloom in the foreground.

He is appraising me.

'I have done it,' I say.

Those dark eyes.

'Remember *"the moment of dispassionate understanding . . ."* '

–*Ah.*

'I hope you will be pleased.'

I want him to be proud.

'What if you don't like it?'

Then he won't like it. He still understands it is something that I had to do. *For* him.

And despite him.

'It is all I have to give.'

He knows that. He has always known that.

A little laugh. I send it down the table to him, teasing, passing it across: ' "–*Nature still defeats the frowsty silence of the cloistered men*".'

Indeed.

His brow has always been satirical. There is a slight crinkle at the corners of his eye, the finest lines of laughter. I had not noticed them before. I had been so absorbed by gravity – and by his fine, patrician nose.

I tilt my head, ' "*. . . their theories, their deceits!*" '

He allows me the liberty today. He allows me my own conceits. He is laughing with me as I go across the quad.

There is a last task.

Just as I have given my thesis into the prof's keeping, to see it to its end, I must find the painting of the *inala* cow on the rock.

If it is there – the restoration will have been complete.

And if it's not?

I telephone Mrs Trollip to ask her if I can come and see her and if, perhaps, I can spend the night at the little house by the store.

'*Ag*, man,' she says. 'I don't know that it's too safe there, now. The store's mostly closed since you were here last year. We only use it as a depot for rations. Arthur goes there sometimes. He's made a shed for all his old machines that were lying around.'

'Just one night,' I say. 'There's something I must look for in the *veld*. It might take a little time to find it.'

'If you say so.' She is dubious.

'I also need to give Delekile some money for a few of the things I've sold. I wish it was more.'

'Come and get the keys from me, then.'

'I'll be there on Tuesday morning.'

She is brightening. 'Make sure you're here for tea.'

'Can I bring you anything from town?'

She insists that there is nothing that she needs but I buy some fresh fruit and salads, chocolate and a bottle of wine.

She is waiting, in her red Fasco dress. Her plaits are just the same, pinned up on to her head. Perhaps a little wispier and sparer than before. She smiles in welcome, looking up at me through the bifocals, which magnify her eyes, first one and then the other. It is the same gap-toothed smile, the same gruff chuckle in her voice.

'Man, it's nice to see you,' she says, exclaiming over the gifts. 'It gets very quiet around here.'

The tea tray is already laid out in the living room. She must have been listening for me and heard my car turning down past the cattle byre. The pot is under its embroidered cosy. A plate of biscuits is covered with a doily.

–*Dulcie's Peanut Biscuits.*

They are still warm from the oven.

'How's Mr Trollip?' I say.

'Not so good, but the machines make him happy. You'll see his new shed down at the store when you get there. He made it with that *skelm*, Delekile, out of old corrugated iron. They got the stuff all over the district. Most of it's rather buggered, just like the machines, but it's better than having them lying around in the bush. I don't know what Arthur thinks he's going to make on them, but it keeps him out of trouble.'

We sit in the living room, in the same chairs as before. Dulcie is searching for her cigarettes. Her cough is worse. The ash still scatters wherever she moves.

'The house has been closed up for ages,' she says. 'It will be very musty.'

'I've brought a camp bed.'

'And there'll be no hot water. I can't even tell you to get Delekile to stoke up the donkey because I know he's off checking fences on the boundaries and putting down jackal poison. He won't be back tonight.'

'It doesn't matter,' I say. 'I'll be off in the morning as soon as I've got through what I have to check. I'll leave Delekile's money with you, shall I? It's not very much. It's the best I could do. The art shops seem to like stuff made from telephone cable these days, in nice bright colours.'

'Don't tell Delekile that,' says Mrs Trollip. 'He'll be cutting up the wires all over the district and there'll be hell to pay!'

She pours the tea and I take a cup from her. The sugar spoon has a little crest on it, commemorating some long-gone prize ram.

'I also have a primus stove that you can borrow. It's a terrible old thing. And a kettle.'

'Thank you. I would like that.'

'And I have some nice fresh eggs. My fowls have been laying well lately and the *nywagis* seem to have been leaving them alone.' She looks at me then: the mention of predators has unsettled her, a little finger of doubt. 'Why don't you stay here?' she says. 'It will be no trouble, really . . .'

'It's important to be there.'

'I don't know what it is about that old *pondok* . . .' she says, half absently.
—*It is Godfrey, Mrs Trollip. It is Grace.*
—*It is the inala cow.*
—*It is the whole mythology of love.*

I make no reply. Then I say, brightly, 'My thesis is finished. I have just handed it in.'

'That's wonderful, my girlie,' says Mrs Trollip. 'Man, I'd like to see it.'

'So many people have been contacting me about Ngunis,' I say. 'Everyone suddenly seems to want them. They're all very disappointed, though, when I only know about colour-patterns and poems. They want to hear about beef and milk.'

'And about time they sat up and took notice!' She sniffs, ruefully. 'I'm so sad my old Dad isn't here to see the work. He really did his best to make people interested, you know. So did I. It was such a long uphill battle all those years ago. He always said, "They're the breed of the future, Duls." ' She dips a biscuit in her cup. 'I'm too old for it now,' she says, 'but my son has a really nice herd near Vlakfontein. You should call in and have a look. He's got some beautiful little heifers this year.'

—*Nice little hocks?*

'He's quite a big shot on the Nguni Cattle Breeders' Society. He's off to sales all over the show these days. I can never understand why it took so long to recognise the breed. Now, all of a sudden, prices have rocketed. The poor old blacks, who should be farming with them, can't afford them any more. Everything is *deurmekaar* these days.' She fishes a bit of floating biscuit out of her tea with a spoon. 'If my Dad had only been a chap who could write and talk at meetings, he'd have got things moving years ago. He told Dr Godfrey to spread the word and Dr Godfrey wrote a very interesting paper about it. But it was so highfalutin, I don't suppose any of the farmers that read it understood much, though I should think it might have made an impression on the blokes in the Department and things.' She lights another cigarette. 'Did you ever see it? Man, there was something in the way he wrote it . . .' – she pauses – 'it was very beautiful, like poetry.' She glances up and out of the window where the swallows' nests sit snugly under the eaves. 'I wonder if there was anyone who understood it.'

'I've seen it,' I say quietly, not wanting to startle her away. 'It was written for many people to think about – but for only one person to understand.'

She touches her hand to her plaits.

'Grace Wilmot,' I say.

Dulcie Trollip reaches over for her teacup. Then she says, quite brusquely, 'I sent it to her myself. I made sure she knew.'

Far away, the sounds in the yard drift in: someone emptying a bucket, goats, at a distance, the faint stirring of the palm tree on the front lawn.

'You were a wonderful friend to her.' I am tentative. I need her to respond.

She looks across at me. She draws herself up. She is defending Grace. 'She was a very strong person,' Dulcie Trollip says. 'She did an amazing amount for education and feeding schemes and things. But she wasn't the "do-good" sort – you know those kind of urging people who make you want to run a mile. It's just that everybody loved her. All the down-and-outs around the place. She had streams of them at her door the whole time. Endless patience, never got cross. Cats. Dogs. Kids. Anyone who seemed bewildered. You name it, they loved her! That's what I heard from people who knew her there.'

'Did she ever say anything about the paper?'

Dulcie Trollip is silent a moment, then she says, 'She didn't need to.'

Grace puts the paper in a box which had belonged, once, to her grandfather. She folds it carefully. She knows what the original would have looked like, scrawled on lined paper, torn from an exercise book, probably written in pencil – the long looping words, joined, as he pushed for the end. The turn of phrase. She can hear his voice exactly.

She had never heard him lecture, but she knows – beneath the brisk, articulate, assured manner – would be the wryness, the self-deprecation: a lightness of touch. He is having a joke at himself, for any lurking pedantry.

She knows that voice, pitched gently in the dark, the falling tone, the pause, the closing phrase.

It is the thing that she remembers best.

It has radiance.

She closes the paper into the box. It will settle into its folds, Dulcie Trollip's note appended: *'I know this will interest you.'* She has weighted it with the little stone that he had given her – small and smooth and curved exactly to the caress of a thumb, perfectly balanced in her palm. There is also a scrap of *impepho* which she had kept from the time that they had made the *inala* cow their ancestral beast. She put it in the box with the only picture which she had of him. The boy, budding into neck and shoulders, a spike of fringe across his forehead, the lip firm – but just a little tender.

It will be Ruth's one day, when she is ready to apprehend it. Or to let it go.

As she chooses.

If she chooses.

I get up to take the plate of biscuits to Mrs Trollip. She seems suddenly frail, sitting in her chair among the putty-coloured cushions. I would like to kneel beside her and put my arms about the small frame. She is bird bones, perched within the stiff folds of her frock. The vigorous young woman at the cattle show – strong legs, strong hips – the bride upholstered into satin in the picture, is left only with a gap-toothed smile and a crown of plaits which has slipped into cobweb.

Out on the lawn I can see the old bird bath. It stands forlorn on an empty patch of earth and the irises in the bed by the wall are dry and spare. All the abundance of the garden has gone and the sweet-thorn is encroaching.

'I only heard from her once after that,' says Dulcie Trollip. 'When I wrote and sent her the notice of Dr Godfrey's death.'

I have always known the date: *February 2nd, 1963.*

He was only sixty-four.

'What did he die of?' I ask.

'Lungs,' she said. 'He was gassed in the war. He smoked a pipe. What can you expect?' She lights another cigarette. 'You've got to go somehow. The same will happen to me.' And she wheezes a laugh.

The letter is lying in the postbox along with a couple of bills and a handwritten notice from a painter, looking for work. Grace puts the bills in her pocket and looks at the letter.

She knows the writing.

The envelope is light.

She glances up. Her children are playing on the lawn. Ruth and Jack are teaching little Hugh to ride a bicycle. Ruth is running along behind him holding on to the carrier, Jack yelling, 'Keep pedalling!'

Little Hugh is wobbling wildly, shouting, 'Don't let me fall!'

Grace is standing in the driveway, between the edgings of marigolds.

The afternoon sun is hot and flat. There is nothing distinctive in the day. She tears the envelope and opens the letter.

3rd October 1963.

Dear Grace,

I am writing to tell you that I heard that Dr Godfrey passed away some time ago on Feb. 2nd. Dr Humphreys of the Vet. Department told me. He was a friend of Dr Godfrey's from the old days here and from school. I saw him at a cattle sale earlier this month. He said that he had read it in his school magazine. I wrote for a copy. I am enclosing a cutting.

I am glad my old father saw him before he passed away himself. He was very fond of Dr Godfrey. He said he was a very fine man. I thought so too.

I hope this finds you and Mr Wilmot and the children well.

Please visit any time you are here. I will always be so glad to see you. The kiddies from the school that you taught have all gone on to do well in high school. I remember that funny little chap called Desmond. He never took to me. He was always asking when Mrs Wilmot was coming back.

Dulcie had pinned the death notice to the letter:

Clement John Godfrey (1898-1963).

Grace reads it over and over.

–How will I know when you die? How will I know?

The cryptic script, taken from the school Register: academic, athletic and other sporting achievement. Military service. His lectureships and publications, his awards and honours, his work for human rights, his activism, lobbying, from a distance, for justice in his country. It lists his fellowships of this Institute and that. Places she has never heard of, abbreviations which she cannot decipher.

One of the most distinguished of our old boys, he is buried at St Barnabas, near his home in Cambridge, where he and his wife, Stella, used to worship. Our condolences and heartfelt sympathy go out to Mrs Godfrey, their two sons and their three grandchildren.

Grace will never go to the graveyard where he is buried.

Nor will I.

We have no business there.

It is in a place we do not know, a landscape which Godfrey has absorbed without us. Stella, their sons and grandchildren, will take him flowers sometimes, become familiar with the names on the stones around him. They are his company now. They will be his company forever.

Such things are private matters between him and Stella.

At no time – at no time, ever – did Grace or I have any claim on 'Clem'.

Perhaps, for us, it does not matter where he is. We know he did not find his mother, either in her room or at the place of her memorial. He found her in the gesture of a woman:

–in whose protection is that embryonic soul, if not in hers?

Grace holds the printed slip caught between her palms.
　This Godfrey, is Godfrey-the-Golden.
　This Godfrey, is Stella's.
　A man with a name that she does not use.
　But, her Godfrey – her Godfrey – is a hunter of the southern skies; a clean-bladed swordsman. He knows the stars of Hoeing and of Harvest; the stars of Famine and of Death. He knows the turning of the planets in the sky, their long migration – and, on earth, the routes navigated down across the eastern plains by men: savannah, forest verge and upland, where their cattle graze.
　The white bull of heaven and all his heifer stars, the abundant herds below, their pastureland.
　–As Bibleman says.
　Her Godfrey is a man who lives alone in the shadow of the Ridge of Jackals.
　A man of ironstone and aloe.

He had been dead eight months and she did not know.

Grace searches her diary and finds *February 2nd, 1963*. There is nothing written in on that day. No appointments, no reminders. It is a small blank space on the lower right hand corner of the page.
　It had passed away like any other day.
　Without a sign.
　She sits on the step of the veranda and watches the children on their bikes. Ruth is standing with her hands on her hips. Young Jack is pushing his brother, launches him off over the grass, tipping him, almost gently, into the marigolds.
　Hugh comes through the door and Ruth calls, 'Dad, come and look' – turning – 'get up and show Dad what you did.'
　Small boy toiling up and out of the flowers, Ruth running to help him mount and send him, with a shove, back across the lawn. Jack chasing, Hugh striding awkwardly beside the bike, his cockscomb of hair on end, his face red and eager, hands out to steady the child before he falls.

Grace goes quietly into the house.

She folds the letter and puts it in the box. She takes the box from its usual place, withdrawing its presence, and puts it at the back of her cupboard. She lets her fingers linger just a moment at its lid, pulls an edge of shawl across it, as though she is protecting it.

The room is very still, the summer light lies thinly on the floor. And somewhere, at the other end of the house, the telephone is ringing.

Such incongruities and irritations do not matter any more.

He is simply apprehended in everything she does. Not self-consciously, but in the quiet recess of herself.

Kusegazini: you are in my blood.

Which cannot be divided.

'Is Grace Wilmot still alive?' I say.

Dulcie Trollip shakes her head.

'No,' she says. 'She died not so long ago. Hugh Wilmot was a lot older than her but he lasted well into his eighties. He was such a funny old stick,' she laughs. 'But he was devoted to her. That's what I heard. And she shook him up a bit. Got him – how can I say it – to get "with it" . . .' The idea seems to amuse her. 'He was very old fashioned when he was married to Doreen. She was always going-on-sixty. But Grace was fun. She jollied him up. And then, Mr Wilmot was devoted to Ruth.'

'Ruth?'

'The daughter,' Dulcie Trollip says.

The daughter.

I say, meeting her eye, hazarding my own belief, 'Did she ever know?'

Dulcie Trollip's glance is swift and shrewd. 'Sometimes the truth is best left alone,' she says.

'And sometimes it needs to be told.'

'It was up to Hugh Wilmot to tell her, then,' says Dulcie Trollip. She looks across at me. 'Hugh was a happy man and Ruth a loved child. Grace did what she thought was right. It was the best she could do.'

She took the burden on herself – for all of them – and lived with it. I lower my eyes from Dulcie Trollip's gaze. I wonder if I could have done the same?

'I believe Ruth's a practical sort of girl,' says Dulcie Trollip. 'A scientist or researcher of some kind. Very clever. Very independent. Old Hugh Wilmot lived with her family until he died. She'd never have stuck him in an old-age home. I heard he just popped off one morning while he was reading his Bible and one of the grandchildren found him and said, "Grandpa's gone to God".' She puts her cup on the tray. 'And life goes on,' she says.

It does not sound trite.

–*Whatever kind of Right is the Truth*.

Without it, nothing would be sacred.

And so, their lives – the record of a family, another generation, the remembrance of friends – find a new response to love.

I only know one Godfrey and one Grace, circumscribed within a time, linked immutably to place. And, as Gert had tried to gather up the stars, I – believing – have tried to gather up their story in my arms, allowing it its moment and its conformation.

Its quiet truth.

That has been my task.

The rest is beyond my interpretation. Or my interference.

Dulcie Trollip and I walk along the path to the car. She has to stop every now and then for breath.

She seems to be surveying her garden as we go. There is nothing to see, except the older shrubs which have grown into tangles, in need of pruning.

I am carrying the old primus stove and a container of eggs. 'If you see Arthur in his shed, send him home before it's dark. I don't want him falling in a *donga* like the padre that I told you about. And you make sure you lock up properly, when you go to bed.'

She allows me to embrace her. She pats my hand.

'It is nice to talk,' she says. 'It is difficult to live with somebody who never speaks.'

I drive away. This time Dulcie Trollip does not watch me.

She is walking with her back to me, down the path towards the house, taking her words with her. She will go to the kitchen and wash the cups. She will turn them in her hands, in the soapy water, and she will wring out the dish towel and hang it on the drying rack.

Like Grace, like Gert, like me – she knows the value of prosaic things, the small and simple actions that protect the heart.

Chapter nineteen

For the biographer, there are facts. But there are also conversations, thoughts, events, that have to be imagined – even conjured – to make those facts take life again and breathe. Godfrey and I know well that shadow-dance between us: instinctive gestures, palm to palm, sensing, hardly touching. It is delicate, and fragile. Sometimes reckless.

Without it, neither can exist.

It is done by instinct.

It is done with faith.

But mostly, it is done for love.

At the end, the ebb and flow of a reality – and the mind-map of imagining, of synchronicity and sign, need resolution.

Whatever kind of Right is the Truth.

They are not always the same thing.

I knew that I would make this journey. As Godfrey had for Grace.

And I will tell the last day as it was. Nothing will be added for effect.

The store still stands. And the little house. Juxtaposed, Arthur Trollip's shed.

The herd of old machines, like patient oxen – *imijendevu* – are gathered in their corrugated byre where once the packstone kraal had stood. Beyond, the open *veld*, the river-bed and – to the south – *uqolo lwezimpungutye*, the ridge of jackals, deep in shadow, rearing up before the rising sun.

Yesterday afternoon, when I arrived, I did not find old Arthur Trollip in his shed. His truck had already gone. I went to the door and looked in at the gloom. The light of late afternoon was coming through the latticework of

295

holes of his strange construction. All across the architecture of those old machines, the light shafted down, like sunlight filtering through broken rock to subterranean water. They were venerable engines, their makers' names embossed – so far, so distant from the place of provenance. Above the floor, up a steel stair, was Arthur Trollip's office on a platform, with a lopsided desk and chair. He could sit up there and survey the strange marooned detritus, pay homage to the workmen who had gone.

–*I don't know what he thinks he's going to make.*

It is something of a sanctuary. As much as the little house with its whitewashed walls had been a sanctuary for another kind of love, for harvesting the things that move the heart.

Grace and Godfrey had recorded words, gathering them in: Arthur Trollip is curator of the works of iron-loving men, gone long ago.

In a corner, on a workbench, lay scraps of iron and tools and wire. Half finished on a wooden stand, was one of Delekile's own creations. A jackal running in the *veld* – and behind, a dog and a man. Touch a leg, and the thing is set in motion: dog chases jackal, man follows. It is a perfect synchronicity of movement, so deftly engineered.

I picked it up and looked at it.

Small relief man, head back – hunting stance – arms alert, legs stretched forward.

The jackal was extended in the last dash for freedom.

But it will always run, equidistant from the man and dog, pinned forever to its plinth of wood.

Ultimately, there is no escape.

I left the shed, laced on my boots and went in search of the painting of the *inala* cow.

Godfrey's map was in my mind.

Standing at the door of the shed, I could trace, without hesitation, the simple lines of his cartography.

Here is the ridge and here the *krantz*. Here, the river-bed.

Here is the *witgat* tree and there – to the right and down – the place which he had marked with 'G', pencilled up against the tapering fault. Above, the twin *koppies* rise from the upland plain beyond the ridge.

I followed the river-bed. I followed it all the rest of the afternoon. I went up and down.

Up and down.

There are places where water oozes. There are places where the rock is black as flint. There are places where it is red and where the soil between is mauve, then dun. The *witgat* tree has died but its roots divide round rock. Its trunk sends a gibbet of shadow across the *krantz*.

Cactus had grown up in the disturbed land. The spines were needle sharp and long. I took them from the soles of my boots, pulled them from my trousers.

I explored the rockface with my eyes but a strange exotic had covered the *krantz*. A cleft took on a shaft of early evening shade.

I could hear my own breathing.

It must be here.

It must be here.

It must be here where Godfrey had once stood, rapt in quiet contemplation of colour and proportion and design.

It must be here.

When the light had almost gone, he would have crossed the empty river and walked away with Wilton Mayekiso. They would have traversed the flatlands of this barren stretch, sharing tobacco and matches as they went, speaking of the restoration of their herds.

—There are cattle in the sky and under the earth.

—And on the rock.

If Delekile was here now, he would surely show me. He would know, as Wilton Mayekiso had known before him.

The light was going down behind the ridge. I heard the first faint evening sounds from the bush. The sky was high and white – the throat, the underbelly of a reptile, soft-scaled and moist. The clouds were building to the north.

I ran my eye along the edge of the ridge; I ran it down, remembering that Godfrey had diminished height with cross-hatched shading.

There was the *witgat* tree. There was the rock-face. There was scree at its foot, the fallen boulders, the jumble of exotic spines.

But the painting was not there.

I could not find it in the fading light.

It had dissolved into the shadow of the *krantz*, into the rising dusk.

Into imagination.

I stood at the door of the sanctuary and I could not go in.

—Godfrey?

But there was no answer. He was not waiting for me.

He has already left: it has been enough.

I walked back across the empty camp towards the house and unlocked the door.

I stood at the threshold, in the desolation.

The floors were infested with fleas. Old furniture had been piled into the room where Grace and Godfrey used to work. It was stacked in the bedroom. The spares of Arthur Trollip's engines squatted on the back *stoep* behind a mesh of flyscreen, stretched across between the pillars, holding up the lean-to roof.

I put my provisions on the table in the kitchen, clearing a space. I lit the lamp. The flame wavered round a heart of indigo and blue, a thin black wisp of smoke darkened the funnel. I sat on the upright chair, and drew my journal and my pen towards me.

> 'There is a saying in Zulu, "if you were in my flesh, I could tear you out, but you are in my blood, which cannot be divided".
> Which cannot be divided.
> For her it was the tragedy. For me, the consolation.'

I write through the early hours of evening. I write far into the night.

In this small white kitchen, in the gold and blue of lamplight, I write as Godfrey had once written, long ago.

For both of us, it is a confession of love.

And, for both: a recessional for grace.

In that little house, in the dark hours before the morning, I heard the wind. I could hear it far, far off. It came down the valley, moving in a body, sweeping through. Things were alert to it: trees, the battalions of aloes on the slope, blood-dipped bracts, breasting it. Ground birds, sensing it, must have crouched, knowing its force.

The house turned its back on it, hunched down.

And so did I.

It came from the north-west, dragging cloud and bringing rain. I lay and listened to that rain, its unsteady, restless beating. Here, then gone; coming back again. Uncertain. A voice lamenting in the dark. And then, a wild and moving sky, the hooves of the storm, the black-cloud bull, breaking from the moon's byre.

—his voice descends on the ground like the thundering of the morning rain.

—his bellow trumpets like the gourd of the wind.

I lay in the cocoon of my sleeping bag, afraid.

I could hear the birth of that wind, underneath the ground. It came up and circled the little house like the leguaan, curving the corners, licking at the doors.

Beyond the clouds, the Ridge of Jackals would be clear against an empty sky. Above, the stars of Hunting and of Famine and of Death.

And then, I heard the tapping.

Tap-tap-tap.

—Godfrey?

An inexorable little sound. I stared into the dark but there was no light anywhere.

—Godfrey? Are you there? Come, Godfrey, come.

Tap-tap-tap-tap.

I was limp with fear.

I lay for a long, long time.

The wind died and it stopped. Just like that.

—Don't leave me, Godfrey . . .

I went to the window. I could see the faint blur of my own face. Outside, was the tumult of sky and the silhouette of the sweet-thorn by the back door, bending in the wind. Sometimes still, sometimes shaking.

It must have been the tap of the thorns, the little cipher of a branch nudging at the door.

Perhaps it was Delekile, come for his money.

But why so small, so insistent and so late?

Or was it?

I will never know.

The morning is pale. The ridge is spined against the sky.

I am packing the car when Arthur Trollip comes. He parks beside the shop. He raises his hand when he sees me but he is far away. A woman, with her head-scarf pulled across her eyes, is sitting in the back of the truck. She gets down slowly, feeling her way with her feet. She is bowed an instant against the tail-gate, holding on. Then she straightens.

She turns away and Arthur Trollip shambles into his shed.

The woman walks towards me on the road.

She greets me in Xhosa with the smallest husk of voice. She passes. I turn and watch her.

She walks in the shadow of the sweet-thorns, leaning in. She moves across its lattice-grid. It takes her up and lets her go, dissolving and reassembling her shape. She reaches open ground. Her shadow goes beside her, steady at her feet.

I turn back to the shed, making my way past the barred double doors of the store and the yellow sign with the handcuffs and the salivating dog, the rifle raised.

I am standing at the entrance. 'Mr Trollip?'

Arthur Trollip is halfway up the stairs to his suspended platform, high above the engines on the floor.

He nods. He has a wayward eye. His hair is standing up in tufts. A disjointed face, hinged together. 'My girlie,' is what he says.

He half turns, in his workman's overall, using the iron balustrade to support himself. He comes down heavily as if he needs an arm to hold him. He stands at the foot of the stairs in his stained boots. He is an old, bewildered man.

I approach. He takes a nut and bolt from his pocket, turning them in his fingers, twisting them this way and that. He looks about. He says, 'I must clear

299

this mess. I must have it ready for inspection.'

'Is someone coming?'

He does not answer.

Then he says – a voice that seldom speaks, words at random. 'I must open the store and phone again.'

'Is something wrong?'

'The police said that they would come.'

I am close to him. His hands and fingers are clumsy with the bolt, some of his nails are crushed into the tips of his fingers. 'It is Delekile,' he says.

'Delekile?'

'His mother came.'

I wait.

'Delekile drank jackal poison in the night. He gave it to his wife. He drank it himself.'

The drifting motes of light are laid about us on the floor.

'They are dead,' Arthur Trollip says. 'His mother came to tell us.'

The tapping in the night. The sound of the sweet-thorn branch knocking at the door.

Tap-tap-tap. Tap-tap-tap.

Appalled, I follow him to the store. He finds his keys and opens it. He pushes back the heavy double doors against the wall. The light floods in across the pallets on the floor. He goes behind the counter to the telephone and picks it up. I watch him, a silhouette against the dark, empty shelves.

I stand suspended – so still, a bird alights in the dust on the porch, foraging unconcerned.

I let my eyes rest on the counter, on the sacks of meal hunched, one above the other, on the glass display case with the penknives and the mouth organs.

I see the wedding and engagement ring in their square of plush, the plastic dome protecting them.

The box is still there, after all these years.

A pledge of love.

I can see the little tag, attached by a string: R3.50.

So small a price – and never paid.

I stand and hear the strange disjointed conversation – a man, searching for signals.

'Hello? Is that the police? Hello, can you help me? Hello?' His voice, crackles down a line which may have been cut – long ago – by wire thieves looking for plastic tubing in red and green and blue.

I remember Delekile wanting a cellphone, how he had said, when I had paid him last, that he would buy one, when – one day – he got a lift to town.

– *Hello God. This is Delekile. Can you hear me, God? Can you hear me?* Turning

300

this way and that to find a signal – the red and white finger of God on a hill, pointing at the sky, wrapped around with razor wire, to keep the copper-thieves away.

–*This is Delekile, God.*

–*This is Delekile, God. Do you know me?*

I wait with Arthur Trollip. 'Just his wife and him.' Arthur Trollip says. 'She was a quiet woman. Didn't drink.'

So strange a phrase, as if it vindicated her for living.

He sits on the bench in his store. Next to him are the little bits that Delekile made. He fetches a box and puts them into it.

The jackal and the dog and man, striding out, nailed to their slip of wood.

As the morning light flattens into sameness, the police drive by. We see the van stop and park beside the road where the small path leads down to Delekile's house.

Life has been suspended in that place: so sudden, so silent and so terrible.

I can see Delekile's mother, standing in the yard now.

She waits.

The lament – unheard – invites no consolation. Not from those who have never grieved the grief of a lifetime's desolation.

–*In whose care is that embryonic soul, if not in hers?*

Arthur Trollip looks about, searching. He is bewildered. 'I must work,' he says, picking up a spanner and turning it in his hands. 'There is too much to do. All this cleaning and Delekile gone.'

We hear another vehicle. A battered yellow van sidles to a stop beside the store, settling its weight into the dust. Men get out, women and a child. They walk in single file towards Delekile's house. His mother turns and waits for them. One hand – by a slow gesture, with ritual grace – is drawn down across her eyes until they reach her.

And so I go, numbed and humbled, driving up and away from the strange corrugated byre where the oxen-engines drowse in shadow and the light drifts down; away from the store and whitewashed house, the low wall, the insidious poison of the yellow sign, *'Ingozi: Danger'*, proclaiming ownership.

Of what?

In so implacable a place – *of what?*

I do not look back.

–*A great desolation will overtake us here.*

That is what Godfrey had written.

–*A great despondency. Drought and more. I have seen the last real spring.*

Even then, he had known.

301

That is the truth of how it was.

I lay it down now, restored – in part – to its belonging.

I leave it for another.

Perhaps for Ruth. Perhaps for a child of my own.

In another time, in another way: the eternal echo-step of love and loss.

So cruel, so tender.

Godfrey might have said: *–Chos', chos', kuphelaphela ke:* it is finished now.

Except that it is not.

–Kanti: and even yet.

That wry, that ambiguous reminder of resurgence, of belief: Wilton Mayekiso – with another, older wisdom than our own.

At the curve, where the camber of the track is banked with sand – the first bow of the steel road – I can see the river-bed below. Above, the *krantz* rises steeply to the ridge. There is the *witgat* tree, white against the fissure in the rock.

On the bank, browsing in among the thorns, a small herd of heifers graze.

At the sound of the car, one raises her head, looks back across her red and ochre-speckled shoulder.

It seems that she is beckoning.

The conformation is exact: the white face, the dark eyes, the flanks scattered with the rust of dappled spots.

She is an *inala* cow.

She is pale. Vivid. Poised.

A little toss of the head: *–I am abundance*.

And then – as suddenly – she turns.

Cryptic in the colouring of sand and stone and shadow, she disappears among the thorns.

Above, the ridge rises black against the morning sky. A lyre-horn of aloe transforms from ironstone to dust.